The Awakening of a Forbidden Love . . .

Charles refilled my wineglass. "We have to talk about your wife's illness," I reminded him, too much aware of him next to me on the dock.

"We will before we go back. But not yet."

There was a different note in his voice . . . He touched me, the lightest trace of his fingers at my temple, following the smooth line of hair behind my ear, the pressure increasing as his fingers moved beneath the heavy twisted knot at the base of my skull. And then he pressed the very sensitive hollow there, and a hot flame shot straight through me.

"How long is your hair?" he asked.

I couldn't look at him, couldn't speak. With one hand I removed the hairpin that held the knot in place. I tossed my head and my hair fell its full length, nearly to my waist.

"A river of burning gold," he murmured. He spread his fingers and ran them slowly, sensually, through the length of my hair.

I closed my eyes. This was wrong. I knew that later it would cause me terrible pain, but I wanted Charles Charpentier as I had never wanted another man in all my life . . .

DIANNE DAY

OBSIDIAN

PUBLISHED BY POCKET BOOKS NEW YORK

This novel is a work of fiction. Names, characters, places and incidents are either the product of the author's imagination or are used fictitiously. Any resemblance to actual events or locales or persons, living or dead, is entirely coincidental.

Another *Original* publication of POCKET BOOKS

POCKET BOOKS, a division of Simon & Schuster, Inc.
1230 Avenue of the Americas, New York, N.Y. 10020

ISBN: 0-671-63990-0

First Pocket Books printing July 1987

10 9 8 7 6 5 4 3 2 1

POCKET and colophon are registered trademarks
of Simon & Schuster, Inc.

Printed in the U.S.A.

Author's Note

The geographic area in which this book is set is real; so, too, are places mentioned specifically by name such as All Saints' Waccamaw church, Brookgreen Gardens, and the Hammock Shop. Everything else is the product of my imagination.

Dianne Day

OBSIDIAN

Chapter 1

I FELT AS IF I had been here before, even though I knew that I had not. It must be, I thought, the strangeness of approaching over water, the boat silently slipping through water as black and smoothly rippled as volcanic glass. A word formed unsought-for on the edges of my mind and flowed through unguarded spaces across the border from the unconscious into the conscious: obsidian. A strange word.

I looked down at the black water and it was at once both alien and familiar, and then I lifted my eyes and saw the house, my destination. It seemed to rise straight up from the water, glowing in the afternoon sun, victorious in its age as if it had stood forever while time slipped, like the river, around it.

Dizzy with déjà vu, I stepped back from the railing and sat on the nearest wooden bench. The old, flat-bottomed boat was little more than a floating platform with two rows of benches filling up the deck. In the stern there was a sort of shack where the captain stood at the wheel. The unseen motor throbbed. I had become accustomed to its muffled sound and felt its throbbing as if it were the beating of my own heart. In the normal course of events this boat would have carried tourists, but there had been a terrible, unseasonal storm that had disrupted the normal course of events. I longed for my car; I felt as if in leaving it behind I had left

1

behind a part of myself—the part of me that belonged to the 1980s, to the real world.

Honestly, how ridiculous, I scolded myself. I blinked, automatically and unnecessarily smoothed my hair back above my ears, and put myself through the kind of reality test I'd been taught to use with confused patients. I felt that *I* needed it! What is your name? I asked myself. Rosamund Hill. How old are you, Rosamund? I'm 26. What day is it today? It's Wednesday, the 23rd of March, 1986. Do you know the name of this place where we are? This is the Waccamaw River in South Carolina, and that house ahead, where I'm going, is called Charpentier after the Charpentier family. I'm going to live there and work there for Mr. Charles Charpentier. With a part of my mind I reflected that the next question in the strict order of the reality test was Who is the president of the United States, and I smiled at the seeming absurdity of the questions. But with another part of my mind I did feel reassured, more in touch with the reality that I knew.

The house, glowing, dignified, was close now, and I could see a dock at the river's edge. I stood and walked back to the wheelhouse.

"That's Charpentier, isn't it?" I asked the captain. I enjoyed the feel of the soft French syllables on my tongue.

"Yes, ma'am."

I didn't like being called ma'am by this man who was probably old enough to be my father, but I had already learned that here it was useless to say so. Captain John, whose boat bore a weathered sign that said "Captain John's River Trips," was paunchy, his skin permanently lined and tanned. His captain's cap was old and faded, and it clung to his head at an odd angle, as if it had grown there.

"It was good of you to make this trip just for me." I watched as he cut the motor and turned the wheel with big-knuckled hands, gliding the boat easily toward the dock.

"Didn't do it for you," he drawled, "did it for Mr. Charles Charpentier. You a relative or somethin'? You don't look much like the Charpentiers."

"No. I'm going to work there." The boat edged up to the dock and stopped with a soft thunk.

"Is that right?" He measured me with a skeptical eye, and

then his face softened. "Well, it don't make no nevermind to me, I guess. Come on, I'll take your suitcase up to the house for you." He threw a thick rope from the boat to the dock, which had wooden steps descending into the water. Then he stepped across and gave the rope a few twists around a post, and came back for my bag.

The glassy black water was motionless beneath the boat. I didn't need the hand he extended to me, but I took it anyway, not to offend him.

"Thank you, Captain John."

"You're welcome. Watch your step now. Old houses don't use the river much no more. Can't tell how the path is gonna be, but one thing's for sure, it's gonna be wet. Good thing you got boots on."

I had indeed worn boots because of the wet weather—the same good, strong leather boots that had seen me through all but the coldest weather in Boston. Under my trench coat I wore a sweater and jeans, not what I had intended for my arrival. But then, I had not intended for my arrival to coincide with the storm.

The big storm the day before had forced me to stop in Myrtle Beach in midafternoon, even though I had planned to reach Charpentier before nightfall. It had been simply impossible to continue driving through rain so thick that the wipers could not clear the windshield. Thunder had boomed and lightning had cracked, along with a wind so strong that it nearly swept my new Reliant wagon off the road. On the south side of Myrtle Beach, Highway 17 had been awash. I had turned back and found shelter in one of the many motels that lined the road. From my room I'd called my new employer and explained. He'd said I should stay in the motel, that he would call back when the storm cleared. Lightning had struck at least one of the trees on his property, and he would have to check the condition of his private road.

He did not call back until nearly noon the next day, and I had grown anxious from a night of fitful sleep and a morning of waiting. His road was blocked, he said, and I would have to come by boat. He gave me directions to Wachesaw Landing near Murrell's Inlet. Such strange-sounding names! But I had found them on my map. I left my car, as he had instructed, at the Landing. Charles Charpentier's voice had been strong and deep, and had held an edge of anger. I wondered what face, hands, and body went with that voice.

Captain John was apparently a taciturn man. He made no attempt at conversation as he trudged ahead of me. From the boat at a distance the house had seemed to rise up out of the water itself, but that was an illusion. Actually it was on a bank, many yards from the river which curved out and around it. The path up the bank was raggedly overgrown by grass, slick on top and soggy underneath from all the rain. It was a steep climb. When Captain John reached the top he stopped and turned, as if to wait for me, and when I was beside him he raised his free hand, pointing. I turned to look.

"Yonder's the old rice fields," he said.

Between the bank on which we stood, with the big house behind us, and the river, which from this vantage point I could see swept away in a great arc to the left, lay a vast sea of high grass the new-green color of springtime.

"I've never seen anything like it," I said truthfully. Though there was no wind now, the grass moved as if it were alive.

"From up North, ain't you?" asked Captain John, tilting his head to one side. His cap, if it had not been such a permanent fixture, would have fallen off.

I smiled at him. "Yes. I'm from Boston. Cambridge, actually."

"Thought so." That seemed to satisfy him. He turned back once more to the path and strode along, swinging my heavy bag as if it weighed nothing.

For some reason I did not want to look at the house. I looked instead at the path, which gradually became less overgrown and therefore more muddy. Soon it was bordered by plants I vaguely recognized, and my mind supplied a name, liriope. Now to the right and to the left other paths intersected; I allowed my eyes to range farther and saw that the paths formed a pattern. We were walking through a garden, and it was filled with flowers, their yellows and pinks and whites still bright though they had been lashed by rain and wind. Their fragrance reached me on the washed air. I thought of Cambridge, where, when I had left three days before, the streets were still bordered by dirty snow turned to ice.

I thrust my hands into the pockets of my trench coat and forced my eyes up to the house. Charpentier. I rolled the syllables in a whisper across my tongue, I let them out in a sigh. My steps slowed as I drank in the ivory-colored walls, the tall, many-paned windows, the long porches above and below supported by slender columns, the great brick chimneys rising many feet above the roof. *Home,* I thought without volition, and I felt the sun warm on the back of my head like a blessing.

But in the next moment I whirled away, turning my back on the place with such sudden movement that my leather shoulder bag swung out and slipped down to the crook of my elbow. I was appalled, even frightened, by the strong feelings the house evoked in me. It was *not* my home, I had never seen it before, never heard the name Charpentier until three weeks ago. But I felt I knew it, I felt as if there loomed over me a huge, unknown reason why it was *here* that I had come. . . . I brought my hands up to cover my eyes, pressing the heels of both palms hard against my cheekbones. I breathed deeply, from my diaphragm, and counted to make the breaths even. One, two, three . . .

"Ma'am?" Captain John's inquiring voice sounded to my ringing ears as if it came from another planet.

"I'm all right," I said, willing it to be so. "I'm just a little out of breath. I'll be there in a minute." I repeated silently to myself, I'm all right. It had almost happened again: the certainty, the inexplicable knowledge of things I could not possibly know, just as it had happened in the hospital. But that was why I had left the hospital, left medical school, so that it would not happen again. Not here, not anywhere.

I tugged the purse back up to my shoulder, put my hands again in my pockets, and tried to smile. I lifted my chin and was rewarded by a puff of soft spring air upon my face. I reached out with my legs, striding. Whatever the life this house held for me, I would meet it with confidence.

The door opened as I climbed the wide steps. Already on the porch, Captain John put my suitcase down and raised a hand to the brim of his cap.

"Afternoon, Regina. Mr. Charles asked me to bring this lady, and I brung her safe and sound."

"Thank you, Captain. Good afternoon, Miss," said the

woman in the doorway. She was tall, her skin a golden brown, and she wore a gray dress with a wide white collar that looked almost, but not quite, like a uniform.

"Hello," I responded.

Captain John apparently considered his job done and was already shambling off. I extended my hand to him, and he looked at it for a moment in surprise, then enveloped it in a hearty, callused grip.

"I enjoyed the ride on your boat," I said. "You must let me pay you for bringing me."

The captain pumped my hand, grinned, and all the lines in his face curved upward. "No need for that. Mr. Charles Charpentier will take care of it, and if he don't, well then, he'll owe me one, won't he?" That thought seemed to amuse him and he winked at me, pumping my hand one last time before he continued on his way.

"Goodbye!" I waved as I watched him go. Then I turned to the woman who still stood in the doorway, and tried out my smile. "I'm Rosamund Hill."

She didn't return it. "I am Regina. I keep the house for Mr. Charles. Please come in. We were expecting you." She stepped back into the darker reaches of the house.

I picked up my suitcase. She made no attempt to take it from me. I could feel her eyes on me as I passed her, and heard her close the door behind me. Then, as before on the path, I could take in my surroundings only by small degrees. I focused on my feet, saw that my muddy boots rested on an oriental runner. Age had muted the colors to pastels. On either side of the rug wide planks of dark wood, dark enough to be mahogany, gleamed in a high polish. I heard the ticking of a large clock, softly resonant in the hushed, high hall. Then I heard the swish of her clothing as Regina moved.

"Mr. Charles is out on the road where the big trees fell. I'll take you to your rooms."

I hesitated. "I, ah, I think I should take off my boots. They're muddy." She made no response to this, but stopped where she was, at the foot of the stairs, and stared at me. I scanned the hall, looking for a place to sit, and when I saw none I put down my suitcase and sat on it while I removed first one boot and then the other.

She could at least offer to carry something, I thought as I struggled with boots in one hand, heavy suitcase in the other, and my shoulder bag that kept sliding down my arm. I followed as she mounted the stairs.

"This is the oldest part of the house, built in 1835. It's one of the few that survived the War without much damage."

"You mean the Civil War?"

"The War Between the States" she corrected.

The distinction was lost on me. She was continuing.

"The North Wing was added in the 1880s, and the South Wing at the turn of the century. These river houses do not have a front and a back; instead, there is the East Front which faces the oak alley and the road beyond, and the West Front—where you came in—which faces the river." She had reached the top of the stairs and turned, looking down at me.

I thought how curious her voice was, not at all Southern Black, but precise, with an almost European cadence.

"In the future when your feet are muddy, you should use the south side door by the kitchen." Regina's tone implied that she condescended to forgive me a grievous error.

I felt like the new kid on the block, ignorant and clumsy, as I gained the final step and paused, facing her. "I'll do that," I promised. I saw that I was nearly as tall as she, which made me feel better. New kid I might be, but she would not intimidate me.

"The North Wing burned ten years ago," she said. "It has been rebuilt entirely, so it is quite modern. Mrs. Charpentier occupies the North Wing, and that is where your rooms are." She turned away and started in that direction.

"What about the South Wing?"

She stopped and turned back to me. "On this floor, Mr. Charles has his rooms. Downstairs in the South Wing," she enumerated precisely, "are the kitchen, the pantries, the flower room, the laundry room, and my room."

"Oh, I see." She resumed her pace and I followed, down a hall that was dimly lit by a long window at its end. The doors on either side were closed. "I had no idea the house was so large."

"There are twenty-seven rooms," said Regina. She turned in front of the long window, with me close behind her, and we were in the North Wing. It was very pleasant, a long, narrow gallery-like hall with floor-to-ceiling windows along one side and on the other, doors to the rooms.

"These two rooms are yours." She opened the first and then the second door. "There is a bathroom between them."

I went through the first door into a sitting room, large, square, high-ceilinged, with a beautiful Chinese rug on the floor. "It's wonderful!"

Regina came in after me. "There are a few things I must show you." She crossed to a wall dominated by bookshelves above and closed cabinets beneath. She took keys from her pocket and proceeded to open these one by one. "Here in the center cabinet there is an electric heater. There are no fireplaces in this wing. After the fire, Mr. Charpentier did not want them here. There is central heating, but sometimes it is inadequate and you may want to use the heater. On the left there is a television set on wheels, so you can move it where you wish. On the right is a small refrigerator, both for your own use and to store Mrs. Charpentier's insulin. Her other medications are kept in the drawers next to the refrigerator. Her syringes are also there, in the top drawer. The rest should be empty." She pulled out the drawers one by one, checking.

I was beginning to find Regina's precision and thoroughness tedious, but it was apparently her way and I tried to be patient. She was not yet finished with all she had to say. She fixed me with eyes that were a curious, tawny brown, much the same color as her skin. She had the coloring and the intensity of a lioness.

"It is very important that these cabinets, all of them, be locked whenever you are not in this room. Even if you are only in your bedroom or your bathroom. And you must keep these keys with you at all times." She held up the three small keys, from which a long, thin chain dangled. "Do you understand? *At all times!*"

"I understand." I understood the words, but not the reason behind them. A *why?* was on the tip of my tongue, but I bit it back. Already I sensed that Regina would tell me only what and when she wanted. I held out my hand for the keys, and when she had given them to me, I slipped the chain over my head so that I wore the keys around my neck. This pleased Regina.

"Good," she nodded. But still she did not smile.

I am somewhat reserved myself with new people, but under the circumstances I felt that she could have made me feel more welcome. Instead, I felt a definite chill. It came from Regina, and I wanted her to leave me.

"Will you introduce me to Mrs. Charpentier now? Or shall I go ahead and unpack?"

"It is for Mr. Charles to decide when to take you to his wife. I will send the maid for you when he returns to the house. Leave your muddy boots in the hall, and she will clean them for you." Regina had taken her cue and was leaving the room when she paused. "We have had no electricity today, but the water is perhaps warm enough for you to bathe, if you wish."

I accepted this as if it were a peace offering. "Thank you," I said and was relieved to be able to close the door after her.

I cleaned my own boots in the bathroom sink, too late realizing that I had ruined a white washcloth in the process. I was not used to having a maid. As I scrubbed, I wondered if I would ever adjust to living in someone else's house, even a house as grand as this, if I could get used to having servants. . . . What was wrong with me? I didn't have servants. I wasn't a guest here, I worked here. Just like Regina and the maid, whoever she might be.

I looked up at myself in the mirror above the sink, in dismay. I realized that I had been unconsciously feeling like a guest come for a long visit. I was in a new role now, one that I knew nothing of, not even how I should act. All my life I'd been a student of one kind or another. The only job I'd ever had was as a summer camp counselor, and that was certainly no help now.

I put my boots on the floor to dry and left the washcloth soaking in the sink. I took off and hung up the towel I'd wrapped around myself after a tepid bath, and put on my robe. I slipped my hand into the pocket, making sure that the keys were there. Already I was concerned that I not lose them. I went into my bedroom, recognizing that I must do some hard thinking.

I sat in a soft chair, a silly little chair with ruffles around the bottom, a chair I would never have chosen for myself. I looked across at the bed, which was a four-poster with more ruffles, and I felt so out of place that I wanted to cry. Where was that déjà vu now when I needed it? At least it had made me feel that I belonged here.

I hugged my knees and put my forehead on them. I knew I must not let myself cry. There were things that I wasn't ready to deal with yet; I had packed them away tight and solid inside myself, and tears would weaken the package. On the practical side, crying would surely turn my too-fair skin blotchy. I must not cry. I pressed bone of forehead against bone of kneecaps and concentrated. Think, don't feel. I thought about why I'd come to this place. I thought carefully, so as not to disturb the things packed away.

I needed a break from medical school, so I'd told my faculty advisor, Dr. Frances Windsor. She was a stern woman who had fought her way up when women were scarcely accepted in medicine. I could tell she thought I should be made of hardier stuff, but I stuck to my request for a leave of absence on the grounds that I needed to rethink my commitment to medicine. Dr. Windsor attributed my inability to continue the third-year clinical rotations to shock and grief over my aunt's recent unexpected death. I didn't tell her it was more than that.

Finally she'd granted my request. Then she asked what I planned to do. I replied vaguely that I wanted a change of scene, and I would get some sort of undemanding temporary job until I could make a decision about my future. "Perhaps . . ." Dr. Windsor had said, and with that one word set into motion the chain of decisions that had brought me to Charpentier.

Dr. Windsor had a family friend, a lawyer, in Boston on business. She had promised to help him find a particular sort of person with medical background to be a companion for a client's chronically ill wife. The job was in South Carolina. She'd been thinking in terms of a nursing student, but in view of my circumstances, perhaps . . .? I was interested, and she made the contact.

I went for an interview with the lawyer at the Boston hotel where he was staying. I took my curriculum vitae, as he requested. He'd seemed more than respectable, and when he called and offered the job a week later, I accepted.

Now I realized how few questions I'd asked in the interview, though I'd answered many. But that was all right. All that had mattered then and all that mattered now was that Charles Charpentier's need for a particular sort of companion for his wife coincided with my need to get away from Cambridge and medical school. I needed time and distance, and money to support myself. I didn't dare spend any more of Aunt Henry's small legacy than what my car had cost. The job would give me what I needed.

I raised my head and massaged my temples briefly, then I stood and stretched, reaching for the ceiling until I felt my joints loosen and I tingled all over. I was myself again. I felt better than I had since I'd driven into the awful storm. This job was a godsend. If the house and the people in it seemed anachronistic, well, I would handle it. What was most important was that I had made a commitment to care for a chronically ill woman. There was still enough of the would-be physician in me for such a commitment to have meaning. I did not yet know exactly the nature of her illness, but I would in time. I focused on the commitment, knowing that I was already honor-bound to keep it.

Chapter 2

I ANSWERED THE KNOCK on my bedroom door.

"Mr. Charles says, will you please come downstairs when you are ready," said a small woman, younger and much darker than Regina. She looked at me with bright, impertinent eyes.

"Thank you. I'm Rosamund," I said, determined to be friendly. "And you are . . .?"

"My name's Phyllis. I'm the maid. Miss Regina she say, if you need me to iron your clothes for tomorrow I could do it, but after that you do your own. You got anything you want me to iron for you?" Her accent was thickly Southern, and she was the friendliest person I had yet met at Charpentier.

"No, thank you, Phyllis. Perhaps tomorrow morning you could just show me where things are. I'm sure I'll get along just fine," I said. "Oh, and please tell Mr. Charpentier I'll be downstairs in just a moment."

"Yes, ma'am. I'll see you tomorrow morning!" She grinned and sashayed away.

I went back into the room, feeling obliged to check my appearance in the mirror, although if I was unsatisfied with it, there was not much I could do. The green sweater-dress I wore was the only thing that had come out of my one suitcase unwrinkled; the other bags I'd brought, along with boxes of books and other things I'd thought I would need for an extended stay, were locked in my station wagon at the Wachesaw Landing. In the full-length mirror on the inside of my closet door, I looked at myself. Normal. My impossibly straight, thick, red-blonde hair was neatly pulled back in a twist at the nape of my neck, as usual; my eyes looked a little too big for my face, as usual; my only makeup was a peach lipstick, as usual. I had, however, put on gold earrings for the occasion. And I'd remembered the keys—they were on their chain around my neck, under my clothes, because there were no pockets in my dress. My camel-colored leather shoes were good and had been expensive, as was almost always the case because my feet were so long and narrow. And there were no runs in my stockings. There was nothing else to check. I went downstairs.

The third room I looked into had a fire burning in the fireplace and was obviously a library. All the walls were lined floor to ceiling with books. It seemed as unoccupied as the dining room and the breakfast room had been, but I was attracted by the warmth which, for me, came from the many books as well as from the welcoming fire. I went in.

A man rose from a large leather wing chair that faced the fireplace and had hidden him from view. He rose—and rose, and rose. This man was no mere six feet tall, he was easily four or five inches taller than that. His chest and shoulders were massive. I knew that he must be Charles Charpentier, but he did not fit the mental picture I had subconsciously built to go with that very French name. I supposed I had expected him to be small and slim and elegant, and certainly there was nothing inelegant about his soft-looking gray pullover sweater whose V neck revealed a white open-collared dress shirt, or his dark trousers. But the total effect of him was primitive, elemental. His hair was thick to near-shagginess, and very black with gray at both temples; his forehead was broad and prominent, eyebrows dark and heavy over deepset eyes whose color I could not at the moment determine; long straight nose, well-defined jaw, shapely mouth. It was a mature face, marked with lines that suggested strong feelings often held in check. I remembered the voice over the telephone, strong, authoritative, but with an edge of anger. Now I heard it again.

"Miss Hill. I am Charles Charpentier."

"How do you do," I murmured. He had taken my hand and I was off-balance until I stepped forward, toward him.

"Please, join me here, by the fire."

"Thank you." I took the companion chair and held my hands out to the yellow-orange flames. "It's a nice fire." With my peripheral vision I saw him sit and cross one very long leg over the other. I could feel his eyes on me. For a few moments he said nothing, and I continued to pretend great interest in the fire.

"I'm having a drink before dinner. Bourbon and water. What can I get for you?"

I forced myself to look directly at him. "Something less strong, if you have it." I could not remember when I had been less at ease in a new situation.

"A glass of dry sherry?"

"Fine." I gave my attention back to the fire. Soon the sherry appeared near my fingers, glowing like a topaz in its cut crystal glass. I accepted it. "Thank you."

Charles Charpentier resumed his chair, moving more gracefully than I would have thought a man of his size could. I turned slightly toward him, ready to talk as I knew we must. He was looking me over, very thoroughly. I shivered, and quickly sipped at my drink to cover it.

"If the electricity doesn't come on soon, it will be uncomfortable in the North Wing," he remarked.

So, he had seen my shiver. I replied, "Regina told me there were no fireplaces. She said there was a fire there, some time ago."

"Yes, that's right. Well, we won't worry about that for the moment. I expect we'll have power again soon, and there are more important things to talk about. Let's start with a few ground rules. I want us to be on a first-name basis. Of course you've already met Regina and Phyllis, and you've probably noticed that they call me Mr. Charles. I want you to call me Charles. My wife's name is Arabella, but I call her Bella, and I want you to do the same. I have gone out of my way to find someone whom my wife will regard in a different light than she has looked on her aides in the past. There have been . . . difficulties with the others, who were more like Regina and Phyllis. You are different. Your use of our first names will reinforce that. Do you think you understand what I'm trying to say . . . Rosamund?" He pronounced my name as if he were trying it out on his tongue.

"I think so. Your lawyer Mr. Parker, told me at the interview that you wanted someone with, ah, a higher level of education than is usual for this sort of job. He didn't say why, and I didn't ask."

Charles was silent. He regarded me darkly, seeming to measure me. "You may as well know right off that I tend to be blunt. I'm not a pussyfooter."

I can certainly see that, I thought. But I did not interrupt.

"I graduated from Harvard myself, about twenty years ago. Parker was going to Boston on business, and I thought while he was there he might find the kind of person I wanted to help with my wife. I hadn't had much luck here, and Parker said he could get his friend Frances Windsor to help. When he read me your resume over the telephone, I agreed with him that at least on paper you were even more suited to what I wanted than I could have hoped for. I had to trust his judgment on the personal interview, and Parker's usually a pretty fair judge of people. But . . ."

He fell silent and scanned me with such intensity from head to foot that I instinctively stiffened, sitting straighter in my chair. My complexion, which so recently I'd sought to preserve from the red blotches that crying always brought, was going to betray my discomfort under his gaze. I could feel the hated warmth of a beginning blush.

"But," he repeated, "now that I see you for myself, I wonder if this time he may have made a mistake."

My cheeks flamed. "I beg your pardon?" I hoped the ice I put into my voice would quench the fire in my face.

"Exactly why did you drop out of medical school?"

"I didn't *drop out.* I took a leave of absence."

"Why?"

"Personal reasons!" I snapped. I knew that I was blushing furiously.

"Oh? A failed romance with one of the doctors, perhaps?" His lips curved in a mockingly sensual smile.

"Mr. Charpentier," I began, deliberately avoiding the use of the first name he'd requested, "that question was rude and uncalled for, and I do not intend to answer it. My personal reasons for leaving medical school have no bearing whatever on my ability to do the job I thought you hired me for. And what is more, you doubtless already know that, since I told Mr. Parker, who was more courteous, the same thing. He checked my references, I know. Now, if you want to change your mind about me, I will expect reimbursement for my travel expenses here and back to Cambridge, and severance pay in compensation for the time I have already spent readying myself for this job!"

Charles Charpentier threw back his head and laughed. His laughter was rich and throaty, and like his physical presence it filled the room, pressing on me. I felt claustrophobic, but I stood my ground, glaring at him.

At last he looked again at me, no longer mocking, no longer measuring. "I take it all back. You look delicate, with your fair skin that turns such a lovely shade of rose. Do you suppose your mother knew that when she chose your name?"

I had never so much as thought of my name in connection with my lifelong tendency to blush. I knew it was a rhetorical question, but I found myself shaking my head.

"And then there is your hair. Such an unusual color. I don't believe I've ever actually seen anyone with hair that color, strawberry blonde I've heard it called. It's very striking, in spite of the way you have it all bound up. In short, I thought you too pretty to have the strength I need in the person who must contend with my wife. But, by George, you have spirit! You're not as delicate as you look, not by a long shot! I've been put in my place. I apologize, and I salute you!" He raised his glass.

He smiled, a sincere and warm smile, and for the first time I saw what a transformation a smile could bring to Charles's face. For the first time I felt the effect of that smile on me. I melted, my anger was gone, nervousness was a thing of the past. I smiled back at him.

"You apology is accepted. Does that mean you do want me to stay?"

"Oh, yes," he said, his voice hushed and deep in his throat. "I do want you to stay."

I felt trapped in his dark eyes. Everything else, the fire, the room, the house, the world itself, simply disappeared.

And then, in an instant, it was over; I felt disoriented, not sure what had happened or if anything had happened at all.

I heard Charles clear his throat, I blinked, and turned back to the fire. My voice wavered a bit. "Ground rules. You said first names. Are there other ground rules?"

"You'll have your meals with me, except lunch when you'll be with Bella. I've told Regina this. I hope you don't mind eating with me, there really is no other alternative. You'll have two days off a week, but Sunday must not be one of them. My wife is always restless on Sundays, and I want you with her. You may choose which two days you want, and I'll get someone else to come in on those days." He gulped at his drink. He didn't seem to enjoy the giving of instructions as Regina would have. In fact, he seemed uncomfortable.

"Mr. Charpentier, I mean Charles, what exactly is your wife's condition?" I felt it was time for me to know, and I was also simply curious.

"The storm, all the thunder and lightning, upset her. I had to get the doctor in. He sedated her heavily, and she's had a nurse with her around the clock since noon yesterday. Dr. Barkstone will be here to check her tomorrow morning, and he will talk with you afterward, give you all the details. When you've finished talking with him, then I'll take you to her and stay with you until I see that the two of you are comfortable together."

More anachronisms, I thought, a doctor who makes house calls. "You still haven't told me her ongoing illness, her major diagnosis," I persisted.

Charles released a deep sigh that was almost a groan, and he slumped down in his chair, letting his feet sprawl. He did not answer right away, and as I waited I could almost see a heaviness descend upon him.

"My wife is a manic-depressive," he said at length. "Unfortunately she has proved to be one of the few who do not respond to lithium treatment. Gradually over the twelve years we've been married, her highs have become higher and more frequent. The lows are about the same. Then, two years ago we discovered that she is diabetic. She requires daily insulin injections, but she resists them. She wouldn't let her aides give her the injections and she wouldn't learn to do it herself, so I've had to do it. I'm hoping that from the beginning you can change that. I need to be able to travel for business reasons, and I can't stand being tied to this place day after day for the sake of those injections. . . ." His voice drifted off into his own private thoughts, and he ran his hand fiercely through his thick hair, making it look even shaggier.

A sad story, simply told. I felt with him the weight of it, pressing him down. "Of course I will," I said quietly.

From behind us came a low, European-sounding voice. Regina. "Dinner is ready, Mr. Charles."

"Would it be wrong for me to ask what kinds of things Regina does?" We were finishing a delicious if cold meal, and I'd remarked that Regina was a very good cook. Charles had said that I was mistaken, Regina did not do the cooking. There was a cook who came in. I continued, "I think I'll be able to fit in better if I understand how things work here, who does what."

"Hmmm. Yes. Well, you're probably right about that. Regina does the things my wife would do if she were well enough, and at one time, Bella did do some of them. Regina plans the meals, does the shopping, puts flowers around the house, keeps up with my schedule, things like that. I believe she does a certain amount of the housework too, since I doubt that little Phyllis could do all of it herself—"

I had heard enough, and interrupted. "I understand. Really, that's very helpful. I'll be careful of my relationship with Regina." I surely would! He had said it all when he acknowledged that for purposes of running the house, Regina stood in place of Arabella Charpentier. My unruly mind insinuated a thought I pushed aside: did Regina stand in the place of his wife for purposes other than the running of the house?

At that moment Regina appeared with dessert and coffee on a tray. Quietly and efficiently she moved about the table, clearing it, then setting down the final course. I wondered why she chose to serve the table herself. Perhaps she liked to watch over "Mr. Charles." Perhaps she resented my being there, usurping time she might have had him to herself.

A sidelong glance from her lioness eyes gave me the ridiculous feeling that she could read my thoughts.

"Regina is really rather unusual, isn't she?" I asked when she had left the room.

"She's an octoroon," pronounced Charles, as if that explained everything. He began on his sherbet.

"Oh, yes, Massa!" I said drily. He had sounded racist to me with that remark, and I didn't like it. I met his eyes in the silence that followed. They were dark, dark blue, like sapphires with tiny flames of the candles mirrored in them. A smile tugged at the corners of his mouth.

"Your sense of humor will take some getting used to, Rosamund. She *is* an octoroon. I couldn't give you her exact lineage, but she is more white than black, which accounts for the color of her eyes and her skin."

"I didn't mean her appearance, necessarily. I meant there's just something different about her. It's in her voice and the way she carries herself. I expect, actually, that you do know what I mean." I made it a mild challenge.

"She came here from another plantation, my mother brought her here. Regina is older than she looks. She is my age at least, and maybe a few years older. She came from Patton, south of here, and I believe that she spent a number of years in Europe and had some of her education there, which accounts for her speech." Now it was his turn to challenge. "Why are you so interested in Regina?"

I pushed the lime sherbet around in my dish. "I don't know. I suppose I'm just trying to get my bearings still. Your way of life here is very different from anything I'm used to. And Regina is a very, ah, dominant presence."

"I don't think of her that way," said Charles with finality. "Brandy with your coffee?" He reached for the decanter Regina had brought from the sideboard to the table when she served the dessert.

"No, thank you. How do you suppose she made coffee with the electricity off?" I asked the question even though I sensed that Charles had dismissed the subject of Regina. An almost unquenchable curiosity is both a virtue and a fault with me.

"A propane gas ring, kept for emergencies." He glowered

at me from under his heavy brows, and went on as if to forestall any further questions from me. "Power outages are common here, especially during the summer months when we have a lot of severe thunderstorms. Now, if you don't mind, I'd like a little silence with my brandy."

I didn't mind. There had been other silences throughout the meal, and I'd learned quickly that Charles Charpentier was not interested in polite small talk. That suited me, for I am not very good at it. I enjoyed the silence now. Even my ever-busy mind quieted as I sipped my coffee and watched the smoke from Charles's cigarette curve back upon itself above the glow of the candles.

Eventually Charles pushed his chair back from the table and stood. "I'm going to walk up the road and see if the men have finished removing the fallen trees. Would you like to come with me? It's about a mile each way."

"I'd like that. I'll need to get a sweater."

When we left the candlelit dining room we walked into near-darkness in the hall. The house was still without power. I stopped, then felt his hand at my back.

"Since you're still unfamiliar with the house, I'll go with you to your room to get your sweater. I'm sure it will be lighter outside than it is in here." With a gentle pressure of his hand he guided me along the hall.

My eyes adjusted to the dimness as we climbed the stairs together. I was very much aware of the man beside me, and I wondered why he affected me so strongly. I was not exactly attracted to him; it was more precisely a physical awareness, as if he had a physical aura so strong that it reached out and encompassed me. This puzzled me. I was accustomed to spending most of my waking hours with more men than women, many of them powerful doctors, and I had long ago learned to hold my own with them. I simply did not usually think in male/female terms. It was not part of my agenda, I had no time for it.

We made the turn into the North Wing, and I caught myself about to release an exasperated sigh. I held my breath to keep it in. I would rather turn blue, I thought, than let Charles Charpentier know that his physical presence confused me!

"You, see, it's much lighter outside," he observed. The wall of long windows shone blue-violet with twilight.

I opened the door into my bedroom. "I'll just be a minute!" I said brightly, slipping through, intending to close the door behind me. But Charles, the master in his own house, had no compunction about following me into the room.

Well, just come right in! I thought in annoyance. I pulled out the drawer where I'd put my sweaters with rather more force than was necessary. From the corner of my eye I saw Charles cross the room, hands in his pockets, and stop before the little chair. He poked at its ruffles with one foot.

"Silly little chair!" he mumbled.

"That's exactly what I thought." In the half-light I identified the sweater I wanted by its feel, and pulled it out.

"What?" asked Charles, turning.

"The chair, the bed, all the ruffles. It's not really my kind of decor." I pushed the drawer closed with my knee.

Charles came to me, grinning down at me while I self-consciously put on the sweater.

"You're not the ruffles type. I should have known. No curls." He looked pointedly at my hair. "No ruffles. A sensible woman. Pretty, but sensible. And strong, too, I think." The grin disappeared. "You have no idea how glad I am that you've come."

"You shouldn't say that until we see how I get along with your wife."

"At the moment I wasn't thinking of my wife." His hand went out as if to touch me, but then he thrust it down into his pocket. "Now, let's go see if the road is clear. After you." He gestured me out of the door.

"Wait!" I cried. I took a few steps backward. My first sight of the oak alley before the East Front overwhelmed me. Like everyone else, I had seen *Gone With the Wind*, but this was real. The live oaks were the largest trees I had ever seen, so beautifully shaped, their balanced rows of trunks topped by branches that spread and arched to meet above a path where Charles already stood.

He held out a hand for me. "Come on, it will still be here

tomorrow and all the days after that. But right now we haven't much light left."

I felt like a tourist, but I could not stop myself from craning my neck upward as I joined him and walked beside him through the "alley."

Charles was amused. "A lot of the houses around have them. You've never been to the South before?"

"No. Well, actually that's not true. I lived with my grandparents in Vicksburg, Mississippi, until I was four, but I don't remember it. When I was four years old my Aunt Henry—her name was really Henrietta—took me to live with her in Cambridge, Massachusetts, and I don't remember anything before that." I was having trouble keeping up with him. I have long legs, but his were much longer.

"What happened to your parents?"

"My mother is dead, but she had left me with my grandparents long before she died. She never told anyone who my father was. Aunt Henry legally adopted me, so I grew up with her last name, Hill. She was both a mother and a best friend to me. She was the most wonderful person, but my grandparents didn't understand that. They had more or less thrown her out of the family. They said both of their daughters had disgraced them, which was ridiculous because Aunt Henry was a Radcliffe professor and a fine scholar. . . ."

Suddenly I realized that I was babbling and I stopped, embarrassed that I'd been pouring out this family history to a stranger. And to make it worse, I tripped on the uneven bricks of the path, and my ankle buckled. Instinctively I grabbed at Charles's arm to keep from falling. I felt the softness of his sleeve in my fingers, and then his arms were around me, holding me safe. I felt the cashmere of his sweater against my cheek. For just a moment, the comfort of being held became more important than anything else, and I let my head rest against the broad chest that felt so soft beneath my cheek.

"I'm sorry," I murmured. His arms tightened.

"Did you also lose your Aunt Henry? You speak of her in the past tense." His voice was strong yet hushed.

Unwanted tears pricked at my eyes. If I spoke, they would come. I moved my head in a nod against him.

"She died . . . recently?" asked Charles perceptively.

Now I pulled away. "Yes. A couple of months ago." I swallowed hard. "I'm sorry I tripped. Thank you for catching me."

"We'll be out on the road soon. Perhaps we should have walked up the driveway. It's not as rough as this old brick path, but the way is shorter through the oaks."

"No, really, I'm fine. And this is so beautiful!" I took a step, ignoring the twinge in my ankle. We resumed our walk in silence and emerged onto a paved road that looked wide enough for only one car. I could see that it curved around the live oaks, presumably becoming a driveway up to the house.

Charles was walking away from me; with my ankle hurting, I couldn't keep up. He seemed unaware of it, focused now on the reason for the walk. He strode on. Suddenly I did not want to be left behind. It was very nearly dark, and though I was no longer under the great live oaks, other trees on both sides of the road loomed oppressively. I hurried to catch up.

When I did, I saw why the road had been impassable.

"A sycamore and a couple of old pines. Apparently the sycamore was half-dead, and it took the pines down with it," said Charles. There was a large amount of wood and greenery hastily cut and pushed to both sides of the road.

"What a mess!" I commented.

"Yes. The storm did almost as much damage as a hurricane. My brother had damage to his house. I'll have to go over and look at it tomorrow."

"Your brother?"

"Louis. Lives on the place next door." Small branches and a multitude of pine cones littered the road, and Charles scuffed and kicked among them.

I turned and looked back the way we'd come. The dark bulk of the house was a massive shadow at the road's end. "You can see the house from here."

"Yes." Charles came up behind me and quietly put a hand on my shoulder. "It looks threatening, even to me, without lights." His hand on my shoulder tightened. "I'm afraid I've done a very poor job of welcoming you to Charpentier, Rosamund. A dark house, a blocked road, a sedated wife. And I've been a slave to our abnormal, isolated life here for so long, I've lost what few social graces my mother trained into me. I'll try to make it up to you. I want you to like us enough to stay."

I was grateful for the touch of his hand. I am not easily frightened, but I felt something very much like fear as I stood, hemmed in by the trees, looking at the dark house.

Charles let his hand move from my shoulder down my arm. "I'd best hold onto you as we walk back." His hand found mine. "Night has fallen, and I don't want you to trip again."

I said nothing as I tried to match his long strides. The pain in my ankle had subsided to numbness. I struggled with a myriad of feelings, the predominant one a sense of loss that came to me whenever I thought of Aunt Henry. Her death from a myocardial infarction, a heart attack, had been so sudden, so completely unexpected, I still could hardly comprehend it.

The way was indeed longer by the drive. Charles did not interrupt my grieving silence until we were near the house. Then I knew that he understood, for he said, "I'm sorry your aunt died. I can tell, from the way you spoke of her, that you loved her very much."

"Yes, I did," I admitted. The pressure of his fingers on mine was warm and comforting.

Chapter 3

I BRUSHED MY HAIR, long, even strokes, and counted as I lifted lock after heavy lock. It was my bedtime ritual, reassuring, soothing. But there was something archaic about dark mirrors, flickering candles, and tall white-curtained windows that worked against my best, most disciplined efforts. An ever-growing part of me was in close touch with childhood terrors I thought I had long ago forgotten. The thing in the closet that comes out when you close your eyes at night. The thing that lives under the bed and will grab your ankle just as you touch your bare foot to the floor when you get up to go to the bathroom. The thing that stays in the mirror, that you can see only out of the corner of your vision, that can reach out and pull you in. . . . I had not been a fearless, happy-go-lucky little girl. I could not even remember how old I'd been when I finally stopped being afraid of the dark.

It was Henrietta Hill who'd been the strong, sensible woman. All I'd ever wanted was to be like her. What had gone wrong? What was happening to me, had started happening even before her death? Was I still the person I had strived to be, or was that person just a facade, an outer shell maintained by habits and learned behavior?

I looked in the dark mirror, and saw what Charles Charpentier must have seen when he'd questioned me, doubted me. I looked fragile, breakable. He was more astute than I'd been willing to give him credit for—even if he had phrased his doubts in sexist terms. My chin quivered involuntarily; I clamped my teeth down over my lower lip and turned away from the mirror. I carried the three-branched brass candelabra and put it down on the bedside table, then got into bed. Quickly, before I could change my mind, I blew out the candles.

God is merciful, even to those of us who think we are not believers. The next thing I knew, it was morning. Sun streamed through the tall window, diffused by the sheer white curtain. The ghosts of the night were gone, and in their place, birds singing. My travel clock on the bedside table said 7:30. For me, I had slept late, and I felt rested.

Ignoring the cold room, I washed and quickly dressed in the yellow sweater I'd worn for yesterday's boat trip. Instead of jeans, I reached for my gray skirt, which was full and had pockets hidden in the side seams. The worst of the wrinkles had hung out overnight. But shoes were a problem. Most of them were still in the luggage locked in my car, and since boots would hardly do, it would have to be the camel-colored pumps. As I was leaving my room I remembered the keys and went back for them. I put them in my pocket and went downstairs.

Coffee and orange juice waited on a painted sideboard in the breakfast room. It was pleasant and bright, with a round table set in front of a bow window. I served myself and sat at the table. Through the window I could see daffodils blooming, nodding their frilled golden trumpets.

I felt Charles's presence before I turned to him as he spoke.

"Morning," he said. One look at him told me instantly that morning was not his favorite time of day. He threw back his orange juice while standing at the sideboard, as if it were whiskey at a bar. Then he poured coffee for himself and, ignoring the little bell on the table, bellowed, "Jenny!"

I bit back my question, Is Jenny the cook? I settled for a polite "Good morning," which he did not acknowledge. He stared out of the window. His eyes had a hollow look, as if he had not slept well.

"Morning, Mr. Charles, and Miss . . ." Jenny was, for a

cook, surprisingly thin, but she had a voice that should have come out of a woman three times her size. It was loud in the quiet room as she came up to the table.

"Rosamund. Rosamund, this is Jenny, the cook," said Charles with some effort. "I'll have ham and two eggs and some biscuits, Jenny."

"No biscuits, Mr. Charles. 'Lectricity not on yet."

"Damn!" he growled. "Then make it three eggs and scramble them."

"Yassuh. Here's the paper." She handed the folded newspaper to him. "What you want, Miss Rosamund?"

"I'll have the same, but just one egg, please, Jenny," I replied.

"Yes, ma'am." Without being asked, she added more coffee to our cups before she left the room.

Charles had spread out the paper over most of the table. One corner of it covered my now-empty juice glass. I didn't mind. I was finding that I liked the evidence of his monumental self-assurance. Perhaps some of it would rub off on me, I thought as I sipped my coffee. Then I realized with a pang that such a thought never would have occurred to me until fairly recently. In spite of the brightness of the morning, a memory spilled out of that tightly packed-away place inside me. The brightness of the sun became the artificial glare of OR lights, and I no longer saw the flower-filled lawn but white-tiled walls and a hospital-green-draped small body on the operating table; and above the boy hung a bag of rich, dark red blood, the wrong blood. . . .

"Rosamund? Rosamund!" Charles's deep voice held an edge of command that I heard, though as if he were far away, in another world. "What's the matter with you?" he growled.

With a great effort I brought the room back into focus, and the clarity of that terrible memory faded.

"You look like a goose walked over your grave," Charles observed, sounding more irritated than concerned.

"Is that a Southern expression?" I asked acidly. I intended to keep my memories, bad or good, my own business.

"I suppose so. It's irrelevant. Are you all right?"

"I'm fine. I thought you were reading your newspaper."

"I *was* reading my newspaper, and I happened to look up and saw that expression on your face. And I thought . . . well, I'm not sure what I thought," said Charles. He ran his hand through his already-rumpled hair, then looked at me piercingly. "Did anything happen last night, Rosamund?"

"I slept very well, thank you," I replied. Jenny's advent prevented further probing. "That smells so good, Jenny!" I exclaimed, realizing as she set the plate in front of me that I was very hungry.

"I can do a whole lot better when I get the stove back on," she said, but she grinned. My compliment wasn't wasted on her.

"I'm sure it won't be long now. Thank you, Jenny," said Charles, folding up his paper and putting it aside.

"Welcome, Mr. Charles," Jenny responded. Once again she replenished our coffee cups before leaving the room.

We ate our breakfasts without further talk. To keep memories at bay, I filled my mind with thoughts of what I would do during the day: talk with the doctor, get to know my patient, and hopefully, make a trip to Wachesaw Landing for my car. Regina came into the room so quietly that I was startled when she spoke.

"The power has been restored, Mr. Charles," she said, flicking the overhead light on and off again to emphasize the point. She wore the same white-collared gray dress, or one exactly like it, that she had worn the day before. I thought how particularly it suited her, uniform or no.

"Good!" declared Charles, his attention still on his food.

"And Dr. Barkstone's office called. He had to go to the hospital on an emergency, so he won't be out this morning. I've seen the nurse. She said she will stay until noon. I must have your keys, Rosamund," said Regina, holding out her hand. I withdrew them from my pocket and gave them to her.

"How is my wife this morning?"

"She's quiet. She and the nurse are having breakfast now, but she will need more medication. And she will need you to administer her insulin," Regina said, ever precise and attentive to details.

It will wear on me, this need of hers to spell everything out, I thought.

"You know I'll take care of that!" said Charles sharply. So, she could irritate him, too.

"Yes sir," said Regina, turning her back on us.

But Charles was not finished. "Regina. I hope you remember what we talked about last night." She turned to him and nodded. She said nothing, but her tawny eyes flashed. "So, when you asked for the keys, that was just a slip of the tongue?"

"Yes, sir," she said.

"All right. Go on, then," grumbled Charles.

"What was that all about?" I asked when we were alone.

Charles looked thoughtful, running his hand through his hair again. I liked the way he did that, and the way his thick, unruly hair softened the almost harsh lines of his strong face. He turned his dark blue eyes on me. "Last night, after you went to your room, I had a talk with Regina. I reminded her that before you arrived I'd told her that you were to be treated as a friend of the family and as a medical professional. In other words, she was not to treat you as one of the help. Just now, when she asked you for the keys, she didn't do that, so I brought it to her attention."

"What do you mean?" I was genuinely puzzled.

"I mean, specifically, that to her you are not just Rosamund, but Miss Rosamund."

"Oh, honestly!" All these quaint Southern manners had thoroughly exasperated me. "I don't care about that. In fact, I don't like it. And I hate being called ma'am, too. It makes me feel a hundred years old!"

"I understand better than you think I do," said Charles, narrowing his heavy brows. "I went to Harvard, remember? In fact, generations of the men in my family have gone North to school, for which we have often been criticized. But believe me, it's different here, and I know what I'm doing. You're young, and if my wife is to respect you, as she must or we will get nowhere, she must see that Regina treats you with respect. Unfortunately, Regina seems to have taken a dislike to you for some reason, and I wanted to put a stop to it. Immediately."

"I've been here less than a day. How can you tell?" I'd sensed Regina's dislike from the first, but I'd hoped I was wrong.

"When we came back last night from our walk, Regina hadn't put so much as one candle in your room. It was a deliberate oversight. It had to be, because that woman forgets nothing."

"There was no harm done. I had the candelabra we brought up the stairs," I argued stubbornly. I did not want my fears confirmed.

"Don't be obtuse, Rosamund! The point is, I told her to treat you as a guest on your arrival and as a member of the family thereafter. And she didn't do that, did she?"

"No, I have to admit she didn't. I just hope you didn't make things worse by talking to her about it."

Charles was quickly losing patience with the subject and with me. "Let me make something clear. You're a bright woman. I think you probably understand it already and for some reason only God knows, you're just being stubborn. We are quite a few years behind the times here, whether you like it or not. That's a fact of life. I'm not personally behind the times, nor is my business, but I'm an exception. My wife is, and so are most of the people who live and work on these plantations. I didn't bring you here as a member of the American Civil Liberties Union to reform us all, I brought you here to help me in a very difficult situation. You must accept things as they are. And you must realize that I'm doing my best to get you started out right!"

On conclusion of this speech, Charles flung his napkin down on the table and glared at me, as if daring me to challenge him. I saw that he meant every word, and I wondered more than ever what I had gotten myself into. It was hard to swallow the sarcastic "yes, Massa" that had sprung to my lips, but I did it.

"All right. I know you're right about Regina's attitude toward me, but since I can't think of anything I've done to cause it, I didn't want to believe it. I suppose if you can bear to be called Mr. Charles, I can stand Miss Rosamund. Perhaps when I get to know your wife, I'll understand why this, this respect thing, is so important," I conceded. I wanted to make peace, to have again the sunny serenity of the morning. I changed the subject. "Since the doctor isn't coming this morning, shall I go with you when you give Mrs. Charpentier, Arabella, her insulin injection?"

"No. Not yet. I expect the doctor will come along about noon, before his afternoon office hours, and the nurse is still here. So, you can do whatever you like for an hour or so, and then I'll drive you to the Landing for your car. All right?"

"Yes!" I agreed enthusiastically, "I'd like that very much!"

I returned briefly to my rooms, looking curiously at the closed doors along the way. Perhaps if I asked Regina to show me the house, she might warm to me a bit. But for now, I wanted to explore outside. It was too beautiful a day to stay indoors! I opened the windows a few inches in both of my rooms, and looked around with satisfaction. The sitting room was very pleasant, and already I felt more at home.

"Good morning, Miss Rosamund!" It was Phyllis. She bobbed into the room, her young face smiling, cheeks shining.

"Hello, Phyllis. We were going to see where I can wash and iron my clothes this morning, weren't we?" I was glad she was here, because I had forgotten. I wouldn't have wanted to hurt her feelings.

"Yes, ma'am, we was. But now Regina change her mind. She say, I take care of your clothes and your rooms and everything, just like I does Miss Arabella's. She say, Mr. Charles said so!" Phyllis' eyes sparkled with mischief, and I got the impression she enjoyed seeing Regina have to change her mind, even if it made more work for herself.

"Oh, really, I . . ." Automatically I started to say that I could do it myself, then remembered how insistent Charles had been. So in midsentence I took a new direction. "That's very nice, Phyllis. Most of my clothes are still in my car where I left it at the Wachesaw Landing, but I think Mr., er, Charles will take me to get it this morning."

"Yes, ma'am. Don't you worry. I can take real good care of your things!" She looked very eager, and I feared she would be disappointed by the lack of finery among my "things." I had never been much interested in clothes. Somehow I was sure that Arabella Charpentier, despite her illness, must have closets full of frilly, feminine "things."

Suddenly I wondered if she were beautiful. The temptation to lure Phyllis into gossip was strong, especially since I was sure she would be a lively, innocent informer. There couldn't be a malicious bone in that round body! In contrast there was Regina, who surely would never gossip; and yet I was certain Regina could lie when she chose, without so much as a blink of her strange eyes.

I decided I had best remove myself from temptation. "If you don't need me for anything, then, I'm going outside. It's such a lovely day. I thought I'd explore a little."

"You go right on, Miss Rosamund. I'll just tidy up in here," Phyllis said.

I left the house by the West Front door, intending to wander through the flowers along the intersecting paths of the garden. Instead, I was drawn to the river. The flowers were colorful, their fragrance enticing, but the glassy black water pulled at me until I stood on the bank. I stared at it, as into a dark mirror. Something about it made me feel very small, very young and yet at the same time very old. I felt that if I could reach out and touch it, it would not be liquid and yielding to my fingers. It would be hard and cold and smooth . . . and . . . and round. Round, like a ball. What a bizarre thought! And with it I felt a mixture of fright and fascination that left me breathless. I slowly backed away from that black water.

Perhaps I would do better to stay away from the river, I counseled myself. I turned my back on it and began resolutely to walk toward the house, looking steadily at it as I had been unable to do yesterday. It was handsome in the clear morning light, well-proportioned, not overbearing. This was no Greek Revival museum piece, though I supposed the slender columns owed something to the Greeks. In spite of its size it had the look of a home, a place where generations of the same family had lived out, still lived out, their lives. Now I, too, would live a part of my life in this house.

I did wander through the flowers and eventually through bushes as high as my head and covered with fat, tender buds among glossy dark green leaves. I guessed they were camellias. The azaleas I recognized. They were everywhere in bloom, masses of them in white, coral, all shades of pink, deep red. I breathed deeply, enjoying.

I left the paths and took to the grass to circle the house. I recognized the patch of daffodils and the bow window of the breakfast room as I passed it. I skirted the long leg of the South Wing, wanting to look into the windows but not daring to. I looked up to the second floor. Regina had said Charles's rooms were upstairs. Of course, it must have been a long time since he had shared a room with his wife, I mused. Though, in this different culture, this new world I'd come to, perhaps it was usual for husbands and wives to have separate rooms. Separate suites of rooms, even. How long had they been married when Charles found out about Arabella's illness, I wondered. I knew from books what there was to know about manic depression. The workings of the human mind fascinated me. I'd intended to specialize in psychiatry, when the time came. . . . Now I had to think, *if* the time comes. Well, it would be good experience for me with Arabella Charpentier. It occurred to me that my intended specialization was mentioned in my c.v. Possibly, though neither Charles nor Mr. Parker had said so, this had had something to do with my being chosen for the job.

I had reached the end of the wing. Now I could see the U-shape of the house, the half-circle of the drive as it dipped to the East Front, and opposite, the oak alley. I wondered what had inspired the forefathers to plant those trees in that way? Surely there were no such trees in England or France? I really didn't know. My education had always been heavily skewed toward the sciences I'd needed as a background for medicine. I didn't know enough of history or architecture to fully appreciate this place. I'd lived for twenty-six whole years without ever hearing of a rice plantation. What must it have been like a hundred, a hundred and fifty, years ago?

"Well, do you like it better in the daylight or in the twilight?" Charles had come up behind me, and I had not heard his footsteps through the soft grass.

I knew that he referred to the live oaks. "Both. They're magnificent like this, in the sun, but last night there was something"—I searched for the right word—"primeval about those trees. Almost mysterious."

"Yes, that's true. When I was a boy I used to think that if I sat among those trees very quietly, for a long enough time, they would tell me great secrets. Of course, they never did. Even now, I'm forty years old and I know there are no secrets here, not so much as a family ghost, but sometimes I still feel it. The mystery." He stood with his hands in his pockets, for a moment lost in his thoughts.

"Ghosts? Do other people think they have ghosts on their property?"

Charles chuckled. "Sure. My brother has one. His wife, Lynda, swears she's going to catch it some day."

"How interesting," I said skeptically.

Charles raised a heavy eyebrow and tilted his head to the side, looking down at me. "You're not a believer in the supernatural, Rosamund?"

"No, I'm not," I replied firmly. But then my natural honesty forced me to say, "But last night I could have been persuaded."

"Oh? Are you sure nothing happened to you last night? You looked so strange for a few minutes there at breakfast."

"Nothing happened last night except that I was in a new place and it was dark and I was overtired. My imagination tried to run away with me, but it was brief. I got into bed and blew out the candles and went right to sleep. I slept very well, really."

I hoped he would let it go at that. I didn't want him pressing me, I didn't want to think about what had happened at the breakfast table. The memory had been so strong that it had almost been a vision, or a hallucination.

"Good. But in the future if you're uncomfortable, or concerned about anything, come to my room. I'm a night owl anyway."

"I doubt I'd do that, but I'll remember."

"Well. Are you ready to go for your car?"

"Of course. I'll have to get my purse; my car keys are in it."

"While you're doing that, I'll bring the wagon around." Charles set off down the drive as I hurried into the house.

Charles's wagon was a Volvo station wagon that looked at least twenty years old.

"I have another car, but this is what I drive most of the time. I hope you don't mind," he said as I slid into the front passenger seat. "Seat belt," he prodded.

"I'm surprised you use them." I pulled the seat belt around myself and snapped the buckle.

"Why?"

I wanted to bite my tongue. "I suppose you just don't look like a very safety-conscious person."

"Hm. In the car I am. But, you're right. I'm usually a risk-taker, and I don't give a damn what other people think." I could believe that. He continued, "Fortunately, my risks have always paid off. All except one."

He muttered his last words, as if he had lapsed into talking to himself. I tried to become absorbed in the view from the car window. Trees were thick on either side of the road, as if we were in our own private forest. But I was too curious, I had to ask.

"All except one?"

"Arabella," Charles replied without hesitation. "Marrying Bella was a great risk. My mother refused to accept her, as I must have known she would. Mother wanted me to have the marriage annulled, and when I would not, she moved out of the house. She's lived in Charleston since, and she seems happy there. There's much more for her to do in the city, but sometimes I still feel that she should be here. I'm sure my father never thought Mother would live out her life anywhere but Charpentier."

We had passed from heavy woods into sparser growth and soon turned onto a highway that I knew from my map study must be 17, also called the King's Highway. In the motel I'd read in a free travel-entertainment guide that it was so called because originally it had been built in anticipation of the King of England's visit to his colonial coastal towns, a visit that had never happened. The history of the region interested me, but not nearly so much as Charles himself. He seemed inclined to talk of himself and his family, and I was more than willing to encourage him.

"Is the house your mother's, then?"

"No. My father left the house and all the land to me. Mother got a trust, and so did my younger brother. He wasn't pleased with that, of course. He's quite a bit younger than I, and until he met Lynda he was always irresponsible, which accounts for Father's decision. When Louis and Lynda decided to marry, I gave them the place next door, Leighton. They're doing a good job of restoring the old house. To be truthful, I think Lynda has done most of the work, but at least since he's had the house Louis has been less bitter toward me."

No wonder he seemed so solitary. There was no one in his family close to him. I cast about in my mind for a question to keep the conversation going.

"Do you still raise rice?"

"Good Lord, no!" Charles exploded in rolling laughter that filled the car. "Rice is as long gone now as indigo was by the time of the Civil War! No, what I do is profit from the foresight of my grandfather, who bought up the plantations of his neighbors when they failed after the turn of the century. And of my own father, whose major contribution was that he held onto all the land while he played around on the stock market. Profitably, fortunately. Now I'm developing the land, which doesn't endear me to the remaining neighbors, no matter how carefully I do it. As I told you, most of the folks around here are years behind the times."

He fell silent, thinking, I supposed, about his business. Or his unpopularity. I wanted him to talk again of his family and of the past. I was not much interested in whatever he did to increase the family fortunes. I waited for him to speak again. As the silence continued, I felt a building physical awareness of the man beside me. It was almost too much to be enclosed in the small space of a car with him, though the wind rushed through the open window and tugged at my securely knotted hair. I felt I must say something, anything.

"Is your wife's family also from here?"

Charles's reply was guttural, deep in his throat. "My wife says that she has no family." And then, after a pause, "I am, unfortunately, all she has."

I turned my head and looked at him, at the hard line of his jaw, the large hands locked in a tight grip on the steering wheel. I felt anger in him, repressed and yet near the surface. There had been a lack of sympathy in his voice that somehow did not surprise me.

"I'm sorry," I said. "Your wife's illness must be very difficult for you. Although, of course, it must be even more difficult for her."

"I thought that, too. In the beginning. I thought she must suffer much more than I suffered for her—and believe me, I did suffer for her." He shot me a quick, piercing look. "You will probably think me a hard-hearted man, Rosamund. For many years now I've believed that Bella enjoys and exploits this so-called illness of hers. She is the most completely amoral human being I have ever known."

"Amoral?" The word was so unexpected, I wasn't sure I'd heard him right.

"Totally, completely without a sense of morality!"

"And yet, yet you married her. You've stayed married to her," I protested. Though I had not yet met Arabella Charpentier, I already thought of her as my patient, and I felt a need to defend her.

Charles gave a short, sharp bark of a laugh as he swung the station wagon into a side road. "Oh, yes. I was so crazy in love with her, I thought I couldn't live without her. My mother said Bella put a spell on me, and I think Mother really believed that. But I knew what I was doing. I wasn't put off by her lack of family or by the fact that she was ten years older than I. Her wildness was exciting to me then. I married her—I'm responsible. Still responsible."

He spoke with a grim passion that shocked me and prevented further questions. In silence we drove along a two-lane road, passing small houses weathered to gray, set well back among trees draped with gray Spanish moss. Suddenly the road opened out into a place I recognized, the Wachesaw Landing.

"Where did you leave your car?"

"That way," I said, pointing. "It's a Reliant station wagon, cream, with woody trim. There it is!" Finding my car was like finding an old friend, even though it was brand-new and I'd only had it for two weeks. In my eagerness I leaned forward from the waist, and immediately the seat belt tightened across my chest. I reached down to release it.

Charles brought the Volvo to a halt behind my car. He turned to me. I was still jabbing at the release button on my seat belt, which had jammed.

"Of all the stupid things! I'm, it's stuck!" I felt like a prisoner, a very clumsy and inept prisoner.

"So I see!" Charles's lips curved in a one-sided quirk of amusement. He reached out and trapped my left hand, stilling its futile efforts. "No one has sat in that seat for a very long time—it's probably just balky from lack of use. Let me help you." In one fluid movement he had slipped from his own encumberment and moved across the seat toward me, still holding my left hand. He reached across me with his free arm, a motion that brought his body over mine. "Needs some slack," he said softly.

I felt the webbing tight between my breasts and understood his intention. "I'll do it," I said quickly, raising my right hand above my head to pull more of the belt from its holder, but his hand was already there. My breath caught in my throat. I could feel my heart pound and color rush into my face, all from his nearness, and there was nothing I could do about it. I was truly trapped. Don't let him look at me, don't let him know that his body affects me this way, I silently pleaded as I slowly lowered my right hand and placed it in my lap.

But he did look at me. Though I felt the strap loosen across my chest, Charles did not move. I looked up at him and met the intensity of his very dark blue eyes, inches above mine. For an instant they blazed, a flare of naked emotion that made his face look open and vulnerable. Then it was gone. His bushy brows drew together. He dropped my hand that he had been holding as if it had suddenly burned him.

"Have you out of there in a minute," he said gruffly. His hands now worked swiftly, impersonally, and the stubborn clasp was no match for his strength.

"Thank you," I said. Quickly I opened the car door and slid out, shutting it behind me. I needed the solid metal between him and me. "You needn't wait. I'm sure I can find my way back," I assured him, leaning to the car window. But he was not inside. I looked around in surprise to see him rounding the front of the Volvo wagon.

"I said . . ."

"I heard you. I want to make sure your car starts." He

peered into the back window. "Nice car. I think it suits you."

That won him a smile from me as I unlocked the door on the driver's side. I wasn't sure what he meant by that, but I would take it as a compliment.

"I like it. It's new—I just got it a couple of weeks ago, for the trip down here, really, but I've needed a car for a long time anyway." I stood ready to slip behind the wheel, realizing that I should thank him for bringing me. He must have things to do, and I was taking his time. "Thank you for bringing me to get it."

"It was the least I could do, after putting you through the inconvenience of an extra night in a motel and the boat trip." He walked up to stand near, leaning against the side of my car with his hands in his pockets.

"I enjoyed the boat trip. And Captain John." I edged into the seat. "Well, I'm sure it will start," I said as I inserted the key and turned it.

"Rosamund." Charles reached out a staying hand as I was closing the door. He moved into the open space and sank to his haunches. "There's something I want to tell you. I haven't been able to talk with anyone about my . . . situation with Bella for a long time. There's something about you that loosens my tongue, and I wasn't very careful what I said. I know I've needed help, of a quality I don't know how to describe. I just didn't know that when help came it would be . . . someone like you."

The vulnerable look was back upon his face again. It discomforted me more than even his physical nearness could do, but in a different way.

"I hope that doesn't mean you're going to tell me again that you think I'm not equal to the task," I said.

"No. Not at all. I'm not sure what I'm trying to say," he admitted, running his hand through shaggy, wind-blown hair. "I guess I'm just very glad you've come."

I wanted to touch his face, still his lips with my fingers, tell him that somehow everything would be all right. I held on to the steering wheel with both hands as I assured him, "I'll do my best."

I was relieved when he rose from his crouched position

and closed the door. Without another word, he went back to the old Volvo. I waited as he moved it out of my way. Whenever I looked into my rearview mirror on the drive back to Charpentier, the battered old Volvo followed behind, as if Charles were guarding me.

Chapter 4

D R. BARKSTONE WAS A small man with large, watery blue eyes and a fringe of white hair around a shining bald head. He had delicate hands and smelled of soap. He exuded meticulousness. Why, then, was he avoiding my question?

"Let me phrase it another way, Dr. Barkstone. Is Mrs. Charpentier a manic-depressive, or is she not?" I could not understand his prescribing of a tranquilizing drug for a woman in the depressed cycle of that illness.

The little doctor sighed and settled himself more deeply in his chair. We were in my sitting room. I had the distinct impression that he had wanted to confine our conference to a quick review of his patient's medications, and what I wanted and felt entitled to, was a deeper discussion of the case.

"That is the diagnosis that was made by a consulting psychiatrist I called in, let me see now, it was ten years ago."

"And you concurred in the diagnosis?"

He nodded his shining head. "I did. Though Mrs. Charpentier has never seemed precisely depressed to me. Rather, she has periods of quiet and withdrawal, alternating with periods of, er, heightened activity."

I remembered Charles's words: her wildness excited me. The doctor was continuing.

"We tried lithium therapy, and she did not respond to it, even at levels where I feared toxicity. The manic-depressive diagnosis is more a label of convenience in her case, than an indicator for specific treatment. I think it has helped Charles when he has needed to explain her behavior to others, or to himself."

I regarded the aging internist with growing respect. I knew that it was far better to base treatment on individual observations than to blindly follow a diagnostic label. "Has she ever been hospitalized?" I asked.

"Once. After the fire. You have heard about that?"

I nodded. He continued.

"She was in shock. She was not badly burned, which seemed almost miraculous. But her hair was singed, even her eyebrows and eyelashes. Her skin, on her hands and arms and about her face, was comparable to a very severe sunburn. It blistered and peeled, and then was as good as new. Her eyebrows and eyelashes grew back of course. Oh, that's something you should know about her: since the fire, Mrs. Charpentier has insisted on wearing glasses with tinted lenses at all times. Do not attempt for any reason to take them from her—she will become dangerously agitated. It's even difficult for me to persuade her to remove them when I must examine her eyes."

"I'll remember," I nodded. "But that hospitalization after the fire, it was not a psychiatric hospitalization?"

"No. It was not, though I did call in a psychiatrist to examine her. Taking into account the experience she had been through, he found no abnormality. When Mrs. Charpentier is in one of her periods of heightened activity, she is uncooperative in the extreme. There is no possibility that she might submit to hospitalization."

"And she is not dangerous to herself or others?"

"Apparently not. Certainly she is not suicidal. Charles thought she must have started the fire, but there was no proof. Nothing like that has ever happened again, so Charles may have been wrong." He shifted in his chair, crossed his legs, and looked at me intently. "I think Charles was right in bringing you here, Miss Hill. Whatever your reasons for interrupting your medical education, you will be a most valuable observer. I understand that you plan a residency in psychiatry?"

"Yes, I hope so." I refused to follow that with the thought that was always so near the surface: If I continue in medicine. I rushed on, "Dr. Barkstone, I'm not sure what's expected of me. Oh, I have no question about the management of Mrs. Charpentier's diabetes, or administering whatever medication is required. But surely the previous nurse's aides could do that. What more is it that you want of me?"

"He has not told you?"

"No. Mr. Charpentier has told me very little. I think it is difficult for him to talk about his wife. I believe he expected you to instruct me in all the details of her care."

"Well. I think you must verify this with him, but I will tell you as far as I know. You will soon discover that Mrs. Charpentier is a difficult patient, a difficult woman, extremely strong-willed. Regina is very effective in obtaining her cooperation, but Charles . . . oh, how shall I put it? Charles desires that Regina's time be kept free from demands by his wife, free for other things. She did not need an aide before the fire, and probably there are times when she does not really need one now, but Charles does not want her left alone. The first woman stayed quite a while, two or three years, I think. Then one day she just disappeared, with no notice. Since then there have been many. Frankly, it has become impossible to find anyone locally, even as far away as Charleston. When I suggested that we try out of state, Charles had the idea to use our contacts in Cambridge, which brought you to us. I must say, I never thought someone with your qualifications . . ."

I interrupted impatiently. "So she is difficult and strong-willed. Charles did tell me that was the reason he wanted someone she would not regard as a servant. But beyond that?"

"You can be an informed and intelligent observer, far more so than anyone with only an aide's level of training. Charles and I want you to observe and document his wife's behavior. She has bizarre ideas and fantasies in her so-called manic phase. Over the last two years these periods have come closer and closer together, and there is some suggestion that now even in her quiet times these ideas persist. She is too cunning and intelligent to reveal them to me when I am here. You can do most by your observations."

"I see. I'm sure I can do that. Are we hoping for some particular goal or outcome?"

He looked uncomfortable, shifting again in his chair. "No. Perhaps Charles . . . but he has not told me anything specific."

"Well, then. Did you bring her chart for me to record my observations?"

"Very professional question. I'm sorry to say I didn't think of it, I keep only the medication record here. Her chart is in my office. I'll send you some log sheets, and if we decide to include them in her chart they'll be in the correct form." He looked pleased. "Now, shall we go and meet the lady in question?"

I was quickly on my feet. "Yes. I've been wanting to do that, it seems, for a long time now." Eager with anticipation, glad that my curiosity would soon be satisfied, I left the room in Dr. Barkstone's company without a backward glance. I did not remember that he had put a fresh supply of medication in the cabinet, and that I had failed to lock it with the keys Regina had so scrupulously returned to me.

We briskly walked the length of the windowed gallery and down a stairway at the far end that I hadn't known was there, then into a large, long room below. I felt a little light-headed as I followed the doctor into the room. My height, which was greater than his, made me feel exposed. I supposed the light-headedness came from nerves.

Charles sat with his wife at a table in a corner, and he stood as we approached, and addressed his wife. "Bella, this is Rosamund Hill; Rosamund, my wife, Arabella Charpentier."

"How do you do," I said, ready to offer a handshake as I would have done in my former environment. But she neither moved nor spoke. She had masses of very dark hair, here and there shot through with strands of startling white. Her face was narrow, her neck long, and her skin either intentionally or unnaturally pale, untouched by the sun. She wore a purple gown with ruffles at the throat and at the hem of its wide sleeves, and her tinted glasses, very large and very fashionable, shaded from lavender to purple. Though she said nothing to acknowledge my presence, I could feel her eyes on me behind those glasses.

"Join us for lunch," said Charles, resuming his seat. "You too, Dr. Barkstone."

The table was set for four. I sat, but Dr. Barkstone declined, gesturing with his small hands. He seemed nervous and eager to be on his way. "No, thank you," he said, "I must get back to town. I have office hours this afternoon." Already he was backing away.

"Well, then, you know your way out. Thank you for coming," said Charles.

"Yes, thank you," I seconded, turning toward the doctor's retreating figure. "It was good to meet you, Dr. Barkstone."

"Likewise," he nodded, stopping for a moment. "And Mrs. Charpentier, I think you are very fortunate in your new . . . er, companion." He gave her a little nod, looking like a courtier leaving the presence.

"Good-bye, *doctor*," said Arabella, with chilling emphasis.

She does not like him, I thought. I turned back to the table, and caught Charles's eyes on me. He sat opposite me, his wife next to him.

"Well, we have a head start on you, Rosamund," he said, handing me the salad bowl.

It was an awkward meal, with Charles doing most of the talking. Under Arabella's scrutiny, which I sensed but could not confirm, I began to wish that I too had tinted glasses to hide behind. Twice I addressed her, trying to be relaxed and friendly, but she ignored me. Arabella ate her meal slowly and deliberately, with an air of detachment, as if she were alone. Or wished to be alone. The air around Charles fairly crackled with his exasperation.

At last he gave up. "I'll leave you two to get to know each other," he said, pushing back his chair. He looked at me, and I tried to read his look but could not; it seemed at odds with the harshness of his voice.

"I'm sure we'll get along well," I said, with a brightness as false as my words. As I watched Charles walk from the room, I thought how unlike me it was to say something just because it seemed the expected thing. I disliked myself for it and decided I would not do it again, regardless of the consequences. Even silence would be better, no matter how awkward.

There were pears and a wedge of cheese for dessert. I took a pear and cut it in half. It was fragrant and juicy, and I enjoyed removing the skin and cutting it into smaller sections. I offered half of these to Arabella, well aware that she watched me.

"Will you share the pear with me?" I took her silence for assent and divided the pear between two dessert plates, then added a small piece of the cheese to each. She accepted the plate with her long, thin, too-white fingers. The purple ruffle of her sleeve fell back to reveal a wrist so thin it was little more than skin over bone. A death-hand, a hand to be afraid of, I thought.

"Thank you."

Nothing could have startled me more. I would have been less surprised if she had thrown the plate, pear, cheese and all, in my face.

"Charles says we are lucky that you are able to spend some time with us." Her voice was unexpectedly beautiful, low and thrilling.

I wondered what he had told her about me. I recalled his insistence that I establish a relationship of equals. I said, "I feel fortunate that I shall get to know your lovely home. I've never been in this part of the country before."

"You come from the North?"

"Yes, from Massachusetts."

"I've never been there. I was in Virginia once. That was a long time ago." She said this with a certain wistfulness, then applied herself to consuming the pear and cheese with that single-minded deliberation.

I also finished the fruit and cheese in silence. I felt challenged, and fascinated. I wondered how Arabella would look with color in her cheeks, a smile on her well-shaped lips, and without the glasses obscuring her eyes. She was still rather beautiful in all her gauntness; in her youth she must have been dazzling. But there was something about her that chilled me, without reason.

"What do you generally do after lunch?" I asked.

"I always rest for two hours in the afternoon. Come, I'll show you my bedroom."

As Arabella led me from the long, rectangular room we'd occupied, through a linking powder room to her bedroom, I had for the first time a mental picture of the entire North Wing. Somehow I had assumed that her bedroom was upstairs, like mine. Rather, it was beneath my bedroom and since it was larger, it occupied almost the whole space below both of my rooms. I supposed the difference was accounted for by a large closet space.

"Do you like it?" Arabella gestured dramatically with a sweep of her arm in its flowing, ruffled sleeve.

"It's . . ." I could not say spectacular, though that word came immediately to mind. I said, "It's impressive."

Arabella chuckled—a low, almost ugly sound, out of keeping with the rather cultured tones of her speaking voice. "I chose everything myself. I had a decorator come from Charleston."

The bedroom spoke almost violently of the manic side of her personality. Pale gray walls and a darker gray carpet anchored a mad kaleidoscope of too-rich colors. The furniture was all black-lacquered chinoiserie, traced and painted in scarlet and gold. At one end of the room, nearest where we stood, was a Turkish divan piled with velvet and satin pillows in green, gold, purple, and turqoise. At the opposite end was her bed in its massive black lacquer frame. Its four posts were squared, more like pillars, and supported a canopy which was nearly as high as the twelve-foot ceiling. From the canopy hung scarlet draperies, matching the scarlet spread. How anyone could sleep in such a place I couldn't imagine.

"Charles hates this room," she hissed, as if sharing a great secret. "He won't even come in here!" she chuckled, evil, full of malice.

I hated it too, but I sensed she was testing me. I trailed one hand across the pillows on the divan. I would not have been surprised if their lurid colors had come off on my fingers, staining them irreparably, but of course they did not. Slowly I walked across the room and stopped to examine the painted scenes on a secretary-desk that was higher than my head. In itself, it was an exquisite piece.

"This is lovely," I was able to say, for I meant it. But its beauty was buried amid mad opulence. Next to the desk, in a heavy gilt frame, hung a large painting which I studied as if I knew something about art. The subject was medieval, that much I could tell; it was all very dark, with gargoylelike creatures lurking in the background, peering out at the viewer, and in the foreground a robed figure hunched over a great book. It revolted me. I declined to comment upon it, and decided I had put up enough of a show of interest. I turned back to Arabella, who stood like a frilled, purple column in the center of the room.

"After you've rested, perhaps you'd like to go for a walk? It's really very nice outside today."

"No. I don't feel very well today. I may sleep the rest of the afternoon." She walked up to me and stood too close. It was hard not to back away. "They drugged me, you know, that doctor and the nurse." She sounded whining, complaining.

"I'm sure they only meant to help. I know the storm upset you."

"Ah, you don't understand at all—what's your name?" She was a couple of inches shorter than I, and she craned her neck to bring her face closer to mine.

I saw myself a tiny reflection in her lenses. "Rosamund." It was hard not to flinch, to return the stare from eyes I could not see within their purple sheath.

"Yes. Rosamund. Pretty name. You'd be pretty too, if you didn't make yourself so plain. Such hair—I like your hair. Do you always wear it knotted up like that?" She touched my head.

"Yes. Well, almost always." I lowered my eyes. The touch of her hand made my skin crawl, and I didn't want her to see the rejection in my eyes.

"That's a pity. Well, it's none of my business if you want to look plain. What were we talking about?"

"The storm."

"Oh, yes. Well, you see, Rosamund, the storm didn't upset me. I loved the storm! I always love storms. Storms give me power—wonderful, delicious *power!*" She raised both hands in the air above her head, sleeves falling back, and twirled away from me.

Now I saw without doubt the abnormality in Arabella Charpentier. In the moments before she had twirled away, her lips had quivered with her intensity. I had no doubt that her eyes glittered behind the glasses.

"That's why they drug me, to keep me from the power." She stopped, once more in the center of the room. "Oh, this time it wasn't too important, so I let them do it. To please Charles. Sometimes I still like to please Charles. But when I want to, I can get around them."

"Oh, I see," I said offhandedly. I vowed she would not be able to get around me. But still, she had my sympathy. I could imagine, after almost forty-eight hours of heavy sedation, that her head felt heavy and her tongue thick. "I'm sure you do need a good rest, and we'll see how you feel when you wake up. Do you need any help? Can I get your robe or anything?"

"No, no, I can do it by myself. You go and do whatever you like." With a wave of her hand she dismissed me.

"All right. Sleep well," I said. Once again I marvelled that anyone could sleep at all, much less well, in that bedroom.

I was not sorry to be out of it. When I returned to the big room, already looking forward to some time alone to digest what had just happened, I found that I was not to be allowed the luxury. Regina was there, clearing the table.

"Hello, Regina. Mrs. Charpentier is taking her nap." I was as polite as I could manage. Too late I remembered I was to call her Bella. I would never be able to do that, it didn't come naturally to my lips somehow. But from now on I would be careful to say "Arabella." Perhaps this one slip wouldn't matter. The situation strained me. I would much have preferred to be friendly, to offer to help Regina clear the table and stack the dishes on the little cart beside her. Instead I stood and watched, feeling awkward.

"She will sleep all afternoon," Regina declared.

"So she said." Rather than stand there uselessly, I went to the french doors and looked out onto a slate-floored patio bordered with azaleas, all red and in full bloom. It would be pleasant to sit there on the cushioned lounge chair and read while Arabella slept. But I had not brought a book with me, and I did not want to leave her alone.

"You do not need to stay while she sleeps," said Regina, as if she knew my thoughts. It was another annoying habit of hers.

"I prefer to be here," I said, still looking out at the patio.

"None of the others stayed with her while she took her naps. After all, you won't be with her when she sleeps at night. You won't even take supper with her. You'll be with Mr. Charles at the end of the day." Was her tone slightly nasty, or did I imagine it?

"Regina, I am not one of the others. I do not intend to leave Arabella alone when she naps, not today or any other day. However, since you are here at the moment, I am going to my room to get a book. I'll be right back." I made it a statement, not a request, and I started for the door. Her voice stopped me, and I turned back.

"Then, while you are upstairs you had better do something you forgot earlier." She came to stand less than two feet from me, and her strange eyes radiated superiority and hostility.

Instantly I remembered. I had failed to lock the medication cabinet! My hand went to my pocket and closed upon the small keys. "Of course." Don't explain, I told myself, you don't owe this woman any explanations. My chin went up a notch, as if to compensate for our equal height. I challenged her.

"Regina, you've never told me why it's so important that I keep those cabinets locked and the keys with me. What is the reason?"

Her lip curled in derision. "Those are the orders of Mr. Charles."

"Then, I will ask him." My eyes locked with hers. She very nearly snarled at me. Adrenalin pumped through me, the ancient instinct for fight or flight flaring within me as I had never felt it before. Controlling every movement, I withdrew the keys from my pocket and let them dangle from my fingers. Then I turned and walked slowly to the door. I stopped and looked back at her.

"I'll be back in a moment," I said.

"I will not be here. There is no reason for it."·

I refused to respond to that. I turned my back and left the room. That was Round One, I thought when I gained the hall, and it was a tie.

Three weeks went by quickly. I was settling in at Charpentier; my days and nights had developed a routine that was a pleasant change from anything I had ever known. One thing was clear: Arabella liked me. She allowed me to give her insulin injections from the start. I had practiced first on a grapefruit and then on myself, and was confident that I would not hurt her. I simply told her on the morning of my first full day with her that I would be doing the urine test and giving the injections, and she accepted it. I felt I had achieved a major victory, and to Charles, I had. More than once he said that he had not felt so free in years. He bestowed his thanks on me along with the smile that so transformed his face, and I felt as if he had given me a gift so precious it should be refused.

By a great stroke of luck, I decided to ask Arabella to show me the house in the afternoons after she rested. This inspiration came in my second week with her. At first she acted as if she hadn't heard. Already I had learned that this was characteristic, when she was presented with something new, she would ignore it completely. The fact that I was not uncomfortable with long silences was thus a great asset for me with Arabella. For the most part I adopted a go-with-the-flow attitude—I wanted to see how she motivated herself rather than try to impose my ideas or wishes on her. But it was important to me that I get her to leave her suite once in a while, and since she refused to go outside, I persisted rather deviously. "Well, I'm sure Phyllis will show me around, but I had hoped you would do it. After all, you're the mistress of the house. You must know so much more about it than Phyllis does, since she's only a servant," I said. And she took the bait.

Arabella made a great production of it. She changed from her usual long dressing gown into a street-length dress of very bright blue silk and shoes to match. Of course she had glasses to match too; she had them in every color. She made up her face, a bit garishly for my taste, but expertly. And so we began, and every afternoon until we were done, Arabella, each day in a different dress, took me through two or three rooms. Everything had to be examined in minute detail. Often she might have been alone, speaking a soliloquy that to me sounded like disconnected thoughts but to her had meaning, while handling objects and exploring them with her thin white fingers and single-minded deliberation. Then, in a lightning-swift change she would become the gracious hostess, instructing me with names and loads of detail, as if she were a docent trained by the local historical society.

I seldom paid close attention to her. I was gaining my own appreciation for the house through this slow exploration. In the older rooms in the main part, I was drawn always to the long windows, eight feet high, their sills level with the floor. Houses in New England do not have such windows, and standing before them I felt some of the wonder of a child with a new discovery. While Arabella prattled on about objects and furnishings, it was the architecture itself that absorbed me. I looked at crown moldings, at wainscots and panelling, at ceilings that varied from room to room, some plaster carved with rosettes in the center, some painted in colors now faded to palest pastels, some wood laid in intricate patterns. I looked at the wide wood planks of the floors, such beautiful wood and so highly polished it seemed too fine to walk upon.

My interest was caught, and at night after dinner I found books in the library from which I learned that the tall windows were made not just for their proportions but for maximum ventilation, that the floor planks were cut from the trunks of huge trees usually felled on the plantation itself, and that these houses had been built with slave labor. The books totally absorbed me. I would forget Charles's presence at the large library table he used for a desk, but sometimes I'd look up and find him watching me with the smallest of smiles on his lips.

The books satisfied my intellectual curiosity, but they could not provide one answer I craved: why did I feel that I had been in this house before, not the whole house but only the oldest part? Why, when I hovered in that borderline state that was almost but not quite the déjà vu I'd felt on my first day, was it accompanied by both fascination and fear?

The exploration of the house took almost two weeks, allowing for my days off on Mondays and Tuesdays. At Arabella's insistence we had seen every one of the twenty-seven rooms. Now I knew the house, and what I thought was more important, Arabella trusted me. By the third week I was able to get her to walk outside in the late afternoons. I was pleased, I thought I was making progress and so was she. Though toward what, I wasn't sure. It was frustrating to share my feelings of accomplishment with Charles during my daily reports at the dinner table, only to have him answer with a monosyllabic grunt.

"That's not good enough, Charles!" I said in exasperation on my third Saturday. "What exactly does it mean when you say 'ugh'?"

"It means," he replied with a wave of his fork, "that I heard you, I registered what you said."

"You told me yourself that Arabella hasn't been out of the house in two years, and now she's walked up the drive with me, and up and down the oak alley, and through all the paths in the garden, for three days in a row! And all you say to that is 'ugh.'" I was indignant. He just continued eating, but my appetite had vanished.

He changed the subject, not too gracefully. "My brother and his wife are about your age. And there's a new priest at All Saints'. I hear he's young and unmarried."

"All priests are unmarried, Charles. They're supposed to be," I said archly.

"All Saints' Waccamaw is an Episcopal church, not Catholic. Perhaps I'll give a dinner party, introduce you to some people your own age. Here, have some wine for a change. After all, it's Saturday night." He scowled at me, pulling his bushy eyebrows together, and reached for the tall green bottle.

"Oh, all right," I relented. "But I'm not going to let you get away with changing the subject, and I don't need to meet people my age. What I need is to talk about your wife *with* you, not *at* you!"

Charles leaned toward me, his voice so low I could barely

hear it. "All right, but later. The walls have ears." He straightened and said in a normal tone, "Now drink your wine."

I drank and half-heartedly resumed eating. The meals at Charpentier were always larger than I wanted. "I'm not bored here," I said, "I have a lot of things to do."

"I'm glad to hear it."

"What I'm trying to say is, you don't have to entertain me. That's not why I'm here."

"Sometimes," said Charles in a rumble, "I wish you could forget why you're here! At least while we're eating dinner!"

I blinked in surprise. I felt rebuked. I reached for my wineglass. It was a white wine, cool and slightly fruity. I drained it before I realized what I was doing.

"Do you want dessert tonight?" Charles asked, knowing that I often refused it.

"No, I don't."

"Neither do I. Bring your glass. Let's take this wine and finish it down by the river."

"That sounds like a nice idea," I said. And possibly not a very wise one, I added to myself. Then I remembered, he'd said we would talk about Arabella. And down by the river there was no possibility of Regina eavesdropping. That was probably the reason for his suggestion. I decided to check it out. I scampered to catch up with Charles as he walked ahead on the path through the garden.

"Charles, were you referring to Regina when you said the walls have ears? Is that why you didn't want us to talk about Arabella in the dining room? I thought you trusted Regina."

He looked down at me without breaking his stride. "I do trust her. I have no question of Regina's loyalty to me, to Charpentier. In fact, I don't know what I would have done without her these last years. So, I choose not to antagonize her. She's jealous of your growing relationship with Bella and perhaps of the, ah, time you and I spend together. That's all."

"I see."

We had reached the top of the bank, and I paused. It was a lovely April evening, the air felt soft, the sun was setting across the river and turning a line of wispy clouds all shades of pink. Whatever the reason that had brought us out, I was glad we had come.

"Oh, Charles, it's really beautiful!"

"Yes, it is, this time of year. In a few weeks there will be mosquitos, and if we tried to sit by the water we'd be eaten alive." He went down the steep path and automatically reached a hand back to help me.

I ignored his hand, preferring to navigate on my own. In my low-heeled shoes I managed the descent with no problem.

"You fixed it up!" I exclaimed as we reached the dock. The wood looked new, and there was a railing all around and benches on two sides.

"Tore the old one down and built a new one. Captain John told me it was in pretty bad shape after he brought you out, and I came down and took a look and saw he was right. So, here you have it!" Charles grinned, pleased with himself. "I should have brought a bottle of champagne. We could christen it!"

"I thought you only did that to boats." I walked across the new boards gingerly. In spite of the beautiful setting, I was still a bit afraid of that river. I knelt on the bench and peered over the railing, down into the water. At this time of day, it did not seem so threatening. Perhaps it was because Charles was with me. I heard him approach, and got to my feet.

"Here, hold out your glass," he said, "I think we should have a toast."

I held it out obediently and watched as he filled both mine and his, and when he raised his arm I did the same.

"To Rosamund, without whom this new dock probably would never have been built!"

I laughed. Our glasses touched with the delicate ring of fine crystal, and we sipped. Charles's eyes met mine, and held.

"Do you know, I've never heard you laugh before?"

"I didn't realize," I admitted, turning away to sit on the bench.

Charles followed and sat at the corner, where he put one foot up on the adjoining bench, and put the wine bottle there, too. "It's true. You're far too serious, Rosamund, for one so young."

"I'm not that young!" It was the second time in a brief period that he had mentioned my age, and I didn't like it. "I'm twenty-six. Do I seem so young to you?"

He sighed and leaned back, his arms draped across the railing. Then he turned his head and looked at me. "Sometimes you do, yes."

It was not what I wanted to hear, not in that soft air, filled with the heart-tugging feel of Spring. I looked away, and a wave of sadness rushed over me out of nowhere. I looked at the river. The setting sun was low now, too low to see, but the reflection of its fiery orb burned a red glow on the glassy water. I remembered the wine in my hand and took a long, hard swallow.

Charles moved across the bench and filled my glass again, though it was less than half empty.

"I have to work tomorrow," I protested, looking at the glass, needing to remind not him, but myself.

"I know, but you work for me. Besides, it's only a little wine." He did not move away. He sat only inches from me.

"For me, a little is all it takes!" I was too much aware of him. "We have to talk about Arabella," I reminded him.

"We will before we go back. But not yet."

There was a different note in his voice, its usual harshness softened by something else I tried not to hear.

"The sun is turning your hair red. It looks like burning gold."

I bowed my head. My stomach was knotting. My skin was tingling in anticipation of his touch. I tried to deny it, to push the thought away, but oh, I wanted him to touch me.

He touched me, the lightest caress of his fingers at my temple, tracing the smooth line of my hair behind my ear, the pressure increasing as his fingers moved to the back of my head and beneath the heavy twisted knot—a Psyche knot, it was called—at the base of my skull. And then he pressed the very sensitive hollow there, and a hot flame shot straight through me. I knew that he could do that to me with just the touch of his hand. I had known it for days, but I had tried to reason it away, to tell myself it could not be so.

"How long is your hair?" he asked, removing his fingers. My neck felt their loss.

I couldn't look at him, couldn't speak. With one hand and the ease born of long practice, I removed the tortoiseshell hairpin that held the knot in place. I tossed my head and my hair fell its full length, nearly to my waist.

"A river of burning gold." He spread his fingers and ran them slowly, sensually, through the length of my hair. "It feels like heavy silk," he murmured.

It was I, not my hair, that burned. I closed my eyes. This was wrong, I knew that later it would cause me terrible pain, but I wanted Charles Charpentier as I had never wanted another man in all my life.

"Rosamund . . ."

I opened my eyes, knowing that they revealed my willingness. His hand was still buried in my hair. I turned to him, and the look on his face devastated me. It was naked with wanting. My lips parted, but I could not speak.

He bent to me, his lips covered mine, gently moving, persuading. His hand, tangled in my hair, moved to the back of my head, pressing me into the kiss. My world tilted and spun into a hot, moist darkness that was Charles's lips and tongue, probing, seeking, finding, filling, and I felt as if my whole life poured into that one joining.

At last he moved away. I felt his hand caressing, slowly leaving my hair.

"I know I shouldn't have done that," he said.

"I know. Nor should I."

Neither of us could speak further. I supposed he was just as lost as I in the implications of what we had done. We finished the bottle of wine in silence, still sitting side by side, not touching. By that time it had grown quite dark, but there was a moon. We had traded red light for silver.

"How long can you stay with me?"

Not with us. With me, he said. I seized that small distinction, and then I put it aside. "I don't know. I hadn't really thought. Several months. As long as it takes . . ." I couldn't finish the sentence. I didn't know what we were moving toward, didn't know what the goal was for Arabella. As I thought her name, I felt a stab of pain. So, I thought, the pain comes so soon.

"I'm afraid Bella may hurt you."

So, he was thinking of her, too. Of course he was, she was his wife. But the kind of pain he had in mind was not the pain I felt.

"Not physically," he went on, "but she has ways." Charles turned to me and put both hands on my shoulders. "Are you really willing to share this with me, Rosamund? You could leave. Now, before anything else happens."

"No. I can't leave. I've made a commitment."

He drew me to him and wrapped me in his arms. "Oh, God. I hate myself for doing this to you."

Something in me, some basic, sensible part of me, forced itself to the surface. I became rational again. I pulled away and made a space between us.

"It was just one kiss, Charles. I wanted it too, but that's all it was." I began to twist my hair around my hand into a long coil. I could do it in the dark or with my eyes closed. I found the large hairpin in my pocket and secured the knot. "I'm not the child you think I am. You haven't done anything to me, certainly not with one kiss." I lied, trying to believe it, and even to my own ears my voice sounded cold.

"Very well, then." There was the hardness, the edge of anger his voice could hold. "You wanted to talk about my wife, and I'll do it. Bella is a cunning, devious woman. She seems to like you now, but she will turn on you sooner or later. I admit I haven't watched her closely enough in the past, but I began to, not long before you came. I have good reason to believe that she's building to a crisis much more serious than anything that has happened before. You've encouraged her to go out of the house with you, and it worries me for you to be alone with her like that. If . . ."

"If what?"

"I don't know!" He ran his hand through his hair roughly. "Sometimes I think the years of living with her have twisted me too, and I don't entirely trust my own judgment. I know you're good with her and that she seems to trust you. But you must not trust her. She grows more animated every day now, you see that, don't you?"

"Yes, but I thought . . ."

"You thought it meant she was getting better. I haven't wanted to discourage you, that's why I've been so noncommittal. But her animation is a sign that she's moving back into her most dangerous state. You must be careful, Rosamund, especially if you continue to take her out with you. God—or the devil—only knows what she's capable of."

I felt bombarded by all this, especially by the urgency Charles conveyed. I took my time to absorb it, and then I said, "So you think that sometime in the near future she may require institutionalization."

"That's one way you could put it, I suppose. But it sounds too neat. It's not that simple. I think something . . . decisive will happen, and when it begins. . . . Well, you know Bella well enough by now to know there will be nothing neat or clean about it."

"You think she will become violent."

"Worse than that."

"Worse than violent? What could be worse?"

"I think, I *believe*," Charles said slowly, "that my wife is evil."

The words hung in the air as definite as a solid object. They shocked me and filled me with a deathly cold. The would-be psychiatrist in me wanted to argue, but I found that I could not. Everything was suddenly more than I could deal with.

"I'm cold," I said, "I want to go back to the house."

Chapter 5

AFTER A HOT SHOWER I wrapped my old terry-cloth robe around me and belted it tightly, even though I knew it would do no good against the chill that came from inside me. I took my brush from the dressing table and sat down on the little chair to brush my hair. I couldn't bear to look at myself in the mirror, didn't want to see the color that Charles had called "burning gold."

If only I could talk to Aunt Henry! If only she hadn't died, none of this would be happening. Or, if only I had told her about the strange experiences I'd had at the hospital before she died, she'd have told me what to do. Then I could have stayed in Cambridge. Why instead had I told a doctor, a psychiatrist no less, who was no help at all, when I could have told Aunt Henry? Aunt Henry, who had been more than just an aunt, she had been my best friend! If I had just stayed in Cambridge none of this would be happening to me.

I was thinking in circles, thinking the thoughts of a child, not an adult. And I was brushing my hair too hard, hurting myself. I put the brush down.

Aunt Henry was dead, and it was true that she had been my best friend. I missed her terribly, and a part of me still raged at the suddenness of her death. Perhaps it had been a mistake not to tell her, but it was too late now and so I mustn't think of that. What I really wanted, really missed, was her good sense and her comforting presence.

I went to the chest of drawers and opened the walnut box I'd brought with me—my treasure chest, I'd called it, ever since I'd made it myself in a woodworking class in middle school. I took out the letter she had written to me, that I had found in her desk drawer after her death. I climbed onto my bed with it and sat cross-legged in the middle, half-realizing that I did so because as a child I had always felt safe sitting in the very middle of my bed. Once again I read Aunt Henry's letter. She had written it just before Christmas, and in January she was dead.

Dear Rosamund,

I hope you will never have to read this letter. I write because lately I have begun to think I made a mistake by not telling you something you have a right to know. I would tell you now, but I see that something is troubling you, something you haven't yet chosen to share with me, and so the time is not right. I want you to be "in a good place," as we used to say, when I tell you. I hope that will be soon, and then I can tear up this letter. But in case something should happen to me suddenly, be it accident or act of God, the letter will be here for you to find.

I know you do not remember the first three years of your life, the years you spent with your mother; nor do you remember the year between three and four when you stayed with your grandparents in Vicksburg. When you were four and I came to take you back to Cambridge with me, I learned that my mother and father had told you your mother was dead. That was not the truth, Rosamund. All these years I continued to let you think she was dead because it seemed kinder. But lately I have begun to think that you have a right, as everyone does, to know the truth about your parents. Even if that truth is uncomfortable.

Your mother, my younger sister Margaret, was different, even when we were children. Not so much in looks, for she got her dark hair and smaller stature from our mother, just as you and I resemble your grandfather. Margaret was different in the way she acted. From earliest childhood, she liked to be alone. Even as a

61

toddler she would wander off by herself, and often I was sent to bring her back. I confess I grew to dislike her. She was such an obstinate, independent little girl, very hard to like. In adolescence she became very pretty in a dark way, and terribly moody. She was bright enough, but she wouldn't study and she hated school, the exact opposite of me. She continued to wander off alone, and sometimes would be gone for two or three days at a time. She had worried our parents so much that I think they were relieved when, at eighteen, she wandered off and simply did not return. No one saw her again until she was about twenty-eight, and then she came back to Vicksburg with you, three years old.

I think she deserves credit for realizing that she was unable to take care of you. She never said who your father was or where she had been living, but your grandmother said she had driven a car with a Louisiana license plate. You had decent clothes, you were clean and healthy. The only thing to indicate you might have had less than a normal life to that point was that you were too quiet, you seldom talked. Your mother did not die, Rosamund. She took you to her parents, then she just went away and never came back. She may still be alive today. You know your grandparents from the way they have shunned me for my "mistake" of marrying a Yankee and staying in the North after he deserted me; you can easily imagine that they never tried to locate your mother.

I believe she loved you as much as she was capable of loving anyone, and she demonstrated that by taking you to the only people she could be certain would take care of you, her own mother and father. I think now, looking back, that the reason my sister always seemed so different was that she had—has, if she still lives—a mental illness of some kind. I can see no purpose that might be served by your trying to find her. But that is for you to decide, now that you know the truth.

I do hope you will never have to read this. If you do, it means that I am gone. Know, dearest Rosamund, that I have always loved you as if you were my own.

—Henry

I folded the letter and put it in the envelope, and then the tears came. I cried for Aunt Henry, for a mother I could not remember, and for myself. Once again I felt sick, as I had the first time I'd read it and every time thereafter—sick because it was possible that if my mother had been mentally ill, and it certainly sounded as if she had, she might have passed on the defect to me. And in me, it might have lain dormant for years, manifesting itself at last in those three inexplicable episodes of the previous fall. Knowing about my mother seemed to confirm that there was something really wrong with me.

I cried until I was exhausted, and fell asleep on top of the bedspread, still wearing my old robe, curled in the fetal position. Something happened as I slept. Perhaps it had already happened, since my coming to Charpentier, and it took the strong emotions and the release of so many tears to bring it to my awareness. All I knew was that when I awoke the next morning, the lamp still on beside my bed, I was stronger and more certain of myself than I had been in months. I knew that I was not mentally ill; there was another explanation. And though at Charpentier my life was more complex than it had ever been before, I would meet the challenge. I would work everything out somehow, one step at a time.

Charles was already at breakfast, which on Sundays consisted of sweet rolls and fruit left on the sideboard by Regina. Jenny and Phyllis had the day off and so did George, the gardener. As I spooned orange slices and cut-up fresh pineapple into a bowl, it occurred to me that Regina never took a day off. She was always at the house.

"Doesn't Regina have a regular day off?" I asked as I sat down at my place and pushed aside pages of the Sunday *New York Times*.

"Good morning to you, too," growled Charles, not looking up from the paper.

"Oh, yes, good morning," I said abstractedly.

"She has Fridays."

"What? Oh, you mean Regina." I had been looking at him and marvelling how my heart beat faster just at the sight of that shaggy head of dark hair, and the hard line of his jaw, and the sensual curve of his lips. Why had I never noticed until now how very sensual his mouth could be, when he was not angry or brooding over something? Regina had instantly gone out of my mind, and good riddance.

Charles glanced at me as he turned a page noisily. Immediately I dropped my eyes and started on my fruit. One step at a time, I told myself, everything will work out, even this. The memory of that kiss will fade, my heart rate will return to normal, I won't feel his eyes on me when they aren't, it's just my imagination because I know he's reading the *Times*, he gets lost in it every Sunday. . . . I stole a look, and he caught me, and I blushed. I grabbed the nearest section of the paper and opened it all the way, hiding behind it.

"I haven't seen you do that in a long time." Charles sounded amused.

"Do what?" I asked from behind my paper, even though I knew very well what he meant.

"Blush, you know that thing you do that turns your face so *rosy*, Rose-a-mund." He drew out my name with teasing emphasis. "Did anybody ever call you Rosie?"

"Of course not!" I scoffed. I folded the paper so that I could hold it in one hand, though my cheeks were still flaming. If he was going to tease me anyway, there was no point in trying to hide.

"No, I guess they wouldn't—not a serious person like yourself."

"Umpf," I responded. I had no time for this. I was due in Arabella's room soon. That thought proved to be very good for cooling my cheeks, and I settled down to eat my breakfast in earnest.

"Okay," Charles said, "I'm sorry. I didn't realize you were so sensitive about blushing. You shouldn't be, you know." His voice grew husky. "It does things to a man."

He got up from the table and went to the sideboard, coming back with the coffee pot. He stood a fraction of an inch behind me—I could feel the heat of his body. "Do you want more coffee?"

"No. Thank you. Honestly, Charles! Most mornings you don't even talk at breakfast. There must be something wrong with you today!" My heart was tripping again, and I certainly didn't want him to know.

"Your point is taken," he said, moving away to sit in his own place. He filled his own cup and set the pot on the table. "Maybe there is something wrong with me today," he said somberly.

I let it pass. I finished my sweet roll and fruit, and Charles went back to reading the paper. When I asked for a second cup of coffee, he turned the handle of the pot in my direction and nudged it a bit.

"Help yourself."

"Thanks a lot." I had to half rise to reach for it. "I'm glad to see you're back to your normal self again."

"Humpf!"

I turned toward the window so that he couldn't see my grin. I enjoyed bantering with him. I sipped my coffee and thought how good I felt, and how nice it was to be able to look out the window at breakfast and see such a profusion of green and masses of flowering bushes and the beautiful dogwood trees in bloom. If there were dogwoods in Massachusetts, I had never seen them. The reality of what Charles had said the night before about Arabella seemed at that moment very far away.

"I'm going to have that dinner party."

I turned away from the window. "You mean, the one with Louis and Lynda and the unmarried priest?"

"That's the one. On Saturday, I think, if Jenny and Phyllis can stay."

"What about Arabella? Will she join us?" My automatic reaction was to think of it as an opportunity for my patient, a chance to give her a more normal life.

"I doubt it, though you can never tell with her. It will be the first time I've entertained in a long while, and of course I'll have to tell her. Frankly, it would be a great deal easier if she would stay in her room."

"Oh, Charles, it will be a party. It might be good for her!"

Charles tipped his chair onto its two back legs and looked at me thoughtfully. "You don't really believe what I told you last night, do you, Rosamund?"

"It's not exactly that I don't believe you. It's that you want me to take care of her and observe, and I'm doing that. I have to trust my own observations, and so far, what I see is a woman who is reclusive and eccentric, whose thought processes aren't always sequential. That's all. And do you know that the only medication I've had to give her in almost a month is her insulin? I can't help but think, perhaps if she were just happier with her life. . . ."

Charles looked as if I had slapped him in the face.

"I didn't mean it like that!" I was instantly contrite.

Charles released a heavy sigh and let the chair settle down on four legs once more. "I know you didn't." He reached across the table and took my hand. "You're so innocent in so many ways, Rosamund. You must have had a very protected life with your Aunt Henry."

"I never thought so, but I suppose that's true in a way," I admitted. I'd begun to realize it for myself, first during my clinical rotations in the hospital, and increasingly since Aunt Henry's death. Charles squeezed my hand.

"Well, as sad as it seems, we all have to lose our innocence sometime, or else we'd never survive. I know you're stronger than you look; you've proved that more than once already. Come on, Rosie, we'll go tell my wife about the dinner party right now."

He did not let go of my hand until we reached the breakfast room door.

I bought a new dress for the dinner party, going shopping on my day off. It had been expensive—all the shops in the area seemed expensive—but it was worth it. It was silk jersey in a gorgeous shade of periwinkle blue that lent color to my too-pale gray eyes. I was pleased with the simple cut of the sleeveless bodice and the way the skirt hung in graceful, fluid folds. With it I wore my go-with-everything high-heeled beige suede sandals and the tiny diamond stud earrings that had been my twenty-first birthday present.

At the last minute I decided my hair wouldn't do. The severity of the Psyche knot looked wrong with the dress. I took it down and brushed it out into fullness, then piled it on top of my head in a sort of Victorian pouf. Not bad, I thought, it seemed softer, anyway. A few wisps escaped around my ears, and from habit I started to smooth them back, then changed my mind. I liked the look. The woman I saw in the mirror surprised me. My self-image had been formed in adolescence: a skinny girl with colorless skin and pale bug-eyes and too much funny-color, absolutely straight hair. At Radcliffe and at Harvard Med I'd never found any reason to pay attention to my looks—nobody that I knew paid attention to their looks—and nothing had altered that self-image. But tonight, it was different. I cared. I liked the way I looked, and I was glad of it.

I went downstairs alone. Arabella had refused to say whether she was coming to the party or not. In her erratic fashion she had alternated between extremes of showing me what must have been every party dress in her wardrobe, and withdrawing into total silence as she played for hours with a deck of cards. Since Regina usually served Arabella dinner in her room, I presumed that if she decided to join us, Regina would see she got there.

Louis and Lynda Charpentier had already arrived and were sitting with Charles in the south parlor. There were two parlors, living rooms to me, and like everything else the house had two of, they were named for their geographic orientation in relation to the river. The room looked handsome and gracious, with the late afternoon sun flooding in through the long windows. I heard the grandfather clock strike the quarter-hour as I entered the room.

"Here's Rosamund!" Charles announced. He walked toward me and his sapphire eyes swept me from head to foot. As he approached, he smiled for me that rare, wonderful smile. My heart turned over, and I knew I glowed as I smiled in return. I thought, I mustn't look at him like this, but I felt too good, too happy to conceal my feelings.

"Hello, Charles," I said.

"Come and meet Louis and Lynda." The light, guiding touch of his hand at the small of my back sent shivers through me.

I accepted what the others were drinking, a martini, and settled down to be sociable. I learned that the unmarried priest was expected at seven-thirty, and that he did have a name (I'd begun to wonder!), which was Timothy Durrell.

Louis was a younger, softer version of his brother. Everything about Louis seemed a little blurred around the edges, even his voice, which was decidedly and pleasantly Southern. Lynda was remarkable, small and pretty, with short, wavy brown hair and brown eyes that sparkled with wit. She had a delightful way of saying very direct, sometimes outrageous things in a soft, courteous voice. In five minutes I saw that she could wrap Charles around her little finger. I envied the ease with which she flirted with him.

Father Durrell, who immediately said he would only answer to Timothy, arrived precisely at 7:30. He wore the round white collar and pleated black shirt of his calling, but with a gray suit so well-tailored that Charles in his gray slacks and navy linen blazer looked almost shabby by comparison. Priest or not, Timothy would have turned any woman's head. Nearly as tall as Charles but thinner and more elegant, he was blond and blue-eyed and had a faint cleft in his chin. He, too, accepted a martini, acknowledged that he already knew Louis and Lynda, then gravitated to me. He was easy to talk to. He surpassed me at being a good listener, a quality I rely heavily on in a group of new people. He soon had me talking about myself.

We went into the dining room at eight o'clock. A place was set for Arabella, the appropriate place at the opposite end of the table from Charles. I was seated next to it, with Louis opposite me and Timothy on my right. We had just sat down, when Arabella appeared. Actually she made a dramatic entrance. The men stood, and I froze.

"Oh, am I late?" she asked in a voice too shrill, not the low, rather beautiful voice I knew she possessed. She was dressed well and yet she looked frightening, in black lace that made her too-white skin look like death. She had teased her hair to impossible fullness, and its white streaks were shocking. Her mouth was slickly scarlet, and her glasses were like mirrors.

Charles took her arm and ushered her to her place. As I watched them I understood much that I had not understood before. He was no longer the relaxed host, nor was he as he often seemed to me, the big man so unconscious of his own elemental sensuality. His face had become a craggy mask, his large body radiated steely tension. And yet he was all polite control.

"Sit, please sit," shrilled Arabella, but as she did not, the men still stood politely.

"Bella, I want to introduce Father Timothy Durrell from

All Saints', whom you have not met. Timothy, my wife, Arabella Charpentier."

"Madam," said Timothy formally.

"A priest! How delicious!" said Arabella in a much lower tone, dripping sarcasm.

I silently blessed Louis for jumping in immediately with, "Good evening, Bella. How nice to see you again."

Arabella still stood, her chin high so that the cords of her thin neck stood out. She looked like the wicked queen in a contemporary fairy tale.

"Will you be seated, Arabella," said Charles definitely—it was not really a question. Probably only I saw the subtlety with which he pressed down on her shoulder as he brought the chair edge behind her knees. Slowly, under that pressure, Arabella sank to her chair.

How good he is with her, I thought as I watched him return to his place. I felt the pain that must have been his pain as I realized how many countless times he must have done this, never knowing what his wife might say or do.

"I'm glad you decided to come," I said to her.

"Why, Rosamund, look at you! What have you done to your hair? Trying to make yourself look nice for the pretty priest?"

I couldn't believe the venom in her voice. She had not spoken to me this way since my first afternoon with her, when I'd thought she was testing me, deliberately trying to shock me. As I had then, I refused now to be shocked. I merely said, "Your dress is lovely, Arabella."

"Yes, it is." She splayed a bony hand over her small breast. "Black lace. I thought it would be very appropriate." She paused. "Black is appropriate for death, isn't it, *priest?*" The candle flames danced in the mirrored lenses that were her eyes.

"My name is Timothy," he said evenly. I sent him a swift glance of approval.

"Charles is going to die." There was silence at the table. "Lynda is going to die, and Louis, and dear, sweet Rosamund, and even the priest!"

"And so will you, Arabella," I said.

"Yes, that's right. We're all going to die. And so, you see,

I have dressed appropriately!" She laughed, a shrill peal of mirthless sound.

I decided the only thing to do was to eat, and I began mechanically to work my way through each course as it was served by a careful, solemn Phyllis. Regina was nowhere in sight.

Timothy was rather magnificent as Arabella continued to bait him, refusing to call him by name. When she said priest it became "priessst," a venomous hiss. He turned away her provocations effortlessly, though his eyes were alert, watchful. He even managed to converse with me between Arabella's taunts.

Midway through the main course I'd had enough of her rudeness to Timothy. "Arabella," I said clearly, "you are the hostess. I believe you've forgotten your manners."

It stopped her. I talked across the table to Louis and found his soft drawl a welcome change. With Arabella silent, conversation became general around the table. I discovered that I liked these people.

Arabella maintained her silence through dessert. Then she stood and in a perfectly normal voice said, "I'm sure you would all like to have brandy and liqueurs in the parlor. Charles, please take me to my room now."

He came to her and offered his arm, and she placed her thin, white hand on it. She took a step, then halted and bent over me.

"Rosamund, dear," she whispered into my ear, "it is not necessary to be polite to one's *enemy*."

"Have a nightcap with me. It's still early," Charles urged. The others had not stayed long after dinner, which was not surprising.

"All right. Just a little more brandy." I was tired, but wound up tight as a spring. I slipped my sandals off and curled my feet under me on the sofa.

Charles came, dangling the brandy bottle by its neck from one hand and loosening his tie with the other. I watched him settle onto the couch and stretch his legs, and thought how gracefully he moved for a person his size.

"What was it my wife whispered to you?" He poured brandy into my snifter.

"Enough!" I put my hand over the glass. "Sometimes I feel like you're always plying me with alcohol."

"Mmhm. Well, what did she say?"

"You wouldn't understand unless you knew what was going on between her and Timothy earlier."

"I heard some of it. And I heard you tell her she'd forgotten her manners. I was impressed by that—you've got balls, girl!"

"As a matter of fact, I don't, and don't call me girl!"

"Okay, Rosie. Seriously, what did she say to you?"

"She said, 'Rosamund, it is not necessary to be polite to one's enemy.' "

"Oh, God." He put his head back on the couch and rubbed his forehead with his hand, hard, back and forth.

"You know," I ventured, "my first day with her she acted a little bit like she did tonight. And there were, I don't remember exactly, little things that gave me chills. Like her hand. I had this sort of flash—I thought, 'This is a hand of death, a death-hand,' but then I told myself it was silly."

"Go on." He was giving me his full attention.

"At one point she chuckled. It was horrible. She sounded . . . well, evil."

"I know that sound. Anything else?"

"She showed me her bedroom. That room is just bizarre. She said you wouldn't go in there, and she sounded malicious. Like she did with Timothy tonight, only tonight it was worse. Much worse." I shook my head, remembering, and a long strand of hair came tumbling down my neck. It distracted me. I swept it back up, but it fell again. I said, "Damn!"

A smile tugged at Charles's lips. "Leave it. It looks delightful. I like your hair that way—but then I just like your hair."

"Charles, don't get me off the track. This is serious."

"I know it's serious, but I'm not really surprised by anything Bella said tonight, including what she whispered to you. I have a confession to make. I did invite Timothy for you, but I had another motive—I wanted to see how Arabella reacted to him. If she joined us, and I thought she'd be too curious to stay away. What she told you is the truth. He *is* her enemy."

"How could he be? He's just a nice, young—"

"Handsome," Charles inserted.

"Thank you. Handsome, intelligent Episcopal priest. She doesn't know anything about him. She never even met him before tonight."

"Rosamund, you're thinking like a psychiatrist. I tried to do that for years with Bella, and it only confused me. She's abnormal, all right, but she can be perfectly sane when she wants to."

"Even the so-called insane are sane part of the time," I argued. In spite of what I'd seen and heard during dinner, and my earlier, instinctive reactions that I'd just recapitulated, I didn't want to believe what I knew he was going to say again. That Arabella was evil.

"Nevertheless. I won't argue with you, you're too stubborn. Keep making your own observations. Do you think it's easy for an unimaginative businessman like me to admit that there is such a thing as objective, real evil in this world, especially to think of his *wife* that way?"

"No." I looked at him. "I'm sure it isn't easy."

Charles leaned forward, putting his elbows on his knees, warming the brandy snifter between his hands, though he seemed to have forgotten it. He wasn't drinking. "At first, after we were married, I denied there was anything really wrong with Bella. I made excuses, said she was just different. I was obsessed with her, and some of her differences excited me."

I couldn't help but wonder what she had done that excited him, but I kept quiet.

"Then about six months before the fire she went out of control. That was when Barkstone called in the consulting psychiatrist who made the manic-depressive diagnosis. Then came the fire. I still think she caused it, whether she started it outright or not. And after that, this business about her eyes."

"What is it? Why does she always wear glasses?"

"Actually, she has beautiful eyes, very, very green, like emeralds. But it has nothing to do with vanity. Her eyebrows and eyelashes were singed in the fire, but her eyes weren't damaged at all. For weeks she wouldn't believe that her eyes were all right, and then when she finally realized they were, she got phobic about protecting them. She said that if anything ever happened to her eyes she would kill herself. She started wearing the glasses all the time, for protection, she said. But that gets me off the track. After the fire our relationship changed, and I wanted her to get well or at least to stabilize this manic-depression so that we could have a normal marriage." He laughed harshly. "God help me, I even thought we might have children!"

"I'm sorry," I murmured. He seemed not to hear.

"Of course, that didn't happen. Then I went through a stage of wanting her to get well enough that I could divorce her, get her completely out of my life. That stage lasted a long time. Then, something happened and I realized that I'm responsible for Bella. I can't just turn her loose on the world."

"You said something happened. What?"

"She killed the animals."

"What . . . do you mean?"

"I had two dogs, golden retrievers—I really loved those dogs. And there were two or three cats that came and stayed, had kittens, and so forth. One by one about a year ago I found them dead, their necks broken."

"How do you know she killed them?"

"I saw Regina coming from the direction of Bella's patio, carrying the last dead cat, and I put two and two together. I accused Bella, and she laughed. I told her it wasn't funny. And then she told me the animals wanted to die, that they were 'willing sacrifices.' "

Charles seemed to realize the brandy was in his hands and took a long sip. Then he looked at me. "And that, Rosamund, is a concise history of my marriage. Enough background, I hope, for you to understand where we are now."

As horrible as the part about the animals was, this 'concise history' had a continuity that rang true. To my other feelings for Charles, I added respect.

He held out his arm. "Come to me, Rosamund. Come sit by me."

I uncurled my feet from under me and slipped across the couch, into the half-circle of his arm. It seemed natural to rest my head against his shoulder.

Charles stroked my hair. "You're a blessing in this house," he said softly, and he kissed my temple.

"What a lovely thing to say." I lifted my face to look at him and saw tenderness in the dark blue eyes. "I didn't know you could be so gentle," I said truthfully.

He kissed me, a soft, lingering kiss that made me glow with warmth. "It's you. I learn something about myself from you almost every day."

"Like what?" I whispered.

"Like I've been missing you all my life, and I didn't even know it."

I reached for him, to bring his head down to me, and I kissed him. I knew I loved him so much that my heart could break with it, and it very well might. When my lips left his, he buried his face in the curve of my neck. I felt a touch of dampness on my skin. Tears. Charles's tears. Then he kissed my neck there, taking his own tears away.

"I'd like to take you to my room," he said when he lifted his head.

I took his face in my hands—his dear, strong face. His eyes were still damp, and I kissed them. "No. It's difficult enough as it is. That would only make it worse." I had a terrible thought. "If Regina should come and see us like this . . .!" Reluctantly I moved away from him.

Charles ran his hand through his hair. "Yes, it would be bad. My reputation was ruined long ago, but I should think of yours."

I was putting on my sandals, smoothing my skirt.

"I never did tell you that I like your dress," Charles smiled.

"That's all right. I figured it out!" I held out my hands and pulled him to his feet, and we went from room to room, turning out lights, closing windows, locking both front doors. Then we climbed the stairs and went our separate ways.

Chapter 6

I WALKED ALONG THE beach. How wonderful it was to be under the open sky, to be able to look out on a horizon that seemed infinite! Even if both sky and sea were gray today, and the wind so strong that there was not a boat to be seen in the choppy water. I stretched my arms over my head and breathed deeply of the ocean-smell. I'd been foolish not to come here sooner on my days-off explorations, especially since the beach was only across the road—the road being Highway 17—and just about four miles from the house.

Though the sky was cloudy, the air was warm. I rolled my jeans up to my knees, left my sneakers on the sand, and waded into the surf. It was low tide, and the sand beneath my toes was hard-packed, barely shifting as the waves tumbled in, pulled out. I was completely alone, just me and the seagulls.

The beach was private, a part of the original tract that over two hundred years ago had given the Charpentier family the land "from the river to the sea." From the books in the library I'd learned that in summer months the families from the big houses on the Waccamaw River would transfer their entire household to their beach "cottages" for relief from the oppressive heat and the mosquitos. For the first hundred or so years the roads through the thick woods had been mere tracks, and so furniture and provisions and trunks of clothing had been loaded onto barges and floated down the river, into the Winyah Bay, around the tip of land called North Island, into the Atlantic, and then up the coast to their destinations.

I could see the old Charpentier cottage from where I stood, but I would explore it another day. Today I savored open skies and the vastness of the sea. It was a welcome change from Charpentier's many rooms and its surrounding woods and gardens. The lushness of all that growth could be cloying, at times claustrophobic. I was glad to escape.

The previous day had been Easter Monday, a week plus two days since the dinner party, and I needed to think about Arabella. I needed to do it away from the house and away from Charles. Something very strange happened on Easter Sunday, and I had not yet told him, nor had I recorded it in my daily notes.

Arabella had been avoiding me since the party, as much as it was possible to avoid someone in the same room. She wasn't really withdrawn; in fact, the restlessness of her movements and the shortness of her attention span to the TV, reading, and solitary card-playing that were her usual activities, indicated agitation. Perhaps I should have medicated her, but I did not. She stayed in her room at nap-time longer and longer each day, though I doubted that she slept. She declined my suggestions that we go out afterwards. On Sunday I thought she was probably aware that it was Easter, though I couldn't be sure since it was not a household in which church was mentioned. Knowing that it would be a subject she found distasteful, I decided to use it to push a response from her.

"Today is Easter Sunday," I said, coming to sit with her at the table where she played cards. "I'm surprised you don't want to go to church."

She looked at me. That, at least, was something. She was wearing a red dressing gown trimmed in ecru lace, and her glasses shaded from pink to red.

"Don't you ever go to church, Arabella, not even on Easter?"

There was a tremor in her hands that transmitted itself to the cards she held. She said, "I'm not Arabella."

I tried not to show my astonishment. "You're not Arabella," I echoed.

She continued her game of solitaire, but I could feel she hadn't shut me out. She was alert and waiting.

"You aren't Arabella. You look like her, and you sound like her, but you're not Arabella."

Her response was a prolonged eerie chuckle.

I got up and walked across the room. I'd taken up needlepoint to fill the hours I spent with her, and I got the bag that held my canvas and colored yarn, and brought it back to the table. I was doing a picture of a unicorn in a garden. I sat down again and began to work on it, stitching green thread for the grass. I did not look at her.

"Who are you?" I kept my head bent over my work.

"I'm not going to tell you."

"Do you know my name?"

"Your name is Rosamund."

"Yes, it is. What's yours?"

"I will not tell you," she said, her voice low and intense. "It's not for you to know my name!"

I wove my needle with its tail of green in and out, in and out. "How can I be your friend if I don't know your name?"

Laughter came out of her mouth, shrill and mirthless. "*You* can't be my friend! You with your clear eyes," she sneered, "and your bright hair, you . . . *maker of unicorns!*"

"You don't like my unicorn?" I asked innocently.

"Hah! You know, don't you, you're trying to provoke me. You know your unicorn is a symbol of Chris-s-s-t," she hissed. "You with your talk of *Easter!*"

The symbolism of the unicorn had not occurred to me, but I kept that to myself. I noted that in fact she did not sound like Arabella. She did not frighten me. I thought of multiple personalities and wondered if this had ever happened before.

"Does Charles know your name? Or Dr. Barkstone?"

"Maybe they do, and maybe they don't." She sounded petulant, and I sensed that I would not get her to talk much longer.

"How about Regina?"

"Regina knows," she said immediately. She began to gather up all her cards.

"Where is Arabella now?"

"Oh," she turned to me, "she's here, but she's asleep."

"I see. It's remarkable, you look so much like Arabella."

She leaned toward me, bringing her face too close to mine. She whispered harshly, "She and I are one. I see through her eyes!"

That was all. She had shuffled her cards and gone back to her game. She had not spoken to me again that day, nor had I seen her since.

I hooked my thumbs in the pockets of my jeans, feeling them ride my hip bones as I sloshed along in the surf. I wanted to feel loose and lanky, like a long-haired, suntanned California girl in a soft-drink commercial. But I didn't, I couldn't. My mind and my muscles felt as tight as the thick french braid I'd woven of my hair.

Somehow I didn't think Arabella would tell the licensed practical nurse who came in on my days off that she wasn't Arabella. My first impulse, of course, had been to tell Charles the whole thing, word for word. But I hadn't been ready to listen to more talk about evil, and certainly not about demonic possession. That thought had forced itself into my mind when she'd said, "I see through her eyes!" But intellectually I couldn't acknowledge such things.

I left the water's edge, walked a few steps to dry sand, and sat. The ocean was not entirely gray under the cloudy sky, in patches it was green, like light jade. The ceaseless rhythmic sound of the breakers comforted me. I picked up a stone from the sand near my hand—it was flat and smooth and cool, soothing to rub between my thumb and fingers. I couldn't pretend to know what was wrong with Arabella Charpentier. I did know that Charles was right about one thing, that she was building up to something, and I felt oddly protective of her. I wouldn't tell Charles, not yet. I'd write the observation as a late entry in the log, that would be enough. I simply could not believe that Arabella was dangerous. Merely bizarre.

Actually, I thought as I slowly rubbed the smooth stone, for me it was Charles who was dangerous. Emotionally dangerous. I'd been in love before, or had thought I was, but those experiences were mere shadows compared to what I felt for Charles. For me, the very quality of the air changed when he was near. Inside or out, it didn't matter, I could feel his presence, that physical aura he carried with him, and I did not need the confirmation of my eyes to know when he approached. The slightest touch of his hand was electric, and if that touch were prolonged, my very bones began to melt. That was why he was dangerous. All my attempts to analyze my feelings away, to tell myself, for example, that the attraction was so powerful because he was older and I'd never had a father, didn't really work.

It was the first time in my life that I couldn't put my head in control and keep it there. That was the problem, because I knew that Charles did not, could not, care for me as deeply as I did for him. It was just that he'd been too long in an impossible marriage and I was young, and I was new, and I'd come into his life at a time when he particularly needed me. When this situation with Arabella reached some conclusion, if not before, the small, sweet attraction he felt for me would fade.

Damn! I got to my feet and hurled the little stone with all my strength out into the sea. I wouldn't let myself be in love with Charles Charpentier. I simply could not! I stamped along the beach, back to where I'd left my sneakers. Maybe I'd start having dinner on a tray in my room, at least part of the time. Certainly I must stop sitting with him in the library after dinner, and walking out among the oaks at twilight, and . . . anything that allowed me to be alone with him when it wasn't absolutely necessary for carrying out my responsibilities to Arabella. I shoved my feet into my sneakers, gritty sand and all. As I climbed the dunes back to where I'd left my car, I decided to check out All Saints' Waccamaw Church in what remained of my afternoon. Timothy Durrell just might be the cure for what ailed me.

The church was not hard to find, though along the way I was surprised as always by the way trees and vegetation closed in so quickly along undeveloped parts of the smaller roads. My explorations were always marked by these moments when I felt lost, cut off from the familiar, though I knew I had only to keep driving and soon all would be well again.

The church grounds were marked by a long, low brick wall. I parked along the opposite side of the road, noting that someone else had done the same. Timothy, perhaps? But I saw no one as I located a wrought iron gate and went through it. The church building was on my right, smaller than I'd expected, but classsically proportioned with four stone columns supporting the pedimented roof of a shallow porch. The door was closed, and I didn't feel inclined to enter. Something about it struck me as odd, as if something were missing. In a moment I realized there were no steps; the building sat flat upon the ground looking like a small temple brought too suddenly to earth. All around it, all around me, there was an atmosphere both mysterious and peaceful, larger than life.

I stood very still, listening, feeling. There was a presence here I could not define. I looked about. The church grounds had been carved out of the surrounding woods, and the brick wall enclosed not just the church itself but also a graveyard. Dark green live oaks strung with the gray of Spanish moss stood among weathered headstones, with an occasional bit of color scattered here and there by bushes still in bloom. Almost in a trance, I walked among the graves. Over and over the same names were repeated. Many I recognized from my reading; many were so old and worn it was almost impossible to decipher them. Most were simple stones, but a few were ornately carved or topped by a stone figure. One of these was an angel who knelt with wings outspread upon a marble block that said simply CHARPENTIER. I stood reading the names and dates of Charles's ancestors inscribed upon marble plates set into the ground around the angel, and I wondered what it would be like to be one of such a family, I who did not even know my own father and mother.

I wandered on, now skirting the graves along the far side of the enclosure. All the markers here seemed very old, as did the low brick wall, which crumbled in places as if worn out by its effort to keep back the encroaching trees on the other side. It was darker here too, because of those same trees. I strained to make out names and dates. And then it happened.

There was a roaring in my ears and a pricking in my scalp, down my arms to my fingertips, and down my spine. A part of my consciousness split itself off and became an observer. I knew something was beginning, and I was powerless to stop it. My peripheral vision was disturbed. At first it wavered, then it darkened, and everything around me receded until I was looking down a long, dark tunnel. Wind howled around me; it slapped and shoved at my body in a ceaseless assault. A wall of water came rushing down the tunnel, filling it with a roar. Above the roar rose high-pitched cries of women and children. I could smell it and taste it, bitter and salty—they were drowning in the sea. And over all, a man's voice, anguished, sobbing, "No, no, no!" Sorrow! Terrible, terrible sorrow!

I felt sick. My knees were weak. I staggered backward. I had to get away from all that sorrow, it was more than I could bear. I felt an arm come around my shoulders, supporting me.

"Rosamund! It's all right, I'm here. It's Timothy."

My eyes were still darkened and I could not see. He sounded far away. But I could feel his arm and his hand, strong and real, gripping my shoulder. I leaned into him.

"I have to get away from here," I managed to whisper.

He wasted no words, just led me slowly away. After a few steps everything was normal again. Whatever it was, it was linked to that one particular spot in the graveyard. I blinked, glad to be back in the real world, and found that my eyes were wet. I stopped to wipe my cheeks with my fingertips.

"Here." Timothy handed me a folded handkerchief. "You were crying. Sobbing, actually. What happened?"

I dabbed at my face with his handkerchief and then returned it to him. "I don't want to talk about it."

"We'll see about that. At least, you should sit down for a while."

That was true. The experience had left me feeling depleted. We went into the dim coolness of the church. It smelled of hymnals and polished wood. I sank into a back pew and covered my face with my hands. The cries of the women and children and the anguish of the man's voice still haunted me.

Timothy's voice was gentle. "I really want to know what upset you so much. It might help to talk about it."

Maybe he was right. At least, I thought he might believe me. I told him everything, exactly as it had happened. "I'm glad you came along," I finished.

"I was showing the church to a couple I'm going to marry

next month—the fiance's from out of town and he'd never seen it before. When I walked with them to their car, I saw a wagon with Massachusetts plates and I was hoping it belonged to you. So I looked for you."

"Thanks. I'm glad you did."

"You'll be all right here for a couple of minutes, won't you? I want to check something out. I'll be right back."

I nodded. While he was gone, I studied the interior of the church in an effort to blot out memories of other experiences that tried to crowd into my mind. It was too dark inside to see much, and I was glad when Timothy returned quickly. I slid over in the pew to make room for him, and he sat next to me.

"The gravestones near where you were standing—did you have time to read them before these things started to happen?" he asked.

"No. No, I was trying to make them out, and then my vision started to go funny. I have no idea who's buried there."

"That's what I thought." He was silent for a moment while he looked at me intently. "There are several families— men, women, and children—who lost their lives in the Great Storm of October 1893 buried in those graves. And one man who survived his wife and children and was buried next to them when he died many years later. That storm was a terrible tragedy, Rosamund. It destroyed all the cottages on Magnolia Beach, what's called Litchfield Beach now. Many people died."

I felt stricken. I did not want to know these things. Yet I couldn't deny what I'd seen and heard, even smelled and felt.

"Does it frighten you?" Timothy took my hand. "You look a little frightened."

"Yes," I admitted, "yes, it does. But . . ." I bit back my words. Those other memories were too dangerously close to the surface.

"You're psychically sensitve, Rosamund. You experienced the terror of that storm for the people who died in it, and the tremendous sorrow of that one man who survived. It's a gift that you have, not something to be afraid of."

"Easy for you to say," I said bitterly. I withdrew my hand

from him and crossed my arms tightly, hugging myself for comfort.

"Has something like this happened to you before?"

I looked at Timothy's handsome face, classic lines of high cheekbones and straight nose, perfectly formed mouth, and the barely perceptible cleft in his chin. His eyes were intelligent and caring. Perhaps I decided to trust him because of the symbolism of his roman collar, or perhaps it was because I desperately needed help with these things I didn't understand. My mouth felt dry with anticipation of risk. I moistened my lips with the tip of my tongue.

"Do you," I ventured, "do you know anything about these, ah, psychic things?"

"A little. Parapsychology is an interest of mine. It seems to me to be related to the spiritual side of life, which makes it a legitimate concern for a priest."

"All right, I'll tell you. But I'm afraid you'll think I'm a bit crazy."

"I doubt that. Go ahead, I'm listening."

"Three times over the last several months I've had experiences that were, well, out of the ordinary. Not exactly like what happened today, but I expect it's all related somehow."

"Never before these last few months?"

"No, never. It all started after I began my clinical rotations. You know, in the third year of medical school you go into the hospital and see patients for the first time."

Timothy nodded. "I understand."

"The first thing that happened wasn't so terribly unusual, except for the effect it had on me. On rounds one day we saw an old man who was semicomatose. The main thing wrong with him was simple old age; he was ninety-four, and his body was worn out. But his heart was surprisingly strong. He had recently begun to refuse nourishment, and the question was whether or not to start tube feedings. He had no relatives, no one close to him. The other medical student and I were told to feel his pulse, and as the intern had described, the old man's heartbeat was strong and regular. When I stood by his bed with his wrist in my fingers, something happened to me. It was as if my consciousness split in two, and one part of me was the med student counting pulse rate and watching the second hand on my watch, and another part was observing the man on an entirely different level. Observing, and in some way communicating not with his body, but with another part of him."

"And what did you observe?"

"There was a struggle going on inside him. I don't know how, but I could feel it. A struggle between his worn-out body with its strong heart, and his . . . I guess I'd call it his spirit, that was trapped in his body and wanted to be free. While they were discussing his case, I stayed in that sort of split-consciousness state, and I became certain that he would die that night. His spirit-part would win the struggle. I don't know how I knew, I just knew. So when it was my turn to talk, I said I thought we should hold off on the tube feeding for twenty-four hours, to give him an opportunity to tell us what his wishes were in case he regained consciousness. That was what the attending doctor decided to do, and that night the old man died."

"How did you feel about that?"

"It shook me up. I tried to tell myself I had imagined what went on between him and me, that his death was just a coincidence. You see, Timothy, I'm not a religious person. I was brought up by my aunt who was a classics professor at Radcliffe, and she called herself a Stoic. I've never believed in a soul or a spirit world or an afterlife, or anything like that."

"I'm sorry that your aunt brought you up a Stoic. It's such a joyless philosophy. But that's rather beside the point now. Did that experience with the old man change your mind about souls, or if you prefer, spirits?"

"No. It just confused me, and then after the other things happened, I thought I might be cracking up, losing my mind."

"Tell me the others."

"The second was about a month after the first. I was on twenty-four-hour duty and I was very tired. I was in the doctors' lounge, drinking a cup of coffee. I was alone, and all of a sudden I felt my mind go funny, with that pricking I told you about, and the visual disturbances. And then all I could see was a patient's chart and a doctor's hand writing orders in it. Then it was like a zoom-lens kind of effect, and I was seeing the chart close up. I could read every word, and the doctor had written the order wrong. I wasn't familiar with the patient or the medication, but I knew the order should have been 10 cc, and he had written 100 cc. Then my vision cleared up. I sat there and finished my coffee and tried to shake it off, but I couldn't. I simply had to go to the floor and look at that chart, and when I did, it was just exactly as I'd seen it. So I took it to the charge nurse. She looked at me suspiciously but she said I was right, the dosage must be incorrect. Since it was to be given at six A.M., she called the doctor and woke him up, even though it was the middle of the night. That episode got me in trouble with the nurse, who said her nurses would have caught the error and questioned the order anyway; and with the doctor, who wanted to know what I was doing in his patient's charts when I wasn't even assigned to his service."

"So, nobody thanked you for your intervention, even though you may have saved the patient's life."

"Far from it. There was no way I could explain why I had looked at the chart, and I was blamed for not minding my own business, and most of all for violating one of those unwritten codes of hospital behavior. A medical student just doesn't do what I did."

"I see." Timothy's eyes were grave.

I almost wished now that I hadn't started this, for the worst was yet to come. I shifted on the hard pew. "There's one more. It was by far the most powerful experience, and the worst of it all was that I was completely helpless." I rubbed a hand across my forehead. The very memory hurt.

"If it's too painful, you don't have to tell me."

"No, maybe you'll understand. Two other med students and I were observing surgery on a two-year-old boy who had a congenital intestinal malformation. It turned into a nightmare for me, but much more so for the boy. The surgery was done in one of the older ORs, so we had to observe from in the room itself. We were wearing scrub suits, and so forth. I felt strange from the minute I went in there, but I put it down to nerves, loss of sleep, the glaring lights, and the fact that I knew the boy because I had rotated to pediatrics by then. The surgery went off just fine, the surgeon had finished, the resident was closing, the nurse hung a bag of blood to replace what the boy had lost, and then WHAM! It hit me. All at once my ears roared. This time there was no pricking, it was like an electrical charge went through me, and my whole field of vision was instantly taken up by that blood bag. It became a terrible, awful, blood red thing, it seemed to pulse and have a life of its own, hanging there in the glaring light. A part of me was screaming inside, it's the wrong blood type, it will kill him! Another part of me could see the label on the bag that said A positive, which was the boy's correct blood type. Somehow I believed the screaming in my mind, I believed that it was the wrong blood. But there was nothing I could do. Nothing! It nearly tore me apart. I had to get out of the OR, and I ran out, which I shouldn't have done, and threw up in the scrub sink. It was horrible!" I shivered, remembering. "The boy died of a transfusion reaction. An adult or even an older child would probably have survived, but he was too small, too weak. Of course they investigated it and found that the blood had been labelled in error. They had given him B-negative blood."

"That was a terrible experience. You never told anyone what you had seen?"

"I did go to a psychiatrist in private practice, outside the hospital, and I told him all three things, as I've just told you. He said it was only stress, that the first clinical rotations are often traumatic and the mind can play tricks on a person. He suggested that I'd made up the wrong-blood business after the fact and convinced myself it really happened that way."

"And what did you think?"

"That he didn't believe me and didn't understand. I knew those things really happened, but I also knew they were abnormal. Then, a couple of weeks after the boy died, my aunt had an MI, a heart attack, and she didn't survive it. There was no warning, none at all, and after her death I just couldn't cope. I had to get away. I thought those strange experiences of mine wouldn't happen outside of the hospital. I was also half-afraid I might be mentally ill. But now, you see, it's happened again. This was different because it was from the past and the other things were in the present and the future, but it felt very much the same to me."

"Oh, Rosamund," said Timothy, taking both my hands in his, "no wonder you sounded bitter a few minutes ago when I said you have a gift! It's too bad your classics-professor aunt wasn't a Platonist instead of a Stoic; that might have helped you. But perhaps I can help, a little. I've heard it said that once the validity of just one experience of this sort is undeniable, it alters one's view of reality forever. I was there this afternoon, I watched you, and I wouldn't deny what you experienced today, would you?"

I shook my head.

"So, given that I know today's experience was valid, I can believe the others. I'd believe them anyway, because I'm sure there is a spiritual as well as a physical reality. That's what has you hung up. You've had experiences that don't fit your belief system, and instead of questioning the system, you questioned yourself."

"That's true." He was helping. I'd never thought of it that way.

"Your aunt's death, coming just on the heels of the other things which had already shaken you, must have been devastating. You must have felt very insecure, and yet you left everything that was familiar to you and came to the Charpentiers. And in spite of everything, you seem to be doing very well. I saw how you handled Mrs. Charpentier at the dinner; you're very good with her."

"Thank you." He was giving me a lot to think about. I said slowly, "I have felt a little insecure, and especially before Aunt Henry died, I doubted myself. But you see, she taught me to accept things as they really are, that's a big part of Stoicism. All I knew was that I didn't understand anything except the fact that she was gone. I thought what I needed was time, to get away until I could understand. I knew I couldn't continue in medical school if it meant more experiences like the one in the OR, not without understanding. So I asked for a leave of absence. Coming here was just an accident. A happy accident, I think." I smiled at Timothy.

"I'm happy that you came. But some people, the ones who believe most strongly in the spiritual side of life, say there are no accidents. Perhaps you were meant to come."

"You mean, like karma?"

"Exactly." He gave my hands a squeeze.

The look in his eyes said that his idea of karma at this moment was whatever brought me and him together. I freed my hands and reached behind to tighten my french braid, though it didn't need it. "That's a little too mysterious for me. For now, I'm going to have my hands full with the concept of a spiritual reality, not to mention karma! But it does help, you've helped me. I appreciate your listening, Timothy, and what you've told me. I really do. And now"—I got to my feet—"it's getting late, and I really must go back."

"Of course. I'll walk you to your car." Timothy locked the church door behind us, and we went through the gate and across the road.

I stopped beside my station wagon. "Is your car here, or could I give you a ride home?"

"No, thanks. The rectory is just up the road and I enjoy walking. There is one thing you could do for me, though."

"Which is . . .?"

"Have dinner with me tonight. That is, if you don't have to be with the Charpentiers."

"I don't," I smiled, "and I'd love to have dinner with you."

"Wonderful! I'll come for you in about an hour."

"That will be fine," I agreed as I got into my car. Timothy stood out of the way, and I made a U-turn in the road to head back the way I'd come.

I felt rather pleased with myself. Going out with Timothy was surely a step in the right direction. Away from Charles! I'd show him that I wasn't one to get caught up in hopeless fantasies, no sir, not I, the sensible Rosamund! But an annoying hitch in my heartbeat when I thought of Charles eating alone at the long mahogany table robbed me of some of my satisfaction.

I entered the house through the south side door and stopped in the kitchen to tell Jenny I would not be in for dinner. Then I hurried up to my rooms. Washing and drying my hair in less than an hour wouldn't be easy, and in addition I had no idea what to wear.

As it turned out, what to wear was not such a problem; it had to be the brown silk, my one good dress until I'd bought the blue one, which I thought was too dressy. The problem was my hair, so long and heavy, and so difficult to dry in the humid South Carolina climate. But there was an unexpected benefit: that same humidity gave the ends a tendency to curl, and so when time grew short and my hair was still stubbornly damp, I decided that for once I would wear it loose. I swept the sides up and back, and secured them on the crown of my head as I'd used to do in childhood. Charles would like this, I thought, and then I made a face at myself in the mirror. The whole point in going out with Timothy was to forget about Charles. It shouldn't be the *whole* point, I chided inwardly as I rummaged in a drawer for Aunt Henry's favorite stole of pale-pink Scottish mohair; that wasn't fair to Timothy.

Through the windows of the gallerylike hall just outside my door I could see any approaching car. I hadn't long to wait, and I sped through the halls, down the stairs and out the East Front door, hoping that I would encounter neither Charles nor Regina. I didn't, and I opened the door just as Timothy raised his hand to the knocker.

"Hello." I stepped out and closed the door behind me.

"Hello, yourself! You're very prompt!" His blue eyes crinkled at the corners with his smile.

"It's either a good habit or a neurotic compulsion. I don't like to be late." Resisting an impulse to look over my shoulder to see if anyone might be watching, I started for the gray car waiting in the driveway.

"I appreciate that. I admit this house isn't one of my favorite places, so I'm just as glad not to have to come in and wait."

We had reached his car, and Timothy opened the door for me. Now I did look back. "Really? But it's such a beautiful old house!" I felt a proprietary need to defend it.

"Umhm. That was a tactless thing for me to say. I'm sorry. Let's be on our way."

I gathered my long self into the passenger seat as gracefully as possible. I knew the polite thing would be to accept Timothy's apology and let the remark pass, but I was too curious. As soon as he was in his place and starting the car, I pounced. "What is it you don't like about Charpentier? And besides, how could you have an opinion? I thought you were new here!"

Timothy raised an eyebrow as he turned his head briefly to look at me. "Why did you think that?"

"Because Charles said there was a 'new priest' at All Saints, when he was planning that dinner party."

"Oh. Well, it's true I'm new at the church, but I'm certainly not new to the area. Maybe to people like the Charpentiers the Durrells might seem new, but my family has had a place on the Pee Dee River for thirty years. It's right next to Lynda's family home. We grew up together, her brother was my best friend. Lynda has always been like a little sister to me."

"I see. But you don't sound like you grew up here."

"I know. That's because my parents came from New York. Long Island. And because I went to prep school and college and seminary all in the Northeast. Now, where would you like to go for dinner?"

"Anywhere. I haven't eaten out since I came here—I've had all my meals at Charpentier. I'll trust your judgment."

"Good. If you haven't been to any of our restaurants, then we'll have many nights of culinary adventure ahead of us. Not to mention other types of adventure! I want us to get to know each other . . . well, Rosamund. And I know just the place to start."

I looked at Timothy, surprised by the silky note of seduction in his voice. In spite of his almost-too-perfect good looks, he'd always seemed so completely upright. And besides, he was a priest. But he was also a man, about my age, a very eligible bachelor. For the first time I noticed he wasn't wearing his roman collar. He wore a blue-gray suit with a white shirt and a darker blue tie. "Are you incognito tonight, or what?"

"Incognito?" Again the raised eyebrow.

"You aren't wearing your collar."

"Oh, that." He grinned, and a little dimple flashed on the cheek next to me. "I'm more often without it than with it, I'm afraid. I guess you don't know—I'm not really a parish priest."

"Oh. So it's not that you're incognito, it's that you're a fraud."

Timothy's laugh was a pleasant, light baritone. "I'm ordained all right, but I'm really a teacher. I'm just at All Saints' while the rector is on sabbatical. It makes a nice change, and keeps me in practice, so to speak. But the real reason I'm doing it is that my father hasn't been well, and I wanted to be near my parents for a few months."

I was aware that he'd deftly steered the conversation away from whatever it was that he didn't like about Charpentier, but it didn't seem to matter so much now. I was enjoying his company. "What do you teach? And where?"

"History. Especially early church history, at a small college in Virginia called Mount Saint Andrews. I'm sure you've never heard of it, but it's a good little school. When I finish my doctoral dissertation, who knows?"

"Tell me about your dissertation."

"It's slightly esoteric. Christian Gnosticism. I doubt you'd be interested."

But I was, and so he told me. It was almost like having a piece of my old life back again. Academic people are all much alike, and I discovered that Timothy was above all an academic. Like Aunt Henry, like so many people I'd known for so much of my life, and I was comfortable with him. We ate at an inn across the Winyah Bay, in a tiny, intimate dining room, and watched night deepen over the water. With coffee and dessert I brought up again the question that had remained at the back of my mind.

"Will you tell me now why you don't like Charpentier?"

Timothy frowned. "That's a bad situation there. I'm sure you know that, and you're making the best of it. But I hate for you to be so isolated in that house. I'd like you to get to know Lynda. She's a normal, sane person, and she has a great sense of humor. I'm sure you'd like each other. She would give you an out, in case you ever need it."

He sounded like the voice of reason, crying in the wilderness. Stubbornly, I resisted. "I don't feel isolated. Arabella is strange, of course, but she's fascinating to work with. It's valuable experience for me. When I get my M.D.—I keep forgetting that I should say *if* I get my M.D.—I'd planned to specialize in psychiatry."

"I wasn't thinking of Arabella Charpentier." Timothy's eyes held such a quiet intensity that I felt heat and, I knew, color creep across my cheeks.

"Then, you must mean Regina. I have to grant you that Regina's difficult."

"No, Rosamund. I mean Charles."

"I know quite a lot about the Charpentiers. I made it my

91

business to know when Lynda became serious about Louis. As I told you, she's like a little sister to me, and her own brother—he's an engineer—was in Saudi Arabia at the time. Still is, in fact."

"I had the impression that Louis was sort of a . . . a ne'er-do-well."

"He was. But he's okay. He's basically a gentle soul, fun-loving, harmless, a comfort-seeker. And he's completely nuts about Lynda. It's Charles who's the dangerous one."

"How do you mean?"

"There's a dark streak in the Charpentier family. It has been there since the first, over two hundred years ago, It shows up in at least one male in every generation. It's a kind of ruthlessness that has made them the great landholders they are, but they've been neither well-liked nor trusted. It's said around here that the Charpentier men always managed somehow to attract and marry the right sort of woman, a woman who could temper and offset their darker qualities. There's a locally famous story about how Charles's great-great-grandmother saved the house during the Civil War. Perhaps you've heard it?"

I shook my head.

"Almost all the rice plantations were devastated, not by the Union soldiers, but by mobs of freed slaves. In all fairness to both whites and blacks, it was probably shortage of food that caused the madness, and everyone, landowners and slaves alike, was starving. Anyway, when the mob came to Charpentier, Charles's great-great-grandmother went out alone and stood on the West Front porch to face them. Apparently it was her quiet courage and her dignity that got them to listen to her. At that time the Charpentiers owned three plantations, one of them on a large island where the Pee Dee winds into the Waccamaw. She stood there on that porch and gave the whole island to any freed slaves who wanted to live there, if they would leave her home alone. They had already burned the house on the island, which she may or may not have known, but the cabins and the slave chapel were still standing—the chapel is still there today—and it's good farm land. So they took her word, and they went away, and that's how the Charpentiers survived the Civil War with their wealth and most of their property intact.

They were the only family on the Waccamaw who did. And that's ultimately the reason for Charles's present land empire, because that is how his grandfather as a young man had the money to buy up his neighbors' plantations when they'd tried for a generation to recover and finally failed."

"That's fascinating," I said, "but I don't see that it has anything to do with me."

"You're that kind of woman, Rosamund. It's exactly the sort of thing you would do. You'd go out there on that porch, looking every inch a lady with your fair skin and delicate features and those great, clear gray eyes, and you might be trembling inside but you'd stand your ground. I know you would."

I supposed he was right, but I didn't think I wanted to hear where all this was leading. "Timothy," I began.

"Let me finish." He held up a monitory hand, a serious expression on his face. "Maybe I'm out of line, God knows I didn't mean to get into all this, but I'm concerned about you. It's not Louis, but Charles who has the Charpentier dark streak, and in him it's intensified because he made the wrong marriage. I'll give him credit where credit is due: he's not a womanizer, as so many men would be in his situation. He seems to work off all his frustrations in his business dealings, where he has the reputation of being even more ruthless than his famous acquisitive grandfather. I think the truth is that Charles is rather inexperienced with women—I confess that idea isn't original with me, it came from Louis who, before Lynda, had considerable experience of his own. Louis said if Charles hadn't had this romantic fantasy of a great love at first sight, he'd never have made the mistake of marrying Arabella. Louis was probably right, but if so, that only makes Charles all the more dangerous. Rosamund, you're exactly the kind of woman the Charpentier men have always married. I saw how Charles looked at you the night I was there, and I felt the atmosphere in that house. It feels like an explosion just waiting to happen, and you're right in the middle of it. Now do you understand why I didn't want to go into the house? Why, the more I know you, the less happy I am about you being there at all?"

I was shaken. I didn't doubt that Timothy's perceptions were accurate. Even the protection of my swift tongue had deserted me. "Yes," I said at last, "but I need to think about what you've said before I can make any response." I took the napkin from my lap and put it down on the table next to my half-eaten pecan pie. "Please finish your dessert. I'm going to the ladies room, and then perhaps we can start back."

On the long drive home, Timothy remained considerately silent, leaving me with my tumbled thoughts. At one point he grasped my hand, raised it to his lips, and feathered a kiss across my knuckles. The perfection of his gesture touched me but could not still my struggling mind. Timothy had sought to warn me; he couldn't know that he had given me a powerful insight into the very man he sought to warn me against. I understood the women who had married the Charpentier men Timothy had called dark and ruthless; I felt a kinship with those women. I had gone looking for Timothy that afternoon because my head told me it was the right thing to do, and then he himself had given my errant heart the ammunition it needed to begin its assault anew. It required a tremendous effort to put my head back in control, as I wanted it to be.

When Timothy turned his car onto Charpentier's private road, I knew the time had come for me to give him some response. "Could we stop along the road here, before we get to the house? I want to tell you something."

"Sure." He pulled over and killed the headlights. Only the glow from the dashboard remained, turning him into a silhouette. "I was beginning to think I'd said too much, and you were never going to speak to me again!"

"No, not at all. It's hard for me to say this, but the truth is that you told me some things I probably need to know. I want us to be friends, so there's something I need you to understand. I've made a commitment to take care of Arabella Charpentier. To me, that commitment is the most important thing. Charles thinks she's building up to something, that something decisive will happen, and I believe he's right. As far as I'm concerned, the only person in that house who's in any danger is Arabella herself, and I intend to be there for her. Even if it's difficult, even if I'm uncomfortable, I can't leave."

"Not even if Lynda, or I, could find you another job?"

"No. I have to see this through. It's very important to me."

There was a soft click as Timothy released his seat belt and moved toward me. He stroked my hair gently. "You will be careful, won't you, Rosamund?"

"Yes, I will." He was going to kiss me—I wanted him to kiss me. I wanted to be so overwhelmed by his kiss that I would fall instantly, totally in love with him, and Charles Charpentier would be wiped from my mind, from my heart, forever. But Timothy hadn't moved. He still stroked my hair, that was all. I said, "I do want your friendship, Timothy."

"You have it." His hand stopped its stroking and cradled my head.

I lifted my face to him, and he kissed me. Light, but lingering. It was over before I felt anything, and he moved back behind the wheel.

"Thank you for dinner," I said when he stopped in front of the house.

"You're welcome. I'll walk you to the door."

The outside lights were blazing. After the dark of the drive, I felt as if I were onstage as we went together up the walk. At the door I took my house key from my purse. It was the first time I'd used it, but it slipped easily into the lock. Timothy's hands on my shoulders turned me around.

"Good ni . . ." I tried to say, but Timothy's mouth covered mine, and his hands pressed me to him, molding my body to the length of his. It was a deep, possessive kiss, there in the blazing light on the doorstep of Charpentier. I was astonished.

"I'll call you," he whispered against my cheek as he released me. He reached into his inside coat pocket and brought out a business card, which he pressed into my hand. "In the meantime, if you ever need me, for any reason, you call me. The church number is on the front, my private number is on the back."

I looked up into serious, caring blue eyes. "I will," I promised. Then I turned the key in the lock and went into the house. I closed the door and leaned against it for a moment. That kiss had taken my breath away, but whether from surprise or something else, I didn't know.

Chapter 7

CHARLES WAS ALREADY AT the table when I came into the breakfast room, something that had never happened before. As I'd observed early on, he was anything but a morning person.

"Well," I said from the sideboard as I poured a glass of orange juice, "this is a first!"

"You don't have exclusive rights on being the first one down in the morning, *Miz* Early Bird!"

I sat down with my juice in one hand and an empty cup and saucer in the other. Charles had already brought the coffeepot to the table. "I can't help it, you know. One of the requirements for admission to medical school is the ability to wake up spontaneously at the crack of dawn. God, Charles, you look terrible!"

"Thanks. It's nice of you to notice."

His hair was shaggier than ever, and his square jaw was darkly shadowed with a day's growth of beard. His newspaper was still folded, untouched. He sat with his huge shoulders hunched, brooding over his coffee cup.

"You haven't even shaved. Is something wrong?"

"Maybe I'm growing a beard. Jenny!" he bellowed.

She came and then left again, and I repeated, "Is something wrong?"

"If you must know, I stayed up all night. Drinking."

"Oh. Well I must say, you look it. Please pass the coffee-pot." To my surprise, he did it. I'd expected him to tell me to get it myself. I poured into my cup slowly, watching Charles from the corner of my eye. He looked like Thor, hunched and hidden in dark thunderclouds. "Do you do that often?"

"What?"

"Sit up all night, drinking."

"No, I don't. Last night I was provoked." He shot me a powerfully malevolent look that hit me just as hard as if he'd hurled a thunderbolt. I decided I'd best leave him alone.

Jenny returned with a tray laden with fluffy biscuits, butter, scrambled eggs, and fragrant country sausage. I ate with pleasure. Breakfast had become my favorite meal in this house. I thought Charles couldn't have too much of a hangover, because he was working his way through his usual amount of food.

He pushed his plate away. "How long has that been going on?"

"How long has what been going on?"

"You and What's-his-name."

"You mean Timothy Durrell?" This was what I wanted, wasn't it, I wanted Charles to know that I had a life of my own, apart from Charpentier. But now that he'd brought it out into the open I was distinctly uncomfortable.

"Yes, him. How long?"

"Not long. And nothing's going on. We just went out to dinner. You wanted me to have friends, remember?"

Charles put his elbows on the table and clutched his hands into his thick hair, head bowed. A heavy, dark shock of hair tumbled over his forehead. When he spoke, his voice came out a low rumble. "Friends? Out to dinner? I saw the way he kissed you, on *my* doorstep!"

My face burned scarlet, and my tongue leapt automatically to my defense. "Is that why you left all the outside lights on, so you could spy on me?"

"I left the lights on as a matter of courtesy. And I wasn't spying on you. I heard the car, and I looked out my window to see that you got in safely."

"You don't have to watch out for me," I snapped, "you're not my father!"

The sapphire blue eyes flinched, his sensual mouth turned

down bitterly at the corners. I had wounded him, though I hadn't meant to. But it was too late to call back my words.

"Is that what you really think, Rosamund? That I'm old enough to be your father?"

"No! I . . ." But he wasn't listening.

"This morning I feel old enough. Damn it all to hell!" He hurled himself away from the table and stalked to the door. But then he turned around and heavily retraced his steps.

I sat stricken. Everything was out of control. Teasing had turned to real hurt, and my own feelings were tearing me apart.

Charles sat down again. All the anger had gone out of him. "I'm sorry, Rosamund. I couldn't get it out of my mind, seeing you with him like that. All night long I drank and cursed, and it didn't do any good. I kept seeing you in his arms, his hands on your magnificent hair, his mouth coming down on yours. But I have no right to you, none at all. If things were only different . . ."

His anger was so much easier to deal with than this. My eyes filled with tears and I turned my head away, but not before he'd seen. He leaned across the table and with his fingers under my chin, turned my face back to him. My tears welled over and spilled onto my cheeks.

"Ah! So you do have some feeling for this old man after all." He smiled, but it was a sad smile.

"Yes," I whispered, "I do."

"Someday, somehow, I'll make this all work out. I swear to God I will! Will you wait for me, Rosamund?"

Slowly, I shook my head. My voice broke on the words, but I said what I had to say. "I can't promise anything, Charles. Nor should you." I wiped away my tears with the back of my hand.

"So much wisdom in someone so young, and so beautiful. Nevertheless, I do promise you I'll make it work out. I have to. I don't think I'd want to live if I lost you. I learned that last night, and it was a hard, bitter lesson, believe me." He stood up, then swiftly bent and kissed my cheek.

"You'd better go and shave," I said.

"That's exactly where I'm going."

I stared after him. I felt as if I'd walked into a wall or been run over by an eighteen-wheeled truck. I was dazed, unable to think, which was just as well. The things Charles had said were unbearable to think about. Arabella was waiting, I had a job to do—thank goodness! I went to do it.

I went straight from the breakfast room to Arabella's suite in the North Wing, not following my usual routine of returning first to my own rooms. I didn't want to be alone with my thoughts, not even for a few minutes, and I didn't think Arabella would mind if I was those few minutes early. But as I approached the door at the far end of the first-floor corridor, some sixth sense told me to be cautious. The North Wing, unlike the rest of the house, had wall-to-wall carpet and my footsteps made no sound. I turned the doorknob slowly, and silently opened the door just enough to look into the room.

Regina stood over a seated Arabella. There was something menacing in the angle of Regina's body, and the tone of her voice chilled me though I couldn't hear her words. There was no doubt that Arabella did not like whatever Regina was saying. She raised her thin, white hands to the sides of her face as if she would cover her ears, but instead she paused in midmotion, seeming to recover her composure. She ran the fingers of her raised hands through her hair at both temples, lifting it up and out as if to more fully display those shocking white streaks. She raised her chin and arched her neck, and turned her head from side to side—self-contained now, utterly disregarding. I knew how impossible it was to break through that self-containment, and so did Regina. But still she gave it one parting shot, and this time she spoke loudly enough for me to hear: "I know that you could do it, if you would only try."

I decided it was time for me to make a legitimate entrance. I closed the door as silently as I had opened it, then opened it again and strode breezily into the room. "Good morning!"

"Good morning, Miss Rosamund," said Regina, "I did not expect you so soon."

"Am I early?" I pretended innocence and looked at my watch. "Well, only ten minutes. And it looks like you've finished breakfast. I hope you slept well last night, Arabella."

A thin smile touched her lips, but she did not reply. She wore her mirror glasses today and a mossy green dressing gown of rather gauzy material. With her white skin she looked like a vampire of the forest. I smiled back at her, amused by the thought. That was one thing I didn't have to worry about, her teeth at least were normal.

I turned toward Regina, who had crossed the room and begun to clear the breakfast dishes. "I'll see to Arabella's insulin now."

Arabella's bathroom with its red porcelain fixtures and black-enamelled vanity was only slightly less shocking than her bedroom. I'd learned to ignore it, as every morning I went in to test the urine specimen before preparing her insulin injection. I did the strip test once and found I had to repeat it. There was no doubt—the results were not the same as usual, which meant that her diabetes was no longer stable. The difference was slight, not a big problem yet and I could adjust for it, but I'd have to report it to Dr. Barkstone. And I'd have to talk with Regina too, because I suspected the cause of this was that Arabella wasn't eating properly. I'd have to make Regina understand how important the proper diet was, and that she would have to help me watch what Arabella ate.

I went upstairs to get the insulin, deciding that I would call the doctor while Arabella had her nap. But talking to Regina could wait. It was bound to be difficult, and after that breakfast conversation with Charles, I'd had all the difficulties I could take for one day! What I needed now was a nice, quiet time with my patient, the quieter the better. After I'd prepared a syringe with the corrected insulin dosage, I got my needlepoint and the novel I was reading. I was ready now for my quiet day.

The morning was the best I could have hoped for. There was a good old movie on television, and Arabella and I both became absorbed in it. When it was over I went to the kitchen, as I often did, and brought back our lunch. The less I had to see of Regina today, the better, I thought. In spite of the uneventful morning, I hadn't quite lost the vague uneasiness I'd felt when I'd found Regina bending over Arabella, as if she were threatening her. But that was absurd! Regina was strange, all right, but one thing I was sure of: she was absolutely devoted to her mistress. Devoted and possessive. Besides, Charles trusted her completely.

I continued to muse over these things as we ate our lunch, but I also watched what Arabella ate. She seemed calm today, almost placid, and she was consuming her meal in her methodical manner. She was never one to initiate conversation, nor on this day was I. I preferred to work with my own suspicious thoughts.

The relationship between Arabella and Regina was a peculiar one. I didn't quite understand it. My instincts told me something was off, but I had no idea what it could be. Maybe Charles was wrong about Regina. He hadn't seen what I'd seen that morning. On the other hand, I could have misinterpreted. Surely Regina's body language had been threatening, and her tone of voice. But the words themselves, the few I'd been able to hear, could have applied to anything. I should give Regina the benefit of the doubt, even if I didn't like her. Perhaps, like me, she wanted to get Arabella involved in some new things. Like what? Well, like flower arranging. Regina could certainly use some help with that!

I turned my head and pretended to look out of the window so that Arabella wouldn't see my beginning smile. I'd discovered that it was not Regina, but Charles—the dark and ruthless Charpentier, according to Timothy—who loved flowers and wanted them all over the house. Often my fingers itched to get into one of Regina's haphazard conglomerations of flowers. One could hardly call them arrangements! I'd seen her method one day when I went to the flower room to ask if I might fix some for my own room. She mixed different varieties in a bunch which she grabbed in one hand, then cut all their stems straight across the bottom in one slash, and thrust them into a container of the right height, whether or not it harmonized. On behalf of the flowers, I'd felt insulted as I'd watched her. How different this was from the reverent appreciation Aunt Henry had shown for her flowers! She had taught me to treasure each individual blossom's perfection, had shown me at an early age which stems should be cut straight, which at an angle, and which should be crushed so that they would live longer.

It was clear that Regina took no real enjoyment in her responsibility to keep fresh flowers in the house. So, it would be no wonder if she wanted to get Arabella to take it over, and she very well might have said, "I know you could do it, if only you would try." It was a very sensible explanation. I didn't believe it for a minute.

I had finished my lunch, and Arabella was nearly done as well. She was so quiet, perhaps too much so. I roused myself to make an effort. "After your rest today, would you like to do something different? We could go to Brookgreen and look at the sculpture."

She did not reply, and I wished for the thousandth time that I could see her eyes through the glasses. Was she thinking about it? Had she even heard me? I would have to learn to be more sensitive if I was ever to decipher the puzzle that was my patient's mind.

At last she said, "I don't like this weather, Rosamund."

A rare statement for her. She usually seemed oblivious of her surroundings, and that included the weather. Or so I'd thought, but I was soon to learn that I was wrong.

"I have to agree with you," I said. "I don't like it much either." It had been overcast and very, very humid for several days. The air felt so full of moisture that it seemed if you could get hold of it and squeeze it, drops of water would fall from your hand. "But still, that's no reason to stay here. There's no rain in the weather forecast. So how about it? Shall we go to Brookgreen?"

"A storm is coming," said Arabella, and her voice was low and thrilling. "Soon. Tonight, or tomorrow. I don't have to go anywhere. The storm is coming to me."

I looked at her. She was still calm, she made none of the tiny, restless movements that indicated agitation. Yet she had been, prior to today, so often agitated that I had become accustomed to it. This stillness seemed unnatural. I said, "Arabella, you're impossible. You haven't even considered going to Brookgreen this afternoon, have you?"

"No, Rosamund. I only want to have my rest." She stood up gracefully, and the soft green material of her gown rippled about her thin frame.

"All right, then," I sighed. At least I'd tried. I stacked the dishes on the tray. Though Regina had never said anything to me about it, I'd quickly learned that if I brought lunch from the kitchen, I was also expected to take the dishes back. Anything to keep the peace, I thought as I walked through the long hallways, but then I corrected myself. No, not anything—there were limits. I had a feeling that one of these days soon I'd find out where the limits were.

Jenny always kept a radio on in the kitchen to sing along with her station's gospel songs in a strong, rich voice that could be heard through much of the house. When I'd put my tray of dishes on the counter next to the sink, I asked her if she'd heard a weather report on her radio station, anything about a storm coming.

"Ain't this weather somethin'?" She paused in her work—she was rolling out a piecrust.

"Is it unusual for this time of year?"

"Yes, ma'am, it shore is. Mostly we has lots and lots of rain in the spring, but not this year. Everythin' dry as a bone. Peoples gardens doin' nuthin'. Air so heavy a body can't hardly breathe, and nuthin' come out of it. Not since that there big storm when you came, no more'n a couple of piddly showers since then." She shook her head somberly and went back to rolling dough.

"Arabella says a storm is coming, and I just wondered if you'd heard anything on your radio station about it."

"No, they ain't said nuthin' 'bout a storm." She turned to me, interested. "You say Miss Arabella say a storm comin'?"

I nodded.

"Then likely it'll come. But it's gonna take more'n one storm to end this drought we got. You hear 'bout them forest fires up in No'th Ca'lina? Well, could happen here too, if we don't get some good rain. One thing go wrong an' it all go up, whoosh, just like that!" She snapped her floury fingers, and bits of white dust floated on the air.

"Is Arabella good at that kind of thing, predicting the weather?"

Jenny deftly picked up the thin round of dough, turned it, and slapped it down again. "Oh, yes'm. Some peoples has the gift. There's some folks say Miss Arabella she be a witch, but I says she has the gift, that's all. I believes in the Lord, don't wanna believe in no witches!" She flashed a wide smile.

I returned it. I knew as soon as I left she'd break out into song, praising the Lord she believed in, but I lingered. Jenny had never talked to me so openly before—but then, I hadn't done much to encourage her. I said, "I don't believe in witches either, Jenny."

"Didn't think you would, Miss Rosamund. You not the type."

"I know some people think Arabella is crazy, but I'm not so sure about that. What do you mean, she has the gift?"

Now Jenny doubled her circle of dough over and flopped it into a glass pie plate. A crease of worry appeared between her eyebrows. "Regina don't allow no talking on that. I already said too much."

"But surely you can talk to me. The whole reason I'm here is to help Arabella, and I only want to understand her better. I think you can help me do that."

Jenny stopped the swift, sure movements of her fingers and looked me straight in the eye. "You a nice young lady, Miss Rosamund, and I like you. You makes a big difference 'round this place. I been cookin' here all my life, and my Mama before me, and my Grandmama—we goes all the way back to when my people was slaves to the Charpentiers, and I reckon nuthin' would make Mr. Charles let me go. But it just ain't worth it to cross Regina. You understand what I'm tellin' you?"

My breath caught in my throat. "I think so." I could see by the expression on her face that she wasn't quite sure I did.

Her eyes swept the room, then she said in a hushed voice, "You be careful, Miss Rosamund. Remember, it ain't worth it for *nobody* to cross Regina 'less it's Mr. Charles hisself!"

"I'll remember. I've enjoyed talking to you, Jenny. I guess we'll find out pretty soon if Arabella's right about the rain, won't we?"

She nodded. On impulse I winked at her, and she was delighted. "Miss Rosamund, you a mess!" she called after me as I left the kitchen.

I'd been away from Arabella's suite longer than I liked,

but I still had to call Dr. Barkstone. I couldn't take the chance of Arabella overhearing, so I made the call from my sitting room. I was put right through to him and was relieved when he said what I'd thought he would say, that such a small change was no cause for alarm, but her food intake would bear close watching.

I returned to the big room downstairs. Arabella would rest for another hour at least. I settled on the couch with my novel, but I couldn't get into it. I put the book aside. I was definitely uneasy, I might as well admit it to myself.

Charles's face came into my mind—shaggy dark hair tumbling over his broad forehead, the touch of gray at his temples, deep blue of his eyes, the sensual expressiveness of his mouth, the strong lines of his jaw and chin covered by the blue-black shadow of a day's growth of beard. I was seeing him as he had looked that morning, when he'd said things I'd forced from my mind. Now they came rushing back. My stomach flipped over. Charles wanted me! With an intensity that alarmed but did not surprise me, for that was the way he was. If ever the word *passionate* had suited a man, it suited Charles. The words I least wanted to recall were imbedded forever in my brain: I don't think I'd want to live without you.

Oh, God, what was wrong with me? Promises made after a sleepless night, a night spent drinking, are worthless. Any fool knows that! I simply could not, would not, allow this to go any further, not even in my thoughts. It would be better to think about who called Arabella a witch, and why.

Immediately my uneasiness increased. Thinking about Charles had been a distraction apparently—the real reason for my disquiet lay elsewhere. I got up from the couch and went to the open french doors. The very air felt ominous. I stepped out onto the patio and looked up at the sky. It was a uniform, pale gray. No thunderheads. The feeling of omen did not come from an approaching storm. But it had something to do with Arabella.

All my senses were alert. There was something here, in this place. My head turned as if pulled by an invisible cord. And then I saw them.

The mourning doves, a pair of them. Always together, I'd seen them from my window every morning and again in the evening, making a slow, dignified progress through the grass, softly cooing to each other. Now they were dead. Their plump, buff-colored bodies with their dark-spotted wings lay side by side at the edge of the patio. I walked slowly across the slate and knelt beside them. These birds had died no natural death—their once-bright button eyes looked up at me from an impossible angle. Their heads were twisted around backwards. Their necks were broken. I reached out and touched the curving breast of the one nearest my knee. The feathers were soft, but cold, and the flesh under the feathers was hard. So, they had been dead for several hours.

A shudder ran through me. This was what I'd felt—death. A small death, but death all the same, untimely and unnatural. It was somehow the more horrible for its purposelessness. No animal had done this; it was too neat, the necks grotesquely screwed to exactly the same angle, the bodies arranged side by side in a mockery of their togetherness in life.

I was revolted, and then I was angry. What kind of person would kill these gentle, harmless creatures? I got to my feet and turned away, wiping my fingers on my skirt as if I could wipe away the touch of death. Charles would say that Arabella had done it, as he'd said she killed the dogs and cats. I stared at her bedroom windows, open and scarlet-framed by their drapes inside. Had she done it? Was that why she'd been so quiet? Did the act of taking innocent life calm something inside of her? I had to know.

I went into her bedroom without knocking, without any consideration for the privacy she insisted upon when she rested. I was so angry that I wanted to scream at her as soon as I was through the door, but I got myself under control. I'd assumed that Arabella seldom really slept during her naptime, but perhaps she rested. I forced my steps to slow and approached her quietly. She lay in that great black-pillared bed, on top of the red quilted satin spread, apparently sleeping. Her eyes were closed, her mirror glasses on top of an elaborate black-and-gold bedside table that looked like something taken from an Egyptian tomb. She still wore the green gown, the matching slippers were on the floor where she had stepped out of them, and in spite of the warmth and mugginess of the air she had covered her legs with a lacy rainbow-colored afghan that clashed with the setting and with her—not a rainbow person, our Arabella.

"Arabella!" I said sharply, "You must wake up!"

She moved her head from side to side on the pillow, but she did not wake.

"Now! Wake up, Arabella!"

Her eyes opened. For a moment I forgot everything except those eyes, seeing them for the first time. They were so very green and an unusual, elongated shape. The lashes she'd lost to the fire had certainly grown back, dark and thick. With those eyes she was an exotic creature, and in the instant I saw unusual beauty that had attracted Charles, would have attracted any man.

Those eyes were as expressive as I'd thought they would be. They quickly passed from the blankness of sleep into a blaze of annoyance. "What are you doing in my room!"

"Something has happened," I said firmly, "and I want you to come outside with me. Right now. It's important."

She sat up and reached for her glasses. She might as well have slipped a mask over her whole face, so completely was it altered. "All right," she grumbled, "I'm coming."

I turned my back on her and led the way. I didn't stop until the dead birds were at my feet. Then I turned and watched her approach. She walked stiffly, without her sometime-grace, and stopped in the middle of the patio.

"These are the mourning doves. You remember, don't you, Arabella? I told you how I liked to watch them out of my window in the morning when I'm getting dressed. And then they would come again in the late afternoons, just before Regina brings your dinner. I've called you to the window to watch them with me. You do remember?"

Her face was impassive. I watched for the slightest sign of emotion, but I saw none.

"They're dead now, Arabella. Look at them! These beautiful doves are dead. Someone killed them!"

She turned away and sat on one of the wrought iron chairs. I went and sat next to her. Still she said nothing.

"How did it happen? These are wild birds. Who trapped them? Who . . . killed them?"

Her nervous hand movements had returned. Her fingers

plucked at the folds of her skirt. She looked at me, and I saw my reflection in her glasses. "They weren't trapped. I made them come. I know how to do it, you see." An odd smile twisted up one corner of her mouth.

"How do you do it?"

"It's my secret." She laughed her eerie chuckle. "Mine, and hers."

"Hers? Who do you mean?" I couldn't stop my questions. I was so angry I wanted to shake the answers from her. "Do you mean Regina?"

"No. Not Regina. I didn't kill those silly birds. And that's all I'm going to say." She rose stiffly and started back to the house.

I called after her. "I'm going to tell Charles. I'm going to bring him to see this with his own eyes!"

There was a slight hesitation in her gait. I was sure she'd heard me, but she went through the french doors without a word.

With a last, shuddering glance at the birds, I went to look for Charles. He was probably out, visiting one of his developments or whatever he did during the day. The most reasonable way to start would be the garage, to see if his car was there. I walked rapidly through the house, though my anger had cooled a little, and out the East Front door. I followed the drive around to the garages. All the cars were there, so I went back to the house.

The more I walked, the more I dreaded telling him. But it had to be done. Arabella had to know that I would not let this sort of thing go by. He was probably in his office, one of his rooms in the South Wing. I'd seen it on my house tour with Arabella, with its ceiling of dark and light wood laid in an intricate pattern—Victorian herringbone, or something like that. I found that my teeth were clenched with tension, and I paused to take a deep breath before I went through the open office door.

"Excuse me for interrupting you."

Charles sat behind a desk which suited him well, it was massive. At the sound of my voice he looked up and smiled. "Rosamund!" Then his expression changed. How swiftly it could alter, as a dark cloud obscures the sun. "Damn. Something's wrong."

He came around the desk and took my hand, pulled me over to a leather two-seater couch just as I realized a reaction was setting in. All my anger had drained out of me, and with it the adrenalin. I felt suddenly cold, clammy, and my knees were like water. "This is ridiculous!" I said, but I sat down very quickly anyway.

"You don't look so good, Rosamund. No, don't tell me anything yet. Put your head down for a minute. No, not that way! This way." He shoved my head down onto my knees. "I thought you were supposed to be a doctor!"

"I'm not going to faint. It's not that big a deal," I said into my lap.

"Don't talk!" Charles commanded. He sounded as if he was across the room. Then he was back, rubbing my neck beneath the knot of my hair, with gentle pressure encouraging me to lift my head. "Here, drink this. Straight down, all at once."

I tossed it down without even looking. The effect was immediate, like swallowing liquid fire. I felt the blood rush to the surface of my skin in a warm glow. "Wow! What *was* that?"

"Vodka. Very good Russian vodka. Now, what happened?"

"It's not that big a deal," I repeated. "Or at least, it shouldn't be, but I thought you ought to know right away. I'm glad you were here and not off someplace."

"Get to the point, Rosamund."

"I found two dead birds on the patio. Mourning doves. I know this sounds silly, but I felt as if I knew those birds. They came at the same times every day, always together. . . ."

"I know. When mourning doves mate, they mate for life."

"Well," I tried to lighten up, "at least they died together, then. But they didn't just . . . die. Their heads were twisted around backwards. Somebody killed them."

"Oh, Lord. Arabella."

"I don't know. I'm not sure she did. I made her come out on the patio and look at them. She said she didn't kill them. She said the oddest thing, Charles. It was so odd, I think she may be telling the truth." I paused, thinking about it. "She said she made them come to her, but she didn't kill them."

"Made them come to her. I hadn't thought of that—it would be damn near impossible to catch a pair of wild birds, even doves who usually walk around on the ground. Not like the dogs or the cats, who'd come when you called. . . ." Charles was musing. "Although, come to think of it, the cats didn't know Arabella. They were strays, and they wouldn't have anything to do with anyone except me and Jenny—she fed them. You're right, it is odd. How could she do that, make them come to her?"

"I asked her, and she said it was a secret that only she and one other person knew. She wouldn't say who the other person was either, except I asked if it was Regina, and she said no. Then she said she didn't kill the birds and that she wasn't going to talk anymore. Charles, I want you to come down and look at them. I want Arabella to know that you know, that you've seen. Even if she didn't do it, I'm sure she knows who did. They must have been killed early this morning, probably while we were at breakfast."

"And while we were at breakfast, Regina would have been there. So Regina would know, too. But couldn't it have happened earlier?"

"No." I shook my head. "I always see—always used to see—the mourning doves from my window when I was getting dressed. I'm sure they were there when I was dressing this morning."

"All right, let's go down. You're feeling better now?"

"Yes," I said, "I'm fine."

Charles and I walked quickly through the house, side by side, through Arabella's living room, and onto the patio. Regina was there, and the birds were not.

Charles was scanning the slate, but I knew exactly where the dead birds had lain and I wasted no time. "What have you done with them?" I demanded.

"I beg your pardon, Miss Rosamund?" Regina's yellow-brown eyes were as cold and as hard as glass, and so was her voice.

Charles explained. "A pair of dead mourning doves. Rosamund found them here just a little while ago. You must have seen them, Regina."

Oh, she was a cool one, all right. She stood there in her simple white-collared gray dress, with her high cheekbones and her golden skin, holding herself like a queen, and she lied with great facility.

"I didn't see any birds, Mr. Charles, alive or dead. What I *saw* was Miss Rosamund running away from the house and leaving Miss Arabella alone, when we know Miss Arabella's not well enough to be by herself. So I stopped my work and came to be with Miss Arabella. I looked in on her and saw that she was all right. I just came out here to check on the weather. I think a storm's on the way"—she raised her face to the sky, showing off the long line of her throat—"but I don't see any storm clouds yet." She smiled, well satisfied with her own explanation.

"I don't believe you," I said. "You knew those birds were here!" In my mind suddenly I could see her as clearly as if I'd been there watching. "You laid them there precisely, side by side—you probably hoped I'd find them. Why else would you have left them there?" I took a step toward her and nailed her with a stead gaze. "And what's more, Regina, I think you are the person who killed them, not Arabella. You took each dove in your hands and twisted their necks until they were dead!"

She didn't even blink. "Miss Rosamund, I never lie. And I have better things to do than killing birds."

Charles ran an exasperated hand through his hair. "This is getting us nowhere."

"I'm going to get Arabella," I said. "She knows what happened, what you really did this morning." It was a big gamble, I knew, to turn to Arabella for help—and I'd lost before I'd even had time to take a step toward the house.

Arabella came sweeping through the french doors. She had changed her clothes, and she looked the best I'd ever seen her. She wore an old-fashioned dress of white organza, the kind Southern ladies used to wear on hot, muggy afternoons like this one. It was all tiny pleats in the bodice and inset lace, and a billowy midcalf skirt showing off trim legs and ankles in white stockings, and thin, elegant feet in white kid shoes. She looked ten, maybe fifteen years younger.

"Charles," she gushed, "how nice of you to come and see me! We must sit down. Regina, we could have lemonade, couldn't we, on this awful afternoon? Such dreadful weather!"

I felt like asking her why she hadn't a fan to flutter, to make the picture complete. It was a performance I recognized, like her lady-of-the-manor act when she'd shown me the house. Only this one was better. In my old chino skirt and loose blue cotton-knit sweater and flat shoes, I felt like a mediocre commoner. Charles, I saw, was temporarily at a loss—she'd hustled him to the wrought iron love seat and pulled him down beside her, and she'd ignored me as if I were not there at all.

I couldn't have this. There was something awful about it. From the corner of my eye I saw Regina move, likely on her way to get the lemonade. "Wait, Regina!" I put more authority into my voice than I felt. "We're going to finish what we started here."

Arabella turned her head regally, as if searching for the source of this disruption. Her glasses were pale blue, a good choice to go with her innocent-looking outfit. "My goodness! Don't you want to sit down and have some lemonade?"

"Not right now, Arabella. I want you to tell Charles about the two dead birds I showed you just a little while ago, before you changed your clothes. I'm sure you remember."

She lifted her hand daintily and pressed it to her bosom, Vivien Leigh playing Blanche DuBois. "Dead birds? How . . . distasteful! I haven't seen any dead birds, have you, Regina?" She stuck to her role, but I heard a quiver in her voice and I was sure she *was* performing. She hadn't flipped into another reality where she really was this Southern belle.

"Of course not," said Regina. Every word dripped scorn. "I told Miss Rosamund and Mr. Charles. It's only Miss Rosamund who says she's seen these dead birds, and I think she made it up just to cause trouble."

Ah, she has given me the cut direct! I thought. There was silence—nobody said anything. I needed time out, to give myself time to think. "Oh, all right." I pretended defeat. I slumped into the nearest chair, a picture of dejection. If Arabella could act, then so could I.

"Yes, of course, that's it." Arabella pulled her face into a smile so falsely bright it was grotesque. "Rosamund was being naughty!"

Regina put her up to this, I thought. On her own, Arabella

might well have told the truth, as she had told the truth to me. But there was that peculiar relationship between them, and now Regina was trying to use it against me. First she'd wanted to shock, maybe even frighten, me with the birds, and now she wanted to confuse me. Embarrass me. I was willing to let them play their game.

"Do send her away, Charles," simpered Arabella.

I was willing to let them play, but Charles was not. He stood and shook off Arabella as if she were no more than a mischievous puppy. I kept my head down, still trying to look defeated, but I could see what was going on. Regina stood near the french doors, Arabella subsided in a white froth on the love seat, and Charles was gathering power. He positioned himself halfway between me and his wife, and he looked even taller than his six feet five inches.

"That's enough!" His voice rolled out like thunder. "Regina, there will be no lemonade. Come over here." She came. "Now, I don't know what this performance is all about, but I do know one thing. Rosamund is a responsible person with a great deal of integrity. If she says she saw dead birds on the patio, I believe her. In fact, if she said she saw a sea serpent in the Waccamaw, I'd believe that too."

Don't, Charles, I pleaded silently. Don't say too much. I hadn't expected this impassioned defense. Nor had Regina. At the moment, she looked stunned.

Charles was not finished. "Now, I don't know that it's worth my time to find out what happened to those birds. But I want it understood that *no one* is going to undermine Rosamund's position in this house! Do you understand?"

"Yes, sir," said Regina. She wasn't stunned now. She looked from Charles to me with pure hatred in her eyes.

Arabella exploded. She was no longer acting. "Her position in this house!" she sneered. "And just what position *is* that, Charles, on top or underneath? How about on her hands and knees like a doggie? You think I don't know this beautiful little girl is your *whore?*" She advanced, stalking him.

"That's enough, Arabella!" But he couldn't stop her, I knew. Only physical means, a slap in the face or something like that, would stop her now, and I didn't think Charles would do that.

"You said she was a friend, a friend of a friend of the family, you said—"

"That's true," I inserted, trying to distract her though my cheeks flamed from her crude accusations. "I *am* a friend of a friend!" It was like trying to talk to an avalanche. Here were the remnants of a younger, healthier Arabella, fiery, earthy. I watched her in horror and in awe.

"You brought her here to help me, you said. But you lied. You're the liar, you—Charles Charpentier! You brought her here for yourself. You think I'm too crazy to notice, you think just because I wear glasses I haven't got eyes in my head? Well, *see*, I do have eyes! She's seen them now, you might as well see them too!" She ripped off her glasses and flung them down—they skittered across the slates. Her magnificent green eyes blazed. Charles took an involuntary step backward. "There was a time you loved my eyes! I know you. I know what kind of man you are. You haven't been in my bed for years. You're not a monk, Charles. You've got to get it somewhere, but at least you never brought them home before."

She stopped, and now she looked at me. I couldn't say anything. The psychiatrist in me was too impressed with the near-accuracy of her feelings, and for the moment I'd forgotten myself. There was a gloriousness to her fury, and I was absorbed in her.

Her attention went back to Charles. "Maybe you think she's different, is that it? Oh, I admit she's nice enough to me—I even like her sometimes. Maybe you brought her here because you think you're really in love with her, and that's why she stays."

There was anguish in Charles's strong face. He tried again. "Arabella—" And once more she overrode him, her voice scaling higher.

"That's it! I see it on your face. I know it because I know you. You're in love with this girl, and now you want to get rid of me! You and Rosamund, both of you, together, you want to get rid of me! But you can't do it, you'll never do it, because I have the power. I have power you never dreamed of. It's been growing and growing all these years!"

Arabella was slipping over the edge into her madness. I could hear it, I could feel it, I could see it now in the green glitter of her long eyes. And I myself had had all I could stand. If I didn't do something now, it would be too late, for both of us.

I jumped out of my chair. I had to match force with force, or she would never hear me. "Now, just a goddamn minute, Arabella Charpentier!" She turned to me, away from Charles. Good. "You're wrong, wrong, *wrong!* I do not have a sexual relationship with your husband, do you hear? I never laid eyes on him before I came here. I came here for only one reason, and that's to help you. To help *you,* Arabella. And now you've insulted me, you've said terrible things about me. You called me a whore, for God's sake! I don't want to hear any more. I certainly don't want to hear that I'm plotting with Charles to get rid of you when nothing could be farther from the truth!"

I had her full attention, and she was calmer now, much calmer. "I come from a good family," I continued, a concept I thought she would understand. "I was well brought-up, and I don't know if I can stay where anyone says such terrible things about me. I'm going off by myself for a while now. I have to think about this. I may come back, and I may not." I turned my back on them all and strode away. I meant every word that I'd said.

Chapter 8

I CLEARED MY MIND as I climbed the stairs to my room. I visualized a surface of clear blue, a pure sky without cloud, and I held it before me to the exclusion of all else. Later I would think, later I would deal with feelings that might overwhelm me if I let them in now. Later, when I was away from this house. For now there was only the endless blue filling my mind, calming me.

I picked up my purse and checked to see that my car keys and house key were in it. Then I made the long walk through the house and to the garages, looking neither to the right nor the left, seeing only the blue, the blue, the blue. At last I was in my car. My car was my friend, I was glad to be there. But it was not until I'd driven the whole length of the private road and turned onto the highway that I gave a long sigh of relief. Then I did the reality-things: I looked at my watch and saw that it was only three-thirty. I turned on the car's air-conditioning, and the blast of cool, dry air felt wonderful. I could breathe again! I wondered if Charpentier had central air-conditioning. Surely, in this climate, Charles would have had it installed. When I got back, I'd ask him about turning it on. . . .

I pressed my lips together in a rather grim smile. So that was the way it was with me—as soon as I let my mind go, it went right back to Charpentier, to Charles. In spite of all that

116

had happened! Well, we do not necessarily have to turn all our thoughts into actions, the voice of Henrietta Hill said inside my head. It was one of her favorite bits of advice, and I'd internalized it. "Thanks, Aunt Henry!" I said aloud.

Nevertheless a great deal had happened, and I did need to process it. I did have to decide what I would do, and right now I needed to go somewhere that I could be quiet and alone to do that. I wished I were one of those people who can do their thinking on long drives, like a woman I'd read about in the newspaper who dictated an entire mystery novel into a tape recorder while she was commuting to and from work. But I'm not like that; when I drive it's to go somewhere. So where would I go? Brookgreen, I thought. I'd been thinking of going there anyway, and I was already headed in that direction.

I turned into the entrance marked by a large metal sculpture of two rearing horses, the *Fighting Stallions,* and presented the season ticket I'd bought after my first visit. I'd known I would want to come back again and again. There was an enchantment about the place, all the more so because I'd discovered it all by myself. Not that it was hard to find, with its giant horses right at the side of the road! But no one had told me about it, no one had said oh, you must go to Brookgreen Gardens and see this and that, and so I'd had no idea what to expect. I felt again the magic, like a child in a new world, as acre after acre unfolded before me. Brookgreen had been a rice plantation—more than one, actually, though now it had a unity that made it seem like one. The main house and whatever other houses there had been were long gone, and now it was all an incredibly beautiful park and gardens. The gardens were a setting for outdoor sculpture of exquisite variety, from massive forms like the huge winged Pegasus of white marble, to delicate small carvings in stone of little children and animals. It could take years to see and appreciate all of it.

I parked my station wagon and began the long walk through the oak alley. It was not unlike the one at Charpentier; the mystery and the peace of the great trees felt the same, dripping with Spanish moss which always looked to me as if it were native to another planet. In fact, it reminded me so much of Charpentier that I didn't want to let it influence me before I could sit down and really think objectively. I hurried through the oaks and on up to the alligator pool on the site where the original plantation house had stood. I'd read a plaque there that said the house had been destroyed by fire a long time ago. I chose one of the paths that radiated from the pool and walked along, resolutely refusing to be drawn in by the statuary which today would be a distraction. Soon I found an ideal place, a little stone bench that was almost hidden by a rhododendron as tall as I. I sat down and, finally, let my mind run free. And my feelings as well.

At first everything was just jumbled confusion. Then I had a moment of pure, sheer disbelief. Just a few months ago I'd been a serious medical student, who never wore makeup, pretended men and women were all the same, didn't believe anything without scientific—preferably clinical—evidence, whose primary problem in life was getting enough sleep. Now the only thing remotely the same was that I still preferred to go without makeup! No wonder I had such a boggled mind. I'd had experiences I couldn't deny, experiences that could only be called psychic, a word that hadn't even been in my vocabulary until recently. Feelings of déjà vu were always just around the corner, ready to leap out at me with no warning. I lived in a house that was straight out of the ante bellum period, and the whole way of life was so different that I felt like a fish out of water. Or did I? I admitted I hadn't thought about the differences in a long time, so I must be getting used to it.

But there was more, so much more. Not just the place, but the people. Regina—an unusual person who might be intriguing if I weren't so convinced of her malevolence. Arabella, a woman of such rich complexity and strangeness and tragedy she made my mind whirl. Timothy, priest and teacher, island of sanity, with the kind of looks that would be right at home on television. Honestly! I thought in disgust, this whole situation would be right at home on television. Especially by the time you add Charles—ruthless, romantic Charles married to bizarre, crazy Arabella—and me, half in love with him but caring deeply about her as well. What was a nice, intelligent, sensible person like me doing in all this? It all seemed so, so . . . what? So unreal. And if I were as sensible as Charles gave me credit for, surely I'd just turn my back on all this, say the heck with it, and leave. Go back to the real world.

Go back where at least the air was breathable! The humidity was so cloying I could hardly stand it. The knot of hair on my neck, in the way I'd worn it for more years than I could remember with never even a thought that it was there, now felt heavy and even soggy. I looked up at the sky, searching the open patches through the trees for any sign of a change, but there was none. I dripped perspiration and I realized I was terribly thirsty and probably becoming dehydrated. I just wasn't used to this climate. I got to my feet. I would walk slowly back to the car and finish my thinking on the way. As I walked, I paid attention to what I was feeling. There was the physical discomfort, but there was something else as well, a kind of thrumming vitality singing in my blood. I had never, ever felt so alive. The truth was that I loved it here—loved Brookgreen, loved Charpentier, loved the beach and the ocean so nearby. And in a way I didn't understand, a way somehow linked to the ever-near déjà vu, I felt at home.

I walked around the gilded statute of a young, decidedly undebauched Dionysus. I'd been paying so much attention to what was going on inside me, not looking where I was walking, that the great oak alley took me by surprise. It was, in both the truest and the currently popular sense, *awesome*. I stood there, absorbing it, letting the reality of it seep into me through my every pore. This, too, was real—as much the real world as Cambridge and the hospital and the old life I'd left behind. This, and all that waited for me at Charpentier, was reality with a deeper dimension than I'd known existed, strange but also exciting. The inexplicable could be understood. Difficulties could be overcome. In time. And I knew that I would not willingly leave, not now. The decision was made.

The thought that, after what had happened earlier in the afternoon, Charles might want me to leave, never even occurred to me. I was completely though unconsciously secure in my place at Charpentier, and it was a good thing.

That secure grounding which I never thought to question would later enable me to survive many things.

Charles sat on a mounting block outside the garages, which had once been the stables. Adjacent was a carriage house, which sheltered two shabby old carriages and had room for more. He rose as I pulled up. He'd obviously been waiting for me, and he looked like the hounds of hell had been giving him a hard time. He opened my car door.

"Thank God you came back! We have to talk, Rosamund."

"Yes, you're right, we do." I let him pull me from the car. There was a moment when I thought he might take me in his arms, but he didn't, and I pushed down the lock and shut the door.

"You're . . . you're going to stay, aren't you? You didn't just come back to get your things and leave again?"

"No, Charles, I didn't just come back to get my things." I gave him a reassuring, comradely pat on the shoulder. "Yes, I'm going to stay, and we will talk. But first things first. My body needs attention. I feel like I've perspired so much I've lost ninety percent of my body fluids! I need water, in me and on me. A glass of water to drink and a long, cool shower. And please, please tell me the house is air-conditioned and we can turn it on!"

Just seconds before he'd been scowling, with his broad shoulders hunched under unspeakable burdens. Now he smiled down at me, that very, very special smile, and I knew the meaning of the poet's cliche: He pierced me to the heart.

"You're amazing, Rosamund. Thank you for coming back. Thank you for just being who you are."

He'd been doing his share of perspiring, I saw. His hair curled in damp little tendrils over his ears and on his forehead, his shirt looked damp, and he had unbuttoned it halfway down the front. My eyes strayed to the dark curls on his chest, but I jerked them back to his face—I was hot enough already! "You're welcome," I said. "So, can we talk later?"

"Mostly, yes. But there's something you should know

before you go in—that's why I was waiting for you here. Partially. The other part—"

"Skip the other part. Just tell me what it is I have to know right now, before I go into a coma from severe dehydration!"

"Okay," Charles chuckled, "okay. It's Bella. How can I explain it? She's completely out of it. After you left she went rigid. She closed her eyes, wouldn't talk, wouldn't move. I sent Regina away, put her glasses on her, picked her up and carried her to her room and put her down on that divan with all the pillows. I kept on talking to her, and finally she came around. Only now she says she's not Arabella! I don't think she even remembers what happened this afternoon, the things she said."

"That's wishful thinking on your part, Charles."

"Maybe. But I don't think so. Anyway, I called the agency for a private duty nurse for tonight, just in case. And I do think it would be better for you not to see her until tomorrow. Seeing you might just stir her up again."

I looked at him critically. "Charles, do you still trust me to take care of your wife?"

"Of course I do."

"All right. The nurse is a good idea, because Arabella should be under observation if she had a catatonic episode, which is what it sounds like from your description. And I doubt if I could stay awake all night to do it. But I need to see her, I need to talk to her, because I have to let her know I've come back. I have to reestablish trust with her as quickly as possible, or I'll be no good to her at all. We, you and I, will talk more later. All right?"

Charles sighed. "All right, do what you think best. Come on, we'll go in by the kitchen so you can get whatever you want to drink. I already turned the air-conditioning on in the whole house. Believe it or not, I'm as uncomfortable in this weather as you are!"

"I seriously doubt that!"

We grinned at each other, and it seemed the most natural thing in the world that he put his arm lightly about my shoulders as we walked to the house. It was so natural that Charles might not even have realized he'd done it, because I knew he'd never consciously do anything to put me in danger. We were only a few steps from the side door when I thought of it, that any physical contact between us was not a good idea—not after Arabella's accusations. I said as much to Charles, very quietly, and he dropped his arm. But it was already too late. I saw a curtain twitch in a window, and I knew we'd been seen.

Between the cool water in the shower and the cooler air in the house, plus twelve ounces of ice water from the kitchen refrigerator and a tall glass of mint iced tea from the pitcher Jenny'd insisted I bring up for my own small refrigerator, I felt much better. I put on one of the two summer dresses I owned, a pale yellow cotton oxford cloth with roll-up sleeves. I really would have to do something soon about my clothes. I had so few, and they were all wrong for this climate. It was only late May, and already it felt like full summer to me.

I brushed and blow-dried my hair until I ran out of patience, which didn't take long. Of course it was still quite damp. The most sensible thing would be to cut it. Immediately I thought, Charles wouldn't want me to cut my hair. I looked severely at myself and told myself to stop thinking like that. But what was I going to do with it? The idea of twisting it into the Psyche knot was about as attractive as having a small furry animal on the back of my neck. If I braided it damp, it would dry all kinky and look like a nest of snakes tomorrow, and I certainly didn't have time to achieve the Victorian pouf. The important thing was to get it off my neck. The only thing I could think of was the old reliable ponytail, so I pulled it all back and up to the crown of my head and secured it with an elastic band. Not bad. It still hung halfway down my back, but it was a lot cooler. I tossed my head to be sure the elastic would hold, and my betraying mind said, *a river of burning gold.* Shut up! I replied, and stuck out my tongue at the face in the mirror before I put on my peach-colored lipstick.

Now I had to see Arabella. I wouldn't stay long. And then I'd have a serious talk with Charles in the library before dinner.

The private duty nurse hadn't arrived yet, and Regina was

with Arabella. I hadn't expected that. They were both sitting on the couch, watching the six o'clock news. I rapped my knuckles on the open door and went into the room.

"Regina, I'd like to be alone with Arabella for a few minutes, please." I circled the couch and turned off the television.

"Why?" she shot back.

"I want to talk to her. In private."

"I told Mr. Charles I'd stay with Miss Arabella until the nurse comes, and that's what I'm going to do."

I had neither the time nor the patience to argue with her. "All right, then. There's no reason you shouldn't hear what I have to say." I pushed an upholstered chair closer to the end of the couch on which Arabella sat, and I perched on the edge of its seat. "Arabella?"

She still stared at the empty TV screen.

"Has she been sedated, given any medication?"

"No. You have the only keys, Miss Rosamund." She made it sound like a crime.

"I do have them," I acknowledged. I'd assumed Charles also had a set, but perhaps this wasn't so. "Arabella." I felt sorry for her. She had seemed so young and so vibrant in her white costume only a few hours ago. Now there was a change in her that went deeper than the fact that she was dressed as if ready for bed, in a pearl gray silk kimono, an elegant garment, but its color made her look old. Her glasses too were gray, and looked opaque, and her skin devoid of cosmetics was a flat, unhealthy white. I pleaded, "Arabella, please look at me. I've come back. I said I might go away or I might come back, and I've come back to stay."

She stirred. She arched her neck and turned her head. "I'm not Arabella," she said in one of her more vicious tones of voice.

"Well, that's all right. You know me just as well as Arabella does, so I'll just talk to you. I'm going to stay, because I want to help Arabella. And I want to get to know *you* better. Maybe one of these days you'll tell me your name."

She laughed. It was a rasping, mirthless sound, but I was glad to hear it because it was a response, she wasn't shutting me out.

"Why are you laughing? Did I say something funny?"

"You're so simple, Rosamund. You pretend to be so good. Or maybe you really are good, I wouldn't know. I know nothing about goodness!"

That voice definitely did not sound like Arabella. It gave me the creeps.

"You probably know a lot about a lot of things," I said.

"Yes-s-ssss. I do. I know we don't want you here. Go away, Rosamund!"

"Who is this *we* you're talking about?"

"Me, and Arabella, and Regina. We don't want you here. Do we, Regina?"

"I want what Mr. Charles wants," said Regina carefully.

I studied her, trying to hide my surprise at her reply. There was a crack in her facade. She looked a shade less confident, and there was a flicker of something in her eyes, not her usual leonine stare. Curious to know what was going on with her, I made a stab in what I hoped was the right direction. "You know the name of this person who's not Arabella, don't you, Regina? I wish you'd introduce me."

"I can't say that I do or I don't. If she wants you to know, she'll tell you herself. You . . . already seem to know her more than I realized." There was the flicker again.

Suddenly I knew where it was coming from. Regina had underestimated me and she didn't yet know what to do about it. "Yes," I said, "this one and I have talked before." I addressed the not-Arabella again. "Well, since I find it hard to converse with someone who doesn't have a name, I'll call you Jane, for Jane Doe."

"Jane!" she sneered. "A trivial, silly name!"

"Nevertheless, I shall call you Jane until you tell me your own name, which I presume you like better."

No response.

I pushed on. "Jane, Regina has said she wants what Charles wants, and Charles himself asked me to help Arabella. That hasn't changed. He knows I've decided to stay, and he trusts that I'll do my best for his wife. As long as you're using her body, or her eyes, or whatever it is you're doing, I guess that means I'll help you, too."

"Do whatever you like," she growled, "but *I* don't want your help!"

"Do you plan to be here long, Jane? Or might we have Arabella back soon?"

"I don't like that name." Now she sounded whiny, petulant.

"Then you know what you can do about it. Will you answer my question?"

"Yes-s-ssss. I'm waiting for the storm, and I'll be here a long, long time. Now go away!"

"All right," I agreed. I'd been reasonable with this unreasonable creature for long enough anyway. "I expect the nurse will be here soon, don't you think so, Regina?"

Regina nodded.

I stood up and nudged the chair back into place with my knee. Then I looked down at Arabella/Jane. "Just one more thing, Jane. The nurse doesn't know about you, and I think it would be better to keep it that way. Just don't tell her you're not Arabella."

Her lips curled in derision as she arched her neck to look up at me. "Do you really think I'm that stupid, Rosamund? I'd never tell one of those nurses anything. I don't talk to them at all!"

"Fair enough. Have a good evening, you two—or should I say you three?" I was more concerned about the change in Arabella than I liked to admit, but for now I had to put that out of my mind. I went through the halls to the library, where Charles had said he'd be waiting. What I had to accomplish with him might be even more difficult than dealing with his wife. I found him waiting, and dropped into the nearest chair.

"Hi! That was some conversation I just had with your not-Arabella. I'm calling her Jane. Regina was there, too."

He didn't pick up on that. Instead, he was solicitous. "Let me fix you a drink. I know you don't usually, but I think you'll agree this hasn't been your usual day."

"Thank God they're not usually like this! Do you have any Scotch?"

He grinned. "You Northerners. Always want Scotch instead of bourbon. What do you want with it—water, soda?"

"Maybe instead I should try some bourbon and, what is it you put with it down here? Coca-Cola? Dr. Pepper? Seven-Up?" Charles looked so surprised I had to laugh. "Thought I was serious there for a minute, didn't you? I was only teasing. Scotch and water, please.''

He crossed the room to do the fixing. "Lynda drinks bourbon and Coke. Seems to thrive on it, so be careful how you make fun of us. Here you are.''

I sipped at my drink and enjoyed the silence that fell between us. I wished it could stay this way, that all the other things could disappear and I could have one night, just one single night, alone with Charles and no responsibilities. I could feel his eyes on me, but I hesitated to meet them. When at last I did, I saw in them a shadow of the anguish that had been there earlier in the day. I couldn't bear it. ''What is it, Charles?''

''I was thinking of the things Bella said this afternoon. I'm so sorry, Rosamund. She can be crude, I know, she's been that way with me before, but to have her say such things in front of you and worse, about you . . .! I apologize for her, and for myself, for putting you in a position to have to hear it.''

''I accept your apology, though it isn't really necessary. She was . . . remarkable, wasn't she?''

''Remarkable?'' He gave a short, harsh laugh. ''She was terrible. Horrible!''

I was quiet, considering. Though I knew how this talk with Charles must end, I did not know how to get there. I had only instinct to rely on. ''I thought in some ways she was rather magnificent. And I also thought that for a few moments I could see the, ah, exotically beautiful woman you married. The woman you fell in love with, all earth and fire. You could see her too, couldn't you, Charles?''

The color drained from his face. ''You're too perceptive, Rosamund.'' He got up and went to the window and stood with his back to me. I knew he was upset and didn't want me to see.

''No, Charles. Not *too* perceptive. Perhaps perceptive enough to be a good psychiatrist, if I ever get back to medical school, that's all. I had a feeling as I watched Arabella that she was burning up the last of her sanity. Like she gathered up all that was left and threw it out at us in a final fireball.''

Charles returned to his chair and sat down heavily. He looked at me with great sadness in his eyes, which I thought was for his wife. He was suffering deeply, and there was no way I could help him.

"You should go back to medical school, Rosamund. You will be a good psychiatrist, and I have no right to hope . . . otherwise. You've never even told me why you left."

"No, I haven't, and now is not the time. I expect I'll tell you eventually, and maybe I'll even be able to work it out so that I can go back. But right now, tonight, this time belongs to Arabella. We both need to talk about her. Don't you see that, Charles?"

"I don't know. I've lived with it, with her, for so long that I'm barely rational on the subject anymore. You lead on— I'll see what I can contribute." He glanced at his watch. "You'd better keep in mind that we have only about half an hour before dinner."

"I know. I think that's enough. What I was most interested in, and most concerned about, this afternoon was that Arabella was—I'm sorry, it's hard to know how to put it. She was close to the mark with her accusations about you and me."

Charles narrowed his heavy brows. "In some ways yes, and in other ways, no. You know how sick she is; is it necessary to dwell on the product of a sick mind? Now that I've apologized to you, I'd like to put the whole episode behind us."

Very quietly, but very definitely, I said, "No. We can't do that."

"Why?"

"Because although she was angry, she was quite rational, and you know it."

The dark clouds we needed to bring us rain were all gathering now, only they were inside Charles. I'd never seen a stormier visage.

"Very well. But if you insist on talking about that, I have to do it my own way."

I inclined my head in assent.

"She made it sound like I've had women all the way from here to Georgetown to Charleston and back. That isn't true,

Rosamund. There have been a few, I admit, but damn few.''
He leaned forward with his forearms resting along his strong
thighs. "She was right about one thing, though." His eyes
softened in an unfathomable look, and then he hung his
head.

I waited, full of joy and fear.

When he looked up again at me, the softness was gone.
His eyes blazed. "Oh, hell, Rosamund! I don't want to tell
you like this!" He twisted his great, muscular body out of his
chair and stalked across the room where he began to make
himself another drink.

I followed him, stood beside him, handed him my glass.
"You don't have to tell me." I looked up at him. His hand
reached out to touch my long hair, and his eyes came to
mine. In their dark blue depths I saw again the anguish. That
he wanted me, I knew. If the intensity I felt from him had its
roots in more than wanting, I had to turn it away. It was the
thought of being loved, truly loved, by Charles Charpentier
that filled me with both joy and fear. I had to turn it away.

My heart was a live thing caught in the cage of my body. I
had to be mind, all mind, and reason. "I . . ." My voice
wasn't working. I moistened my lips with the tip of my
tongue and began again. "I know there is some feeling
between us, Charles."

"Some feeling," he agreed flatly.

I rushed on. "The incredible thing is that Arabella sensed
it somehow, that she came to her own not illogical conclu-
sions. I'm very concerned about that!"

Charles abandoned his drink-mixing task. "Come over
here," he said, drawing me with him to stand before the cold
fireplace, "as far away from the door as possible. I don't
want us to be overheard. Now. I think Regina must have
seen us together and said something to Bella."

"No. I'm almost certain she didn't. Did you notice the
expression on Regina's face when you were defending me?
She was stunned. You were so, well, passionate about it, and
it took her completely by surprise. Regina got a whole new
set of things to think about today. You know how precise she
is—she hasn't got it all in order yet, and that bothers her. I
could see that just a few minutes ago when I was with her
and Arabella."

Charles's hand closed over mine. No more than that, the strong warmth of his fingers, and I burned, melted, the secret places of my body opened to him. "No," I whispered, "don't touch me. You mustn't touch me, Charles. Especially not in this house."

"Rosamund. You can't mean that."

I searched desperately for the right words to explain. "Don't you see, if Arabella really did do what I think she did today, if she used up the last vestiges of her sanity, then you and I are responsible! You saw her, you heard her. She was like . . . like any other woman, angry because she thought she'd been betrayed by her husband. But then she went over the edge; it was too much for her!"

Slowly Charles released my hand. He looked as if my words were a slap in his face, and still there was more I had to say. I had to make him understand. "I'm fond of her, Charles. I care deeply about her. If there's anything at all I can do to help her over the next few weeks, if there's any way I can help you to find a decent life for her in the future, then I have to do it. She must never again have cause to think those things about us, the things that pushed her over the edge."

Now he backed a step away. "You want me never to touch you again, is that right?"

I nodded.

"And essentially what you're saying is that you care more about my so-called wife than you care about me."

"I, I didn't think of it that way, Charles." But now, too late, I could see that he might.

He was a strong man. Sensitive, yes, and easily hurt, but in any challenge his strength came boiling to the surface as it did now. His features hardened. He could have been one of the statues at Brookgreen. A warrior. Or a god. "You said you care about Bella. In fact, you said you care deeply. You've never said you care deeply about me!"

"I can't, Charles. Not now, now is not the right time. M-maybe later, when Arabella's crisis is resolved. She's going into crisis now, and there's no way to tell how long it will last—a few days, a few weeks. She needs help! And I need you to help me help her!"

His voice rang out. "You're asking one hell of a lot!" He

attacked the room, eating it up with great strides of his long, angry legs, back and forth.

I stood by the fireplace, unable to take my eyes from him, fighting back tears with every ounce of strength. If even one tear fell, I knew my courage would dissolve, and all this pain would have been for nothing. I trembled, but I did not cry.

He came back to me, threatening, his voice like the low rumble of thunder, but he had himself under control. "Let this be understood, Rosamund Hill. I do not say lightly things such as I said to you after breakfast this morning, if you can remember back that far. You don't really know me, do you realize that? You're spending all your time and effort in understanding a woman who is most certainly crazy, who I think is evil, and who—based on what I saw and heard when she said she wasn't Arabella—may be possessed as well. Whatever the hell that means." His voice dropped an octave. "I believe I'm in love with you, woman. What's more, I'm finding out at my age that I've never really loved anyone before. And I'll tell you something, Ms. Psychiatrist, it hurts. Now you want me to agree not to touch you, you want me to put aside what I feel, what I need. You want me to help you with the woman who's been like an albatross around my neck for God knows how many years! All right, I'll do it. But be warned, Rosamund. We may lose our chance. By the time *later* comes, it may really be too late!"

I bit my lip, and swallowed hard. There was nothing I trusted myself to say.

Charles waited. His eyes were hard, as hard as sapphires themselves. When I still didn't speak, he said, "You can eat dinner by yourself. Tell Jenny and anybody else who needs to know that I had to go out on a business emergency. There's no way I'm going to sit across the dinner table from you tonight!"

I stood frozen in front of the fireplace, watching him leave the room and felt as if he were leaving my life. The tears streamed down my face, but it was all right, he was gone, he wouldn't see. He slammed the front door so hard it shook his hundred-and-fifty-year-old house.

I went to my room and called Jenny for my dinner on a tray.

* * *

Something was wrong. I didn't know what it was, I didn't know where I was, but I knew that something was wrong. I wasn't breathing right, I was hyperventilating, struggling . . . and then there was the flash. With a gasp of tremendous effort, I opened my eyes. The room was dark and ominously still. Then I heard it—the great, long roll of thunder. And there was another flash, stark, cold light startling through the white curtains, invading all with a nightmare glare. Now I understood. But I still wasn't breathing right. I swung my legs over the side of the bed, sat up, and waited for the thunder. Closer this time, and louder. I'd been deeply asleep, the exhausted sleep of emotional depletion. The storm had summoned me to fight for wakefulness.

I cupped my hands over my face and breathed into them to stop the hyperventilation. I glanced at the red numbers of the digital clock-radio I'd bought for my room: three A.M., night's nadir, the hour at which, more than any other, people die. I didn't hyperventilate for nothing, something had frightened me. Not the storm—I wasn't afraid of storms, rather the opposite. Even in childhood, when I'd been afraid of the dark, I'd found thunderstorms curiously, wonderfully exciting. What, then? A dream? A premonition? I couldn't remember either one.

The thunder rolled, it went on and on. I walked to the window and held the curtain aside. The windows were closed, of course, because of the air-conditioning. It was a black night outside with a faint glow of light far off to my right—Arabella's patio. The private duty nurse would be inside on her all-night vigil. Even through the closed window I could hear the rising wind. Far across the lawn the massed trees swayed their tops, darker shapes against the dark sky. I waited in anticipation of the first grand sweep of rain, the driving wall of water that would break the tension and the heat. Arabella had been right. By whatever mysterious means, she had known this storm would come.

I shivered a bit in my thin cotton gown and crossed my arms. I didn't want to leave the window, not until it was so lashed by rain that I could no longer see. It wouldn't be long now, the storm's intensity was building. The lightning flashes were longer, brighter, the thunder so close behind I could barely count to two. . . . Oh, God! I drew in my breath sharply, gripped by instant, icy fear. A shape, an apparition, where no shape should have been. I stared, and in the next illumination I saw it again on the lawn, beyond the azalea border of Arabella's patio, a dark figure hooded and robed. There was a tremendous *crack* as lightning and thunder simultaneously struck, and the figure raised its arms to the sky. On the dying thunder-roar I heard its wail, and I ran. That was no apparition, that was Arabella!

I ran in my bare feet, not stopping to retrieve the slippers I'd kicked under the bed in my haste or to locate a seldom-worn bathrobe in the closet. I sped down the hall, down the steps. Where the hell was the nurse? I slammed through the door—why that should awaken the nurse when nothing else had I was sure I didn't know, but it did.

I paused in midflight long enough to look at her. She was very young, she looked about old enough to baby-sit, and she'd fallen asleep at the game table, her head on a book. She was an RN, a very new one from the cap askew on her head, and I'd never seen her before. "Stay there, there's no time to explain!" I threw the words at her as I opened the french doors and went out through them. The slate of the patio was cold and slick on the soles of my bare feet. I'd entered another world, a wild and primitive place.

I crossed the patio slowly as my eyes grew accustomed to the dark. The wind had dropped for the moment, and rain fell in huge drops. Before I'd gone more than a few steps I was soaked to the skin, but the air was warm and thick, and unreasonably I felt a shivery pleasure. I stopped at the azalea border and looked into the dark.

I could just barely see Arabella, but I could hear her. She was singing. No, chanting—I could hear the rhythm if not the words. In the next flash of lightning I saw her, saw the black hooded cloak that covered her from head to foot. White, I thought, she should be wearing white; why I should think that I didn't know. I pushed through the waist-high azaleas and pattered on a diagonal across the soft, wet grass to a little copse of dogwood trees that gave me shelter and put me several yards closer. I was convinced now that she wasn't running away, nor did I think she was trying to get herself struck by lightning. A remote possibility at best anyway, since the trees and the tall chimneys of the house offered much better targets. She was in no danger.

Now the wind rose, and I could feel it coming—the storm's full fury. Arabella also felt it. I had my night vision now and some help from the faint lights in the house since they were no longer directly behind me. Arabella had stopped her chanting. She had dropped into a crouch, and she slowly turned around and around, rising little by little as she turned. She looked as if she were slowly twisting up out of the earth. The wind howled, it pushed at my body, tore at my hair. Arabella turned faster, whirling now, and at the next great simultaneous boom of thunder and flash of light, she threw her arms skyward and cried out a word I'd never heard before. The wind snatched it from her. Her robe whipped about her and its sleeves fell back from her thin, white wraith-arms that reached for the thunder; her hood, too, fell away and her hair flared out about her head with its own white lightning streaks.

Through the lashing torrent she chanted now with her arms held up to the sky, her voice high yet strangely resonant, chanting in a language unknown to me. It could have been gibberish, or it could have been a tongue that only she knew from the depths of her tormented mind—it was full of harsh, gnashing sounds that crashed together in a commanding cadence. It was the performance of a lifetime; I wouldn't have missed it for the world.

Suddenly I realized I was no longer alone in my dogwood copse. Alarmed, I turned and my face was caught in the wind-whipped curtain of my hair. When I'd subdued it, I saw Charles. He was as drenched as I, but he wore a robe and slippers and I was suddenly aware that I did not. I dismissed the thought. This was no time to be concerned about modesty.

"What the hell is going on?" he yelled over the roar of the storm.

I held up a finger to my lips for silence. He glared at me and strode out, but I stopped him, dragging on his arm. I strained on tiptoe, trying to speak into his ear, and obligingly he lowered his head. "Don't stop her now," I said, "we'll talk later!"

He growled, "When you die, I'm going to put that on your tombstone: We'll talk later!" But he was silent, and he waited and watched with me.

We hadn't long to wait. The wind died, the thunder receded, the rain slackened—and Arabella collapsed on the ground. We went to her. Charles reached down to pull her to her feet.

"Wait," I said and knelt to examine her. She was unconscious. I felt the pulse in her neck—it was strong and regular. "She can't get up, Charles, she's out. But she's okay. Will you carry her?"

"Ummmh," he grunted. He gathered her up, voluminous soaking cloak and all, and we went in a very wet procession back to the house.

"Now, what in the name of Great Galahad was that all about?" asked Charles. We had turned Arabella over to the care of the little nurse, who was now most efficient and eager to prove herself.

"Great Galahad?"

"Come off it, Rosamund. I'm not in the mood for your witty tongue." His voice was harsh, his eyes flashed as they raked over my body.

"Well, I'm not particularly in the mood for your bad mood either, if you'll pardon the redundancy," I came back at him. My long nightgown, slightly old-fashioned with its high, square neck and blue ribbon threaded through the white cotton batiste, was not particularly revealing. But it was wet now and it clung to me in places Charles touched with his eyes. I ignored that, and I ignored the flush that rose in my face. "What that was all about, you have as good an idea as I do. She went out into the rain, that's all, nobody could stop her." I saw no need to tell on the little nurse, who probably couldn't have stopped her anyway. "I was watching her, I knew she was safe. Has she ever done that before? How much did you see, how long were you standing there?"

"I saw enough. No, she's never done that before. Storms always excite her, she talks nonsense, and usually we tranquilize her. If you'd given her the medication, she wouldn't have done that." He looked at me accusingly.

"I don't believe in medication unless there's a good

reason for it. She didn't hurt herself or anyone else by what she did. Besides . . . ah-choo!" I sneezed, and sneezed again. "Look Charles, no harm is done. I'm going to get dry and try to get some more sleep, and I suggest you do the same. I'll tell the nurse to come for me if she needs me. And I'll see you at breakfast."

Chapter 9

ONCE AGAIN I FOUND Charles in the breakfast room before me. But the signs were more auspicious to-day—he was impeccably combed, shaved, and dressed in a dark gray suit, and he was already into the newspaper.

"Good morning," I said from the sideboard, and got a grunt of recognition in return. So far, so good. Without even looking at me, he called for Jenny, and breakfast was under-way.

I ate without pleasure, simply chewing and swallowing in the hope that the food would make me feel better. I was light-headed and sandy-eyed from lack of sleep, and I also felt like I'd been used for an emotional punching bag. I thought Charles couldn't feel much better. I glanced at him. He seemed engrossed in the paper spread out on the table. His thick hair was disciplined, the craggy contours of his face were set into seriousness, and I recognized the colors of his alma mater in the crimson-and-white diagonal stripes of his tie. As he slowly turned a page, his eyes never leaving the paper, I saw that he wore a ring on his right hand—a heavy, handsome gold ring set with a square red stone. A ruby. I'd never seen Charles wear a ring before. In fact, I'd never seen *this* Charles before.

I realized I was staring, and brought my eyes back to my plate. Overnight, Charles had changed. This well-dressed businessman, so self-absorbed and self-possessed, was a stranger to me. I hadn't felt so alone since my arrival at Charpentier. I picked up my coffee cup, but it was empty.

"May I give you more coffee, Rosamund?"

"Yes, please." Even this politeness was strange, distancing.

He folded his newspaper carefully, set it aside, and laced his fingers together on the table in front of him. He looked like the chairman confronting the board. The ruby in his ring winked at me, but there was no such levity in his face.

"I'm going to Charleston today to visit my mother. I also will be at my office in Georgetown. I intend to do the majority of my business from there in the future, rather than from my office here. Both of these telephone numbers are in the address book by the phone in the library. If you should need me, my secretary in Georgetown will always know where to reach me."

More distance. I felt a pang that I ignored. "All right."

"Have you seen Bella yet this morning?"

"Yes, when I first got up I went to check on her. She's still sleeping. The nurse said she has slept straight through since the storm."

"If there are any problems when she wakes, you can call Dr. Barkstone. I suggest you call him anyway and set up a time for yourself to go to his office within the next week. I think it's time you discussed your observations with him. It's time we got some clear idea of where this crisis, as you call it, is going. I will not allow this situation to go on indefinitely, I assure you. Of course, I don't expect you to go into town to see Barkstone on one of your days off. When you've made the appointment, you can ask Regina to stay with Bella during that time."

"I'd rather not," I said quickly, "have Regina do anything more than her usual routine."

"Oh?" Charles arched a heavy eyebrow. "Then you can get one of the nurses. It's up to you."

"Charles, about Regina—I didn't think of this until later, after everything was over last night. Don't you think it was rather peculiar that Regina never showed up, that she never even came to see how Arabella was taking the storm?"

"No, I don't. I am not interested in hearing your speculations about Regina, any more than I am interested in hearing her speculations about you."

I felt stung. "But . . ."

"I said I do not want to pursue that line of thought! You can leave Regina to me. I know very well"—here his lips curved in a smile that was both bitter and sensual—"how to handle her."

His voice was heavy with insinuation, and my words flew out without volition. "What do you mean by that?" Instantly, I regretted the question.

"Why, Rosamund, I didn't know you were so naive! I've told you Regina is an octoroon. Surely you understand. No? In New Orleans in the last century men used to fight duels for the attentions of an octoroon. Octoroon women have long been prized for their exotic looks and their remarkable sexual abilities. I believe you've noted my taste for the exotic."

Impossible to know which was worse, the unmistakable meaning of his words or the scornful sensuality on his face. The thought of Charles physically involved with Regina sickened me. Literally. The contents of my stomach were trying to work their way up into my esophagus.

"You bastard!" I spat, just above a whisper. I left the table and walked out of the room. I took the stairs as fast as my shredded dignity would allow, and even so I made it to my bathroom just in time. While my stomach carried on its disgusting revolt, my mind tried to tell me something. It said, you rejected him, Rosamund. How would you expect a man like Charles to handle rejection? He was hurt, he wanted to hurt you back, that's all. And there's probably no truth in what he said about himself and Regina, it was all just . . . just insinuations, nasty to be sure, but just insinuation not confession.

I'm tired and I'm overreacting, I thought. I cleaned up the sink and splashed cold water over my face and neck. I brushed my teeth. I rinsed out my mouth with mouthwash. I could get the taste of it out of my mouth, but the picture Charles had planted in my mind would not go away. I saw the back of his head, his neck, and his heavily muscled shoulders naked, working, as he humped over Regina; and over his shoulder I saw her strange, lioness eyes. They were laughing at me.

I sat in a straight chair near Arabella's bed, watching her sleep, and heard Aunt Henry's voice saying, There's no rest for the wicked. Well, my aunt was wrong for once. Wicked or not, Arabella was getting all the rest. Midmorning, and she slept on. I was not surprised. The nurse's notes, which I would incorporate into my own log, carefully documented the events of the previous night, including the fact that she herself had briefly fallen asleep: ". . . during which time the pt., in a manic state apparently caused by a thunderstorm, went out of doors, attended by her companion R. Hill and later by pt.'s husband. She was brought back by them in semiconscious state, all vital signs within normal range. Pt. refused to respond to reality orientation but was cooperative in changing clothes and drying hair. Refused 6 oz. orange juice. To bed and asleep 4:30 A.M."

The notes went on to record at one-hour intervals, "Sleeping quietly, no problems," just as the nurse had told me earlier. Her notes were good, better than most. I'd thanked her and apologized for her overlong shift, inwardly grateful that on this morning of all mornings I did not have to deal with Regina. My own observations soon confirmed that Arabella was in a deep and apparently normal sleep, and I did not expect her to wake before noon.

I looked with longing at the many-pillowed divan, which was about the shape of a king-sized bed, then gave myself a mental shake. No rest for me! Not until tonight, which at the moment seemed an impossibly long way off.

I could use this time to think, to plan. I'd make the appointment with Dr. Barkstone at the first opportunity. It would be a goal, something concrete to aim for as I picked my way through the shifting sands of all these strangenesses, the strangenesses that centered on this woman. I looked at her. Even deeply asleep, Arabella Charpentier didn't look like anybody's idea of a normal fifty-year-old woman. This morning she looked older, actually. There was nothing average about her. I got lost in contemplating her face. Her papery white skin was so dry that it had no shine at all and thousands of tiny lines that remained invisible unless one were as close as I was now. Her mouth in repose, unadorned by lipstick to give it color, turned downward at the corners. Among the thousands of lines in that face there was not one that could be called a smile line. I had never noticed that before. It was tragic . . . and also rather horrible.

I turned away, twisting my body in the uncomfortable straight chair. It was hard for me to sit still in that room. Something about it disturbed me on the deepest level. There was an atmosphere, hard to define yet palpable; it lurked beyond the bizarre furnishings. Those were just outward appearance, mere material trappings. The reality of the room was deeper, darker. I was sure it was not my imagination. Probably I would never have noticed, going in and out as I usually did, but sitting here hour after hour in silence and in the gloom produced by the thick, heavy red drapes drawn across the windows, I felt that atmosphere. It seeped into me, it made me uneasy, it made my skin crawl.

Arabella stirred, and my attention instantly went back to her. She turned from her side, facing me, to her back. Still asleep, she raised a hand in her habitual gesture, smoothing her hair back from her temple, thin fingers combing through the white streaks. A sense of something like recognition touched me for a moment and then was gone, and I thought only what marvelous hair she had. It was as thick and heavy as my own, and the white streaks were natural, white to the roots and the tiny new emerging hairs. Her profile, sharply etched even in the gloomy light, reminded me that she had good bones as well. She was aging, but with those bones and that hair she would never look less than dramatic, if she chose. She looked like a Medea, I thought . . . or like a witch. As Jenny had said some people thought.

But no, not a witch. In the part of my mind peopled with legend and fantasy, a part which I had neither nurtured nor used since childhood, I found a witch-image. It looked like a hag. Arabella was more like the wicked queen in Snow White; Arabella was the *before* and the hag-witch was the *after*. So, she did not look like a witch, but like someone grander, a caster of spells, a wielder of dark powers, possessor of a magic mirror that could show her things. . . . My mind drew me ever deeper into that unnurtured part, presenting me with half-formed images and whispered, half-heard words, until I rebelled and pulled back with an effort of will.

All this occult stuff was absurd! I tried to smile about it and found that I couldn't. It was not necessarily absurd. My medical training had taught me a meaning for *occult* which was without all the mysterious connotations, as in "occult" blood, blood which is hidden until the proper test is applied. With proper knowledge, that which is occult, or hidden, can be revealed and then a correct diagnosis can be made. I seized the thought with gratitude; it was a firm place to stand in all the shifting strangeness. I needed facts, not fantasy—though I had to admit my fantasies had taken me in the right direction. What were the facts about Arabella Charpentier, who was she, really? Who were her parents, who had given her that long, straight nose, the high cheekbones, the abundant hair? Charles had said she had no family. Were they all dead, or had they disowned her? She seemed well educated, with an inbred kind of snobbishness that I associated with a certain kind of Southern family background, though where I got the idea I didn't know. At any rate, I doubted she could have acquired it after her marriage to Charles. What kind of life had she lived before her marriage? Would it help me to know? Perhaps it would. Perhaps, when things calmed down between us, I should ask Charles.

I shifted again, seeking some comfort in the straight chair. I sighed, I let my mind go still. I was so very, very tired. I felt the presence of the room around me, engulfing me in its heaviness, and I closed my eyes. Just for a moment, I thought . . . and then there was no more thought. Against the black curtain of my closed eyelids, a thin, red line appeared, spinning out of nothingness. With it I felt a surge of energy. The red line thickened, and my eardrums throbbed with a muffled *boom* and another and another, in time with my beating heart. The red line began to turn, it curved back upon itself until it became a swirl, turning faster and faster, a crazy whirligig of red on black. With its whirling, the energy coursing through me magnified to desperation, caught within my body, pushing to break through my skin; my ears pulsed and pounded, my whole body even to the roots of my teeth reverberated like a drum.

My eyes flew open. The figure on the bed was slowly sitting up. Through the fading throbbing in my ears I heard her say, "What have you done with my glasses, girl?"

Any port in a storm, I thought when Regina appeared about an hour later with the lunch tray. I swallowed my pride, not to mention a certain degree of loathing, and asked her if she would have her lunch with Arabella in my place. I explained that I had to call Dr. Barkstone in private, and said I could get myself a sandwich in the kitchen.

"Has something happened?" asked Regina, an unusual look of alarm on her face.

"No, not since last night. You do know about last night?"

Regina nodded. "The nurse told me. I doubt it did her any harm." Regina's eyes glittered. "She loves the thunderstorms. She knew it was coming, you know."

"Yes, I remember." And where were you during all that, I wondered, not for the first time. "You're right, it did her no harm. In fact, she seems to be in unusually high spirits today, but I know you can handle her. Charles asked me to call the doctor, that's all."

"I will stay."

"Thanks. I'll let you tell her you're here—she's in her bedroom."

I went straight to my sitting room an found comfort in the ordinariness of the act of making a telephone call: the familiar dial tone, the little buttons to push in their neat rows of numbers. Thank God for numbers! Always the same, zero through nine. . . . The receptionist answered, and her businesslike voice and the routine manner in which she made the appointment were a healing contact with the world. By the time I'd confirmed an hour the following Monday, I felt much better. It was easier for me to go there on my day off, regardless of what Charles had said. That done, I forced myself down to the kitchen.

"You looks tired, Miss Rosamund," said Jenny.

"We all had sort of a rough night," I admitted, "and I didn't get much sleep."

"Well, you gots to eat regardless," Jenny commented, and set about making me a ham-and-cheese sandwich. "Everthin' be all right today?" she asked as she handed the sandwich to me on a plate. Her curiosity was all over the thin brown face.

I shook my head. "I don't know, Jenny, I really don't know. That's why I asked Regina to stay with Arabella for a little while, I need to be alone. I have a lot to think about. Thanks for the sandwich."

I was not hungry, I was somewhere beyond that. But Jenny was right, I did have to eat. I took the sandwich back to my sitting room and eased myself into a comfortable chair, the plate on my knees. I let the light reflecting off the ivory walls and the high ceiling wash over me; I kicked off my shoes and felt the softness of the Chinese rug, pale blues and yellows on ivory in an ageless pattern, thick and soothing to the soles of my feet. I began to eat. I ruminated, in both meanings of the word. I tried to achieve a cow's placidity.

My strange experience, vision, or whatever it was, had been a terrible shock, multiplied manyfold by coming out of it head-on into an Arabella who was not Arabella. She had awakened that way, already locked deep into the delusion of her not-Arabella persona. At first, she had not even recognized me, and when she finally did it made no difference. She was filled with a new determination, a nameless sense of purpose, and it made her uncooperative in the extreme. She'd sneered that *she* didn't have diabetes, and I'd very nearly failed to convince her that Arabella's body did and as long as she intended to use that body she would have to care for it properly and take her insulin. I scarcely remembered dashing upstairs to prepare the injection, so concerned had I been that even in the briefest absence anything might happen.

Nothing had happened. She had taken the injection. Then she'd gone on a rampage in her walk-in closet, refusing to let me help her, complaining loudly that there was nothing fit to wear. At last she'd crowed, "Ah! There they are!" and disappeared into the adjoining dressing room. When she emerged, gone was the Arabella I'd known for two months. And nobody in their right mind would have called this new creature Jane. Gone were the long, soft dressing gowns trimmed in ruffles and lace. I sensed that I would never see them again. She wore straight, black silk trousers and over them a green tunic with a black abstract design in the center that looked rather like a huge spider. She had brushed all the curl out of her hair, or perhaps the rain had washed it out. Her hair hung straight down her back, well past her shoulders, longer than I'd thought it was. The dark lenses of her glasses were the only link to the past. I hadn't had much time after that to observe her before Regina came, but the fact that her experience of the night before had strengthened her somehow was evident. She looked and moved like a stronger person.

I pondered. So, Arabella had found the power she sought in the storm. Her weird ritual had had meaning for her, and it had worked. Her mind might be beyond recall to the real world, but it all undoubtedly made sense to her.

And what about my own strange experience, my vision or whatever? Now at last I could try to make some sense of it. I had drawn that experience out of the room, from the atmosphere of the room itself. A few weeks ago I'd have said Nonsense! to such a thought, but no more. On a nonverbal level I knew: I had been in touch with Arabella's madness. Perhaps with the very essence of that madness, expressed in the symbol of the whirling, twisting red line on black background. The pulsing, clawing energy I had felt was her desperate, crazy energy. I hoped that in my experience its force had been condensed and therefore magnified—otherwise, how could she stand it? I felt like I had stood on the edge of insanity, I had for a few moments participated in Arabella's madness, and I was not afraid. I was shaken, but I did not feel fear, because although her madness had gripped me, I was not trapped in it.

In retrospect it was oddly reassuring, a privilege to have experienced a piece of her illness and to know that I could do so without fear. Even if she had gone over the edge, perhaps I still could help her, pull her back. Get this not-Arabella to release her grip. It would not be easy, the attempt might even be dangerous. Until now, Arabella had always been strange and unpredictable, sometimes hostile and a bit vicious, but underneath that she'd been biddable because she was fragile and she had seemed to know it. That fragility was gone now, or at least she believed it was gone. And that could be dangerous.

All diseases have a progression, including diseases of the mind. Some can be arrested, and some can be reversed. Arabella's disease had progressed to the point where simple arrest was not enough. But was reversal possible? Could I have been wrong in what I'd said to Charles, that she had flung out *all* her remaining sanity at us in a final fireball? Might there be still a tiny spark left, a spark that could be rekindled? This hope had the colors of my vision, the red on black, a consistency that felt reinforcing. Against all odds, I still wanted to have hope for Arabella.

The afternoon dragged on so uneventfully that it was boring. Arabella stayed in her room. Whenever I looked in on her she was doing something at her desk, and I certainly wouldn't interrupt her. I'd rather be bored than have another dose of her bad temper. Left to herself, she was getting along all right, and I was thankful that she was at least quiet.

When the hands of my watch crept around near the dinner hour, I went as always at this time of day to tell Arabella that I was going upstairs and Regina would be with her shortly. I found her curled up asleep on the big turkish divan, colored pillows around her and under her in bright profusion. I was touched. I cared for her. Quietly, I went away.

From my bedroom window I looked out upon the lawn, feeling that I had forgotten something important. Then I realized what it was. Not anything forgotten, but something lost, the mourning doves. I mourned them as I slowly changed my clothes.

The usual evening routine was for me to join Charles in the library for a drink before dinner. I no longer cared about the unpleasantness between us at breakfast, and I welcomed a return to the routine. I hurried because I was a bit late—the time which had passed so slowly had somehow gotten ahead of me. Through the long corridors I went, down the oriental runners, my hand trailing the smoothness of the mahogany stair rail, into the library. Charles was not there.

I went to the credenza he used for a liquor cabinet and poured myself a glass of pale dry sherry. I sat down to wait, and wondered what I would say to him. What he would say to me. I wanted peace between us, at almost any price.

Charles didn't come. The house was quiet, too quiet. It

felt . . . empty. My imagination, of course. The house was not empty. But when the clock in the hall chimed the hour, its sound echoed solemnly off the walls. An emptiness was inside me and I ached with it. I returned my empty sherry glass to the credenza and went alone into the dining room, because it was time.

Our places were set as usual. No doubt Charles would join me soon. Once again I sat and waited, and once again he didn't come. I should be glad, I thought, trying to work up a little rebelliousness, after he had behaved so disgustingly that morning. The truth was, I wasn't glad at all. I missed him, more than I wanted to know. Much more than I would ever admit.

Regina came in with the appetizer. She wore a black dress, cut a little low in the neckline but otherwise very plain, and her hair was covered by a silk turban in a paisley pattern of turquoise, purple, and black. The effect was almost as surprising as Arabella in trousers.

"Good evening," I said. I looked at the footed crystal dish she put in front of me. It was tomato aspic, and I loathe tomato aspic.

"Mr. Charles called," she said smoothly. "He will be late. He will not be here for dinner." She began to gather up the unneeded place setting.

"Oh." That's why the house feels so empty, I thought, because Charles isn't in it. I could feel his absence, just as I could feel his presence. And the emptiness inside of me? Overtiredness, that's all, I assured myself.

I became aware that Regina had finished her gathering-up and stood looking at me. No doubt she expected more of a response than the "oh" I'd given. "I expect he stayed in Charleston to have dinner with his mother." I picked up my spoon and started on the hated aspic. I would eat in stubborn solitary splendor, and she could serve me just as she would have served Charles.

"He said he was at his office in Georgetown," Regina said with that irritating smoothness.

"Whatever," I replied carelessly, and Regina went on about her business.

The excellence of Jenny's food rescued me—I discovered

that I was really hungry and forgot to be self-conscious. I refused the wine but ate everything, including two of Jenny's homemade Parkerhouse rolls, which were so light they seemed to be made half of air. Dessert was lemon meringue pie and I ate that, too. Then I went out to walk it off in the oak alley.

The meal had done me good, and the walk did more. The timelessness of the great oaks, their balance and symmetry, reduced all human problems to appropriately human proportions. The storm had cleared the air, and the breeze that came with the twilight was soft and sweet. I stretched and sighed, and when the familiar feeling of belonging washed over me, for once I welcomed it without anxiety, without question. I strolled among the trees, losing myself in their mystery, and time passed without my notice until suddenly it was dark and I had to go in. Charles had not returned.

I was refreshed and alert, as I had not been all day. I took off the dress I'd worn for dinner and put on my old terry-cloth robe. It had once been bright yellow but was faded now to the shade of pale butter, many of its tight little loops were frayed, and it had the special softness that comes to good cotton after countless washings. As I belted it around my waist I thought that Arabella, even if she were totally sane, would never wear anything so old and disreputable-looking. I sat at the dressing table and began to brush out my hair, but I soon stopped in midstroke. I'd caught a glimpse of myself in the mirror, one of those unintentional things that happen sometimes when for an instant you see yourself as if you were someone else. The robe *was* disreputable-looking, and with my hair streaming down I looked about fourteen. I'd had the robe about that long, and fourteen had been an awkward age. I'd been all arms and legs and eyes, like a giraffe—not a comfortable memory. I blinked, and was an adult again. The adult thought it was about time to have a new bathrobe.

I gave my hair a few more strokes, then left it hanging loose. A plan was forming in my mind, and I wanted to get on with it. I wanted to prepare for my conference with Barkstone the same way I'd prepare for rounds. I wanted to do the absolute best I knew how, and that meant pulling together everything I'd learned about my patient so far, plus reading whatever resources I could find that might help me understand her condition.

The obvious place to start was with my own log, especially since I had to add the nurse's notes from last night and make an entry of my own. The log was in one of the locked cabinets in the sitting room. My hand went to my breastbone where the keys should have been, on their chain around my neck, because the dress I'd been wearing had no pockets. The keys weren't there. With a sinking sense of guilt I realized I hadn't put them on. And I'd thought that looking after those keys had become second nature to me!

Already at the door to the connecting bathroom, I turned and went back to the dressing table where I always left the keys while I showered. They weren't there either. Not wanting to believe my eyes, I shifted the brush, the comb, the hand mirror, the box of tissues; I opened the little drawer where I kept my sparse supply of cosmetics, even though to the best of my knowledge I'd never put the keys in that drawer. No keys. Then I remembered: I'd been running late, and I hadn't showered, I had only changed my clothes.

I walked around the end of the bed to the bureau, and there on top were the three little keys on their chain. I closed my hand over them and breathed a sigh of relief. Such foolishness over something that probably wasn't all that important! But I held the keys tightly in my hand until I'd opened the cabinet, checked the insulin in the small refrigerator and the medication and disposable syringes in their drawer, and retrieved my log from another drawer. Then I relocked the cabinet and put the keys around my neck. Soon I was settled in an easy chair with my feet propped on its matching ottoman, knees up to brace the log as I wrote my notes for today and the previous night.

The telephone-rang—such an unusual and unexpected sound that it startled me. My hand jumped and the pen made a jagged line across the page. I looked at it disbelievingly. The telephone rang again. It must be for me, a rare call from outside the house.

"Hello?" I answered tentatively.

"Rosamund? It's Timothy."

"Oh. Hi, Timothy." I wondered why I felt so relieved.

What kind of mind-set had I fallen into, that the ring of the telephone could scare me half to death? "It's good to hear from you."

"Likewise, good to hear your voice. How are things over there?"

"They're, ah, interesting. I think you might say things are beginning to take shape here."

"From the tone of your voice, I guess I'm supposed to say 'that's good.' But the truth is, I don't know what you mean. Please define 'beginning to take shape.' "

"Hm. Well, it's like when you're walking in the fog and up ahead of you, you see a sort of vague shape but you can't quite tell what it is, and as you get closer and closer you can see lines and angles and curlicues. . . ." I stopped, not sure where I was going with that or where it had come from. I grabbed the next image that came to mind. "Or, it's like watching a Polaroid picture develop, only very, very, slowly."

"I see. I think I prefer the Polaroid analogy. The other one seems a little, well, sinister. In other words, something has happened, is happening, at Charpentier?"

"Yes." I bit my tongue. I wanted to tell him more, it would have done me good to have a friend to talk to right then. But I didn't dare. Anyone could have listened to us on the intercom, and I didn't dare take the risk.

"I'm not surprised," said Timothy. "The tension I felt in that house is bound to produce some change, rather sooner than later. Do you want to tell me about it?"

"No. Not right now. Maybe the next time I see you."

"That's what I had in mind. How about dinner Saturday night? Or tomorrow night, Friday?"

It was tempting. I hesitated. "Saturday and Sunday are both workdays for me, Timothy."

"I know. I remember, your days off are Mondays and Tuesdays. But you aren't required to have your meals with the master, are you? Surely your evenings are your own. I promise to get you back early." His tone was light, teasing, but with a plaintive note that was charming.

I made up my mind, and I had an idea. "I can't this weekend, I really can't. I have a conference with Dr. Barkstone in his office on Monday, and I need all my nights between now and then to get ready. But I think maybe you could do something to help me."

"Well, if I have to take no for an answer, maybe I won't want to help."

"Oh, come on, Timothy. I hope you're teasing. I really need some help."

"Okay. I'll get my white horse and be right over!"

I laughed. "No, no horses needed. What I want is some books. You said you were interested in parapsychology, ESP, stuff like that. Could you get me a book or two on the occult?"

"The occult what? That covers a very wide range of things."

"Oh, demonic possesion, occult rituals, maybe witchcraft, things like that."

There was a very long pause. "Why, Rosamund?"

"I'm not quite sure. Call it a hunch. There's something going on with Arabella, and I'm not quite sure what it is, but I doubt if the medical books that I brought with me are going to be much help. I'm just trying to get a handle on whatever is going on, and I know nothing about these so-called occult things. I think I need to learn. Please, can you help?"

"I don't like it," said Timothy flatly. "But I do respect your instincts, Rosamund. I have a couple of books that may be of use to you. I'll bring them to you tomorrow, but you must promise me something."

"What?"

"If you learn anything, if you get any ideas from these books, you'll discuss it with me before you jump in and do anything with what you learn. This stuff can be dangerous in the wrong hands. No, maybe I should say it can be dangerous in the *right* hands. Anyone with your innate ability shouldn't mess around with something you don't understand."

"I promise, and anyway I'm not planning to *do* anything. I just want to learn, that's all."

"Okay. Then I'll bring them over to you tomorrow. What time would be good?"

"After dinner, I think. About eight. I'll watch for you. And thank you, Timothy, thanks very much."

"You're welcome. Now, are you ready for the price? You don't expect to get this kind of service free, I hope."

"Name your price," I chuckled. It was good to hear the humor in his voice again. He had really sounded worried.

"The price is that you go out with me for that dinner you won't have this weekend. How about Monday night instead?"

"It's a deal," I agreed.

It's funny how the human mind works. Like when you've tried to remember a name all day and you can't, and then in the middle of the night you wake up with that very name the only thing in your head, and you have to get up and write it down because you know if you don't, it will be gone again by morning. It was like that. Something had nagged at me from the time of the guilt over the keys, but try as I would I couldn't get it to surface. Then in the middle of the night I woke up and I knew. There should have been two bottles of medication in that drawer, and there had been only one.

I turned on my lamp and took the keys from the bedside table. I went into the other room, unlocked the cabinet, opened the drawer. There was a box of disposable syringes in the corner and one brown plastic bottle of tranquilizers, dated March 24, the date Dr. Barkstone had placed them in the drawer himself. I tangled briefly with the childproof cap and got it open. The label said "#50." I counted the tablets and there were fifty. All present and accounted for. I put them back into the bottle, pushed down and screwed the cap back on, then stood looking at the drawer with the bottle still in my hand.

I still had this feeling that something was wrong, but what? Barkstone must have taken the other bottle away. I'd opened that drawer for a syringe every single day, replaced the box of syringes whenever it ran out—surely if there had been two bottles and then only one, I'd have noticed, wouldn't I? It was maddening to be unable to remember, unable to be sure. The trouble was, I'd never given Arabella the tranquilizers, so I never had to count them.

Reason was taking over, telling me that I had started out with a full bottle put there by Dr. Barkstone and it was still full. I replaced the bottle in the drawer, closed it, and locked the cabinet.

But my subconscious mind told me something else, it had awakened me to do the telling. I had not yet learned that my subconscious mind was always right, that these middle-of-the-night communications could be trusted. I dismissed the matter of two-versus-one bottles of medication as an anxiety dream, brought on by feelings of guilt, and I went back to sleep.

Chapter 10

FRIDAY, SATURDAY, AND SUNDAY were very busy days for me. Regina's uncle had died, and she had to go to Patton Plantation to help with the funeral. Charles said the man had been like a father to Regina, and I recalled that Patton was where she'd always lived until coming to Charpentier. Phyllis bravely offered to help me with Arabella in Regina's place, but her eyes were like saucers even as she said the words, and I hadn't the heart to take her up on her offer. So, I ate all my meals with my patient, got her up in the morning, and saw her to bed at night. As I told Timothy when he brought the promised books, it was just as well that we hadn't planned to go out.

The books were extremely unscientific—and they were fascinating. I read avidly, devouring information in the certainty that at some point what was useful would sort itself out from what was not. I was learning things I would previously have thought outrageous, but now I had a certain degree of humility, and I admitted that some though surely not all of it could be true.

It was less easy to learn from Arabella herself, because she just wasn't talking. She spent an unusual amount of time in her room. Or, she would sit on her patio for an hour at a time, still as a stone, seemingly in a trance. The old Arabella I would have provoked into speech, sure that even in anger she would reveal something of the workings of her mind. I did not know yet how to relate to this new person in Arabella's body. She was the same, and yet not the same, and my observations when I wrote them into the log at night seemed meager indeed.

Regina returned on Sunday evening. She came to Arabella's rooms just as we were finishing dinner. I was glad to be relieved of my duties, yet the sight of her strong-boned face chilled me. She received my condolences with cold eyes. "It was time for that old man to die," she said.

I'm a shower person. It's rare for me to take the time for a tub bath, but tonight it seemed like a good idea. Complete with bubbles. I turned the taps on full and poured in a capful of bubbling lotion. It smelled like spring flowers. I added another for good measure, shed my clothes, piled my hair on top of my head, and sank into the fragrant foam. I closed my eyes, made my mind a blank—and immediatley it filled with Charles. I'd scarcely seen him in days, only for a brief moment when he'd come to say that Regina had gone to Patton.

I indulged my fantasies while I pampered my body. Shamelessly I lay in the warm water and behind my closed eyelids made myself a lover who had Charles's face, then Timothy's, then Charles's face again. My lover had a boat, a beautiful boat with sails and a deck of gleaming teakwood. We sailed away on a transparent aquamarine seas and the wind was like soft kisses, and he made love to me for days and days and days. . . .

I opened my eyes and shook my head to shake out the fantasy, to shake away Charles's face with the open, vulnerable look that so haunted me. My billowy bubbles had all gone flat. I fished around in the now-tepid water and found the washcloth, which I applied in a businesslike manner to my body. Fantasy-time was over. I had business to do with Charles, if he was at home. I suspected he wouldn't like it very much. Well, that's just too bad, I thought. I had forgiven him for his insinuations about Regina, but just barely!

Wrapped in a towel, I padded across the room to my bureau. I pulled on soft, faded jeans and my shapeless blue cotton sweater automatically—my mind was already at work on the problem of how to get Charles to talk about things I was sure he wouldn't want to talk about. I went to the dressing table and brushed my hair just as automatically. I smoothed some blusher on my cheekbones, added a touch of lipstick, tucked my hair behind my ears because it had a tendency to get in my face when I left it down like this—and then, unfortunately, I stopped thinking. I got a look at myself, and I looked about fourteen again. Damn! I hated that. How many Sunday nights at home with Aunt Henry had I worn these same jeans, this same sweater which had lost its shape long ago? And what had happened to me, that I should even care?

I made a snap decision: after my morning conference with Barkstone I'd buy some clothes, the right clothes. If I couldn't find what I wanted in Georgetown, I'd go to Charleston. I could certainly afford it. With my room and board provided for, my salary was just piling up in the bank, and I was tired of looking like an impoverished student! It was a satisfying idea, and I felt better for it even if I looked no different.

Shoving the keys into the pocket of my jeans and my feet into my loafers, I went looking for Charles. He was not in the library. He was not lingering over coffee and brandy in the dining room. I opened the east Front door and looked out into the bluish early twilight—nothing, no one walked under the live oaks. I closed the door. So, if Charles was at home, he was in his own rooms. The bear in his lair. I climbed the stairs and at the top went the opposite of my usual way.

All the doors along the South Wing corridor were closed. I knew his office was about halfway down, but he wasn't very likely to be in his office at this hour of the night. I lectured myself: Don't be silly, Rosamund. You're a grown woman, you have business to discuss, and there is no reason for your heart to pound like that just because the man is probably in his bedroom! I knocked on the first door.

The dark old doors were heavy wood, deeply carved in panelling, and I couldn't hear a thing on the other side. I waited. My heart hadn't paid the least attention to my lecture, it hammered away. I shoved my hands, my fingers anyway, into my front pockets over my hipbones. The door opened, and there he was—craggy face, dark shaggy hair with silver at the temples. I felt absurdly glad to see him, as if I hadn't seen him in years. I said, "I need to talk to you, Charles."

There was a hitch in his cheek, as if he'd started to smile and suppressed it. "I suppose it's important, for you to be here at this hour on a Sunday night."

"Yes, it is."

"Well, come in then." He turned his back on me, and I followed him into the room.

"I, ah, I'd better close the door. This is confidential." I went back to the door, which was as heavy as it looked, far heavier than the doors in the North Wing. I shut myself in with the bear in his lair.

The room was enormous, it could have contained the entire apartment of some of my friends in Cambridge. But it was still a bedroom. I disliked the fact that I felt so self-conscious, and so I forced myself to take a good look around, as if I were on a house tour. I remembered Arabella's description when we'd done our own tour. She'd stood in the doorway, with me peering over her shoulder, and said, "This is Charles's bedroom. It's gloomy. Edwardian. Too much walnut panelling," and she had hurried us on. There *was* a lot of walnut panelling, but it was magnificent, rich and glowing, not gloomy. From the tall windows hung panels of ivory lace, strong-patterned Irish lace, old and priceless. Not one but two fireplaces. A vast turkey carpet, its colors worn and muted to beiges, roses, and golds. Warm brown inviting leather chairs, plumply shaped by years of embracing the human body. A drum table cluttered with pages of the Sunday newspaper. A low bookcase filled with books that would be Charles's favorites. I longed to see their titles. And at the far end, a baronial bed, the kind of bed heirs are born in. And conceived in.

"Nice room," I said.

"Humph," said Charles. He'd obviously been sitting at the table reading the paper and drinking. There was a cut-glass tumbler of whiskey among the litter of newsprint. "Join me." He indicated a chair, the mate of his with leather-padded arms and seat. "Want a drink?"

He's a little bit drunk, I thought. His trousers and his shirt were wrinkled, as if he'd napped in them, and his shirt was half unbuttoned, and his feet were bare. I heard myself say, "Yes, please, I'd like a drink."

Charles arched one heavy eyebrow, mockery of surprise. "I don't have any Scotch up here. Just good old American whiskey."

"That's all right. American whiskey will be fine."

His lips curved into something between a grin and a leer. He knew I wasn't much of a drinker. There was a cabinet built into the wall panelling behind the table, cleverly concealed. Charles came back from it with another cut-glass tumbler half-filled with the golden-brown liquid and two ice cubes. And in his other hand, the bottle, which he put inelegantly on the table. I supposed he was making some sort of masculine statement—this is my room and I'll do what I please in it, that kind of thing. "Well, see how you like it. Don't worry, it won't grow hair on your chest."

"Cheers!" I said. Charles slouched into his chair and watched as I tasted, swallowed. The whiskey stung, and then was smooth, golden on my tongue and in my throat, and it spread through me with a pleasant glow. "It's actually very good!" I exclaimed.

Charles chuckled. Even if I'd hated it, it would have been worth it to produce that chuckle. "Yes, it is. This is special stuff, private label, hard to get—my excuse for buying it by the case." He drank too, and then he looked at me intently. "As much as I'd like to sit here and drink with you and swap dirty stories—if you know any—I don't imagine that's why you're here."

Oh, I'd like that, too, you don't know how much, I thought. But I said, "I need some information. I'm preparing for a conference with Dr. Barkstone tomorrow morning. I've done some relevant reading and reviewed all my own notes, and now I need some history. I can only get that from you. Arabella wouldn't be a reliable source."

Danger signals. Deepening line between the heavy brows. "What kind of history? You can get it from Barkstone. He has all that medical history, it's not in *my* head."

Well, I thought, here goes. It was like jumping off the high board into an unfamiliar swimming pool. "I don't mean medical history, Charles. I mean personal history. I need to know everything you can tell me about Arabella's past, how you met her, what she was doing, and how she was living when you met her. Family, schools, childhood, all those things."

"Why?" The one-word question had the ominous resonance of a bass bell.

"Because I'm looking for a pattern, and so far her illness doesn't really fit any pattern. *I don't know who she is,*" my voice rose in involuntary emphasis, "and I feel that I need to know." I leaned toward him, pleading with my eyes, willing him to feel my earnestness. "Please, Charles. You can help. You're the only person in the world, at least the only person that I know of, who can tell me these things."

"She's Arabella Charpentier," Charles said, in a deliberate drawl.

"Damn it, you know what I mean!"

Charles was sprawled in his chair. I thought he might be looking purposely dissolute, trying to distract me or to make me uncomfortable. To a certain extent he was succeeding. I was more aware than I wanted to be of his raw, animal power; it hovered about him in a dangerous aura. His shirt gaped and revealed a wealth of dark hair on his chest. Between his casually spread thighs the bulge of his manhood was plain. He did not answer me, he pierced me with his sapphire gaze. The intensity of his eyes said, as plainly as if he had spoken, Cruel! You are cruel to ask this of me!

I looked away, I retreated into the false comfort of the whiskey in my glass. I didn't want to hurt him, and yet I had to know.

At last he spoke, and his voice was hard. "All right. I don't think it will help you. The truth may disgust you. But I'll tell you everything. I met Bella a little over twelve years ago, during Mardi Gras in New Orleans. I think I was a little out of my head at the time. I was only twenty-eight, and my father had died a year before, died suddenly and left all this responsibility to me. Louis was an irresponsible kid, Mother was so torn up with grief she couldn't remember what day it was half the time, and I'd worked my ass off proving to people who would've liked to rip off a piece of the Charpentier estate that I could effectively hold the reins. I was damn near exhausted, and so I took off with a guy who wasn't even a friend really, just somebody I knew, and we went to Mardi Gras.

"I met Bella at a party." He laughed harshly. "Hell, the whole of New Orleans was the party! But I met her in one of those big, elegant old houses, it belonged to some friend of the family of the guy I was with—you had to have an engraved invitation to get in the door, and he had one. Of course I thought she was a guest. Later I found out she was an entertainer, part of a group who'd done their thing before I arrived. But by the time I found that out, it made no difference to me. It was my first night in New Orleans, I looked into those emerald eyes of Bella's and I was *gone*. I guess I was like an animal let out of its cage—I hadn't behaved like that even in my wildest college days. And I'd never known anyone like her. She was incredible. The most sensual, exciting . . ." He sat up abruptly and plunged his hands into his already-tumbled hair.

I drank my drink. I was close to draining the glass of the strong whiskey, but I didn't care. Charles went on.

"I spent two days with her and it seemed we never slept. I lost track of the guy I'd come to New Orleans with and it didn't matter, nothing mattered except her. She did things to me, made me feel things I'd never felt before. I may as well admit it, you'll have figured it out anyway—it was sexual, all of it. I was like a rutting buck, I couldn't stop. But she was no whore, and I knew it. She could act like a lady when she wanted to, the breeding was in her, all right; yet there was this other side to her, this dark, lawless, sensual side that fascinated me."

Charles tossed down what remained in his glass and refilled it, looked over at mine and filled it too, but he didn't look at me. He resumed his story.

"I took a hotel room for us. The crowds were clearing out, Mardi Gras was winding down, and the next morning I woke up and she was gone. I didn't even know her last name. I had to find her—I prowled the streets and the bars and the back rooms until I thought I'd go crazy—it was an obsession. Finally I went to that house where we'd started out and asked about her; I still thought she'd been a guest. That was when I found out she'd been part of the entertainment. But they didn't know her name. She and the others she was with had come in off the street and done their entertainment for free and left, or so they'd thought. Arabella had stayed on."

"What sort of entertainment, what did she do?"

"They did magic, and she was a fortune-teller or a mind reader, something like that. Anyway, I never did find her. She found me. I'd given up and I was sitting at a table in one of those outdoor cafes, and she just walked up to me, as if we'd had a date all along. I was overjoyed, I said it was a miracle, and she laughed and said it was no miracle, she found me with her 'powers.' That was the first time I heard her talk about her powers—I wish it had been the last!"

"What about family? Where did she live?"

"I asked her all that, because you see, I'd decided I had to have her. I wanted to possess her and keep her all to myself—as I said, an obsession. She said she had no family, wouldn't talk about her background at all. New Orleans, like any city then, had people they called hippies, free spirits, and she was one. She lived with three others, two men and a woman, in a falling-down plantation house a few miles up the river. It looked like a decrepit version of Charpentier, and I was so besotted with her that I thought it was all very romantic. Her friends were a little strange, all of them into this magic and mumbo jumbo, but they weren't on drugs and they seemed to have money and from the way they talked I could tell they were educated. I had enough sense left that those things mattered to me.

"I thought the four of them were paired off, two couples. One of the men looked older than the rest of them, and I figured he was hers. It made me crazy jealous. I can still remember the feeling, like dark blood boiling up inside me, and I was all the more determined to have her, get her away from him. I did it the only way I knew how—I asked her to marry me." Charles fell silent, his eyes blurred over with memory.

"Do you remember their names?"

"What?" My questions seemed to bring him back. "Oh, names. Just the older man, his name was Pierre. I've forgotten the rest. They never used last names, any of them. It didn't seem strange at the time. That's incredible, isn't it? That none of it seemed strange at the time. Anyway, this

Pierre did try to warn me. He asked how old I was, which I found insulting, but I told him and he said, 'She's ten years older than you are." I said I didn't care. Then he said something I should have listened to, he said, 'Arabella is changeable. She has dark moods, when she's not at all like she is now. I want her because she has certain abilities, and I'm teaching her.' And he asked me, 'Why do you want her?' I replied that I loved her. He sneered at me and made an obscene remark, the sort of thing one man says to another—actually it was an appropriate thing to say but I couldn't see that, it only made me furious. Then he walked away. I paid no attention to any of it. I thought he was just being a sore loser."

I moistened my lips with the tip of my tongue, my throat dry. "What did he mean when he said she had certain abilities?"

Charles shook his head. "I have no idea. I guess I thought at the time that he referred to her, uh, skills in bed. That was why I wanted her, why I thought I had fallen in love with her—and it was all I thought of at the time."

"Oh," I said, disappointed. "I didn't mean to interrupt you. Please go on."

His face took on a brooding look. He had his glass cradled in his hands, his shoulders hunched, as if the weight of his past were dragging him down, down. "She said she would marry me. I spent a lot of money on her in a short time, buying clothes, presents, anything she wanted. Her exotic tastes enchanted me. I bought her wedding dress, a filmy white thing, tantalizing—when she moved a certain way it was transparent, but then when you'd look again, it wasn't. And a long, long white veil. I remember how it trailed behind her, over the graves. We were married in Lafayette Cemetery. Imagine that, married in a graveyard! It was what she wanted, and I thought it was so romantic. Her friends were the witnesses and they wore clothes that were like costumes out of the nineteenth century, and I wore a coat with tails and a shirt with ruffles, just to please Bella. I felt like Keats or Lord Byron. Poe would have been more like it—with a raven sitting on top of one of those aboveground tombs that look like little Greek temples—Do you take this woman to be

your lawful wedded wife? Quoth the raven, Nevermore!"
His voice cracked. He left his chair and walked slowly down
the room, down the center of the vast rug.

I waited, knowing he'd come back when he had himself in
hand again. He did. He stood a few feet from me, with his
hands in his pockets. I looked up at him.

"It's no good, you know," he said. "I tried. I even hired a
private detective to try to find out more about her, because
she would never talk to me about the past. I wanted to send
her back to her friends, but they weren't there anymore. I
wanted to send her to her family, if I could find them. The
name she used for the marriage license and the blood tests
was Arabella Johnson. Do you have any idea how many
Johnsons there are in the South? Thousands, maybe mil-
lions. And maybe it wasn't her real name in the first place.
She had no driver's license, no social security number, no
credit cards. She did have a bank account when we were
married with several thousand dollars in it that must have
come from somewhere, but no one sent her any money here
that I ever saw. If she got letters, I never saw them, either.

"My mother was appalled, of course, that I'd married a
woman nobody knew anything about. But I was stubborn—
you can imagine. Finally I had to admit I'd made a mistake;
that was when I hired the detective. I had a wild hope that
the marriage wasn't legal, that the priest Bella got to marry
us was a fake. The detective never found the priest, but he
found all the records, religious and civil. In the eyes of the
law, and in the eyes of God if there is a God, the woman is
my wife." He was still standing. He looked down on me with
sad, sad eyes. "That's all, Rosamund. There is nothing else
to tell. Are you satisfied?"

My own eyes stung, and I blinked. "I guess I'll have to be.
Thank you for telling me. I know it . . . it couldn't have been
easy for you."

He sighed, a great heavy sigh, and the vulnerable look sat
for a moment on his forehead and in his eyes, and then it
passed. "It's all right. Even if it doesn't help you in what
you're doing, getting ready for your conference with Barkstone or whatever, you have a right to know." He paused.
"You have a right to know anything you want to know about
me."

His meaning was clear. Alarms went off inside me, but they were dulled by the several ounces of whiskey I'd drunk. My judgment was blunted, inhibitions dimmed, and I knew it. My mind said, Move! Get out of the chair and go! I got my feet under me, my hands on the arms of the chair, preparing to leave.

Charles understood the meaning of those small motions, and instantly he was over me, his hands on my forearms binding me to the chair, making me a prisoner. His mouth closed over my lips swiftly, brutally, forcing my head back and up, forcing my lips apart for his strong, thrusting tongue. He took my breath, my strength, my will. "Don't tell me not to touch you!" he whispered savagely, "I swear I'll kill you if you ever say that to me again!"

Again his mouth descended, devouring, crushing. I tasted blood, his or mine I could not tell. My body burned with the heat of his nearness. I wanted to struggle but I could not, he was too strong. The smell, the taste, the heat—he was dark, primitive, the rutting buck, and I the doe, trapped, spent. I would run no more. My surrender was complete. I fed on him now as he fed on me, and his power filled me.

His hand, strong and hard, found a way beneath my sweater and cupped my naked breast. His thumb stroked the nipple, and his kiss softened even as a hot knife of new desire stabbed through me. His mouth did not leave mine, but the demanding rhythm of his lips and tongue slowed, hardness gave way to softness, tenderly, tenderly. He went down on one knee, his hand left my breast, and he drew me to rest against him. My hands, free now, went to his chest, inside his open shirt. His skin was damp and hot, the hair not coarse but softly curling. I hung in the balance, eyes closed, my face held up for him.

"Again," I whispered, "kiss me again."

He kissed me again, very slowly, very softly. It was astonishing that such gentleness could follow such force. "I've had too much to drink," he said quietly," and so have you, my love. You're not used to it, but I am, and I should know better." He pressed my head down, my cheek in the hollow of his shoulder. He stroked my hair. "If I take you now, you may hate me tomorrow, and I won't like myself very much either," he murmured.

"Yes," I said into his shoulder, "you're right." I knew he was. I knew I should be grateful, that with all his need and brute strength Charles could still be a gentleman. But he, and perhaps the freeing effect of the whiskey, had awakened something in me. I had never felt such a hunger, such urgent passion, hadn't known my body was capable of such hot surrender. And I still throbbed with wanting him.

Charles took my shoulders in his hands and lifted me away from him. He smiled at me. "You're flushed all over. You're very beautiful and if you don't leave now, I might change my mind."

"You're a beast!" I said, and I left him.

Chapter 11

Dr. Barkstone sat behind his desk, patiently reading his way through the log I'd brought with me. His bald head gleamed under the white fluorescent light, catching it off the ceiling and throwing it back again. I waited, my thoughts idle. My presentation was ready, nothing would be gained by going over and over it in my mind, so I thought about Barkstone instead. He was the squeaky-cleanest person I'd ever seen, and his office was like him. A place for everything and everything in its place. I wondered what it would be like making love with a man so innately neat. Bald men were supposed to be extra-virile—something more below to make up for the something less above, I supposed.

Stop that, Rosamund! I chided myself. I must still be feeling the effects of last night's frustration. Certainly I had never, ever felt like that before. I crossed my legs restlessly. Barkstone turned a page with a squeaky-clean hand. He might be pretty good in spite of his age, he had good hands. If it happened that he was interested in, say, providing a satisfying experience for a woman, he would most certainly be thorough. He'd study, take lessons if he had to. . . .

"Very good. Very good notes." He folded his hands on top of the log. "I have just one question. You've never given Mrs. Charpentier the tranquilizer? I see records of insulin only."

165

"That's right." This was not the time to mention the possibly missing capsules. Other more important matters must come first. I'd remember to ask about it before I left, though.

"Interesting. Well, you may or may not know that I talked on the telephone with Charles at the end of last week. I know what he's thinking. Now I'm most interested in what you have to say, Miss Hill."

"First," I began, "I do wish that we could call in a psychiatrist. I'm not qualified to make the kind of evaluation Mrs. Charpentier probably needs."

"I understand how you feel, I've often felt that way myself. But as you know, Mrs. Charpentier can be most uncooperative, and a psychiatrist can't do much good with a patient who refuses to talk. You've documented her reluctance to talk to you—I think it extremely unlikely she would respond at all to a psychiatrist at the moment. No, no, you're doing well with her so far. Let's proceed with your other points and put the matter of the psychiatrist on hold."

"All right." That was, after all, what I had expected him to say, and so I went on. "I've encouraged Mrs. Charpentier to express herself, to be more active. I've challenged her, trying to find out what her real capabilities are. I don't treat her as a sick person, but as someone whose ideas are just different from mine and interesting to me. I can't say that any real progress has been made, though I thought so for a while. Those are the reasons I didn't medicate her, and also because she never seemed out of control enough to need it."

I paused and Dr. Barkstone nodded his head. I continued. "Though I say there's been no progress in terms of her behavior becoming more normal, it's clear to me that she has some goal of her own and she's moving toward it. I've recorded what I've seen of the development of her not-Arabella personality. It's not like any multiple-personality cases I've read about. I've looked—I'm still looking—for a pattern, and so far I can't find one."

The doctor nodded again. I took a deep breath, about to enter shakier ground. "Certain things she said, and that her husband said, led me to wonder about demonic possession. I know how that sounds, but I've been reading about it. There too, she doesn't quite fit the reported cases. There is one thing I'm sure of. Since the night of the storm, even prior to the storm itself, Arabella Charpentier no longer accepts that identity. If we use 'possession' as a concept, then we can say that Arabella believes she is possessed; or to more accurately describe it, there is a person whose name I do not know, who says she is in possession of Arabella's body. I hesitate to say that Mrs. Charpentier is possessed because it's not a medical term, and because it evokes all this Christian mythology about devils, or demons, and evil versus good. Personally, I don't find that helpful."

Barkstone smiled. "I imagine that puts you somewhat at odds with your employer."

"Then he must have told you he thinks his wife is evil?" The doctor's nodding head confirmed this. "I don't agree with him. I'd say rather she has her own inner morality, it has something to do with personal power. She doesn't acknowledge the Christian concept of 'good' in much the same way a delinquent, a sociopathic personality, doesn't acknowledge authority. I admit I don't understand her new personality yet, she hasn't given me a chance. I can only repeat what I've written in the log: she dresses differently, she talks differently—sometimes in a voice that sounds unlike the one I'm used to, she is physically stronger with no agitation or depression, and her behavior is purposeful and secretive."

"Um-hm." The doctor made a steeple with his fingertips, and over this he regarded me intently out of his clear eyes. "Outcome?"

I shook my head. "I don't want to guess." This was what I had decided on before coming here: I wouldn't be pushed into talking prognosis before I was ready, not by Charles and not by the doctor. I still had my hopes for her.

"All right. That's understandable." He put his hands flat on his desk and leaned across it. "Let me put it to you another way. There has been a definite change in our patient. We might call it a positive change except for one thing: she thinks she is someone else, which is hardly normal. What treatment do you recommend?"

"A full psychiatric evaluation."

"And if she will not agree? She is not dangerous, we can't confine her and force her to submit."

"Then, continue to observe."

"Um-hm. I agree with you. In fact, it's the only course I can see open to us. However, Charles wants her put away. Don't look so shocked, my dear! He has in mind an excellent private sanatorium in North Carolina. It's a beautiful place; take away the attendants and it could be a resort. Very expensive, but he can afford it."

"But . . ."

"I know, I know." Barkstone understood my objection before I put it into words. "We can't do it unless she agrees to go voluntarily, and she won't do that. I'll deal with Charles, and if I may be so bold, Miss Hill, try to understand his side of this. Even a man as strong as Charles Charpentier has a breaking point, and if I'm any judge, he's near his."

"I do understand that."

"For his sake we must come up with a plan that has an end point. A human being can stand almost anything if he knows it won't last forever." He waited, and now it was my turn to nod confirmation. "I will make Charles understand we have no legal basis for commitment. He, too, has used the term 'possession.' He seems to think this automatically makes his wife dangerous to herself or others. I'll explain that isn't so. I like the way you presented that to me, and I think you might talk to him in those terms. We will continue as we are now, with observation, for six weeks. That's"—he flipped the pages of his desk calendar—"July 12th, but let's make it the 15th, mid month. Much neater, easier to remember."

I smiled at Barkstone's outstanding characteristic—neat of body, neat of mind. "And after July 15th," I asked, "assuming there's no change before then, what will we do?"

"I'm going to suggest very strongly that Charles rent a small house somewhere for his wife. Regina could go with her, she's devoted to Mrs. Charpentier. Unless you . . .? I'm assuming you will want to return to medical school in the fall."

Fortunately the doctor was so well satisfied with his own plan that he didn't notice my failure to reply. He continued, "I've been the Charpentier family doctor for many years, and it puts me in a somewhat privileged position. I intend to advise Charles that once his wife is set up in her own household he should seek a legal separation, possibly even a divorce. I know his mother will back me up on this. In case you think I'm out of line, I emphasize that Charles himself is also my patient. Why this situation hasn't given him high blood pressure or ulcers by now, I'm sure I don't know!"

I was careful to keep my voice neutral. "That sounds reasonable," I said. But I was appalled at the thought of Arabella and Regina living alone together. My mind was racing. I meant what I said, it was reasonable, and yet . . . yet I just couldn't accept it. I had to admit the idea of a separated or better yet a divorced Charles was appealing, but. . . . My mind tumbled. I realized Barkstone had stopped talking and was staring at me.

"I'm sorry. I was, I was thinking about Charles being your patient," I lied. "He hasn't been ill lately, has he?"

"No, not him," Barkstone laughed, "I can't even get him in here for a routine physical! Well, my dear, are we agreed? I told Charles I'd get back to him with the results of our little talk today."

"Yes." I stood up and shook hands with the doctor over the desk, acknowledging the agreement. I took the log from him. "Thank you, Doctor, for your time and your help."

"A pleasure, I'm sure. You're doing an excellent job, Miss Hill, excellent!" He beamed all over his kind, shining face.

On the way back to my car, all I could think of was Arabella alone with Regina, what a disaster that would be. Six weeks. I had six weeks. I felt a sense of urgency, as if in six weeks my whole life might come to an end. Of course I had forgotten to ask about that other bottle of tranquilizers.

Of all the people at Charpentier, me included, Phyllis was certainly the healthiest. I wished I had both her simplicity and her honest cheerfulness. She had seen me struggling into the house with more boxes and bags than I had arms and hands, and bounced to the rescue. "Miss Rosamund, you been shoppin' up a storm!" she'd exclaimed, eyes sparkling. Together in my room we'd unpacked the boxes and the bags, and never in my whole life had I seen anyone show so much sincere, unselfish pleasure. Her excitement about my new clothes, which she'd promptly taken away to "press the wrinkles out'n," seemed as much as my own had been in choosing them. Someday, anonymously, I was going to do something very nice for Phyllis.

I sat now looking out the window in my bedroom, wearing my new bathrobe. It was pale pink, full-length in the classic wrap style I preferred, made of a fabric that was new to me—something called terry velour, lightweight, velvety textured, and as soft as a kitten on my bare skin. I was distracted; I'd been distracted all day. I didn't really feel like going out with Timothy, though of course I would go. I'd already asked Phyllis to tell Jenny I wouldn't be home for dinner.

I wished I could have told Dr. Barkstone how much I distrusted Regina. But I had no proof, it was more instinct than anything else, and Charles didn't want to hear anything against her. . . . Charles and Regina—Yuk! Octoroons, indeed! How I wished he'd never said those things. He'd planted that disgusting idea in my mind, and I'd never be able to forget it.

My cheeks grew warm, and my heart tripped over something. You forgot last night, didn't you, Rosamund? taunted the little voice inside my head. Yes, I replied to it crossly, I did, but I was under the influence, so it doesn't count, and I'll never let it happen again! The voice, very tiny, said, Oh yeah?

My date with Timothy suddenly looked a lot better, and it wasn't too early to get ready. The dress I chose to wear was the one Phyllis had liked best, a deep lavender silky fabric in a rather unusual style. It had a high neck with a white lace collar, a yoke of tiny tucks, and no waistline. It was made like a child's dress, but it was deceptively sexy. You could prevent it from clinging in interesting places only by standing perfectly still. I took the time to put my hair up in the Victorian pouf, brushing it upside down first for fullness, and I coaxed a few wisps out here and there. Tiny pearl earrings were perfect with the dress. I was happy, and Timothy would be favorably impressed, I hoped.

I watched for his car, as I'd done before, from the long windows of the gallery-like hall. I was impatient now. Suddenly I couldn't bear to be in the house a minute longer. I decided to go out and walk through the oak alley. It was early yet, and I had plenty of time to reach the far side where it met the curving drive. I could step out and flag Timothy down from there.

I should have stayed where I was. As I turned into the corridor of the old main house, I saw the tall figure of Regina, unmistakable in her usual gray dress, and with her another figure taller yet and equally unmistakable. Charles. They were standing close together at the head of the stairs, talking so quietly I couldn't hear a word. I had to walk past them in order to go down the stairs—simple enough, but it felt like running the gauntlet. I forced out a "good evening" as I passed, looking carefully down at my feet.

"Going out?" asked Charles.

I was two steps down and I kept on going. "Obviously."

"I'd hoped we could talk at dinner. There's something I must discuss with you."

"Really, Charles, it *is* my day off," I said in one of my nastier tones of voice, overcompensating. If my tripping heart had been my feet, I would have fallen to the bottom from the very top step. How I hated the fact that I could not control my physical reaction to him! "We'll talk later," I called after me.

"On your tombstone!" Charles shouted.

I was at the bottom of the stairs now, practically free, but I couldn't resist. I turned around and yelled up at him, "Over my dead body!" And I waited.

'Obviously!" he barked. That satisfied me. I grinned and hurried for the door before anything else could happen.

Even with time out for the badinage on the stairs, I still had to wait. I purposely hadn't worn a watch, but it seemed to me that Timothy was at least ten minutes late when I heard his car. I stepped out of the trees to wave from the side of the road.

"Ah, a purple apparition emerges from the oak alley!" he said from his car window as he pulled alongside.

"Lavender," I corrected. "Hi, Timothy. Don't get out, I can open car doors by myself." I slipped into the car beside him.

"I stand corrected. A liberated lavender apparition." He took my hand and kissed it. He looked one hundred percent the priest tonight—black suit, black shirt, round white collar, black shoes. I felt a little strange having my hand so warmly kissed by someone dressed that way.

He slipped the car into gear. "I apologize for being late."

"That's all right. It just gave me more time to commune with those wonderful old trees." I gestured in their direction as his car completed the sweep of the driveway, heading us back in the opposite direction.

"Yes, they are something special, all right. You look wonderful tonight, Rosamund!"

"Thank you. You look rather nice yourself. Terribly ecclesiastical."

"I hope you don't mind—I didn't have time to change. I had an emergency, that's why I was late."

"Nothing bad, I hope?"

"No, not really. A wonderful old lady is dying, and her family called me because it looked like she might not live through the night. We have special prayers, you see, to say for people at the time of death. I couldn't say it was bad, she seemed to be sleeping peacefully. We should all die so well!"

"I see. That's why all the black." I looked at him thoughtfully. "It must be comforting, to believe like that, to have a priest who will come and say prayers over someone you love."

"We hope so." Timothy was unusually solemn.

I tried to see through his eyes, to think of things I had never thought about before. He did that for me almost continually, presented me with aspects of life, of existence, that I had never even considered. "It must be rather awesome, to be involved in all the significant times of people's lives. Birth, death, marriage. The making of new priests."

"Awesome? It's the events themselves that are awesome, and yet they happen in the life of every human being. The church has its jargon too, just like the doctors—we call these things Rites of Passage, and we have rituals for them. The roots of the rituals aren't even Christian, they're pagan. Ancient. It's a privilege to be a priest in those rituals." Timothy turned his face to me momentarily, with a smile of infinite sweetness. "But before you get too impressed, in all honesty I must tell you that ninety percent of the time, it's only a job, like any other job."

"Hmm. Somehow I doubt it's just a job, to you."

"No. I admit praying over someone about to die got to me. And the service for the Burial of the Dead will get to me, too. But maybe that's because it's not my regular job. I'm just the substitute, remember?"

"Yes, I remember." I felt we needed a change of subject, so I asked, "Where are we going?"

"To a rather unusual place. I'd prefer to let it be a surprise, but I'll tell you this much, it's in Murrell's Inlet. You haven't spent much time there, have you?" I shook my head. "I thought not. Much of Murrell's is still untouched by all this development going on around here. For a good deal of which your employer is responsible, I might add!" Timothy sounded bitter.

"You don't approve?"

"That's right. I don't approve. Of developers in general and of Charles Charpentier in particular. He's greedy, Rosamund. He already owns half the land between Litchfield and Georgetown, and what he doesn't own, he controls. He loans people money and takes mortgages on their property as if he were a one-man bank. He doesn't need the money, so why does he build all these houses and other things? I wouldn't be surprised if he put up condominiums on his own beach!"

I had already picked up that "condominium" was a dirty word to a lot of people here—one good prowl around the Hammock Shop in Pawley's Island, if you kept your ears open, would tell you that. "I don't know anything about his business, but I do know a few things about Charles. He takes his heritage, or whatever you want to call it, seriously. He's not the kind of person who can inherit something and just sit on it, he feels he has to make it grow. My Aunt Henry always said there were two kinds of people in the world, the thinkers and the doers. Charles is a doer. You're a thinker. You and he are just different, that's all. And I think you're being unfair about one thing—Charles isn't a greedy man."

Timothy shot a warning glance in my direction. "I've known him a lot longer than you have, Rosamund. Don't be so quick to defend him."

"Honestly, Timothy, I wish you could put aside this irrational prejudice against Charles and try to have an open mind. He's having a tough time right now."

"His chickens are coming home to roost. What goes around, comes around."

"Whatever. A lot of things are happening, or about to happen, that are hard for him."

"All right, I'll try to have an open mind, but only for your sake, because you asked and because you're involved. These are the things you alluded to on the phone, the night you asked for those books I brought you? And have the books been helpful?"

"Yes and yes. I want to keep them a while longer, if that's all right with you. There's a lot I want to talk to you about."

"That's fine, but later. We're almost there now. Just look out of the window and see if you don't begin to get a feel for this place. To me, it has an atmosphere all its own."

I did as I was bidden. We had turned off the main road and now were on one much narrower, full of shadows. I'd lost my sense of direction because I hadn't been paying attention, but I had a feeling we were near the ocean. Small houses began to come closer together, and soon the nature of our road changed and was more like a small-town street. Timothy parked the car in an open area with a few other cars, not exactly a parking lot but obviously used for that purpose, next to a whitewashed cement block shack with red letters on the side that said "Fish Bait."

"From here, we walk," he said. We crossed the road, Timothy guiding me with his hand at the small of my back.

"Where—" I started to ask.

"Shhh. Don't talk. Just look, and feel."

We were on a kind of path made of crushed shells that crunched under our feet as we walked. The ground on either side was sandy but packed hard. Here and there long stringy blades of grass struggled to survive. There were a number of trees but they too were thin, undernourished, and the Spanish moss that hung from them was scraggly and forlorn. Though the sun had not yet set, its light and warmth did not reach this place.

Then I saw the house. It was old and rather small, but bigger than a cottage. I knew at once no one lived there. It had been kept up, but not painted—all its boards and railings and shutters had weathered to streaky gray. Timothy's hand at my back urged me closer. I took a few steps, but my feet were heavy. My skin began to prick.

"I don't like it," I said.

"What is it that you don't like?"

A narrow front porch ran the width of the house, which was mostly one story, but the roof was peaked in the center and below the peak was a window. There was a room there, like an attic but not an attic, one long room that ran straight through the top of the house. I could see it as though I were inside. On the back of the house at the end of that room was another window, and from that back window you could see the sea.

My voice came out in a croaking whisper. "There's great sadness here. No, something worse than sadness. It's despair. Complete loss of hope, loss of all reason. She stands by the window in the dark, looking out to sea. She's looking for a light, and sometimes she sees it but it never comes."

"Can you see her?"

"No, but I feel her. Oh, Timothy, I don't like it. I'm leaving!" I backed away a few steps and then turned. I would have run but he caught my hand and pulled me to his side, then put his arm around my waist so that we walked side by side, our hips touching. I leaned into him and put my arm about his waist too, glad of the physical contact. In that moment I couldn't get close enough to another warm, living body. But even that did not stop my steps. I had to keep on walking, to get away.

"There's a path through here," Timothy said, "through the garden. We don't have to go back to the road." He pulled me to his left, and I resisted.

"No!" I cried. "That's *her* garden, I can feel it. I won't go in there!"

"All right, it's okay. Through the garden is just a shorter way to the restaurant, that's all."

We kept on walking, our feet crunching on the shell path, and gradually I felt better. When we reached the road, I disentangled myself and stood apart. I was still shaken and almost ready to call off the whole evening. I didn't fully realize what had happened; I only knew I never wanted to feel that way again—never!

175

"What in God's name were you trying to do to me?" I demanded.

"I'm sorry, Rosamund. I didn't know it would upset you so much. But this isn't the place to talk. Come, we'll go to the restaurant and have a drink in the bar, and I'll explain." He took a step toward me, reaching out his hand, and I took a step back and away. We stood on the side of the road and a car passed by, very close, but I didn't budge.

"Come on," he urged, "trust me, Rosamund. We can't talk here by the side of the road."

I shook my head fiercely. "I make it a practice never to trust anyone who says 'trust me'! I'm not going anywhere with you until you tell me what that was all about." I hugged my arms against my breasts and waited, thinking that passing cars meant other people and safety.

Timothy at least had the grace to look distressed. "All right. Really, I had no idea it would be so bad for you. That was a kind of experiment. There's supposed to be a ghost in that house. I wanted to see how you would react, if you would feel anything."

"Oh."

"But the ghost isn't the sort that would do anyone any harm. I never meant to hurt you. The house isn't deserted, there's a woman who keeps a little bookstore and gift shop downstairs, it's open on weekends. It's not as if it were a haunted house."

"Maybe not in the popular sense, but the woman doesn't live there, I'm sure of it."

"No. I guess she doesn't."

"And I suppose she sells ghost stories in her bookstore." There, I was starting to feel better. My sense of humor was returning.

"Well, yes, she does. I've bought some from her myself. Including the story of the ghost in that very house."

"I guess I forgive you," I said, holding out a reconciling hand to him, "and unless this restaurant is haunted too, I'm ready to go. I admit I could use a drink after that! I've become a true believer—there most certainly is a ghost in that house. You can tell me the story while we walk to the restaurant."

"It would have been shorter through the garden. Do you want to get the car?"

"No, I don't mind walking. But I wouldn't have gone through that garden for anything. Tell me the story?" We began to walk.

Timothy looked down at me. He was almost as tall as Charles, and in my high heels I still had to look up a couple of inches to meet his eyes. He looked puzzled. "You practically told the whole story yourself just now. Don't you remember what you said?"

"No, I only remember the feeling, and it was horrible."

"The story is that the house belonged to a man who had a large fishing boat. This was sometime in the early 1800s. He lived there with his wife and they had no children, so when he was gone she was alone. But he wasn't an ordinary fisherman, he was a smuggler. There were lots of smugglers here, and earlier there were pirates too, because of the way the creeks wind through the marshes. That's another thing I want to show you, and you'll get a wonderful view from this place we're going. Anyway, smuggling was a dangerous business. For one thing, they had to come back at night and on the high tide. Often they'd be gone for a long time. For obvious reasons they didn't tell anybody when they were coming back, not even their wives. This woman would wait for her husband every night, she'd stand by the window in the upstairs room hour after hour, looking out toward the sea, watching for the light on his boat. And one time, he went out and he never came back. She watched and watched, until finally she died. And after death she still watches. Some people are said to have seen her at the window."

A tremor passed through me. I was quiet, thinking. We walked now up a long, unpaved sort of driveway. There was grass and a lot of trees, some kind of evergreens, and the drive had curves in it so you couldn't see where you were going or where you'd been. There was nothing precisely threatening about this place, but I couldn't say I liked it very much, either.

Finally I said, "Yes, I could see that room and the window where she watches. But Timothy, if you're going to take people like me looking for ghosts, you ought to know that just because it isn't supposed to be the ghost of a bad person, someone who's done evil things—and after tonight I know for sure I wouldn't want to encounter one of those—doesn't mean it isn't dangerous. Feeling what I felt tonight can be dangerous for a person's mind. I've just learned this from experience, and I don't care if the expert ghost hunters ever said so or not, I know it's true. That woman's despair was so terrible, her loss of hope so absolute, that in the end she lost her mind. I'm certain of it. And all that touched me—I was *in* it!"

Timothy stopped walking and stared at me. "You're incredibly sensitive to these things, even more than I thought you would be."

"You sound more pleased than sympathetic!"

"Both, I'm both. Things like this are of great interest to me, you know that. And that, in turn, can be helpful to you. Come on,"—he pulled me along again—"we've only got a bit more to go. I'm sure you'll feel better after a drink or two."

I did feel better, but not by much. The restaurant was fairly new, but it was built to look old. On the outside it was all cedar shingles with a dark brown stain, and it was too big for its setting. You came upon it suddenly, in a kind of shock, like a huge dark brown monster that had come up out of the marshes, sat down, and refused to leave. It was three storys high and the side that faced the marshes was all glass, but otherwise the architectural style was Victorian Hunting Lodge—if there is such a thing.

Some inner sense warned me that it was better not to drink in the state I was in, I still felt hypersensitive in a way I couldn't explain. I had club soda with lime, while Timothy ordered a martini for himself. He obviously found this place fascinating, and I tried to appreciate the view from our tiny window table in the third-floor cocktail lounge. It was true that I had never seen anything like the vast marshes. The sun was setting now and the tide was coming in. I tried to catch Timothy's enthusiasm. The marshes stretched almost as far as the eye could see, then gave way to an expanse of salt water that was the Inlet itself. At the very limit of vision was a narrow whitish line with a few square dots on it—that was a stretch of beach and the dots were houses—and beyond that the blue of the ocean met the blue of the sky. Try as I would, I could not see the break through which boats came and went out to the open sea.

The place was crowded even on a Monday night, and though we had a reservation, they had not called us. Timothy ordered another round of drinks, club soda still for me. He was talking now about the "creeks," twisted canal-like passageways through the tall green marsh grass. The creeks filled and emptied as the tide rose and fell, and it was these creeks that had made Murrell's Inlet a haven for pirates and smugglers. They were more confusing than a maze, having no pattern to them at all, and the smugglers would hide in them while the law enforcement men would become hopelessly lost. Even at high tide a man standing up in a flat boat could see only an endless sea of grass and no way out. There was a lostness, a forlornness about the marshes that spoke to me, though Timothy couldn't hear it at all. It seemed to me impossible that anyone could ever learn his way through there. It would have to be imprinted somehow in childhood so that instinct alone could guide you. I felt how it would be to be lost there, an awareness that sat in the pit of my stomach like an ancient race memory.

The sun was nearly gone now, the marsh grass seemed no longer green but charcoal black, and the winding and twisting creeks like hundreds of snakes appeared red in the glare of the dying sun. The red flash leaped up at me through the window glass, it pierced my eyes and lodged in my soul, and brought with it terror. All the tiny hairs on the backs of my arms stood on end. I couldn't breathe. And then it passed. I turned away from the window. I heard myself say "It reminds me of the old rice fields."

Timothy seemed surprised. "Yes, now that you mention it, I guess it does. All the tall grass, and the creeks winding through."

"A person could get lost in the old rice fields too," I murmured. At that moment they called our table.

Our table was on the ground floor and well away from the windows, to Timothy's disappointment, but not to mine. The food when it came was excellent. But the evening was not going well. I couldn't get interested in the things Timothy talked about, nor could I bring myself to talk about the topics I'd been so eager earlier to discuss with him. I knew why. Midway through the meal I decided it was up to me to do something about this.

I said in a lull in the conversation, "Timothy, I'm uncomfortable with you tonight. It's because I feel like you played a trick on me, taking me to that house. I just don't understand why you did it, and to say that you're interested in ghosts and such, isn't a good enough explanation. What you did was borderline unkind, you know that?"

"Yes, I know that." He looked momentarily like an eight-year-old boy caught playing dress-up in a man-of-God outfit. "Okay. I was working up to it, but after the ghost and all hit you so hard, I've been afraid you'd turn me down."

"Turn you down about what, for heaven's sake?"

"I want you to do something for me. It's a favor, really, for Lynda. But the whole thing is my idea, not hers."

"You made me scare myself half to death, as a favor to *Lynda?*"

"Well, in a way, yes, I guess I did. I can explain. You know Lynda and Louis are restoring Leighton, but what you may not know is that Lynda wants to make Leighton a real showplace, a tourist attraction as well as a home. Lynda has the makings of a successful businesswoman, Rosamund. And she has a kind of mission too, to save a lot of the big old houses by making them pay for themselves again, with tourists. Leighton is the first step—it's terribly important to Lynda."

"Like the Treasure Houses of Britan, only this is Great Houses of the Old South," I said, a little sarcastically. What was really interesting was the emotion on Timothy's face. He felt deeply involved in all this. I did not miss how often he said her name—Lynda, Lynda, Lynda.

"Yes, that's the idea. When you're trying to attract tourists, it helps to have something different, something that will set your place apart. And Leighton is supposed to have a ghost. The trouble is, no one's seen it in this century. The general opinion is it's just a charming story, not like the Gray Man who's been seen so often. Even Louis thinks it's just a local legend. But I thought, if you really do have the ability I think you have—"

I finished the sentence for him. "You want me to check out Leighton's ghost. But you wanted to be sure I could really do it, so you gave me a little test tonight, is that it?"

Timothy nodded self-consciously. "Yes, that's it."

I wasn't wild about his explanation. I returned to eating. At least the crabmeat casserole was delicious. Maybe not as good as Jenny's. With elaborate casualness I asked, "Timothy, how long have you been in love with Lynda?"

He stiffened. I could see him, right before my eyes, retreat into the inviolability of his priesthood. His face became a mask of handsomest perfection. But his blue eyes were wary. "I'm not in love with Lynda," he denied.

What a mess we have here, I thought. Timothy and I, more than a little attracted to each other, with so many things in common, and yet we each had an irrational attraction—call it love, I wasn't sure anymore what to call it—for someone else. And those someone elses were both married. Maybe it only made us all the more suitable for each other. So let him deny, let it pass.

He had recovered his priestly equilibrium. "I love her, but I love her like a sister. Please don't misunderstand."

"I'm sorry," I said sincerely, and my heart went out to him. "I don't have brothers and sisters myself, and I'm no authority on close relationships. It's obvious you care about Lynda and you want to help her, and I'm sorry I misunderstood. So, okay, you gave me the test and I passed. No harm was done. I'll help you with this thing at Leighton. Tell me what you had in mind."

Lynda would call me, he said, Lynda would set everything up; he and other people would be there, it would be like an old-fashioned house party. It would be fun, Timothy promised, not at all like what had happened tonight.

I kept my reservations to myself.

Chapter 12

WHAT WAS IT," I asked, "that you wanted to talk to me about yesterday?"

He evaded my question. "You're sunburned. You look like a tomato."

"Yes, Charles, I know I'm sunburned. I spent the day on the beach." Since Charles had started going to his office in Georgetown every day, we never saw each other at breakfast anymore, and I was finding he could be every bit as rude and difficult over the dinner table as the breakfast table. For that matter, so could I.

"Did you wear your new bathing suit?"

"How did you know I have a new bathing suit? Have you been snooping in my room?" I felt slightly invaded.

"Of course not. Phyllis told me. I daresay everyone within earshot of Phyllis knows you bought a lot of new clothes yesterday. Phyllis idolizes you, you know."

I didn't know—I expected he was exaggerating. I tried to glower at him, but I'm not very good at glowering. "I suppose before you're willing to tell me what you wanted, you'll also have something to say about me going out with Timothy last night. Well, save your breath. It wasn't the greatest time I've ever had."

"Oh?" One dark eyebrow went up. "What a pity. That must be why his good-night kiss wasn't nearly so passionate as the one before. I thought perhaps he was intimidated by the outfit he had on—or that you were."

"You're terrible, Charles Charpentier, you know that, don't you? You were spying on me again! Well, why should you be different? Everybody spies on everybody in this house," I grumbled. As if on her cue, Regina, who I was sure did more spying than anyone else, came in with the main course.

When she'd left again, Charles grew serious. "I wanted to thank you for taking your own time to see Dr. Barkstone, and to tell you that he asked me to stop in his office on my way home. He was impressed with you—said you have fine instincts and good judgment, and he hopes you'll go back to medical school because the profession needs people like you. Not a bad recommendation from a male chauvinist doctor of the old school, like Barkstone."

"Thank you for telling me. But what about Arabella?"

Charles sighed. "Well, I've finally had to accept the fact that the place in North Carolina is out, unless something major happens. I've accepted the plan you and he came up with. It's not what I wanted, but at least it's not too long until the middle of July."

"Charles, don't . . ." I stopped, remembering that what I'd just said about spies was very true. I wanted to warn him not to let Arabella know how little time she had left at Charpentier, because I was sure it would be detrimental. Most of all I wanted to keep him from telling Regina, not only because she would most likely tell her mistress, but also because I simply could not bear the thought of the two of them together, alone, isolated. I said, "Could we go for a walk after dinner?"

He understood. "Of course," he agreed.

Under the oaks I learned that he had already told Regina. He looked satisfied, almost smug, as he recapitulated this for me before I'd had a chance to tell him what I'd wanted so much to say. I was so stunned I could hardly speak. "How, how did Regina take it?"

"To tell the truth, she didn't look too pleased. But I've ensured her cooperation." He had a gleam in his eye.

"I thought you knew so well how to handle her," I said bitterly.

"I do. I told her that I'm bringing Mother back to Charpentier. Something went on between Mother and Regina around the time Mother moved in to Charleston. I sensed hostility on both sides. Regina wouldn't like it here with Mother back—and she doesn't have to know that actually I have no intention of asking Mother back, not that she would want to come anyway. It doesn't matter. They'll go all right, in mid-July, both my wife and Regina." The decisive businessman. Case closed.

I hadn't wanted it closed. I'd thought somehow Charles and Barkstone and I could work together over the coming weeks. My hopes were vague, blurred by my own indecisiveness, and now they were dashed on the concrete of Charles's implacable decision. I was alone again with my doubts and my fears and most of all with my mistrust of Regina. In the set of Charles's jaw and the glint of his eye I saw no room for argument. The spirit was all gone out of me.

"I see," I said, and excused myself. It was early yet for me to go in, but I turned a deaf ear to whatever it was that Charles said as I left him. This was futile, I thought, with an unaccustomed feeling of helplessness. If everything was decided, then I had just become nothing more than an overpaid baby-sitter. I turned on the TV in my room and let the colors and the lights and the noise wash over me as one negative thought after another rolled through my mind. I had no idea what I'd watched when I finally went to bed.

I awoke with a familiar, dull feeling. It was depression, as I'd felt in the weeks after Aunt Henry's death. The new clothes in my closet gave me no pleasure—there was difficulty in the small chore of deciding what to wear. Nor did Jenny's excellent breakfast have any taste for me, and I ate only to ensure that I wouldn't hurt her feelings. My feet, my head, my heart all felt heavy as I went to begin my day with Arabella.

Strangely enough, it was Regina herself who snapped me out of it. She was clearing the breakfast dishes when I entered the suite, and my routine greeting stuck in my throat when she turned her head toward me. Gone was the grudging respect she'd begun to show. In its place was a kind of wicked, scheming triumph, so strong that it broke through my layers of depression. No words were necessary to tell me that Regina believed now that she had the upper hand. She did not even trouble to hide her malevolence, her full lips curled and dripped with it. She was to have her mistress to herself; I was nothing to her now.

My reaction was immediate, beyond the realm of thought. I recognized the evil in her and I hated her. Instantly, totally. My hatred consumed me so suddenly that there was no way I could conceal it, and most oddly, this pleased Regina. Her tawny eyes glittered. Neither of us said a word. All muscles tensed as if ready to spring, and we circled each other like two wild cats. Slowly we changed places in the room and she backed out of the door, never once taking her eyes from me. As I watched the door close after her, my mind filled with one overwhelming resolution: I would prevent it somehow, Arabella would not be confined alone with Regina, never!

I was changed; the depression was gone, zapped by the adrenalin that flowed from the encounter. I took my energy and channelled it toward Arabella.

She responded to my "good morning," which she didn't always. By now she knew the insulin routine as well as I, though for me it had become somewhat more complicated by her unstable glucose levels, and this morning I didn't have to argue with her. She seemed distracted, with a slight edge of her old agitation.

In an off hand manner I asked, "Something on your mind this morning?"

"Of course there is. There's always something on my mind." She said it without the sharpness that the words implied.

Interesting, I thought. "Do you want to talk about it?"

"What?" She turned her head and pulled her chin up to look at me where I stood, used syringe in hand, a few feet from her. The lavender-to-purple glasses shaded her eyes, and I remembered she had worn those glasses on my first day. That seemed a very long time ago. I repeated, "Do you want to talk about what's on your mind?"

"Rosamund, you know *nothing* about these things." A trace of scorn in her tone, but for her it was mild.

"Perhaps you're right." I left her sitting over her post-breakfast coffee at the table in the living room. I was still charged up and if I weren't careful, I could push her too hard. Since her complete transformation into not-Arabella, I had never pushed, never challenged, only observed. I was about to change that, and I thought deviousness would get better results than direct confrontation.

The problem was, devious wasn't in my vocabulary, so to speak. I didn't know how to be devious. I puttered about the room, trying to look busier than I was, and I glanced at her from time to time. Yes, she was definitely preoccupied. It was unlike her to sit for so long at the table. I went and sat with her, deciding to try some old fashioned nondevious conversation.

"Is that a caftan you have on? All the clothes you've been wearing lately seem to be quite different from Arabella's clothes. They're . . . unusual." A bit of an understatement! She wore a red caftan with random slashes of purple and a little bright yellow daubed here and there. The fabric might equally have been done by an exuberant five-year-old, or by a middle-aged painter under the influence of LSD. "Where did you get all these things? I never saw Arabella wear them."

She waved a bony white hand in a noncommital gesture. "She had them for a long time. I made her keep them for me." Now she preened, smoothing the too-bright fabric over her small breasts. "Yes, my clothes are unusual. They suit me, don't you think? I'm unusual!" She laughed, and it came out high, broken, a near-cackle.

I smiled at her. I had noticed, as she preened, how painfully thin she was. Almost pathetic. I really should weigh her more often, I thought, she seems to be losing weight.

Now she held her head cocked to one side, as if she were sizing me up for something. *"You* could help me," she said in the low, thrilling voice she reserved for special occasions.

More interesting! I waited. Perhaps I would not have to be so devious after all.

"I need a candle. You could get it for me, Rosamund."

"A candle?"

She had just the slightest tremors of agitation—or perhaps it was anticipation—about her lips and in her fingers. "Yes," she confirmed, "yes!"

I wondered why she hadn't made this request of Regina, and decided not to ask. "You know we aren't supposed to have any open flames in the North Wing, and that includes candles. Especially in here. You have battery-powered lamps in case the lights go out." But I did not have such lamps in my rooms. I had a whole box of household candles that had been given to me by Phyllis for such emergencies. They were locked up in my cabinets, in the bottom drawer.

"Of cours-s-s-e I know that," she hissed, "but I need a candle, a real candle."

So that was what was on her mind, what had kept her distracted! "What for?"

She tossed her head impatiently. "I need it to practice."

"What are you practicing?"

Her patience was wearing very thin. Her hands fluttered, her voice rose. "*You* wouldn't understand! You know nothing of these things!"

I had to calm her down. "All right. But I do know why I should tell you no. It's because of the fire. You, whatever your name is, living in Arabella's body, do you share her memories? Do you remember the fire?"

Most interesting! If only I could have seen her eyes! She remembered, all right, and it was a bad memory. Very bad. Even without the eyes she looked shocked—mouth open and frozen, a deathlike stillness upon her. She seemed for a moment to stop breathing. Then she shook her head from side to side, tossing her white-streaked hair.

"No," she denied, "no, I don't remember."

"Arabella was burned in the fire. She nearly lost her eyes, that's why she wears the glasses. Surely you know that?"

Her need for this candle was apparently desperate. As I watched her struggle for and gain control over her fear, I saw an opportunity, and I seized it in spite of the risk. I said quietly, evenly, "I will make a bargain with you. You want this candle very much, and I want something from you."

"What do you want?" Suspiciously.

"I want you to go away and let us have Arabella back again."

"No, I can't do that. You don't understand, I can't do that," shaking her head again. Then she had an inspiration, and it visibly pleased her. She leaned toward me across the table. "But I know something else you would like, pretty Rosamund, for your bargain." From her mouth came her low, evil chuckle. "You give me a candle . . . and I will tell you my name!" Triumphantly.

"Your *real* name?"

"Yes! yes, yes, yes, yes, yes."

"All right, I agree to that. You wait here, and I will get the candle." I rose and started for the door.

"Matches too, I must have matches too!"

"Of course, you'll need them to light the candle."

"Yes, yes!"

I didn't allow myself to think that what I was doing could be dangerous. Learning the name, who she thought herself to be, was worth the risk. And if I was right, there was still a lot of the old Arabella left in her, more than I had seen in many days.

I returned with one simple white candle, about six inches long, and a pack of matches. I held them out to her. "Here you are. My half of the bargain."

She had been pacing the room in my brief absence and walked forward eagerly to meet me. She grasped candle and matches with thin fingers, cold when they met mine. Then she stepped back, pressing her prizes to her breast with both hands. She straightened, she seemed before my eyes to grow taller.

"My name," she proclaimed, "is Ashtoreth!"

I awoke so suddenly that for a moment I didn't know where I was. The room was dark, the only light that spilled over my shoulders was from a reading lamp at the head of the bed. I sat up immediately, thinking that I was on call, and my hand went to my waist to shut off a beeper that wasn't there. My movements disturbed a book and it slipped, pages rustling, from my lap to the bed beside me. And then I remembered. I was in my room at Charpentier, and I'd been reading in bed, researching the books still scattered around me for references to "Ashtoreth." I had fallen asleep, reading.

I looked at my clock and watched while a 2 dissolved and

changed itself into a 3. 11:53. The red numbers of the liquid crystal display glowed on their black background. Outside of my little circle of light they seemed lurid, vaguely sinister, somehow connected to my dream. It was bothersome, I couldn't remember what I had been dreaming just before awakening.

There was no time to think about that now. I had come awake with every sense already alert, like a mother with a new baby, and it had taken a minute for my mind to catch up. Arabella—I had to check on Arabella. Never mind that I'd never done it before, I knew I had to check on her, *now!*

My eyes were accustomed to the shadowy dark and I didn't turn on the lights. I pushed aside the books and slipped from the bed, felt briefly with my toes and found my slippers, the new scuffs that matched the new robe I'd fallen asleep wearing. Hurry! an inner voice said, and I hurried, belting my robe more tightly as I half-walked, half-ran. Down the long hall, its gallery-windows white with moonlight, down the far stairs dark by comparison. Then I slowed. I bypassed the door to Arabella's living room and cautiously approached a seldom-used door that opened into the connecting passageway between her living room and bedroom. I listened and heard nothing. I opened the door and stepped into the small passageway. As I stood there I felt emptiness, and I was sure that I was the only living thing in these silent rooms.

Nevertheless, I had to check. The powder-room door opposite me was ajar, and I began there. A pink shell-shaped nightlight glowed, that was all. In the living room, moonlight poured through the many-paned windows and the closed french doors, making small rectangular patterns across the carpet. I scanned quickly over the familiar shapes of furniture. Nothing, no one here.

I knew that Arabella's bedroom would be dark, the heavy draperies would be closed to shut out the moon's illumination. I wished I had a flashlight. Something peculiar was going on here. Wherever she was, Arabella was up to something, and I didn't want to give away my own presence by turning on lights. I went back through the connecting passage to the dreaded bedroom. Don't think and don't feel,

I told myself, just move. I felt my way around the divan to the door of Arabella's bathroom, which backed up against the powder room. It was empty. It, too, had a nightlight, like a white scallop shell—by contrast with the bedroom's blackness, it seemed almost bright.

I left the bathroom door open. A little light was better than none. Don't think, don't feel. I crossed the bedroom swiftly, determinedly. The covers of her bed were folded back, the pillows arranged as she liked them, but she had not been in that bed this night. I did not want to look into the closets or her dressing room, but I did. And then I got the hell out of there. As I gained the corridor I felt the room trying to pull me back, and I shut the door firmly upon it. My breath came raggedly. I felt a fine sheen of nervous moisture break out on the surface of my skin.

Where was she? Carrying across the heavy silence, the grandfather clock struck its hollow chimes. One through twelve I counted. Midnight, the witching hour. I shivered, and told myself it was only the air-conditioning on my damp skin that chilled me. I had to search the house, she had to be here somewhere.

I summoned up a mental floorplan of Charpentier and tried to concentrate on it as I went from room to room. I did reality-things, like counting doors, counting fireplaces. I promised myself that I would buy a flashlight on my next day off—a reminder that there was another world with days off and stores to shop in. But the effort eroded. My search became an archetype of nightmare: long, shadowed corridors stretched before me, flanked by closed doors that I must enter one by one, looking for something or someone I would never find; shapes of trees moved on the cold moonlight through the tall windows, moved into the silent rooms with me; unfamiliar objects humped and huddled in the darkness, ready to come for me, they wavered in my peripheral vision. Everywhere long, white curtains hung like ghostly, silent sentinels.

At last I reached the kitchen. I leaned against the counter and waited for my heartbeat to return to normal. The kitchen was lighter, brighter for its many polished surfaces of white and chrome, blessed with the residue of Jenny's presence and echoes of her gospel songs. I crossed the tiled floor slowly, then went through the swinging doors of the pantry to the flower room beyond. Of course Arabella was not there, nor was she likely to be in Regina's room. I could see no alternative now but to tell Charles that his wife was missing.

I had to go back into the hall and climb the main stairway. Maybe tomorrow, in the daylight, I would be proud of myself for having searched through all the rooms in spite of my fear, but this was tonight, and as soon as I left the kitchen I was again afraid. I fled up the stairs as fast as I could go, tripped and lost a slipper, and like Cinderella I left it there. I pounded on Charles's heavy door with both fists. "Charles!" I called, "Charles!"

He opened the door and I nearly fell in, into the wonderful bright light. I blinked, and gulped, and shivered. He stared at me with an unreadable expression on his face.

"Arabella's missing," I said breathlessly, "she's gone! I've searched the whole house, and she's not here!"

Charles lifted his hand to my face, and automatically in the wake of my fear, I flinched. His hand paused, then continued on its way. He touched my hair, he smoothed it back from my forehead. Only then did I realize how dishevelled I was, hair tumbling all over, nearly covering my face and eyes that I knew were still wide with fright.

"Shh. It's all right." He stroked my hair, gentling me. He gathered it in both his hands and spread it about my shoulders and over my breasts like a veil. "Something frightened you. What?" he asked.

"It was n-nothing. Just the house. I didn't want to turn on the lights. I thought she would be here somewhere, and I wanted to surprise her at whatever she was doing. But she isn't anywhere, and after a while it . . . it got to be like a nightmare, all the rooms, all the shadows. . . ." I shivered again.

Charles held me at arm's length, my shoulders firmly in his hands. His dark blue eyes studied mine, seriously. "Are you sure that's all it was?"

I felt his strength flowing into me and was grateful for it. I swallowed hard and nodded. "Yes."

He urged me with him now to a small leather couch, and I sank down beside him into its welcoming plump smoothness. He looked at my feet. "You lost a slipper."

"It's on the stairs. Charles, we've got to find Arabella!"

"How do you propose we do that?" He leaned back into his corner of the couch and crossed his legs.

For the first time since I'd come into the room, I really looked at him. His feet and his legs were bare. He wore a short robe of thick, loopy terry cloth in a midnight blue color that matched his eyes. His hair was damp, tousled as most of the time, and curling now in tendrils around his face. His crossed legs bared a line of inner thigh. He was fresh from a shower at this hour of the night, and I didn't doubt that under his robe he was naked. I couldn't remember his question. "I, uh . . ." I floundered.

"It would do no good to call the police when she has been gone such a short time," he said, "and besides, if she has left the house, I would imagine Regina has gone with her."

I hadn't thought of that. "Would you go and see, Charles, see if Regina's gone, too?"

He looked at me again with that unreadable look. "All right. Do you want a drink while I'm gone?"

"No. I'll just sit here and wait for you." A whisper of my recent fear brushed me. "You'll come right back?"

"Of course." He went out and closed the door behind himself.

I curled up on the couch, hugging my knees to my chest. I tucked the bottom of my long robe tight about my ankles. My mind was full of questions.

Charles came back almost immediately, and he had my slipper in his hand. "Found it," he said, and dropped it on the floor with the other one. He sat on the couch again. "Regina's gone, too. She'll look after Bella. I doubt there's anything to worry about."

"But where would they go in the middle of the night?"

"I don't know. And to tell you the truth, I don't really care."

"Oh, but Charles, you *must* care! She could get in trouble, she might—"

He interrupted. "Exactly. I suspect the two of them have done this before, and that your being here may have stopped them for a while. My policy with Bella for some time now has been to give her enough rope, and hope that she will hang herself. And that is still my hope." His voice and his face were hard.

I regarded him over the tops of my tightly clasped knees, not liking what I saw. "Timothy said you were ruthless."

His eyes blazed, a cold sapphire light. "Did he?" The sensual lips twisted. "Well, think about it, Ms. Psychiatrist. You yourself would prefer to see my wife in that fancy sanatorium, wouldn't you? Do you think I like the fact that the law requires she do something dangerous before we can put her there?"

Grudgingly, I conceded. "I see your point." But I still didn't like it. I felt defeated again. I put my head on my knees, huddled in a tight ball, all my energy spent.

"Rosamund." His voice was a husky whisper.

I clutched my knees tighter. I didn't move, gave no sign of hearing.

"Rosamund, we're alone. There is no one in this house but us. No one to see, no one to hear. . . ." He lifted my hair, and his lips closed upon my neck, a hard, hot pressure on the sensitive pulse point. Startled, I gasped. He was either draining me or bringing me back to life, maybe both.

"I've wanted you like this for so long," he breathed.

"No," I whispered, as his mouth moved to the base of my throat and his strong hands unclasped my arms from around my knees. His hair felt like damp silk against my chin. I dared not open my eyes.

He parted my robe. The thin fabric of my nightgown was no barrier to his searching mouth. His hot, damp kisses went right through and drowned my skin; through the cloth his teeth seized a nipple and bit.

A current that was more pain than pleasure went through me, my back arched. My knees were weak, they parted, and my arms closed around him. I cradled his heavy head to my breast even as a voice whispered to me from far away, This is wrong, this is wrong. . . .

He moved over me and I opened my eyes, then quickly closed them again, not quite ready for this. All his passion, all his sensuality blazed in an aura around him. He was huge as he bent to me, huge and dark and frighteningly strong. He

193

picked me up as if I were a child and stood with me in his arms. I looked at his face and saw there something primitive, the elemental male animal. Even though it gave me a strange pleasure, I struggled against my unaccustomed helplessness. "Put me down," I said.

"No." His mouth descended on mine, forcing my head back, and I felt my heavy hair falling, pulling my head back farther as his tongue thrust, and thrust deeper. He carried me to his great bed and laid me upon it like a prize, the spoils of battle. Then he stepped back and with one hand he loosed the sash of his robe, and it fell open.

My blood pounded, my senses were garbled, sending mixed messages. A parchment-shaded lamp near the bed bathed Charles's body in golden light. His robe hung from his shoulders like an open, sapphire cloak. He was more muscular than I would have guessed, everything about him large and broad and hard. Dark hair curled in the center of his chest and parted around his flat male nipples, then dwindled to a line which I followed with fascinated eyes until it thickened again, making a nest for genitals that matched his body in their proportions. He was erect. I felt overwhelmed, knowing that he displayed himself for me. I thought irrelevantly that he was doing this all wrong, that he should have undressed me first. I knew that nothing in my limited experience had prepared me for this man, nothing.

I said in a broken voice, "They'll be home soon."

"No, they won't. And anyway, I've locked the door." He came to the side of the bed and untied my robe at the waist. His voice was thick and hoarse. "I've waited for this time with you. I want you now, Rosamund." He pushed my robe from my shoulders and with compelling strength lifted me with one hand as his other hand swept my robe away. "I know you want me too." His eyes were on my body, not on my face.

"I . . ." I tried to speak, but his devouring mouth took my words even as his hands, too strong to resist, took away the last defense of my flimsy nightgown. The small, faraway voice called again: This is wrong, this is wrong. Confused, I could not heed its message nor could I understand why my senses seemed so blunted. Where was the passion I had felt so often in the past? I *did* want him, yet that was not what I felt. I was still overwhelmed, almost . . . afraid of him.

Charles was caught in the force of his unleashed need, urgent, hot, impatient. I lay passive, receptive but un-aroused, lost in lack of understanding. Everything was moving much too fast for me, and when his hand sought to part my thighs, I unconsciously resisted.

For a moment his senses returned. Resting his weight on one forearm he loomed over me, heavy eyebrows drawn together in a face dark with passion. "You're . . . not a virgin, surely?" he asked.

"No," I murmured. But I felt like one. Then, dimly, I realized that I was still half in shock from my nightmare search. That was what was wrong with me. But Charles had once again moved on.

"I didn't think so!" he said in a guttural voice. His lips curved upward in what was meant to be a smile, but it was lost in the rampant sensuality that drove him.

I felt his knee between my thighs and I opened them. I looked down and saw his great phallus glistening; I looked up and his massive shoulders filled my entire field of vision. Suddenly my mind flashed on Regina, Charles humping Regina, her gloating golden eyes looking over those same shoulders, and I snapped.

I twisted my hips sharply just as he lowered himself to enter me, and I felt his hot, straining erection graze my hipbone before he pulled up. Tears of fury and confusion rose in my eyes. "I won't do it," I cried, "not like this! You're practically raping me, Charles!" I covered my face with my forearms and with all my strength I rolled, breaking his hold. I was karate-trained for self-defense, and my body now remembered those lessons, though my mind was still filled with sickening visions of Charles, my naked Charles, with Regina.

"Raping you!" he bellowed from the bed. "My God, Rosamund, don't do this to me. I swear, I can't stand it!"

But I didn't listen. I was too confused, too miserable. I snatched my robe and my gown from the floor by the bed and ran for the door. It was locked, as he'd said. A heavy, old lock with a key, and try as I would I couldn't turn it.

Charles came up behind me, turned me around with a heavy hand on my shoulder. He growled, "What are you, a spoiled child? A cock-teaser? Where do you think you're going?" He was still naked, still erect.

My ravaged hair streamed over my shoulders as I shook my head, and furious tears streamed over my face. "Just let me go, Charles!" With the unerring accuracy of lovers gone wrong, I spat out the words that would wound him most. "Timothy was right about you. You're a ruthless, arrogant man!"

He was stunned. The dark colors of passion drained from his face. His whole body seemed to shrink.

I could only think that I had to get away, had to. "Just open the door for me!" Panic took hold, my voice went out of control. "Open the door, you, you *Regina-fucker!*" I tossed my head wildly, and my hair flew.

Without a word he stepped around me. I looked away from the sight of his strong thighs and tight buttocks. I no longer had a right to see. He opened the door, and I walked through it with as much dignity as my nakedness allowed. He did not close the door. I knew he stood there, following me with his eyes. I wished my hair were a foot longer, to completely cover me. I knew that if I went back now, if I said, Forgive me, he would do it, and we could begin again, and this time it could be better. No, it couldn't. Because even if I found my voice, even if I said, Be patient, slow down, wait for me, and he did, still at the last moment as he hung over me I would see Regina. Regina would not go away. Inexorably my feet carried me into the darkness, farther and farther away from Charles.

The next morning I found a brown paper bag outside my door, and in it were my pink slippers. I was not surprised when Jenny told me at breakfast that Mr. Charles had had to go away unexpectedly on a business trip, and he would be gone for at least two weeks.

Chapter 13

I WAS GLAD CHARLES had gone. I couldn't have faced him. Where Charles was concerned, I didn't know up from down, in from out, right from wrong anymore. It was more than just the business about Regina, though that was what had at last stopped me. I knew, even if Charles did not admit it, that there could be nothing between us until there was some resolution for his wife. Yet still, if I hadn't exactly led him on, I hadn't resisted him either. And no good had come of it, as I'd known it could not. I felt guilty, and ashamed.

But I had too much to do to let myself be bogged down with shame and guilt. I'd made a breakthrough with Arabella/Ashtoreth. I thought of her as Ashtoreth now. I was almost as absorbed in her new personality as she was herself. The fact that I had given her the much-desired candle had made a bond between us, and while she didn't confide in me, she did trust me enough to tolerate my presence in her room. I was subtly included. She would answer occasional questions, and each day I stretched a little further the limits of what she would tell me. Probably I would never know whether Regina had denied her the candle, or whether for some reason of her own Ashtoreth had chosen not to ask Regina for it. I did know that the simple white candle formed a powerful secret between us,

197

for she had told me so, and she had made me promise not to tell Charles, as she in turn promised not to tell Regina. I had inserted a wedge between Regina and Ashtoreth, and I intended to drive my wedge both wide and deep.

On the Sunday following Charles's departure, I stood at the sideboard in the breakfast room and felt uneasy, apprehensive. Why? I scanned the room. The day was overcast but not gloomy, the round table was set for me as usual, the Sunday *New York Times* by my place since Charles was not here. Everything looked normal. I poured orange juice into a glass, filled a plate with croissant and slices of melon—the usual Sunday breakfast fare. On Sundays I always missed Jenny's big breakfasts. I took my plate to the table, and my glass of juice, and then the coffeepot. Then I sat down to begin my meal.

Still the uneasiness did not go away. Had I heard some unusual sound without being fully aware of it? I sat stone-still and listened. Nothing. The house was so quiet I could hear the tick of the grandfather clock in the hall.

Honestly, I chided myself, this will never do! I can't start getting jumpy just because there's no man in the house . . . and no Jenny, and no Phyllis. I dug resolutely into the many folds of the newspaper until I found the *Book Review,* and started to read as I sipped my orange juice.

The glass was half-empty before I realized it didn't taste right. It was bitter, but not bitter with the gone-over taste of too-old juice. As I noted the strange bitterness on the back of my tongue, I realized that my ears felt peculiar, and my eyes, too. My earlier uneasiness zoomed into alarm. My whole body revolted. I convulsed, retching. There was no time even to get to my feet, much less to reach the kitchen or a bathroom. I vomited miserably, helplessly, onto the floor beside my chair, bringing up all the orange juice and finally my own stomach fluids. Still I couldn't stop, but shuddered with dry heaves. My body poured cold sweat.

When at last it was over and I stood shakily, thinking I would clean up the mess I'd made, I found my legs wouldn't support me. I collapsed again and put my head on my arms, weeping helpless tears.

"Are you sick?" The voice from the doorway was hard, cold.

I didn't even raise my head. "Go away, Regina." I waited for her to leave, with my miserable, stinking face on my clammy arms. How long had she stood there watching me? I felt humiliated.

A little voice inside me said, She made the breakfast. Regina tried to poison you!

"No," I murmured aloud. I rasied my head. She was gone, thank goodness. Then I thought how odd it was that she had been there at all. She was never in this part of the house at breakfast. She should have been with Arabella/Ashtoreth.

Moving very slowly, I cleaned up the breakfast room. As I worked, I regained my strength. By the time I'd showered and brushed my teeth three times, I felt much better. Empty and washed-out, but otherwise normal. No achiness, no hint of a fever. It was not the sudden onset of a viral illness that had made me vomit. It *had* been the orange juice, and I had to admit that my little voice could have been right. I dressed carefully and applied blusher to my cheeks. Not for all the world would I go downstairs looking any the worse for my experience!

Regina sat on Arabella/Ashtoreth's couch reading a magazine. She looked up at me with undisguised hostility in her golden eyes.

"Where is Ashtoreth?" I asked.

"In her bedroom." She tossed the magazine aside and stood to leave.

"All right. You may go," I said. "As you can see, I am not sick." I was in her direct path to the door and I did not step aside, as she expected me to do; instead, I stared into her face. Resolve turned my spine to iron, my voice lashed like a whip. "Regina. In the future whenever Jenny is not here, I will get my own meals. I don't want you to have to go to so much trouble for me, as you did this morning. Do you understand?"

In answer she curled her upper lip in that expression of hers that was half smile, half sneer. Her chin went up a notch, and so did mine.

"I understand," she said.

I stepped back and she went past me, moving in her regal carriage. I sagged with relief when the door closed behind her. I almost hadn't made it through that confrontation. I was thankful for our equal height—if she'd been an inch taller than I, I'd probably have lost my nerve.

There was no question that Regina's hostility toward me was more overt with Charles out of the house. I endured it with a stoicism that would have made Aunt Henry proud. I stayed out of her way, hoping to lull her into a false sense of security. Since I was getting all my own meals, both Regina and I were spared the travesty of her serving me in the dining room. We seemed to have a sort of uneasy truce, bound together by our responsibilities to Arabella Charpentier. I didn't think Regina would try to harm me again, but I watched her. And when I left the house on my day off, I did something I'd never done before. I cautioned the nurse against Regina, as I turned over the little keys. If Regina asked for the keys, I said, she was not to have them. Under no circumstances was Regina to be left alone with Mrs. Charpentier. When Phyllis came to clean, that was fine, but if Regina came for any reason, she must be watched. The nurse was the young one who'd been there the night of the storm and was working days for the first time; the others might have questioned this change, but she did not.

That done, I headed for Pawley's Island to shop. In the Hammock Shop, a favorite place, I bought a floppy hat of natural straw and a brightly colored Mexican bag I'd coveted for weeks. At a groceries-and-everything-else store I got the flashlight I'd promised myself and food for a picnic lunch for two—fruit, nuts, cheese, crackers, and a small bag of rich cookies. Then I returned home.

It was a beautiful day, clear and sunny and hot. The drought Jenny had told me about was now an established fact. Everyone complained how dry it was. I could observe for myself that the trees in our woods were looking a bit droopy, but on the whole we were much better off near the coast. I was still avoiding the river, its black water still disturbed me in a way I couldn't define, but George, who did all the outdoor work, said the Waccamaw's water level was dropping. The sunny days followed one after another, and as much as I hated the high humidity, I too began to wish for rain. But not today.

Back in my rooms I changed into my new swimsuit, a peacock blue maillot with scandalously high-cut legs. I'd already braided my hair, which was the best way to wear it on the always-windy beach. Over the suit I dropped a white terry-cloth float, fringed at the bottom, also new. I assembled the picnic food in the Mexican bag, added a tube of sunscreen, topped all with a beach towel, put on my sunglasses and my just-purchased floppy hat, and felt like the Compleat Beach person.

I had persuaded Timothy to take the afternoon off for a picnic on the beach with me. I was driving, since we were going to the Charpentier beach and my car had authorization. I arrived at the rectory just past noon. He had a housekeeper, I knew, but he answered the door himself.

"All ready?" I asked. Chameleon that he was, he was not the priest today. He looked like one of those people who go to graduate school forever—cut-off jeans well-frayed, a thin white T-shirt that said YALE in faded blue letters, and sandals that could only be Earth Shoes, they were too ugly for anything else.

"Yep," he smiled. To the unseen housekeeper he called out, "I'm off!" He jammed an old holey straw hat on his head and picked up a Styrofoam cooler.

I held the screen door for him. "No sunglasses?" I knew the beach routine rather well by now, and the glare off the water could be blinding.

He shook his head as we went down the steps. "Don't need 'em. Strong eyes."

"You'll get squint lines."

"I already have them—see?" He grinned exaggeratedly, and the corners of his eyes crinkled.

"Yes," I laughed, "I see." He was so handsome it was almost maddening, it made me want to mess him up somehow. But how? It would be impossible, he would look good in rags. Or, with his head in a bag . . . good legs, I thought, as he went ahead of me to put the cooler in the back of my wagon.

"I brought beer, Heineken's, and Cokes. Oh, damn! I forgot to bring a towel." He started again for the house, but I stopped him.

"That's okay. You can share mine."

"I meant, to lie on." He looked me up and down. "As much as I'd like to try it, I don't think we'll both fit on one beach towel."

"No problem." I linked arms and steered him back to the car. "I have an ancient cotton quilt I use for that. It's plenty big enough for both of us."

He looked suspicious. "A Charpentier quilt?"

"No. It was my Aunt Henry's. I wrapped some things in it for the trip down here. What difference does that make?" We split as he got in one side of the station wagon, and I in the other.

"It's bad enough I'm going to lie on the Charpentier's sand," he grumbled as he snapped his seat belt, "I'll be damned if I'd lie with you on one of their quilts!"

I started the car. I was not amused. "Honestly, Timothy, come off it! No carping about the Charpentiers today, promise?"

"Okay. I promise."

The tide was half in, half out. I picked a spot where the sand was smooth, just above the high-water line, and spread out the quilt. I sat down and rubbed sunscreen on every inch of exposed skin. I'd learned my lesson about sunburn. I had a light tan now, not easy for me to acquire with my kind of skin, and I didn't want to get burned again.

Timothy had left the cooler and his sandals and gone straight to the water. He waded in to his knees, then came back. "It feels great. A little cool at first, but great. I'm going for a swim," he said, and proceeded to strip. Off came the T-shirt, down went the zipper and he stepped out of the cutoffs. He wore a man's bikini, which is to say he wore almost nothing at all. What there was of it, a triangle well and visibly filled by his private parts, was navy blue.

I was glad of my sunglasses, because for a minute my eyes almost fell out of my head. Such a suit wasn't in character for him, at least not the character I'd thought I knew. "Want some sunscreen?" I held the tube up to him. "You don't look like you have much of a tan yet."

His skin was like mellow ivory, his chest smooth and hairless, the fine down on his arms and legs so pale it was all but invisible. The man with the perfect face also had a perfect body, like Michelangelo's *David*. Young and lean, but not thin.

"Thanks. That's a good idea." He sank to his knees and rubbed the cream carelessly over himself. I watched with interest. He seemed completely unselfconscious about his body, though it was all on display. I was curious how he got to be that way, to take his own gorgeousness so much for granted.

"Timothy, you have a beautiful body. You must know that, or you wouldn't dare to wear that kind of suit."

"So? You don't like it?" He smiled, but a little uncertainly.

"Yes, of course I do. In fact, I'm impressed, not just by your, ah, beauty, but by the fact that you aren't vain or self-conscious. I find that rather remarkable, that's all."

He screwed the top back on the tube and tossed it to me. Then he took a deep breath, closed his eyes, and held his face up to the sun. When he looked at me again, his expression was pained. "Are you playing psychiatrist?"

"I guess I can't help it. I didn't mean to make you uncomfortable."

He stretched out beside me, his swim forgotten. He lay on his side, one hand propping up his head. "It's okay. I don't mind telling you. I had to learn to be like you said, not vain or self-conscious. I grew up always looking more or less like this, relative to how old I was at any given time. I inherited my mother's looks—she's a patrician, the Grace Kelly type, which is fine for a woman. I went to private boys' schools, boarding schools, all my life. To look like I do in that situation is a disadvantage, believe me."

"What do you mean? How can physical beauty be a disadvantage?"

Timothy pulled a wry, sideways smile. "Think about it. Beauty isn't a word that's often applied to men, but I'm afraid it has been to me. I never went through an ugly duckling stage. I had to deal with homosexual advances from the time I was a little kid. I said no out of pure instinct, before I was old enough to understand what it was all about. Puberty was sheer hell for me. I became a loner, studied all the time, went to great lengths to be sure that for athletics I

203

had archery or horseback riding, anything where you didn't have to take your clothes off. Eventually, of course, hormones and heterosexuality caught up with me—but it happened much later than it does for most people. I fell in love, not with a girl but with a woman. I was an undergraduate in college, and it was a disaster. After a couple more disasters, I got some counselling. I literally had to be taught how to appreciate my face and my body as much as I appreciated my mind. It took time and practice, and it wasn't easy. I still practice, that's the reason for the brief suit. And to tell you the truth, sometimes I still don't like to look in the mirror."

"I don't either," I confessed, "but for the opposite reason. When I was a teenager I was truly ugly!"

"I don't believe it," he said, running a forefinger down the length of my thigh, all the way from the edge of my high-cut suit. He looked like he wanted to do more.

I reached out and shoved him, playfully, but hard enough to push him over. "Believe it!" I cried, and I was up and running for the surf. "Come on, no more seriousness. Let's play!"

We swam, we munched, we drank beer. We fell asleep, we woke up, and then we swam again. Somehow the things he'd told me about himself had removed a barrier for me. I no longer felt put off by his perfection. His quiet personality, his even temper were like a balm, soothing upon my abrasions from the tempestuousness of Charles Charpentier. I felt lovely, cleansed and healed. When the time came to talk of the real reason I'd asked him to spend the afternoon with me, I felt reluctant to do so. Timothy was stretched out on his back with his arms behind his head, his holey hat over his face.

I nudged him with a sandy toe. "Timothy, are you awake? I need to talk to you about something."

"Ummm?" he asked from under his hat.

"Concerning Arabella Charpentier."

He put aside the hat and sat up, facing me. "Sounds serious."

"It is." I took off my own hat—it was hard to have a serious conversation from under a floppy hat. "There's been a significant change in her. I would have told you the night we went to Murrell's Inlet, but . . . well, with the ghost business and all, you remember how that turned out."

"Yes, I remember. I've been sorry ever since. I want to make it up to you."

"Today makes up for it. Today is wonderful." I felt a growing affection for him, and I hoped he could tell. "But anyway, I do need some help. She's taken on a new personality, and I've talked with her doctor about it. She says she isn't Arabella anymore. She calls herself Ashtoreth."

"Really? Ashtoreth? That's very interesting."

"Think back on that dinner party, how she treated you. To make a long story short, I want to know if Ashtoreth is a demonic name. In the books you gave me I found one reference to an 'Astaroth,' but it's just a name in a long string of names, part of an incantation supposedly used to summon up the devil."

"I get the picture. You think she's possessed?"

"No," I shook my head. "Actually, I don't. Charles thinks she is, he thinks she's evil, but I disagree and so we don't talk about it. I think it's Regina who's evil—but that gets me ahead of myself. If I knew more about this Ashtoreth, at least I might know if it really is the name of a demon."

"Um-hm. I think I can help. You've probably heard of Astarte. She's the same goddess, called Astarte by the Phoenicians. Ashtoreth is her Semitic name. She's the mother-goddess of the Semites, a fertility figure. Sort of an earth-mother, found in all the old religions. Her equivalent for the Egyptians was Isis, for the Greeks, Aphrodite, whom the Romans called Diana, and for the ancient Celts and other inhabitants of the British Isles, she was the Great Mother or the Great Goddess. You follow?"

"Yes. So it's not an evil name, not the name of a demon."

"I'm afraid it's not that simple." Timothy shook his head rather sadly. "She was a pagan goddess, and when the Christians came along, all the old gods and goddesses were made 'evil' in the eyes of the Church."

"Maybe that's why Arabella, I mean, Ashtoreth, hates Christianity so much!"

"Could be. There's more. The old religions went underground, they didn't completely die. The old knowledge became the basis for necromancy and alchemy and magic, and by the Middle Ages they got mixed up with the concept of the Devil. Maybe not for the great magicians like Albertus Magnus or Paracelsus, but for most people and certainly for the Church. All magic became black magic, and the minor demons of Christian demonology were assigned names of the old gods and goddesses. Ashtoreth was one, and that's why you found a version of her name in that incantation. You see, the Christians condemned the magicians and the necromancers and the alchemists for seeking power in ways that drew upon the old, pre-Christian knowledge. To a Christian, all power belongs only to God: Father, Son, and Holy Spirit. To seek power in any way other than through the Trinity was therefore evil. This led to a lot of abuse by the Church, to the persecution of witches, for example. By the Middle Ages they saw no difference between black magic and witchcraft, although actually there is a lot of difference. Most magicians were learned men, so-called adepts, whereas witches were ignorant, common people. A witch wouldn't know about an Ashtoreth, but a magician or a necromancer would. Is all this any help?"

"Yes," I said excitedly. He had given me the missing piece to the puzzle, and a whole picture was emerging. "I have a theory, Timothy. I'll make you my confidant, but you must promise to keep this just between you and me!"

"I promise." He smiled, amused by my excitement.

"I'll try to give you the whole picture as I begin to see it. It's true that Arabella Charpentier is mentally ill. She was diagnosed some time ago as manic-depressive, though her doctor admitted the diagnosis didn't quite fit. She had been deteriorating for a couple of years before I came, and one of the signs of this deterioration was a delusion, the beginnings of this new personality emerging. What is so fascinating is that since she has completely assumed the Ashtoreth personality, she functions better than she did as Arabella. I don't think she's possessed by a demon, nor do I think she has a multiple personality. I think she has given herself the name Ashtoreth now, just as she probably gave herself the name Arabella in the past—I doubt Arabella was her original name, the one she was born with. I believe Ashtoreth's stronger qualities have been in her all along, more or less dormant."

"What makes you think she named herself Arabella?"

"Some things I learned from Charles. And what you've just told me fits right in with other things I learned from him. Before Arabella married Charles, she lived with some people who called themselves magicians. They were entertainers, Charles said they were into 'mumbo jumbo,' but they may have been more serious, too. Especially one man, the one Arabella was closest to before Charles came along. I think she gave up those things, or tried to, when she married him. Tried to be more normal, more like other people, for his sake. But it didn't work, it couldn't work, she couldn't be like other people because unfortunately she *is* mentally ill, she's not like other people. She had given up something that meant a lot to her, and yet she didn't get what she really wanted. In her saner moments—and I know she had them because I've seen them—she must have realized that her marriage wasn't working, and she remembered a time when she was functioning better. With that healthier part of her mind she identified the part of herself that has become Ashtoreth. You see, it fits. Ashtoreth is obsessed with personal power. She probably remembered the name from long ago, when she used to do magic, or at least was part of a group that did magic. The evil stuff is just part of the act, she's not really any more evil than you or I."

"Be careful, Rosamund," said Timothy. "If she believes she is evil, and if she does have any ability to do magic, it could spell trouble."

I brushed that notion aside, too caught up in my theory to listen. "The real clincher is that Ashtoreth has a whole different wardrobe of clothes, things I never saw Arabella wear, tunics and trousers and caftans and robes in outlandish patterns and colors. I'll bet they are what she wore before her marriage and that she's kept them. She has reached into her own past, trying to recover a time when she was healthier, and the clothes are a symbol of that. And so is the name!"

Timothy looked thoughtful. "All right. There are a few loose ends, but basically your theory hangs together. So, where is it all leading, and where do you fit in?"

It was my turn to be thoughtful. I stared out at the ocean, at water a heavenly shade of blue, touched by dancing points of brilliant sunlight. "I'm not sure yet where it's leading," I admitted. "But I am sure there are things going on secretly that involve both Ashtoreth and Regina, and I'm trying to find out what they are. I'm also sure that Regina is at the very least bad for Ashtoreth; at the worst, Regina herself is the evil one. Whatever that means. And where I fit in is, I have to get Regina *out!*" I realized we had been talking about this for a long time. I checked the angle of the sun and judged it to be late afternoon. "It's getting late. You've been a wonderful help. Thank you. We should go back now, don't you think?"

"Um-hm. In a minute." Timothy caught my chin in his hand and looked long into my eyes. "You're a rare person, Rosamund. One of a kind. Brave, smart, caring." The blue of his eyes deepened, his pupils dilated slightly. He rose up on his knees and clasped me to him.

He caught me off-guard and I had no time to untangle my crossed legs. My arms went around his narrow hips, I pressed my cheek against the warm skin of his lower abdomen. My affection for him flowered. He eased me up until I, too, knelt and he held me against him, thigh against thigh.

"Caring," he repeated. "Could you also care for me?"

"I do," I said, "I do care for you, Timothy."

He removed my sunglasses and kissed my eyelids, my cheeks. I heard the susurant lapping of the waves, felt the sun's heat. His lips found mine and opened them with a lover's kiss, a long, lingering exploration of lips and teeth and tongue that grew increasingly sensual. The kiss deepened when I thought it could not go deeper. I relaxed into him, I gave myself to him. Timothy was safe, and Charles was not. I let him know my need.

Timothy groaned. "Aaah, Rosamund!" He kissed me again, then pulled away. "Would you believe I have to stop?" His eyes shone, his cheeks were radiant. "Will you come to the rectory tonight? The housekeeper doesn't live in, she goes home after dinner. I'll have her cook enough for two. Will you come?"

"Yes, I will," I said.

* * *

I'd had the dream again. There was no longer any doubt, it was a recurring dream, one that had begun within the past two weeks. It was so very odd—no plot, no characters, just an image of fire on the water. Red on black, red flames leaping up out of black, glassy water. Incomprehensible. Water does not burn. It was more of a vision than a true dream, and yet it came to me in sleep. It carried with it some dire message I could not decipher, and I awoke from it each time feeling deep anxiety, terrible unease. At least this time I'd awakened in daylight—it was worse in the dark.

I turned on my side, away from the window and away from the clock. I didn't care what time it was. It was Tuesday, and I didn't have to get up. I wanted to go back to sleep. I closed my eyes and thought about Timothy. Dear, good Timothy. Pleasant memories. They would make better dreams if I could sleep again.

Dinner at the rectory. Sounded like the title of a one-act play, a very civilized sort of play. So it had been, a small, elegant dinner, with all the best touches of civilization: lace tablecloth, heavy silver, candlelight, Mozart. And Timothy was gentle, subtle—he courted me. A smile, a glance liquid with meaning, a feathery touch. I glowed softly in response to him. With Timothy there was not the hot blaze of passion Charles evoked; instead there was warmth, comfort, a feeling of safety.

It was a nice evening. Timothy was a nice person, and most of all, he was *safe*. I snuggled deeper into my bed and was soon asleep once more.

I sat behind the wheel of my Reliant wagon and looked at the building across the street. It was a gray Federal-style structure, with white trim and black shutters flanking tall windows on the ground floor. It looked old and new at the same time, a house turned into offices, or offices masquerading as a house. Neat black letters, discreet yet easy to read from a distance, spelled out CHARPENTIER BUILDING on the space between the middle and top floors. In Georgetown's small business district it had been easy to find; easy, too, to park directly across. Both seemed luxuries to me, not yet commonplace enough to be taken for granted.

Going inside, though, was not so easy. I'd had some idea

that if I introduced myself to Charles's secretary and talked with her face to face, she might favor me with more information than I'd been able to get on the phone. I mentally replayed my conversation with her a few hours earlier. As I'd expected, she'd said first that she would be glad to take a message for Mr. Charpentier, that he called in daily. Then she'd asked, "Is this an emergency?"

I'd wanted to shout into the phone, Hell, yes, it is! Your boss has gone off and left me stuck in the house with Regina the Cobra Woman, and I can't stand it much longer! Of course, I couldn't do that. Instead, I said that Charles had been gone a number of days now and I was concerned that if something did come up outside of office hours, I wouldn't be able to reach him. With sweet, Southern politeness she'd replied, "Mr. Charpentier's instructions are that any emergencies concerning his wife be referred to Dr. Barkstone. Mr. Charpentier cannot be reached directly. Thank you for calling." And with that, she'd cut me off.

I looked at the building again—it seemed a lot of space for one man's business to occupy. I was curious about this side of Charles's life, yet reluctant to intrude where I had no real right to be. Still undecided, I turned off the car's ignition and rolled down the window so that the heat wouldn't build up inside. The back of my neck pricked. I felt as if someone were watching me. Well, perhaps someone was, there was not necessarily anything wrong if people looked at you when you were parked on a street in the middle of town. I got out of the car and looked around. Just a scattering of people, both white and black, some alone and some in pairs, and none of them looking at me. My neck still pricked, and I respected that pricking. I snapped my head around sharply, to look directly behind me—and there was no one there.

I decided to walk two blocks back to where I'd seen a discount drugstore. The pricking had to be imagination this time. The exercise would calm my nerves, and I could buy a few things I needed. By the time I came back I'd have decided whether or not to confront Charles's sugary secretary. I set off, thinking that surely *she* could reach him directly. A man like Charles, obviously so used to making all his own decisions, wouldn't go anywhere he couldn't be reached. For one or two days, maybe, but not for two weeks.

I made my purchases and knew as I walked slowly back to the car that I wouldn't approach the secretary. She was sure to be in person just exactly like she was on the telephone, so polite and sweetly superior, and I'd be damned if I'd let her put me down. I'd be damned as well if I spent any more time wishing for Charles to come back—he would only take Regina's side anyway, he'd never believe what she was like when he wasn't around! I discerned the anger that had peppered my thoughts with *hells* and *damns,* and recognized the defensiveness behind them. The unfortunate truth was that I felt very much alone.

I opened the car door with one hand, the other holding the bag from the drugstore, and I slid into the seat. Then I froze. I gulped for air. There was a dead cat on the dashboard of my car. Its head lolled upside down over the edge of the dash, its sharp tiny teeth displayed in a rictus of death, its pink tongue hanging, its glazed green eyes staring forever.

I dropped the drugstore bag on the seat. My impulse was to run from the car, away from the dead thing. I fought the impulse. Not for a minute did I doubt that Regina had killed this cat and put it here. I wouldn't let her see how much this senseless killing frightened and revolted me! I scanned both sides of the street, looking for the old Volvo station wagon she drove when she went shopping, but I didn't see it. Well, maybe she had someone helping her, someone I didn't know and could never recognize. Didn't all evil queens have their henchmen? There was at least a grim satisfaction in knowing that the pricking of my neck had not been wrong. Regina or her someone had watched and waited for me to leave my car.

"Poor kitty," I said, conquering my revulsion. I picked up the body, cold and limp under its soft black-and-white fur. As I'd thought, the neck was broken. This had once been a pretty cat, not a stray. It would be missed, probably was already missed because it had been dead for some time, long enough that the rigor had come and gone. I put the cat on the floor on the passenger side and drove away.

The Charpentier beach was deserted, as almost always. I'd glanced often in the rearview mirror as I drove north from Georgetown, and I hadn't been followed. I waited after I'd parked, just to be sure. I wanted no nasty surprises in this isolated spot. When I was satisfied of my solitariness, I buried the cat. I dug its grave with my hands in a hollow between two sand dunes. Sea oats stood as markers, waving their golden heads in the steady sea breeze. I wished I could have done as much, or as little, for the two mourning doves. Then I sat for a while on top of the dune, thinking.

Burying the cat as decently as I could, making a small ritual to send it on to cat heaven or to its next reincarnation, had somehow turned revulsion into resolution. My fear was gone. I'd thought Regina was satisfied since Charles had told her she and Arabella would soon have their own house together, that her hostility was no more than simple dislike for me. Apparently, I'd been wrong. Otherwise, why would she try to frighten me off? I wished I knew what she had put into my orange juice—whatever it had been, fortunately, my body had refused to retain it, or I might have gotten very sick indeed. She couldn't do that again, because I no longer ate or drank anything unless it came straight from Jenny's hands or from my own small refrigerator. Now the dead cat. A warning or a threat? What would she do next? Maybe nothing. Charles would surely return soon, and she wouldn't dare try anything similar once he was again at home. If she wanted me to leave before his return, she was fresh out of luck!

Okay, next question. If she was trying to make life so unpleasant for me that I'd leave Charpentier, *why?* I'd have to go in a few weeks anyway, my job would be over. Gut-level instinct, nothing more, told me that she and Arabella were into something, and Regina didn't want me to find out what it was. But I was determined to find out, because whatever it was, I was sure it must be in my interests to know. Which meant, because my main concern was Arabella/Ashtoreth, that I could use Regina's secret against her secure position in the house and with Arabella. She couldn't make me sick, and she couldn't frighten me, not anymore. The only way she could get rid of me would be to kill me. Of course, not even Regina would do that.

My little voice said, She kills animals. Why not people?

I almost ran over George when I pulled into the garage. He was standing partially in my parking place, with his head under the open hood of the Volvo station wagon.

"Hi, George!" I said as I got out of my own wagon and locked the door behind me. "I hope the old station wagon didn't break down with Regina when she went out this morning."

"She ain't been nowheres. It just ain't runnin' right."

"Oh." So, she must have a helper and it wasn't George. I'd thought when I was learning my way around Charpentier that George was the gardener, and he was, but he was more than that. Anything that needed to be done outside the house, George did it. He was gardener, handyman, mechanic, all-around caretaker. He talked little and smiled less, but he was not an unpleasant person, just quiet. He seemed to mind his own business, and since my business kept me in the house most of the time, I knew him scarcely at all. I looked over his shoulder at the exposed workings of the motor. The landscape of the moon made more sense to me. "Well, whatever it is, I'm sure you can fix it."

"I reckon." He poked at something, then opened the door on the driver's side and got in and started the motor. He gunned it a couple of times and left it idling while he returned to his perusal under the hood.

I had a glimmer of an idea. Perhaps it was time to make friends with George. "Would it help you if I sat in the car and turned the motor on and off, or worked the accelerator, or something?"

He stood back and gave me a look that was part surprise and part suspicion. "You sure you want to do that?"

"I'm sure. I have time."

He seemed to ponder, as if whether or not to accept my help constituted a very big decision. Then he favored me with a faint smile. "Reckon it's all right. You gun the motor when I tells you."

I slid behind the wheel and followed his monosyllabic directions. I thought perhaps George was mentally slow. That might account for the fact that, though he was middle-aged, white, and not bad looking, he had never married. He lived alone in a cabin on the far side of the carraige house. It was at the very edge of the woods, at the tail end of the driveway.

My glimmer of an idea brightened. His cabin was far removed from the house, but it was close to the garages. If anyone took one of the cars out at night, George would hear, and if he looked he could probably see, too. He'd make an invaluable ally! I became impatient for him to finish, so that I could talk to him.

"Switch off!" he called out, and I did. After a minute or so, he said, "Now start 'er up."

I could hear the difference in the engine myself. The big old Volvo purred like a well-fed, aged tabby. "Whatever you did," I said appreciatively, "it certainly sounds much better."

"Plugs was wore out, and the timin' was off. Less let 'er run fer a bit," he said, pulling the open car door wider.

I took the hint and got out, automatically smoothing my skirt down over my thighs. "Can I talk to you for a minute, George?"

"I reckon so. It was kindly of you to help."

"You know I'm here to take care of Mrs. Charpentier."

He slowly nodded his head.

"Well, she's been going out late at night, with Regina, and they aren't supposed to do that. I know Regina drives, she takes this old station wagon when she goes out in the daytime to do errands. Have you ever seen her drive out at night?"

George's eyes, like his hair, were medium brown, and they were watchful. "I don't have no doin's with Regina. she goes her way, and I goes mine."

"I know. I do understand that you like to mind your own business. But you see, Miss Arabella is *my* business, and I only want to know if you've seen Regina take any of the cars out at night, maybe with Miss Arabella with her?" I could almost see his mind working slowly, steadily. Come on, I urged silently, tell me what you know! And aloud I said, "You can trust me, George. Anything you tell me will be our secret, just yours and mine."

"I seen her take this ole wagon out after dark sometimes."

214

He frowned in an effort to remember. "But she been by herself. Ain't seen nobody else, just Regina."

My hopes fell, but I persisted. "Was it early or late when you saw her?"

Another frown. "Early, I reckon. I like to set a spell on the porch early of an evenin'. Thass when I seen her."

It wasn't much help, but at least he was with me. I pushed on with a new idea. "You're the caretaker, and I know how Mr. Charles relies on you. Do you ever, ah, walk around the grounds at night, just to make sure everything's all right?"

Now he did smile, an ingenuous, slightly out-of-focus grin. "Oh, yes ma'am! Mr. Charles says thass important. I goes around at least once after dark, me an' my rifle that Mr. Charles taught me how to shoot. Then, if I hears anythin' funny-like, I goes again!"

Now we were getting somewhere! "You could help me so much, if you would, George. You know where Miss Arabella's patio is on the north side of the house?"

"Yes'm."

"Would you, just for the next few weeks, make an extra circle around the house kind of late at night, and keep an eye on that patio? And if you see Miss Arabella and Regina go out of the house by that door, would you watch where they go and tell me the next day? Please? It's really very important! And I'd, I'd pay you for the extra trouble."

George looked doubtful. "Mr. Charles pays me plenty already." He shook his head. "I don' know. I reckon I better think on it for a spell." He turned away from me and started to gather up his tools.

"Please do. It would be such a help to me," I said to his back. I was afraid I'd lost him. "Like I said before, if you help me it will be our secret." Reluctantly, I left the garages.

I wasn't even sure he'd heard my last words, but he had. I was at the semicircle of the driveway, where it curved toward the East Front, when I heard George's voice calling from behind me.

"Miz Rosamund!"

I smiled. So he did know my name after all! Since he hadn't used it, I'd wondered. I waited where I was, and he soon caught up.

"Miz Rosamund, I done thought on it. Mr. Charles, he don't know about, about watchin' Regina?"

My breath caught in my throat. Maybe I'd given too much away. If George was, as I suspected, mildly retarded, then he was probably fanatically loyal to Charles. After all, Charles had given him security, a good job, and a place to live. I felt in over my head, but I wouldn't back down now. "That's right. Charles doesn't know. This, ah, watching is something I'm doing on my own. Nobody knows except me, and now you."

"Thass what I thought. And if'n I sees Regina go out with Miss Arabella, and I tells you, you won't let nobody know George told you?"

"Nobody will know. I said it would be our secret. I promise, and I always keep my promises."

He came a step closer and peered earnestly into my face. "Aw right. Tell you the truth, I don' like Regina none. None ay-tall! But it don't do for folks to know, if'n you doesn't like Regina. I thinks it's all right for you to know, 'cause I thinks you don' like her none either."

I smiled again. "You're absolutely right, George."

He made the faint grin. "Reckon I'll do it, I'll help you, Miz Rosamund!" He grabbed my hand and pumped it vigorously. "George will go 'round late at night and watch like you said."

"Oh, thank you," I bubbled, overjoyed to have an ally. My back was to the house and I was unaware that we'd been seen shaking hands and marking an obvious agreement.

Chapter 14

I SAT UP IN BED, instantly awake, instantly alert. My feet reached cool, soft carpet as my mind told me I was once again alone in the North Wing. I dashed across my darkened room to the window, pulled back the curtain, and looked out. The sky was overcast, no moon and no stars to be seen. By straining my eyes I could make out shapes of small trees and bushes that were blacker than the black lawn, the bulging mass of woods that was darker than the dark sky—but no people-shapes. George, if he were out there, might have seen Regina and Ashtoreth leave the house, but I had missed them.

No matter. This was what I'd waited for. Wednesday night I'd kept myself up well past midnight, thinking it likely they'd go out again on a Wednesday. But they had not. Last night, Thursday, I'd fallen asleep in the chair, waiting. Tonight I'd gone resignedly to bed at the usual time. It was after midnight now. A quarter after, to be exact. On that terrible night of the sexual fiasco with Charles I'd been sleepless until dawn, and I'd heard movement downstairs around three A.M. That was when they'd returned. Tonight I would give myself until two. I didn't want to be caught snooping, which was what I was going to do.

I'd planned this out as well as I could under the nebulous circumstances. I put on my old, washed-out yellow robe and deliberately left my feet bare, for speed and for silence. I stuck my watch in my pocket and took the new flashlight. Plan B was now underway. Plan A was to get something damaging pinned on Regina, definite enough that Charles would be forced to recognize she must not be entrusted to live with his wife. Plan B was different.

I felt excited and scared and a little bit like a criminal as I passed swiftly and silently through the hall and down the stairs, to Ashtoreth/Arabella's seldom-used door. I kept my eyes on the circle of light cast by my flashlight, trained down at my feet. I opened the door and listened. Nothing. I slipped into the connecting passageway, checked the living room as before. It was easier with my light—I swept it around in a wide arc. The room was as empty as I'd expected it to be. I went into the bedroom and shone my light at the bed, which likewise revealed itself empty. I let out my breath in a sigh, I hadn't realized I was holding it.

Plan B: to search Ashtoreth's room in her absence, hoping to find the key to what drove her now, hoping to discover her secret purpose. In part, I was simply curious to know, and in part I thought her secrets might be outrageous enough that they could be interpreted as representing a danger to herself. She would be furious, of course, but I could endure her fury and her scorn and anything else as long as the end result would be the desirable sanatorium in North Carolina.

I checked the drapes at each window to be sure they would contain any light. That Ashtoreth had some plan of her own, I didn't doubt. She had been agitated for the last several days, but in her new personality it was not the diffuse, aimless agitation of Arabella. This agitation had an urgency about it. Her hands trembled as before, but now she verbalized her impatience. She waited, she said; she would not say for what. She had an oversized deck of cards that she would not let me close enough to see, and she played with them over and over, though the game had an ill effect on her. She would cry, "Aah, no!" and fling them down. Once she spat on them. She kept the cards in her desk.

Also in her desk she kept a black-bound book that she wrote in and pored over by the hour, forcing herself to be still though I could almost see the aura of her mad energy about her. She could no longer sit trancelike on her patio, she no longer had the patience. When I saw what an effort it cost her to be still, I suggested that we go for walks again, and she agreed. We'd walked miles in the last two days, every place there was here to walk, and always at Ashtoreth's insistence we ended by the river. There on the dock, seemingly only there, she could rest and be silent. The dark waters cast their spell over both of us, but for me it was the opposite of calming. The river seemed to reverse our roles, and I became the anxious, agitated one.

I pulled down the door of the ornate secretary-desk. Inside was a tensor lamp, folded up. I unfolded it, pulled its collapsing arm up to full height, and turned it on. It was small, but it shed a powerful, clear white light. I switched off my flashlight. Where to begin? With a sigh, I realized I made a lousy detective. My guilty sense of invading another's privacy was strong. I bit my lower lip and forced concentration. This was no time for scruples! I saw immediately that the black book was not here, it must be in one of the drawers below.

Resolutely I pulled papers out of the many tiny cubbyholes at the back of the desk's folded-down writing surface. These were ordinary things, and remarkable for that. Who would have thought that Ashtoreth/Arabella would save recipes on three-by-five cards? The seafood-okra gumbo I could understand, but New York cheesecake? There were ads cut from the pages of the Sunday *New York Times,* mostly from Saks Fifth Avenue, picturing long robes of the kind Arabella used to wear. A motley collection of newspaper clippings, some so old they were turning yellow. I riffled through them, and one caught my eye with its caption: "Magician Arrested." Garth the Great—one of her old friends?—had been arrested in Santa Barbara for performing "lewd acts" at a private party. Unfortunately there was no picture of Garth the Great. I hurried on. More recipes. A small pile of visiting cards, a sad reminder of days when she'd tried to keep up a social life. Three envelopes with no return addresses, all postmarked New Orleans, but no letters inside. I wondered why she'd kept them. Finally, several picture postcards, none with writing on them.

There was a panel, painted in an ornately scrolled design of red and gold, set in the center of all the cubbyholes. I suspected it might hide a secret compartment, and I ran my fingers over it experimentally. I had a sense of where to push, and I pushed. Inside was a small brass key, the old-fashioned kind. That was all. I pushed it closed again.

I angled the neck of the tensor lamp so that it shone over the edge of the desk, and I started on the bottom of the three drawers beneath. Here, apparently, were the kind of personal treasures that have value and meaning only to the person who collects them. More than ever I felt like an intruder. Theatrical programs. One white kid glove, over-the-elbow length. A torn piece of black veil with tiny little stars all over it. Old photographs. Invitations addressed to Mr. and Mrs. Charles Charpentier. I spent little time on this drawer. It was too ordinary, and too sad.

The middle drawer was entirely filled with something white and filmy, wrapped carefully in tissue paper which crinkled when I opened it. A chill went through me. Half knowing what it was, even as my small warning-voice said, No, don't touch it! my fingers lifted out the delicate thing. It was like holding a ghost in my hands: Arabella's wedding veil, ghastly white against the room's surrounding darkness. With outstretched arms I held it up by its headpiece, a circlet of waxy white orange blossoms, and the veil trailed on the floor, it crept over my bare feet and turned them cold, it whispered and moved in the airless room as if it were alive. I stifled a cry as I remembered what Charles had said, how her long veil had trailed over the graves. . . . I had to fight the thing to fold it again, it seemed to resist my trembling hands, and when at last I closed the tissue paper over it, I could have sworn the paper opened again of its own accord. I slapped the paper down and held it with one hand while with the other I closed the drawer, snatching my hand out at the last minute. The hand that had held the paper down was cold as death.

I looked at my watch and saw that an hour had passed, and so far I had learned only that there was, at least for me, something very peculiar about Arabella's wedding veil. I rubbed my cold hand to bring life back to the fingers and realized what a risk I'd taken by ignoring my warning voice. I might have had one of my strange visions, and if so I was sure it would have been terrible. I was glad that that, at least, hadn't happened.

In the top drawer was the black-bound book; another, older, book bound in red, the pages edged in now-tarnishing gold; and the oversized deck of cards turned face down. All I had ever seen of those cards was their backs, covered by a labyrinthine pattern of green, yellow, and dark bluish gray. As curious as I was, I did not expect to learn much if anything from the cards. First, then, the books. I took them out and put them on the writing surface of the desk, and left the cards in the drawer beneath.

I opened the red book, taking the older one first. The opening page was inscribed "Arabella's Book" in her large, spiky hand. There was a date in the bottom right-hand corner: 1965. Pre-Charles. This could be very interesting! I scanned quickly. This was a diary of Arabella's New Orleans years. I wished I had time to read it word-for-word. It reflected a chaotic mind, but an uncanny intelligence. She had a knack for making word-pictures: "D. smells of the swamp." "N. throws her oranges at the moon." There was seldom a complete thought, but the imagery of her seemingly random phrases was striking. Throughout she had a nineteenth-century habit of referring to other people only by their initials. My impression as I speed-read was that she had little understanding of these people, and less true caring for them. In a diary, even Arabella's diary, I would have expected some emotional depth, but there was none, and that in itself was revealing. The only emotion clearly and consistently expressed was anger.

The latter half of the book chronicalled a growing interest in the occult. Page after page was carefully inscribed with strange symbols. There were spells noted down in a symbolic shorthand meaningless to me. Then, surprisingly, came a coherent piece of narrative: "P. says I must guard my eyes, that my eyes have a power I do not understand. He is teaching me to use it. Like hypnosis, but not the same—when I do what he says, it's more like I'm the one hypnotized. I can't remember afterwards, but I feel so strong. I like the feeling, so I keep on doing what he says." And later, "I think P. is in love with me. I would like that because if he loved me then I could make him do what I want, instead of always having to do what he wants. I told him I knew he loved me, but he only laughed. He said he doesn't love me, just my eyes, and my learning how to use them. I hate him for laughing at me. When I've learned enough I'll leave him. Maybe I'll kill him first!"

More pages of jumbled phrases followed, seemingly written in anger, certainly with a great deal of energy. And then: *To call the creatures and bind them to your will.* This page was darker than the rest, from much handling. The spell, or whatever it was, was written mostly in symbols, with some words in a language I'd never seen or heard spoken. I stopped scanning and studied it. The "creatures" were represented by little stick figures such as a child makes for bird, dog, cat, and so on. Paired with each figure was a strange word. Perhaps the name or word used to call the creatures? With a pang, I remembered the mourning doves. "I made them come," she'd said, "I know how to do it. But I didn't kill them." Impossible! Mumbo jumbo, gobbledegook. But the mourning doves had been real. I pressed my fingertips to my temples, hard. I must keep my mind open, *open.*

Only a few pages remained in the red book, and I began to turn them quickly. I stopped. One word leapt off the page, it swam up through the clear white light and entered my eyes, then passed into my brain: *obsidian.* I felt faint, felt as if my soul were leaving my body and I went with it, out into the night, out onto the river where the water was black as night and slick as glass and round, round, round. . . . What does it mean? The need to know, to understand, beat inside of me like a trapped bird which punishes itself with its own beating wings.

Snap out of it! I ordered myself. Read! The answer may be in the book. I blinked hard, and the page came into focus though the black, spiky letters refused to sit still on their lines. "Stop that!" I said aloud, surprising myself, but it worked. The letters settled down, became words, and I read. "I have The Obsidian. It was always meant for me. P. still talks about the child. The child is gone—there is no place here for children. But The Obsidian is mine and I will keep it forever!"

My head swam again, and threatened to fly away. I closed the book without reading further. I got up from the desk and walked away, needing to move. But it was dark away from the focused rays of the tensor lamp, and I returned. Why, why should the word *obsidian* have such an effect on me? Was it, perhaps, a vestige of a former lifetime? I'd read recently about reincarnation, and the concept had made sense to me, unreligious though I'd always been. Obsidian. I mentally searched my vocabulary and came up with what I thought was the dictionary meaning of the word: black volcanic glass. That was why it seemed connected with the river, the river looked like black glass. Yet undeniably the word *obsidian* had a deeper meaning for me. At the moment I was ready to accept reincarnation for the single reason that it provided an explanation, it made sense of something that was senseless, something that filled me with anxiety.

I felt calmer. I looked at my watch. Only fifteen minutes remained of the time I'd allotted myself. Not enough time to get through the black book, to try would only be frustrating. In any event, I'd have to come back again the next time they went out. Tonight had raised more questions than answers. I replaced the books in the drawer, and saw the cards. There was enough time for me to satisfy my curiosity—I took the cards out of the drawer. I turned the pack over with a little sigh of satisfaction, and found it was just as I'd thought it would be. I'd read about these in my borrowed books, but there were never any pictures and I'd grown enormously curious, particularly when Ashtoreth would not show me the faces of these cards she played with right in front of me. They were Tarot cards.

My fingertips tingled as I touched them. They were beautifully made, not slick-surfaced like playing cards, but textured and elegant, printed in many colors, as detailed as fine paintings. There were so many! My heart leapt, I felt as if I held great wealth in my hands. The desk was too small to spread them out, so I took the tensor lamp with me and knelt on the carpet, lost in the mystery of the beautiful Tarot. Pentacles, Swords, Cups, and Wands. I spread them all around me. I fell in love with the Page of Swords—he was so handsome as he stood tall on the green, green mountain, his sword held high and fearless against the blue sky and the gathering clouds. The Three of Cups, three beautiful maidens in flowing robes of bright colors, dancing with their cups in upraised arms, full of joy. So happy, I felt so happy! The Wands I did not like so well, and I hurried through them and on to the best cards of all. I'd been saving them for last. They had such a funny name, the Major Ark . . . Arcana. I counted them out, twenty and the zero, to make twenty-one. The zero was the Fool, a silly, tattery young man, he was about to walk off a cliff, but his dog had more sense and was barking at him. Maybe his dog would save him. The Sun, I liked that; the Moon I liked even better but I couldn't understand why she frowned, and the watchtowers were kind of creepy. Ah, here was my favorite, the second card, the High Priestess. How grand she was, and how mysterious! She looked stern, but that was because she knew so many secrets she mustn't tell. I scarcely looked at the number one, the Magician, he seemed like nothing but a big boy playing tricks; but at the High Priestess I stared and stared.

I played with the cards until a little voice told me it was time to go, and I knew I must obey it. Sadly I gathered up the cards and put them away, put the little lamp away too, and closed up the big desk. I had a flashlight and I turned it on. The little voice said, Hurry! Hurry! and I ran.

Awareness ripped through me like a knife as soon as I was again in the hall, for on the other side of the door I heard voices. Regina and Ashtoreth had returned! But how? Surely it wasn't time. With a sinking feeling in my middle I realized there was a gap in my memory. One moment I'd been sitting at Ashtoreth's desk, and the next I was here in the hall hearing the opening of the french doors, and voices. I had to move! I took the stairs at a run, leaping soundlessly upward, glad I'd had the sense to be barefoot. At the top of the stairs my own door seemed an impossibly long distance away in the dark, nevertheless I switched off my flashlight. Regina could be anywhere by now, she was as quick and silent as a cat, and I couldn't draw her attention to myself. I sprinted through the darkness and found my door instinctively. I closed it behind me and groped for the wall switch, unable to stand the dark any longer. Now if she prowled my way, let her—I could say I'd had a bad dream. I *felt* as if I'd had a bad dream! My knees were like water, my heart pounded, my throat and mouth so dry I couldn't swallow.

I turned on the light in the bathroom, in the sitting room. I opened a cabinet to get at the refrigerator and poured a glass of orange juice with shaking hands. The juice healed my parched throat and tongue. I took my watch from my pocket and looked at it. It said five minutes past three. I didn't want to believe my eyes, but I knew in my gut the time was correct. I'd lost an hour, a whole hour! Even more than that, really—the last time I'd looked it had been a quarter of two, and I should have left Ashtoreth's room at two.

I went slowly back into my bedroom and sat in the very middle of my bed, in the safe place, with my knees tucked up under me. I felt strange, very strange. What had happened to that hour? I must remember, I must force myself to remember. The word, *obsidian,* came back to me—I'd read it in the red book, "Arabella's Book, 1965." Black, spiky writing: *Obsidian.* "I have The Obsidian," she'd written. Then I hadn't wanted to read anymore. I'd looked at the time, I'd put the books away, and then, and then. . . . Blank. A complete blank.

If I didn't remember, surely I'd go mad. But I didn't have a Charles to look after me, so I mustn't go mad. "Aunt Henry, help me," I whispered, "help me to remember!"

Slowly the memory came, and not easily. I had to wrench it out of myself piece by piece. It was the Tarot cards, I'd gotten lost in the Tarot cards. They were so pretty, I'd coveted them for so long. That was ridiculous. I'd merely been curious about them, for a few days, no more. But something in me disagreed. I was torn by conflicting urges, the urge to know and the need to keep hidden, hidden and safe. The battle inside me was so strong it produced physical pain. I doubled over with the pain, and once again I called on Aunt Henry who had always been strength to me. The pain went away, the urge to know won out.

Dimly but with growing conviction I understood that I had recovered a piece of my early childhood, a piece from those years I had blotted out from the greater balance of my life. Rosamund the little child had wanted the Tarot cards, had loved them for their pretty pictures without knowing anything of their meaning. But someone . . . Mama? Yes. Mama had forbidden them, they were not to play with, and she had taken them away forever. Until tonight. Tonight Rosamund the adult had found the beautiful cards. Rosamund the adult had been linked by the Tarot to Rosamund the forgotten child, and my subconscious mind, which had so long protected me from the early memories, had buried the whole hour because of the link from present to past.

Now I'd forced open the door, now I could recall clearly how I'd played tonight with the cards, recognized them joyfully, picked out my favorites. I could not have done that without reliving the past, my own past.

I realized this was a breakthrough. My medically and psychologically trained mind asserted itself and told me that from now on, in the presence of proper stimuli, other such memories might come. But I felt no victory, only exhaustion. I toppled over, curled into a ball in the middle of my bed, and fell instantly into a deep, dreamless sleep.

It was Sunday when I realized I hadn't seen George, and I wanted to know if he'd been watching when Regina and Ashtoreth had left the house on Friday night. Most likely he hadn't, or he would have come and told me, but on the chance he'd seen them and noted what direction they took I went looking for him after supper. First I circled the house, but he was not on the grounds, although, because of the drought, he often watered the bushes and flowerbeds in the early evening. I looked in the garages. The old Volvo station wagon was gone, and of course Charles's newer silver-gray Volvo sedan was gone, too. My Reliant looked a little lonely. I wondered who could have taken the old station wagon. Not George, he had a truck that was usually parked under a lean-to next to his cabin. Regina must have gone somewhere. I'd thought she was with Ashtoreth, but I must have been mistaken.

I walked on down the gravel track that was the vestigial end of the driveway, past the carriage house to George's cabin. His truck, clean as a well-scrubbed baby, was under the lean-to. I went up the two steps onto the narrow porch and noted the rocking chair, where George liked to "set a spell early of an evenin'." But not this evening. The door was wide open but the screen was closed. I knocked on its wood frame and called his name. Twice. A third time, more loudly. This cabin was what they called a shotgun, one room built directly behind another so that a shotgun could be fired straight through from front to back—though why anyone might want to do such a thing I couldn't imagine. I could see all the way to the back door, which was also open. Clearly George was not at home.

I might as well go back. I'd walked a few feet down the gravel driveway when I had to stop. Something felt wrong. I didn't like it. I turned around and retraced my steps, but this time I went to the cabin's back door. I shielded my eyes with one hand and put my nose to the screen so that I could see into the darker interior. "George?" Silence. No, it didn't feel right at all. I opened the door and went into the kitchen. Everything was very tidy. Not so in the bedroom, where the bed was unmade, the pillow fallen on the floor, and the bedclothes looked as if George had tangled with them in the throes of a nightmare. The contrast between the violently twisted sheets and bedspread and the compulsively neat little kitchen was jarring to my nerves. I moved on to the living room, which had a small brick fireplace, an oval braided rug in the center of the floor, a Naugahyde sofa, and another rocking chair that faced a portable TV with a rabbit-ear antenna. Everything here was as neat and clean as the kitchen, even the bricks of the fireplace and its iron grate were scrubbed clean. There was a gun-rack over the fireplace, a prominent place of honor for the rifle Charles had given George and taught him how to shoot. But the rifle was not in the gun-rack.

George could be out taking a turn around the grounds with his rifle, that was the most reasonable explanation for his absence. I wanted to believe that. I wanted to ignore the way his bedroom pulled at me, as if it were a magnet and my shoe soles made of iron filings. I was no virgin voyeur, to be attracted by the sight of a man's unmade bed, the evidence of his violent dreams. Why should I want to go back in there? I went out on the porch instead, to wait.

I sat in the old, weathered rocking chair and rocked back and forth. The motion helped to soothe my growing anxiety. I forced optimistic thoughts. I made up a fantasy in which George had a girlfriend, and he had taken the station wagon to go on a date with her because it was more comfortable than the truck. But why take his rifle on a date? All right then, another scenario: George was out on his rounds with his rifle, and Regina had the station wagon for purposes of her own—and I was in the ideal spot to observe her bringing it back. I rocked and thought, rocked and thought, and every time my mind touched the anomaly of the unmade bed in a cabin that reeked of neatness, I refused to consider it. When I ran out of ideas, I simply rocked and watched the night fall.

Lulled by my own rocking motions, I passed into a state somewhere between consciousness and unconsciousness. I saw the old Volvo wagon back out of the garage. Regina was driving, and George was in the front seat with her. She was taking him somewhere, and George didn't want to go. George was scared, he was scared of Regina, and she had his rifle jammed into the space between the driver's seat and the car door. . . .

"No! No! Come back, you must come back!" I cried, and I ran after the car, wanting to go faster than my feet could carry me, so that I tripped on the rough gravel and fell on my hands and knees. The pain of scraped skin brought me to myself and I stood up, automatically brushing away the clinging bits of gravel. I had chased a car that wasn't there.

Three or four months ago if I'd done such a thing I would have regarded it as further evidence that I was cracking up. Now I thought it likely that I had somehow rocked myself into a glimpse of what had really happened to George. I had no idea how long I'd waited on the cabin porch—time lost its meaning for me in these situations. But regardless of the time, I felt certain that we would never see George or the old Volvo again. The night was pitch black dark around me, none of the outside lights were on. Most likely that was because George wasn't here to turn them on. I walked slowly and carefully back to the house. I didn't want to fall again.

I surprised Jenny the next morning.

"Miss Rosamund, what's you doin' up so early on yore day off?"

"I couldn't sleep," I replied truthfully. "Jenny, when did you last see George?"

"Well, now, let me think." She was making biscuits and she was so good at it she didn't even look as she slapped more flour into the dough. "Was Satiddy." She paused. "I knows why you askin', Miss Rosamund."

"You know where he is?" It was only the question I knew she expected me to ask, I felt none of the hope it might have implied.

Jenny set her usually smiling lips into a grim line. "George has done run off. I never did trust no closemouthed white man," she grumbled. "He's gone up to no good, and that's a fact. Stole Mr. Charles's old station wagon, too. Went off with his rifle an' stole the car. He ain't quite right in the head, you know."

"I don't think George would do that. If he had to go somewhere, he'd take his truck. He had no reason to steal the car, and besides, he was devoted to Charles."

"Well, he's gone. And the station wagon's gone too, and them's the facts." Her voice was just a shade too loud.

"Who told you about this?" I asked.

"Regina. Soon's I got here this morning. And what I want to know is, how'm I supposed to cook with no car to get the groceries? Monday's the shopping day, we be low on everything."

I'd never heard Jenny so ill-tempered. It was almost as if she protested too much. It was out of character for her, and I guessed she was trying to cover up her real feelings. I tried to be reassuring. "Don't worry, Jenny. You make your list and I'll go to the store for you. And I'll call Charles's secretary as soon as their office opens and ask her to get a message to him. I don't suppose Regina can drive the truck?"

"No, I don't suppose she can. Leastways she shore didn't offer to try."

"Well, I'll tell the secretary we have a sort of a crisis here. Although"—I studied Jenny closely, alert to her slightest reaction—"I suppose George could come back any time."

She slapped the biscuit dough hard. There was tension in every line of her thin, wiry body. With the beating that dough was taking, her biscuits weren't going to be as light as usual this morning. "No ma'am, he won't be comin' back. I feels it in my bones." She looked at me now with troubled

229

dark eyes. "Miss Rosamund, I'd be obliged if you was to go to the store. But don't you go callin' Mr. Charles. That's for Regina to do, and it's for Regina to get somebody else to look after the yard and all till Mr. Charles comes back and can handle it hisself. Regina won't like it if you was to call."

"You're right, Jenny. I should have thought of that myself." I slipped down from the counter-height stool where I'd been perched. "I'll just take some juice and coffee and go on into the breakfast room. I want some of those biscuits when they're done." That won me a smile.

I sat at the round table in the bow window and faced an unprovable truth: Regina had somehow gotten rid of George. What I'd seen last night had in fact happened. She had taken him in the station wagon because she couldn't drive the truck, and then she'd had to abandon it so that it would appear he'd stolen it. Where she'd done this, and how she'd gotten back here, I couldn't guess. Surely, please God, she hadn't hurt George. Just frightened him away somehow. George was simpleminded, it wouldn't be hard to scare him. I looked out the window at the lush green grass where earlier daffodils had bloomed, the grass that had flourished under George's care.

It was my fault. I had to face my responsibility squarely. Regina had seen me with George, I was sure of it. She'd seen us shaking hands and smiling, and she hadn't liked it. She must have forced the truth out of him, then made him go away. So she knew, she knew that I watched her and had gone so far as to enlist his help.

I shifted uneasily, sipped more coffee. Well, how bad was that? I lifted my chin even as I bit my lower lip to keep it from trembling. George had agreed to help me, and now George was gone, but that didn't change what I had to do. Nothing would change what I had to do.

My small voice whispered, Regina is evil, evil.

I drained my coffee cup, gazed out of the window, seeing nothing, and at last asked myself the inevitable question: What if Regina had killed George? What if she had shot him with his own rifle?

Chapter 15

I ANSWERED THE TELEPHONE in my room. "Hello?"

"Hi, Rosamund. It's Timothy."

"Hi, Timothy." I felt a twinge of guilt. I hadn't thought of him in days. How could I do that, when he'd been so good to me?

"Don't tell me you've forgotten?"

"I, ah, I guess I have. I don't know what you're talking about."

There was a note of exasperation in his well-bred voice. "The ghost-hunting house party at Leighton. It's tonight! You said you'd come, Lynda planned the whole thing for a Monday just so you could stay overnight and not have to go to work the next day. You're practically the guest of honor, and you *forgot?*"

"I assumed the ghost was supposed to be the guest of honor," I said drily. I was a bit short on patience myself. "Keep your feathers on, Tim. I wouldn't have forgotten. It's just that in working my way through what I have to do today, I didn't get to the evening yet. There's some pretty heavy stuff going on here."

"Business as usual at Charpentier. Is this current heavy stuff anything you can talk about over the phone?"

"Yes," I sighed, "it's no secret. George, the caretaker, has disappeared, along with his rifle and the old station wagon. He seems to have been gone since sometime Saturday. And of course Charles has been away for two weeks, and only his secretary knows how to reach him. My car is the only transportation we have right now, and it seems to be up to Regina to straighten all this out. . . ." My voice quit on me. I strangled on the thought of Regina in charge. But Jenny had been right, the running of the household was Regina's domain, and in Charles's absence the decisions were hers.

"Good Lord! Are *you* all right, Rosamund?"

"Oh, sure. I'm fine. Just worried about George, and frustrated that I can't talk to Charles, and mad because it's my day off but I can't get out of here and leave everybody stranded without a car."

"You know, I think that's exactly what you should do— get out of there. What about the others who work in the house? They must have some form of transportation."

"Jenny, the cook, her husband brings her and picks her up. I don't really know how Phyllis gets here. The LPN who's here today probably has her own car, but that's different. We can't ask her to help, she has to stay with Ashtoreth. So I can't leave. I have to go to the grocery store pretty soon, for Jenny."

There was the silence of Timothy thinking. Then he said, "Somebody should tell the police about this."

"I know. That's what I've been thinking, too. Somebody should, but not me. It would definitely not be a good idea for me to do it."

"I'll do it, then."

"No! Don't interfere, Timothy. Believe me, you mustn't interfere!"

Timothy, most uncharacteristically, was losing his temper. "Rosamund Hill, you can be the most impossible woman! Stubborn, strong-willed—"

I interrupted him. "Now maybe you can understand why a party to look for a ghost wasn't the foremost thing on my mind this morning."

"Yeah," he said grudgingly, "I see."

I placated. "I really am looking forward to the party, and I promise I'll be there. I know it will be good for me to get out of here for a while. We're supposed to arrive at six-thirty, aren't we?"

"I'll pick you up at six-fifteen. No arguments, please. Oh, I almost forgot. Lynda said to tell you to wear slacks and a long-sleeved blouse. Because of the mosquitos—we'll be outside most of the night."

"All right. I'll be ready at six-fifteen. Thanks so much for calling." I hung up the telephone. Damn! I actually had forgotten the house party. It seemed so frivolous, such a waste of time to sit around all night looking for a ghost that probably never existed in the first place. Wear slacks? I didn't own anything with long legs to it except jeans. Not even designer jeans, but the old, bum-around-the-house kind. In a thoroughly bad mood, I stamped down to the kitchen for Jenny's shopping list.

Fortunately the day did improve. For one thing, around noon Phyllis popped into the library where I was reading, and told me a man from Charles's office had brought out a rental car. I felt better immediately. Less isolated. As if, wherever he might be, Charles at least did care enough to provide us with a car when we needed it.

Not us, you idiot! I corrected myself, Regina—he provided Regina with a car. But I felt better anyway. I wouldn't let myself think about George, but I would surely talk to Charles about George. Charles would have to come back eventually. I didn't for a minute think that Regina would report George's disappearance or the "stolen" car to the police, but Charles would do it. Perhaps he had already done it by telephone from wherever he was. That thought cheered me further.

What most improved my day, though, was that I decided to make an occasion out of Louis and Lynda's ghost-hunting party. After all, it was something I'd never do again, a once-in-a-lifetime thing. Real Twilight-Zone stuff. I found the story of Leighton's ghost in the Charpentier library. It was both sweet and sad, and I wondered if the story itself could be true, ghost or no ghost. It seemed that back in the days before the War Between the States, Mama and Papa Leighton had a beautiful only daughter named Alice. Alice was particularly high-spirited and independent for the times, and her father indulged her, allowing her to do such inappropriate things as ride a horse astride and without a chaperone. But Alice turned sixteen and suddenly she was a young lady, and she had to act like one, which meant she had to give those things up. She lost her freedom. She had to wear corsets and hoop skirts and petticoats, and stay at home with her mother and her embroidery. Alice, in secret, rebelled. She fell in love with the handsome white overseer of one of the neighboring plantations. He was not her equal in social status or education, and her father would not permit the match. He confined Alice to the grounds of Leighton, he took away her horse, and even had the oars removed from all the boats and kept under lock and key.

Alice, pining for her lover, decided to run away on foot. The handsome overseer later said he had respected Papa Leighton's wishes, that he had no idea Alice was going to run away and certainly not with him! Nevertheless, Alice chose the night of a grand dinner party for her rash action. While the men were in the dining room over brandy and cigars, Alice, in her party dress with its many yards of petticoats and hoop skirt, slipped away from the ladies. She ran down the lawn toward the river, intending to walk along its banks to the neighboring plantation where she could join her overseer. In the dark she became confused, lost the riverbank, and wandered into the rice fields. She tripped and, trapped by the weight of her wet petticoats, she could not free herself, and she drowned. Her ghost, identifiable by its luminous beauty and the huge skirts of her dress, had been seen crossing the lawn and walking along the riverbank, and in the rice fields near the place where her body was found.

I felt sorry for poor Alice. If she really was a ghost, at least she had not been, before her death, as embittered and crazed by loneliness as the woman in Murrell's Inlet. Did I believe in ghosts? I wasn't sure, if by ghost is meant a spirit who after death stays bound to a particular place, a spirit who can at times be seen by living people. I was, though, able to believe that exceptionally strong emotions can leave an imprint on a place, and on the buildings and objects in that place. Maybe someday there would be a scientific explanation for it, of the E equals MC squared variety. Emotions produce energy, the energy locks onto the matter already present in the place where the emotions occurred. And years later, someone like me comes along and "reads" the still-present emotions. The primitive child in me was as scared of the concept of ghosts as the next person. I'd never actually seen one and I didn't think I wanted to. But I was growing more comfortable with my ability to feel the old emotions in places and things. Yes, this so-called ghost hunt could be interesting, even exciting. I just needed to throw myself into the spirit of it! I smiled at my own unintentional pun.

Such an occasion demanded more elegance than jeans, out of self-respect if nothing else. Also, to be honest, there was the good old American spirit of competition. I wasn't in love with Timothy but if I'd had better sense I would have been, and I didn't want Lynda to completely outshine me. So I went shopping yet again, this time at a boutique closer to home.

Dressing to go out, I realized that all my carefully built-up anticipation was working. I felt good, and I looked good, and I was ready to have a good time. I braided my hair in two braids which I coiled over my ears, like the princess in *Star Wars*. My new slacks were jade green rayon, and the tailored blouse was the same color but of a thin rayon georgette. Under it I wore a flesh-colored camisole, subtly cheating the see-through effect. No earrings, a simple gold chain around my neck. I liked the look. I especially liked the way the jade green turned my eyes from blue-gray to aquamarine.

I'd never been to a house party, staying overnight on purpose with a bunch of adults. I put my best nightgown and my pink robe and slippers into the Mexican bag, hairbrush and toothbrush too. I supposed that was enough.

I was able to really mean it when I said, on getting into Timothy's car, "I'm looking forward to this party!"

"Good," he smiled, "That's the spirit, if you'll pardon the pun."

"You're pardoned. I caught myself thinking the same thing a couple of hours ago." I appreciated my companion's handsomeness. He wore a safari-type shirt, with a lot of flaps and pockets and tabs like epaulets on the shoulders, and trousers to match. And a Gucci belt. His loafers were probably Guccis too, knowing him.

"I was worried about you. I'm glad to see you looking so well." There was a note of intimacy in his voice. He took my hand and kissed it while he kept his eyes on the road.

"Don't worry. I'm tough. Or," I amended, "at least I bounce back quickly. I don't want to think about any of those things tonight. This is a special occasion. Who's coming, do you know?"

"It will be a small group. The house, although it's an architectural gem, is really quite small. Only four bedrooms. So Lynda planned on eight people. One other couple, Fred and Winnie Mandell. He's a doctor, ob-gyn, I think, and Winnie and Lynda were at school together. Everett Billings, he's the arts-and-leisure editor of the local paper, invited for mercenary reasons. Lynda likes him, but I don't. Charles was to have been the eighth, but since he's still out of town Lynda may have invited someone else in his place."

I hadn't seen Leighton, but I had seen pictures before Lynda's work on the place. There was an oak alley, small but in perfect proportion to the size of the house. The house itself was dazzling in a fresh coat of white paint. The architecture was impressive, pure Georgian, a three-story square with the graceful arches of Palladian windows repeated across the facade. The main entrance was on the middle level, and was reached by a curving horseshoe of wide steps. Rather than the usual pillared porch, the house was surrounded on all four sides by a broad terrace. I knew that a great deal of Louis and Lynda's work had been in the restoration of the terrace, which had been torn down by an owner who had wanted porches and pillars like everybody else. Lynda had insisted on removing the porches and rebuilding the terrace, and thus had restored the building's harmonious balance of a square within a larger square. I thought it anything but what Timothy had said, a "small house." The rooms inside must be huge if there were few of them.

"This is perfectly lovely," I said.

"Yes, it is," Timothy's expression as he gazed on the house was one of rapt satisfaction. "Lynda is doing a magnificent job. Of course, the inside isn't finished yet. She'll love showing you around. Come on, let's go in."

I retrieved my Mexican bag from the backseat, and I noticed Timothy's hands were empty. "Where's your overnight stuff? I thought we were all supposed to stay."

He grinned, showing the dimple in his cheek, and pulled a toothbrush out of his back pocket. "I travel light."

I laughed at him. "Yes, I see you do."

Lynda had come out and waited at the top of the stairs. "Come on, slowpokes, everybody else is here!" As we joined her, she kissed me affectionately on the cheek, as if we were old friends. "I thought I never would get you over here, Rosamund. I'm so glad you came."

"So am I. This is lovely, truly lovely!"

Her laugh was like silver chimes. All the sparkle I recalled was still there, in her lively brown eyes, the piquant tilt of her chin as she turned her attention to Timothy. Her hair was different, shorter, in a sleek dark brown cap that emphasized the perfect shape of her small head. She looked like a sophisticated pixie. She managed to flirt with Timothy and make me feel welcome simultaneously, as she eased us through the door.

"Everybody's on the terrace out back. You go on out there, Timothy honey, while I show Rosamund where to put her things."

"I noticed you said 'out back,' " I said as we climbed an elegant circular staircase. "They've so brainwashed me at Charpentier to say 'East Front' and 'West Front' that I've almost forgotten where 'back' is!"

"Well," Lynda confided, "I'm just an ignorant girl from the Pee Dee, and over there everybody knows your front yard is the one by the road, and the back yard is the one you sit on so you can fish in the river. I'll tell you a secret," she lowered her voice to a mock whisper. "I'm not really all the way civilized!" She laughed her silvery laugh at herself.

On the second-floor landing I looked up at the ceiling, which curved in a shallow dome over the circular stairway. "The proportions of this house are breathtaking. It's perfection," I said in awe.

"Yes, they really are. That dome isn't done yet. Would

you believe there's a waiting list for craftsmen who do ornamental plasterwork? I expect it will be after Christmas before we can get somebody here. Now," she urged me along, "up here we have four bedrooms. They aren't finished yet either, but I'm gaining on it. At least they're inhabitable. You'll have a room all to yourself, since you're the only single female. When I thought Charles was coming I had you sharing with Winnie, and Timothy sharing with her husband Fred, but now I've put Winnie with Fred and Timmy with Everett, so you'll be by yourself. Unless, of course," she winked, "my dear old friend Timothy decides to sneak in and keep you company!"

I grinned. "He won't."

"Well, here's the room." She opened the door.

The furnishings were sparse, two pencil-post three-quarter size beds with the reddish brown glow of cherry wood, a nightstand between them, and a huge armoire in the same wood that was one of the most gorgeous pieces of furniture I'd ever seen. The room was very large, the ceilings at least fourteen feet high, and there were four Palladian windows, two on the front and two at the side. As it seemed with everything in this house, the perfection of the space itself most impressed me. I said, "This room is another perfect square."

"Uh-huh. All four bedrooms are exactly like this one, and they're all perfect squares. Exactly the right amount of space was added for the hall and stairwell so that the whole house is a perfect square too, and of course that meant I had to do some fancy mathematics for the terrace!" She wrinkled her nose. "It raises hell trying to add bathrooms!"

I shared her laughter. She was warm, friendly, and easy to like. Her skin was tanned to a deep gold, and she wore a striking jumpsuit in the palest ice blue, with fullness in the long sleeves and in the pants caught up by tight bands at the wrists and ankles. If I'd worn jeans, I'd have felt like a scarecrow next to her. I took my robe out of the bag and hung it in the armoire so that it wouldn't wrinkle. "Shall we go down?" I asked.

"Yes, let's." Lynda linked arms with me and we started down the stairs. Her head came just a little above my shoulder. "You know, Rosamund, my old friend Timmy is really quite taken with you. Too bad Charles couldn't come. Now just suppose, priest or no priest, Timmy ended up overnight in the same room with you—Charles would have a fit. That would be something to see. He'd be mad as a hornet!''

"You're right, he would." We looked at each other and both burst out laughing. She apparently understood her brother-in-law better than I could have guessed. What a relief it was to laugh with someone about it! We were still giggling when we joined the others on the terrace.

I couldn't understand why Timothy didn't like Everett Billings. He was an elegant, silver-haired man, probably close to sixty, with a beautiful voice and impeccable manners. There was nothing of the stereotyped snob about him. I found him a delight to talk to.

Winnie was small, like Lynda. But unlike Lynda she was blonde and so fair that her skin had a translucent quality. Fred was a little too hearty for me and he wanted to talk doctor-talk. I played at it with him long enough to be polite and then moved on. Louis was as I remembered, a softer version of his brother. I wandered over and joined him at the edge of the terrace, watching the blood red sun set across the river.

"We have a bit of trouble at Charpentier," I said.

"Yeah. I heard at the office." He looked at me and saw my surprise. "You didn't know I work there, too?"

"No," I confessed, "I didn't."

"My brother still pretends I'm not there, so how could you know." Louis downed a sizable part of his gin and tonic, obviously dealing with a sore subject. "Charles has a memory like an elephant, but an elephant could be more forgiving. I'm ten years younger than he is, and it'll probably take ten years for me to prove to him I'm not the hell-raising gambler I used to be in my misspent youth. I'm with the Charpentier Company on probation. Been on probation for three years now. Anyway, I heard about George running off with the station wagon. You all get the rental car all right?"

"Yes, we did. But I'd feel a whole lot better if Charles would come back. Do you know where he is, Louis?"

"No. He does this every now and again, least he used to until maybe a year or two ago when things got so bad with

Arabella he felt like he couldn't leave. I expect he's got a woman somewhere he goes to. Begging your pardon, Rosamund, I didn't mean to be crude."

"That's all right, Louis." My burning cheeks told me the color had risen in my face, but the air itself was reddened now as the sun sank with its last rays in a scarlet corona behind the trees on the far side of the Waccamaw. "I daresay there is probably nothing you could tell me about Charles that would shock or even surprise me." I heard and regretted the bitterness in my voice.

Louis heard it too. "Come on, Rose." He placed a soft, affectionate arm around my shoulders. "Let's have one last drink before Lynda gets dinner on the table."

My admiration for Lynda rose even higher as I saw the feast she had set out on the buffet in the dining room. We served ourselves and then followed Lynda's casual directions to sit anywhere we liked at the dinner table. Timothy sat next to me. "I know it's impolite to ask," I said under my breath to him, "but do you think Lynda cooked all this herself?"

"I'm sure she did. She does everything herself. They don't have any help. Lynda says they can't afford it."

I was amazed. The grisly truth was that I knew how to cut up a dead person, but not a chicken. My cooking ability was limited to boiling eggs and frozen things that came in boxes with good directions. On the buffet were a huge glass bowl filled with crushed ice and a mountain of shrimp; a chili-horseradish sauce for the shrimp; a platter of chicken quarters, broiled and rubbed with lemon-tarragon butter; a casserole of wild rice and mushrooms; a tossed salad of Bibb lettuce with cucumber cubes and thin rings of purple Spanish onion; two kinds of rolls; and the dessert at the other end of the buffet, in a matching glass bowl, was that delightful Southern concoction called ambrosia—oranges and pineapple and cherries and coconut folded into whipped cream.

I ate contemplatively, savoring every mouthful. I could see how Charles maintained his lifestyle, he had servants. But here were Louis and Lynda, and Lynda did it alone. The compromises, like serving ourselves from the buffet, were comfortable. She was at ease in this museum of a house; when she said, "our house this-or-that," it was without pretension. She'd joked about having no bathrooms on the second floor and said she just might solve the problem permanently with antique chamberpots under the beds, and I could believe she'd do it and get away with it. She had the style, the flair, to make something like that acceptable; and further, she meant it when she said she'd rather empty chamberpots than spoil the proportions of the rooms.

"You're mighty quiet," Timothy commented.

"Um-hm. I was thinking about Lynda and Louis, and what they have here. It's so . . . different. The best of the old and the best of the new, and it's Lynda's style that holds it all together. Yet she couldn't be much older than I am. I feel sort of humble. She's incredible, isn't she?"

"Yes, she is," said Timothy wistfully, looking across the tops of the candles to Lynda at the end of the table. He looked back at me and smiled, the corners of his eyes crinkling. "But then, so are you. Lynda gets things done. She forges ahead, she makes mistakes and runs right over them and leaves them behind. You're more sensitive, more vulnerable, a thousand times more attuned to other people than Lynda could ever be. Lynda likes people, she enjoys people, and she uses them. She lacks your compassion."

"I think I'd trade my compassion for being able to cook like this," I sighed.

"Don't you dare," he whispered in my ear. "I can always hire a cook. But what you have can't be bought!" His lips touched my earlobe, a feather of a kiss, and I blushed. I hadn't thought Timothy would do something like that in front of other people.

At that moment Lynda stood up. "Okay, everybody, before I bring out the coffee, I want to remind you all that this is a serious business tonight. I've fed you, now I expect some work out of you. I know you're all amateurs, with the exception of Rosamund who qualifies as our resident-for-one-night psychic."

I blushed again as all eyes turned to me. "I think the reports of my psychicness are probably exaggerated."

Lynda's eyes twinkled. "No chance! I got the word from Timothy, and priests can't lie. Or exaggerate. Anyway, I expect all of you know the story of Alice Leighton?" There were nods around the table. "Good. I'm hoping that the festive air of our dinner party, with the house all lit up, the terrace restored and so on, will set the scene to bring her back tonight. After we've had coffee, we'll move outside and break up in two and threes. Louis had the grounds sprayed today, so hopefully the mosquitos won't eat us alive. I've got blankets and sand chairs to sit on and thermoses for whatever you want to take with you to drink, and flashlights. There's a full moon, but take the flashlights in case it goes behind a cloud or something. Have fun, but be sure you stay sober enough to recognize a ghost if you see one. You hear, Louis?'' Louis beamed at his wife, his love for her touchingly written all over his face. She winked at him. ''We'll watch until past midnight, longer if anyone is so inclined. After that, we'll play it by ear. The only rule is, nobody watches alone. If you see a ghost, you want to have a witness. Now please pass around the wine—I'm going to propose a toast.''

The wine bottle came around and I passed it on to Timothy. He looked questioningly at me and I took my water glass in hand to show him that I wasn't drinking. I hadn't been all night, but no one had noticed.

''To Alice Leighton!'' Lynda's clear voice rang.

''To Alice Leighton!'' we echoed.

''I'm glad you're taking this seriously,'' Timothy said, ''but I feel funny about drinking alone.''

''Don't. I've quit for a while. It's not just tonight, it's everything, the whole situation. I seem to be getting more and more sensitive, and I feel the need to have a clear head. I don't tolerate alcohol very well anyway, one drink clouds my judgment.''

We were walking rapidly across the lawn because Timothy insisted he didn't want Everett Billings watching with us. I stopped. ''This is no good, Timothy. I can't rush like this. If you really want me to do this right, I have to walk around by myself and get a feel for the place. That's more important than running away from Billings! I don't see what you've got against the man.''

Timothy shifted his burden of blanket and thermos. I had the flashlight and some paper cups. We'd compromised on the drinks and had a thermos of lemonade, and he had a flask of vodka to add to his. By the light of the full moon I saw the expression of discomfort on his face at the mention of Billings. "I just want to be alone with you, that's all," he said.

"Most likely we will be. You were pretty obvious about steering me out as soon as he started to come our way. Let's forget about him. I want to try to feel out a good watching-place for us."

"You go ahead—I'll follow. You won't even know I'm there. This is going to be interesting."

I smiled up at him for a moment, then I turned away. He was right, it would be interesting *if* I felt anything. I looked back at the house. The dining room windows glowed golden with candlelight. Lynda had turned off the electric lights for authenticity. It must look much the same, I thought, as the night Alice ran away. She would have come down those steps, out onto the lawn. . . . No, not in the middle but to the side, in the shadows where she was less likely to be seen. But to which side? Which direction would she go when she reached the river, north or south? I turned back to Timothy. "What plantation was the overseer's?"

"I'm sorry, I don't know."

Well, I'd try south. I concentrated, wanting to feel like Alice Leighton, wanting to blend into the tall bushes at the edge of the lawn. I walked fast and faster, shutting out the twentieth century, feeling the night, feeling the moonlight, and I was running. I ran into a cold wall of fear. The sensation was so strong it was like having the breath knocked out of me. Then it vanished. I stopped in my tracks and looked around me. The tall bushes were no longer on my left, the lawn was all behind me. I stood on the bank of the river, maybe a yard from the edge. I backed a few steps, and turned around.

Timothy stood a couple of feet away, watching me. The moonlight turned his fair hair to silver. "I thought you were going to run straight into the river."

I shook my head. "No, but I think this is the place to watch." I pointed. "Under that tree, there." I couldn't tell what kind of tree it was, only that it was very big and therefore probably old. And it would be good for leaning against.

We spread the blanket, an old army blanket that blended with the ground and disappeared. I sat on it and hugged my knees to my chest. Timothy didn't talk, and I appreciated his silence. He filled a paper cup with lemonade, held it out to me, and when I shook my head in refusal, he splashed vodka in it and drank it himself.

The river seemed ominous to me by day. At night it was more so. Moonlight gleamed on the slippery black surface. Everything made shadows, and all the shadows seemed to move. The fear returned, not as a wall this time, but as icy fingers that touched me, then moved into me and dwelt there. An invasion, a cold, deadly cancer that grew and grew. I couldn't tell if it was Alice Leighton's fear or my own. I hugged my knees tighter.

The night was anything but silent. Crickets and cicadas and frogs made a noise that hurt my ears. And off to my left I heard a continuous rustling, a rustling that threatened harm. Threatened me. I raised my head and looked in that direction. The pale moon threw the grasses of the old rice fields there into contrast with the black of the river. The grasses moved, heaved, a living, breathing thing. I was very frightened, and I knew now the fear was for myself, though I did not know why. The ghost of Alice Leighton was not here, not now. Perhaps later she would come.

"Timothy," I whispered, "I'm afraid."

Wordlessly he folded his arms around me, eased me back with him until we both rested against the trunk of the great tree. My head lay in the hollow of his shoulder, my drawn-up knees against his thigh.

"Are you cold?" he asked.

Only then did I realize I was shuddering. "N-no, it's the fear. I really am afraid. It's not the ghost, it's just, just me."

"Do you want to go in?"

"No. Just hold me. M-make the fear go away."

He put his hand under my chin, raised my face, and looked into my eyes. Such deep tenderness I felt from him. I clung to him until at last I no longer trembled. Timothy was real, this flesh was real and warm, not cold like the fear, not threatening like the rustling of the rice fields. I snuggled deeper into his warm embrace.

"Have you found any ghosts, or are you just amusing yourselves?"

I knew that hard voice too well. It had a galvanic effect on me. "Trust you, Charles Charpentier," I said hotly, "to be absent when you're most needed and then to turn up at a time like this!"

"Amen," muttered Timothy under his breath. He kept one arm around me. At the sound of Charles's voice I'd sat up instantly, my backbone had become a rod of steel.

"You won't mind if I join you." It was not a quesstion. Charles sank to his haunches, his face a satyr's face in the shadowed moonlight.

"I'd say your joining us right now is most inopportune," Timothy asserted.

"And *I* would say that depends on one's point of view," drawled the satyr. "It looks more to me like I got here just in time."

"Oh, honestly. Just . . . don't!" I warned both of them. I felt Timothy's arm tighten about my shoulder, but I couldn't take my eyes from Charles's face. He must not have had a haircut in the time he'd been gone—his face was framed in a black halo of dark, disordered mane. It spilled over his forehead and mingled with his strong, black eyebrows. The shadow of a day's growth of beard was intensified by the shadows of the night itself. But night's darkness could not obscure the shine of those darkest of all blue eyes as he looked steadily at me. My heart lurched, my breath stopped. I was ridiculously, humiliatingly, traitorously glad to see him.

"You came back," I said belatedly, and heard the note of wonder in my own voice.

Charles heard it too, and responded with an unusual gentleness. "Surely you knew that I would." His tone effectively excluded Timothy, who said nothing but his fingers dug into my upper arm.

"I, I mean we've needed you here," I said.

"Oh?" Charles lips twisted in a bitter grin. "It didn't look much like it to me. "

"I, I didn't mean—" I stammered, but Timothy interrupted.

"He knows very well what you mean, Rosamund." Timothy removed his arm from around me and draped it with forced casualness over his upthrust knee. He challenged Charles. "Your rudeness is inappropriate, Charpentier. You shouldn't have gone off and left Rosamund to cope with such a difficult—one might even say dangerous—situation all by herself."

"I think I have a good understanding of Rosamund's capabilities."

"I seriously doubt that."

"Oh, please—" I tried to intervene, but now I was the one excluded. I might as well have not spoken.

Timothy relentlessly continued. "I seriously doubt you understand anything beyond your monumental self-centeredness."

With dismay and disbelief I saw the verbal shaft hit home. Charles recoiled. His shoulders dropped, his chest heaved out a great breath that was half groan.

"You're probably right about that, Father Durrell. Thank you for reminding me." Charles half rose. "I'll go now and leave you two in peace."

I touched his arm with a staying hand. "No, don't go. Stay and watch with us for Alice Leighton's ghost. Lynda would give us all a tongue-lashing if she heard this foolishness." What could be wrong with him? The rudeness I'd understood, but to accept such a wound, deserved or not, and even to thank Timothy for it?

After a long hesitation, Charles said, "I suppose she would. How about it, Durrell? Are you willing to put up with a third wheel?"

Timothy turned his hand palm up, long fingers open in a gesture of submission. "Since it's what Rosamund wants, all right." He looked at me, his fine face like chiselled marble. "Are you feeling better now?"

I merely nodded.

"Better? What do you mean? What happened?" Charles demanded.

Timothy answered before I could frame a reply. "Rosamund said she was afraid. Just before you appeared. When I touched her she was shuddering, and her skin was as cold as ice."

"Oh. I thought—"

"I know what you thought. Don't make the mistake of using your own selfishness as a basis for judging me. What you thought was only a part of what was going on. To a great extent I'm motivated by a desire to take care of Rosamund, who needs it whether she will admit the need or not."

Charles looked from Timothy to me and back again. "I . . . see," he said slowly. "I believe I owe you both an apology."

"I'll accept your apology," said Timothy.

I murmured, "It really isn't necessary," which they both ignored.

We resumed our vigil, now three-strong, all of us facing the river. The moon declined in the sky and the night became perceptibly darker. Our silence magnified the inhuman night-sounds. In the periphery of my vision the tall rustling grasses of the old rice fields moved endlessly.

Timothy broke the stillness by reaching for the thermos. "Lemonade," he explained, and producing his flask, "vodka."

I shook my head. "I don't want anything."

"Skip the lemonade," said Charles. He accepted a paper cup from Timothy and moved around him to sit on the other side of me. "Did you see the ghost?" he asked quietly. "Was that what you were afraid of?"

"No. I'm not sure what it was." I still could not explain it, even to myself, nor did I want to. I only wanted to forget. "Call it the ambience. Something indefinable. I don't want to think about it. Anyway, it's gone now." I shrugged, a show of nonchalance. My words were like whistling in the wind. Throughout our shared silence my level of anxiety had risen, and it continued. Charles and Timothy sipped their drinks, and I once again pulled my knees to my chest, watching and listening for I knew not what.

The moonlight disappeared, either behind the trees or a cloud. Though my eyes were by now accustomed to the night, the darkness was almost total. My ears strained to compensate.

I heard a new sound that I could not identify. It came from the river, an eerie slithering, as if a monstrous water snake were sliding through the water. "What is it?" I whispered. "What's making that sound?"

Charles stood up and walked to the edge of the bank. He reached back a hand for me—I could barely see him in the darkness. "Man in a boat. Nothing unusual. Come here, I'll show you."

I stretched and took his offered hand, let him guide me until I stood with him at the edge of the bank. I felt rather than saw something large moving, making that sucking, slithering sound. "How do you know? You can't *see* anything! And besides, it doesn't sound like a boat! It's too quiet, it's creepy."

"You can't see him because he's black, and he must be wearing dark clothes. He's poling a flat-bottomed boat. There, now you can see he has a lantern on the back of the boat."

I did see the lantern, like an unblinking yellow eye. "How can he see where he's going? And why would anyone be on the river this late at night?"

"You really are jumpy tonight, aren't you?" Charles still held my hand and his fingers tightened on mine. "I told you, it's nothing to be concerned about. Many people, especially blacks, use the river to get around. It's still the most direct route from one plantation to the next, though we're so fixated on our cars we tend to forget that. As for seeing where he's going, I'm sure he doesn't need to—a lot of people around here seem to be born with a knowledge of the river, the marshes, and the old rice fields. Though I admit Captain John is the only white man I know who can do it. Our friend who just passed can find his way along just by the feel of the pole in his hands, and I expect he's on his way home after a little night fishing. It's not so late, around midnight, I'd guess. Now, are you satisfied?"

"I guess so." I watched until the yellow eye disappeared. Still I stood, slightly disoriented, staring into the blackness. Anxiety threaded its way through my veins, it crawled beneath the outer layer of my skin. Something was out there, I knew it—something terrible, and important to me. My heart thudded and my pulse pounded in my eardrums.

It began as a tiny red point in the distant blackness. The red point grew, a spark kindled and fanned by the breath of a demonic fire-bringer. "Look, Charles," I said hoarsely.

"Look at what?"

"There!" I croaked, pointing upriver. The point had become a spinning ball of fire, about the size of a tennis ball. It whirled faster and faster until it split apart into tongues of flame that leapt and danced on the surface of the river, red fire reflected in the water's black mirror. I watched, locked in dread.

"I don't see anything," said Charles.

Timothy came up. "What is it, Rosamund? What do you see?"

"I . . . can't . . ." The words died in my throat. I was paralyzed. It was the vision of my dreams, but magnified a thousand times and a thousand times more terrifying.

"Rosamund, snap out of it. There's nothing there!" Charles insisted, an undercurrent of alarm in his deep voice.

"Leave her alone, man! We can't see what she sees, but for her it's there, believe me. Be supportive, for God's sake. Can't you see she's terrified?"

The flames multiplied and twined around one another until they became great fire-columns anchored and reflected in the river itself. They crackled and burned. They were far away, but I felt their heat. I broke out in a sweat that drenched my body, fell in droplets from my forehead, and rolled down my face. "The river," I cried in a strangled voice, "the river is burning!" I wanted to run from the vision, but my feet wouldn't move. I wanted to shut it out, but my eyes refused to close. I could only watch in fascinated fear until the fiery columns dissipated, fading into a transparent ruby haze, and then they were gone.

My knees buckled and my eyes closed. I was barely conscious. I felt myself caught up in strong arms. I knew the feel of those arms. It was Charles who carried me back to the shelter of the tree.

"She's dripping wet! Where's that vodka?" he barked.

"She doesn't want it. She said—"

"Damn it, I don't care what she said, she's almost out. Get me the vodka!"

I was too weak to think, too weak to move. I existed on another plane, I heard the men's arguing voices as if from a great distance. The bitter, fiery fluid Charles forced through my lips brought me sputtering and coughing back to reality.

"That's just great, Charpentier. Now you've choked her."

Charles paid him no mind. "Drink, Rosamund," he pleaded.

I opened my eyes to Charles's face, inches from mine. I put my fingers around the cup he held to my lips. His fingers closed over mine one by one, locking them to the cup.

"Little sips," he encouraged. "That's right."

I looked at him gratefully over the cup's rim as I obediently sipped. My eyes felt as big as saucers. Charles had placed me in a sitting position, my back supported by the tree trunk. I could feel its rough bark through my thin blouse. "I'm okay," I said.

"Drink the rest of that anyway, it's not much," Charles said, relinquishing the cup to me. He sat back on his heels, reached into his back pants pocket and thought better of it. "Have you got a handkerchief?" he asked Timothy. "Mine's none too clean."

I looked to my left where Timothy stood a foot or so back, wearing an air of resignation. He unbuttoned one of the many flapped pockets on his shirt and gave his handkerchief to Charles without comment.

The vodka strengthened me, but I still quivered inside. I allowed Charles to wipe the dampness from my face, my neck, my collarbone under the open collar of my blouse. His hands were gentle. When he had finished, I gave him the cup and said, "Thank you. I'm sorry I went to pieces like that." I looked up at Timothy. "I can't imagine what happened to me," I lied, sending Timothy a wordless message: *Charles doesn't know about these things. Don't tell him!*

Timothy knelt down, solicitous. "You're all right now?"

I nodded and stared into Timothy's eyes, repeating the silent message.

Charles returned the now-damp handkerchief to him and said, "Rosamund has had enough for one night. I'm taking her home."

"No, Charles." I shook my head. One of my braids came loose and fell down over my shoulder. I was too wrung-out at the moment to do anything about it. "I don't want to cause any talk, so I'll stay. I'd rather not mention this to anyone."

Without thinking I reached out and smoothed the mane of

Charles's hair from his eyes, allowing my fingers to linger on the trace of silver at his temple. I could scarcely see his face, it was so dark, but I thought he looked haggard. I brushed his cheek with the back of my hand and felt prickly beginnings of beard. "You go on home. You must be very tired. You've come from a long way, haven't you? You were probably driving for hours." I forgot Timothy who knelt so near, and for a moment so did Charles.

He caught my wrist as I withdrew my hand, pressed warm, plying lips into my palm, then curled my fingers over it and held my folded hand within his larger one like a captured, cherished bird. "How exactly like you that is, like the Rosamund who came into my house and into my heart, to be concerned for me when you're half-alive yourself. I . . ." But then he remembered Timothy. His eyes cut away from me and to that silent, kneeling figure only inches away. Charles let go of my hand, reached up, and with his habitual gesture ruffled the hair I'd just smoothed.

He cleared his throat. "Hmmm. Well, yes. I think you're right. I'll go home. You're both staying the rest of the night, then?"

"Yes," Timothy and I said simultaneously.

Charles stood up, so did Timothy, and I would have too, but my knees didn't seem to work. The two men faced each other. For some unknown, masculine reason, they shook hands. Charles said, "You'll take care of her."

"You can be sure of that," Timothy replied.

Chapter 16

THERE WAS A LIGHT tap on the bedroom door. I paused in brushing my hair as the door opened.

"May I come in?" asked Timothy. He saw my nod, came just inside the door and closed it behind him. "I told Billings I snore, and that I'd sleep on the couch."

As tired as I was, I was still curious. "Will you please tell me what it really is you dislike so much about the man?"

"He's gay. It's a well-known secret. And I don't like the way he looks at me. I've had too much past experience with gay men who look at me like that, and I don't want to have to handle a proposition." He was embarrassed, ducked his head, and looked down at the floor.

"Oh. Well, that explains it all right. You can stay here if you want, if you think it won't ruin your reputation." I resumed brushing my hair. The kinks made by the braids were long since gone, but the rhythmic stroking of the brush had a soothing effect. I sat on one of the beds wearing only my nightgown. Leighton's renovation had not extended to installation of air-conditioning, and though I had opened all four windows, the room was warm and sticky-damp.

Timothy looked at me for a moment from where he stood near the door, then shoved his hands deep into his pockets and ambled to a window. "It will rain before morning," he said, looking out.

"Probably just another false alarm."

"I don't think so. I can feel a change in the air. We'd better hope for a real downpour. With the woods as dry as they are, lightning could strike a tree and start a fire in nothing flat. Unless the trees get a good drenching."

"Everything could use a good drenching. Myself included." I put aside my brush. I'd heard a tension in Timothy's voice that I didn't think was caused by anticipation of any storm.

"We'll have to close the windows. Water would ruin these floors." Head down, hands still in his pockets, Timothy turned away from the windows and seemed to examine the bare, highly polished hardwood with great concentration.

I suspected there were enough layers of wax on the floor to protect it from anything short of a flood, but I did not say so. I waited.

Slowly Timothy approached until he stood between the two beds and looked down at me. His face was solemn, his eyes were troubled. "I know you've had a terrible night, but you've never looked more beautiful to me, Rosamund."

"Thank you," I said, waiting. I felt a curious, calm sadness which had its origin in Timothy's blue eyes.

"Charles Charpentier is in love with you," he said. "I wouldn't have believed the man capable of it, but he truly loves you."

"Oh, I—" I began, but Timothy withdrew one hand from his pocket and placed a gentle finger on my lips to silence me.

"As much as I dislike it, I know what I saw. And heard. You love him too, whether you want to admit it or not. It was in the way you touched him, and he touched you, just before he left. A kind of instant intimacy that came to you both so naturally, so completely. In a masochistic kind of way, I felt privileged to be a witness. However . . ."

"However?"

He did not reply. He shook his head, and for once his hair did not fall back into place. It had been a long night, and even Timothy was beginning to look dishevelled.

"What you saw doesn't mean anything, Timothy."

"Really? And Charles Charpentier admitting he was wrong, and apologizing, and charging me to take care of you—I suppose that doesn't mean anything either?"

I swallowed hard, and for some unknown reason felt a pricking of tears in my eyes. I had no answer for that.

"Rosamund, I may be less experienced than a lot of men my age, but I'm sure of one thing. I could love you. We could be good together, I've felt it and I know you have, too. You need to be loved, you're ready for it." He pulled a wry smile. "However, you think of me only as a good friend. Am I right?"

From somewhere in the distance came a low, ominous rumble of thunder. I listened to it, and then I said, "I think of you as a friend, and I feel a growing affection for you."

"Well, you see, the trouble is I've been there before, and I don't want to do it again. I loved one woman and lost her to a Charpentier, and I've been pretty damned noble about it if I do say so myself. Lynda still calls me her best friend. Now there's you, and there's Charles, and I don't feel so noble this time."

The thunder growled again, its sound seeming to reflect Timothy's feelings. "I'm sorry, Timothy," I said. "If it's any consolation, I don't think there's the slightest possibility of a future for Charles and me. What you said about us may be true, but I can't allow myself even to consider it, not now."

"Because of Arabella?"

"Yes, of course, because of Arabella."

The wind rose outside and rattled the Palladian windows in their arched frames. Thunder rolled in waves, under a counterpoint of flashing light. I got up from the bed and went to watch the growing storm. The futility of my love for Charles sat heavy on my heart. I held my face to the night and welcomed the wild, fresh wind into my hair. But when the rain began to fall, Timothy was instantly there to close the window, to protect Lynda's floors as he would no doubt always protect Lynda herself. We stood together, not touching, and watched the rain fall.

When he spoke, Timothy's voice held the same calm sadness I'd seen earlier in his eyes. "I'm going back to Virginia, Rosamund."

The sudden announcement took me by surprise. I wanted to say that he mustn't go, that I needed him, needed his friendship, but I knew that would be unfair. "Can you do that, just leave?" I asked instead. "What about the church?"

"The rector will be back July first, roughly two weeks from now. I'd planned to stay out the rest of the summer at home, but my father's health is stable now. I'll tell Mother I need to go back and work on my dissertation, which in a way is true. The sooner I can finish it the better. But that's not the real reason."

"When did you decide this?"

"Just now. Being here in the room with you, and you in your nightgown with your hair down . . ." He touched my hair. In a white flash of lightning his face looked momentarily gaunt, all bone. "The real reason I'm leaving is that I can't be just a friend to you. There has to be more between us, for me, than simple friendship. Or there has to be nothing. I'm sorry, but I can't stand to stay here while you resolve what you must with Charles."

I nodded my understanding, not trusting my voice. Part of me cried out in silence against this unexpected loss. Part of me felt alone, abandoned.

"I'll still be here for a couple of weeks. If you really need me, you can call me. And I'll call to say goodbye when I do leave. If things really don't work out for you and Charles, perhaps you'll stop in Virginia on your way back to Massachusetts."

I forced a smile. "Perhaps."

"And now, I'm going to spend what's left of the night on the living room couch. Good night, Rosamund." He took a few steps, then turned back and swiftly caught me up in his arms. He kissed me with quick, fierce passion and said, his voice breaking, "Oh, Rosamund! I could have loved you so much!" And then he was gone.

Lynda served a brunch of strawberry waffles in the big kitchen on the ground floor at ten the next morning. Timothy was not with the rest of the group, and Lynda announced that he'd had a nine o'clock appointment at the church. In her informal fashion she offered to drive me back to Charpentier later, if I in return would help her with the dishes. I agreed.

I had an emotional hangover and no appetite. Living up to my end of the bargain with Lynda, I gathered dishes and put them into the dishwasher while the others lingered over coffee and talk. Then I excused myself and wandered out on the grounds. I wanted to see the place in daylight, and more than that, I wanted the sun and the air, still fresh from last night's rain, to restore me.

I looked about with interest. Without my realizing it, I had become accustomed to Charpentier, where the grounds had had the full-time attention of gardeners for more than a hundred years. By contrast, Leighton's lawn was a broad, bare vista. The rain had restored the green of the drought-thirsty grass, but here and there were bare patches that needed seeding. All work apparently had been concentrated so far on the inside of the house.

Of course, all was less mysterious by day. The bushes which had seemed a black thicket were no more than bushes, and rather scraggly ones at that. But the rice fields whispered and moved, a pale green, endless sea. And the river was black. Slick. Obsidian—that word again. I held the tip of my tongue in my teeth and repressed a shiver. Finally I turned and looked upriver, to the site of my vision. There was nothing at all there but the shining black water and the trees on either side.

Lynda joined me. "It's a beautiful morning, isn't it? That rain really helped. I wish we could get more."

"Um-hm. Lynda, what's up the river there, way up? It looks like the trees come out into the water."

"That's a bend in the river, a big one, like a hairpin curve."

"Is there anything on the other side of it? A house or something?"

She looked at me curiously. "Well, yes, in a way. There's an island, a pretty big one. It used to belong to the Charpentier family, but at the time of the War Between the States it was given to the freed slaves. I think they still call it Freeman's Island. There was a house on it once, a long time ago. Now the only thing left of the old plantation that was there is the old slave chapel, and it must be falling all to pieces. Nobody lives on the island now."

"Did the house burn, by any chance?"

"I really don't know. A lot of the old places did burn and some were rebuilt and some not. Why do you ask? It sounds like more than just idle curiosity."

I decided to take Lynda into my confidence. I felt I needed a woman friend, and Lynda was both strong and smart. I told her, "I'm aware that Timothy has told you a little about me, about some of the experiences I've had. Sometimes I see things, things I can't explain at the time, but later there is always an explanation. It's not quite as crazy as it sounds. Last night, though as I told you I didn't see your ghost, I did see something. It was down there. It was like a fire on the water. I've seen it before, but always in dreams. Last night I wasn't asleep, I was standing right here. Both Charles and Timothy were with me, and they didn't see a thing. The trouble is, I don't understand it. I have no idea what it means."

"It upsets you, I can see that."

"Yes," I admitted, "yes, it does. The vision always brings with it a feeling of deep anxiety, or worse. Dread. Doom. The end of something."

Lynda slipped a supportive arm around my waist. "What a bummer!"

"Yeah. The worst of it is, I can't tell if I'm just picking up on something that happened in the past, or if it's a warning of something that will occur in the future."

With our arms linked, by mutual unspoken agreement Lynda and I walked slowly back to the house. She said, "I'm sure these things must be a trial to you, Rosamund, but to me they're fascinating. Will you tell me more? I'm dying to hear."

Thus encouraged, I went back to the beginning, to the first occurrence in the hospital with the old man, and I told her everything. True to her word, she did seem fascinated. She asked intelligent, insightful questions, and as a result I recaptured details and feelings I'd never shared with anyone, and I shared them with Lynda. A bond was forged between us that I felt would last a very long time.

We ended up back in her comfortable kitchen, drinking iced tea while I turned the tables and asked Lynda about herself. She responded with anecdotes about growing up on the Pee Dee, some wildly funny stories about herself and her brother and Timothy when she'd been a prankish kid sister. She told me how she'd met Louis, and finally she shared her hopes and dreams for making a profitable business of the restoration of old plantation houses.

"If only I had more capital," she sighed. "I've sunk everything of my own money into Leighton. And Louis, bless his profligate little heart, had blown most of his inheritance before he met me and decided to give up his wastrellish ways. So he's no help."

"Perhaps Charles would invest in your ventures," I suggested. It seemed a reasonable thought.

"He might. But Louis wouldn't hear of it. The relationship between those two is terrible. I've just about given up trying to make it better. Although, if you were to stay around . . ." She cocked her pixie head to the side and looked at me speculatively. "Rosamund, I have this feeling that you and I could be good friends. The kind of friends that even if we didn't see each other all that often we'd just pick up right where we left off and the friendship would keep on growing. You know what I mean?"

I nodded, smiling. "I do know. I feel exactly that way myself."

Lynda smiled too, and warmth flowed between us. Then her expression became serious. "Okay. So I'll be straight with you. I know Timmy slept on the couch last night, because he was there when I came downstairs this morning. He didn't say anything, of course he wouldn't, not even to me. But Tim's a sensitive person, and my guess would be that he saw the change in Charles last night the same as I did. I just hope you and Tim didn't fight."

"We didn't fight."

"Well, I just have to know: whatever in the world have you done to Charles? When he came storming in here last night at eleven o'clock, looking like the wrath of God, and I told him which direction you and Timmy had gone off in, I expected all hell to break loose. But then he came back through here an hour later and he was just as meek as a lamb."

"Charles? Meek? I can't imagine. He must be sick."

She laughed. "Maybe in a way he is. After last night, Rosamund, I'm convinced that my brother-in-law is hopelessly in love with you."

I didn't want to hear this, not again. I protested. 'I don't think—"

"Hear me out, I'll explain. We all know that Charles can be an arrogant bastard, that's his style. Some of it is an act, and some of it's really him. Well, ever since you arrived, it's been obvious he was interested in you. Infatuated, I thought. He'd come over here and couldn't stop talking about you, that kind of thing. Then I met you and I could see you weren't the type to get caught in a mere infatuation. You're too serious, and too sensitive. So I figured when you started seeing Timmy, that was your way of letting arrogant Charles know you weren't interested."

"Something like that. Only I never intended Timothy to be hurt."

"I do understand that part. Anyway, a month or so ago Louis told me that Charles had started going to the office every day, which he never used to do, and that he acted different. Preoccupied, missing appointments, and so on. Louis loved it at first, 'Big Brother Makes Mistakes,' you can imagine. But Louis is more perceptive than he gets credit for, especially from Charles, and gradually Louis became concerned. He came home one day and told me that he was sure the change in Charles was because of you, that Charles was in love with you and you must have rejected him. Louis has always said that if Charles ever really fell in love, he'd go like a ton of bricks. That was right before Charles went away. Then last night he came back, and well, I've never in my entire life seen Charles like that. He was chastened, Rosamund, all the starch had gone out of him. He sat and talked to me for a while before he went home, asked me to keep an eye on you, and in the next breath said he was sure Timothy would be good to you. And his eyes—oh, my God. The love and the longing and the hopelessness, all right there in his eyes."

My own eyes filled with tears. I blinked them away. I couldn't speak.

"He needs you, Rosamund. I never thought I'd see the day that Charles Charpentier would need anybody, but I've seen. He needs you."

My tears welled up again, but I wouldn't allow them to fall. "Everything is so complicated, Lynda. You're right, that's why Timothy went away. And Charles, I think Charles c-cares enough that he was willing to remove himself because he thinks I prefer Timothy. Maybe it's better that he should go on thinking that."

"But you don't prefer Timothy."

I felt desperately unhappy. "I like Timothy very much. He's been a good friend, and in time the friendship might grow into something more. But right now, it isn't, and right now Timothy felt he couldn't live with it, not once he'd seen how Charles feels. I'm afraid, Lynda. Afraid to say even to myself that I love Charles or that he loves me. Yet I know it's true. I don't see how things can ever work out for Charles and me, and so I try—I try not to think about it."

Lynda placed her small hand over mine. Her grip communicated her strength. "I know the only reason this is any of my business is that we could be sisters-in-law some day, and I know I'd like that. Charles's marriage is nothing short of tragic, and he's paid the price long enough. There are ways. When something is right, there are ways to make it work out!"

I had to smile. So much determination in such a small package! It was like the ghost—she needed one and so there was no question but that it would appear, if not last night, then another time. "I appreciate your optimism, but there's one big problem. I'm not sure it's right for me and Charles to love each other."

Lynda forced a change of mood. "Listen to me, I'm nothing but an old busybody. But I do care about you and Charles, and of course about my friend Timmy. We've beat that subject to death, haven't we? Come on in my office out here, I want to show you something."

Lynda's office was another huge square room, on the ground floor in the front of the house. The two inner walls, without windows, were covered floor to ceiling with shelves. Books and papers, magazines, drawings, and pictures were everywhere. Her desk was a refectory table ten feet long.

The floor hadn't yet been refinished and was partially covered with two very large and colorful rag rugs. An old fanback wooden rocker, painted blue, sat under a floor lamp facing a front window, and next to it on the floor a basket spilled out bright wool yarns and knitting needles. Unmatched ladder-back chairs with rush bottoms and wood worn mellow with wax and age stood around the room, two at the table-desk. The office was pure Lynda, minus her sophisticated side.

We sat in the two chairs at the table-desk, and Lynda showed me glossy eight-by-ten photos of a handsome, huge house across the Winyah Bay which had been built in the 1930s and needed very little work. It had been offered to her through family connections—*her* family, she stressed—for only a fraction of its true value. She planned to get financing and buy it to turn into a conference center, which she was certain she could run at a profit. It was enlightening to see her head for business at work, and I was impressed.

The sound of an approaching car interrupted, and we both looked to the front windows which opened on the driveway. "Sounds like you have company," I said.

Lynda glanced at her watch. "Would you believe it's after one already? I've enjoyed talking to you so much I forgot the time. That's the man who seeded the lawn earlier in the spring, and I want him to do something about those bare patches. I asked him to come today, after our party, because we would have just trampled any new seeds to death. You'll be all right here for a few minutes while I go haggle with him?" She was up and halfway to the door.

"Sure," I waved her on. "With all these books I could be happy in here for days."

"I'll be back soon!" She dashed off.

What an amazing person, I thought. She had enough energy for two. Or three. My own energy was flagging. When Lynda returned I'd ask her to drive me back to Charpentier, and I'd change into my swimsuit and go sleep on the beach for the rest of the afternoon. For now, if I didn't move around some, I might fall asleep sitting at the table!

I prowled about the room, scanning the shelves. Not surprisingly, Lynda had a large collection of picture-books of old houses, not just from the South but the whole country. I chose one at random—at least, I thought it was random—and took it with me to the rocking chair. I sat down and opened the book on my lap, it was too large to hold in my hands. These were houses along the Mississippi River, some grand and famous, others less known but quite beautiful, and still others were stately derelicts, forgotten, forlorn, mysterious in stages of decay. I turned page after page, sometimes pausing to read a few lines of text, mostly just looking at the pictures.

When the déjà vu came, I didn't panic. I went with it. Perhaps on some level I'd expected this. Here in tones of black and white and gray was a house so much like Charpentier that on first glance I thought it *was* Charpentier, seen from the river side where the North and South Wings were not visible. The long porches were there, the slender columns that rose two storys, the tall windows with their sills on the floor. . . . And as I looked I went *into* the picture, like Alice gone through the looking glass. I was inside and I could see the central hall, the two parlors mostly empty of furniture, bare fireplaces, no rugs on the floor. My light footsteps rang and echoed as I ran in and out. It was kind of spooky, but I liked it anyway. I especially liked the way I could walk right out those tall windows onto the porch. But we didn't call it a porch, we called it a verandah. And from the verandah I could see the funny, drippy trees and the tire-swing my mother's friend had hung up there for me, and farther on there was the swamp where I mustn't go because there were bad things in the swamp. I knew the house was old and gray, the paint was all peeling off, but it was still the grandest house I'd ever seen and for a while I was happy there.

I sat in the rocking chair with the book in my lap and remembered these things, with only the slightest dizziness and quickening of breath. It was not déjà vu. Rather, it was the source of the déjà vu that had haunted me at Charpentier. I had lived in this house during the forgotten part of my childhood. I stared at the picture for a long time. I was certain, there was not the slightest doubt in my mind even though the name, Eauclaire, was unfamiliar to me. And I was proud of myself that the memory had come and I'd embraced it so calmly.

I heard Lynda's footsteps in the hall. "I have something to show you," I said when she appeared in the door. She came to look over my shoulder, and I pointed to the picture. "This house—see how much it looks like Charpentier? It could almost be the oldest part of Charpentier, gone slightly to ruin."

"Hmmm." She pulled over a ladder-back chair and sat close, to see better. "Yes, it could. Eauclaire—an ironic name." She giggled, little silver ripples of sound. *"Eauclaire"* means 'clear water,' and this place is on the edge of a swamp." She pointed. "That's a dank tarn if ever I saw one!"

"Yes," I nodded, "that is a swamp. Lynda, I lived in this hosue when I was a little child, I'm certain of it." I told her about the déjà vu I'd experienced so often at Charpentier, especially when I'd first seen it from the river. I told her about the years before I'd gone to live with Aunt Henry when I was four, how I'd never been able to remember them, never *wanted* to remember. About my mother whom I'd always thought was dead until I'd found the letter after Aunt Henry's death.

Lynda took the book from me and studied the picture more closely. "It says Eauclaire is located a few miles north of New Orleans. Doesn't say who owns the house. It looks abandoned. Let's see when this book was published." She flipped to the front. "1978. How old are you?"

"I'm twenty-six. I was born in 1960."

"Well, you certainly could have been there. It could have been abandoned later. You said the only thing your grandparents knew was that your mother's car had Louisiana plates. What a mystery, Rosamund! And how fascinating that you should come to Charpentier and start to remember those early years!"

I shrugged. "Just coincidence."

"More like serendipity, I'd say. And that you just happened to pick this book, and find this picture—you're uncanny, Rosamund Hill! But that isn't your real name, Hill, is it?"

"It is now. Aunt Henry legally adopted me."

"What was your mother's name?"

"Margaret Collins."

"Well," said Lynda, looking at the picture again, "I can't believe your grandparents never looked for your mother. But what about you? Now that you know she could be alive, don't you want to try to find her?"

"I don't know," I said uncomfortably. "I don't think so. My plate is more than full at the moment, so to speak."

"Would you like to keep the book?"

"Oh, no. This is all so strange, I need some time to process it. In fact, I think I'd like to go back to Charpentier if you can spare the time to drive me."

"Sure I can. The grass man will be out there for a while yet. Tell you what, Rosamund. Next time I go into town, I'll make a copy of this picture for you."

"Thanks. I'd like that."

"What a mystery," Lynda repeated when we got into her car.

I smiled. A mystery connected with an old house was obviously irresistibly intriguing to her. For me, it was just one more piece of a puzzle that I'd found and locked into place.

"You know," she mused when we were about halfway home, "all sorts of strange things can happen around New Orleans. That's where Charles met Arabella."

"I know," I said.

Chapter 17

I LAY ON MY stomach and felt the warmth of the sand radiating through my beach towel. The surf sounds soothed me. I slept, and when I woke I knew before opening my eyes that I was no longer alone.

"Don't be frightened." Charles touched my shoulder. "It's only me. I didn't want to wake you."

I turned over, a bit dizzy. I'd been sleeping hard. "How long have you been sitting there?"

"Not long. Less than an hour."

"And you've just been watching me sleep all that time?" He was dressed, or rather undressed, for the beach, in white trunks with a red stripe down each side. They made his tan, and his wealth of body hair, look very dark. He sat on a white terry-cloth robe.

"Yes. You were sleeping heavily. I hope you'll forgive me for following you here, but I want very much to talk to you. Away from the house. This seemed a good opportunity."

I sat up now, and plopped my floppy straw hat on my head as if it might afford some protection from Charles as well as the sun. I felt I needed it. Lynda's words—love, longing, hopelessness in Charles's eyes—came back to me. I was glad now that the dark glasses he wore covered those eyes. "You hardly need forgiveness. After all, this is your beach."

He shook his head. "I do need it. For a lot of things. I

stayed away too long, Rosamund. I'm sorry. I've questioned everyone in the house about George's disappearance, and I've called the police. They'll look for the station wagon, and for George, but I doubt they'll find either one."

"I don't think George took the station wagon."

"It doesn't seem like something he'd do. I suppose I should have known something would happen if I went away, but why George? Of everyone on the place!" He shook his head, his hair the shaggy mane I remembered from last night.

"I know. He was so, sort of innocent." And it's my fault, and I can't tell you why, I thought.

"Well, it will probably be like that first nurse we had a couple of years ago. She just disappeared overnight, but in her own car. I reported her missing because she'd left all her clothes and things behind. Not a trace of her was ever seen again. That was the beginning of all these local stories that got so out of proportion that finally no one would come to look after my wife. Of course, I think Bella's responsible somehow. For the first nurse, for the stories, for George's disappearance, too."

"What local stories?"

"All I know is what Barkstone told me. Obviously no one wanted to repeat them to me. It got around somehow that Bella was putting spells on the aides. That's why none of them stayed very long."

"Oh." It was possible, she might do that, but not without instigation. I wanted so much to tell Charles that it wasn't his wife, it was Regina behind everything, but I couldn't. I had to have proof. "Well, Charles, I can tell you for sure she hasn't put any spells on me. She calls herself Ashtoreth now, did you know? So I call her Ashtoreth, too."

"No, I didn't know that. But like everything connected with her, I no longer much care. Sometimes I think I can't make it through another month, my tolerance for all this is completely used up. Completely! Rosamund, there's something else I want to talk to you about, something much more important to me."

I waited, hiding under my floppy hat. He seemed to want permission. "Go ahead," I said.

"I need to know. Believe me, I need to know or I would

never ask. Are you in love with Timothy Durrell? Are you going to marry him?"

The tone of his voice was so different. So flat. His face too was expressionless. Where was the tempestuousness, the depth and breadth of emotion I'd come to expect from him? What was that Lynda had said? All the starch had gone out of him, chastened. I hated it. Worse than hated it, it nearly broke my heart to see him this way.

"Give me a minute," I said. I got up and walked away from him, I waded into the ocean. I felt the sudden shock of cool water on my feet and ankles, heard the cries of a passing pair of gulls. I concentrated on the waves, on the eternal sea whose very ceaselessness had always somehow put things into perspective for me. Everything became very simple. Later I knew everything would be complicated again, but this was now. The simple truth was that I could not bear Charles's unhappiness. Anger I could have borne, or spitefulness. But this unhappiness I could not bear.

I walked back to Charles, who waited with his great shaggy head in his hands. I sat down cross-legged in front of him, my knees touching his. I took off my floppy hat and my sunglasses. He looked at me and I removed his glasses as well.

"I am not in love with Timothy," I said. "I haven't even considered marrying him." I waited for those things to sink in, watched gratefully as his eyes lost their dullness, regained the sapphire shine I knew so well. "I love you, Charles. You." God help me, I thought. Tears misted my eyes. I swallowed a huge lump in my throat.

He touched my cheek. He looked at me in wonder, as if I had just dropped from the sky and might at any moment dissolve on the wind. "Please," he said hoarsely, "say that again."

"I love you, Charles."

His wonderful rare smile spread slowly across his face. It fell on me and sank through my thirsting skin into my heart. On his knees he bent over me, captured my face in both his hands and kissed me, cherished me. "I thought there was no hope. I've been such an arrogant, selfish fool, I thought I'd lost you forever. And if I had, I would have deserved it. Last night when I saw you with Durrell, saw how he protected you, I was sure you were gone from me. Thank God it isn't true!"

He pulled me to my feet and crushed me to him. His voice cracked on the intensity of his emotion. "Rosamund, I do love you. I love you!" He lifted me off my feet and spun around with me, scattering sand in an excess of joy. "I love you!" he shouted.

I laughed. I tossed my doubts and fears to the wind. At whatever price, this time of happiness was ours. He kissed me again, exploring my lips and tongue with a seeking earnestness I'd never felt from him before, asking before taking what I gladly gave. Then he enfolded me as if he would absorb me completely, and I yielded into him. I wanted to be one with him, bone of his bone and flesh of his flesh.

He said, suddenly solemn, "I love you more than life itself." He pulled away and looked down at me. "I mean that. Rosamund, will you marry me?"

In the happiness of the moment I laughed at this impossible question. My laughter spilled out in a throaty, alto gurgle. "Charles, you idiot! You can't marry me. You're already married!"

"Oh, yes I can. I don't have to stay married. I'll get a divorce. Will you marry me?"

It was still an impossible question, but this was more like my Charles, the real Charles. And he expected an answer. His dark blue eyes searched mine deeply, as if he tried to read my soul.

"If our love lasts that long," I promised, "I will marry you."

"It will last. I swear to you, it will last." His lips descended and took mine, sensually now, as of old. I abandoned myself to the kiss, to the pulse and sinews of his body. We melded together, a single column of glowing, melting blood and flesh and bone, most gloriously human. In love.

"Come on," he said, releasing me. "I have something to make up to you." He took me by the hand, stooped to retrieve his beachrobe and sunglasses from the sand. "Bring your things."

I gathered them up, having to reclaim my hand to do so. "Where are we going?"

"To the cottage."

I followed him to it, a few yards away. "How old is this place?"

"Almost as old as the big house. There are only two around here that are older, and they're on Pawley's Island." He searched through the keys which he had taken from the pocket of his robe. We stood on a broad, south-facing porch. The cottage was built into the dunes, as if it had backed up into them and gotten stuck. "Ah, here's the key. Yes, this cottage has survived a lot of storms, including hurricanes."

The door opened outward, and he stood back for me to enter first. I went into a large room and had time to note that the bare wood floors were smooth and cool, no sand had found its way in, when Charles came up behind me and put his arms around my rib cage. He pulled me back against him and bent his head over my shoulder.

"If you can love me after these terrible weeks, then I know we will survive as many storms as this old cottage," he said softly into my ear.

"I hope you're right," I murmured.

Charles went quickly from room to room, opening the wooden shutters. The cottage was damp and a little musty, but it was clean and the electricity worked. I looked in the refrigerator in the kitchen and found cold bottled water. I took glasses from the cabinets and poured some for each of us, and handed one to Charles when he joined me.

"Who comes here? It looks as if it's used regularly."

"Louis and Lynda. Sometimes we loan it out. But I haven't been here in a long time."

I looked out of a window at the sweep of beach and the sea beyond. "I like it. It has character." I turned back to Charles, and the naked desire on his face took my breath away. He hadn't touched me, yet my whole body flamed.

"I said I have something to make up to you, and I do. I was afraid I'd never have the chance. You were right, Rosamund, right to run away from me that night, the night you said I—" his voice broke on the word, "*raped* you. I didn't understand then how I was forcing myself on you. I could only think that we were alone, and I was half-crazy with wanting you. I was still angry when I left the next morning, it took a few days for me to calm down. But then I went off completely alone and I did a lot of thinking. I've behaved despicably, I know, I'm sorry—"

"Hush, Charles." I went to him and stopped his lips with my fingers. "I'm sorry too. It's all in the past, it seems like a very long time ago."

"Let me make love to you now. Let me show you that I'm not always brutal." His lips were on my eyes, my cheeks, my chin. "I can be sensitive. For you, I can be"—his lips on my throat, between my breasts—"anything. Everything."

"Yes, oh yes!" I put my arms around his neck and he carried me to a bedroom, to a bed. My body was so hungry for him that every touch aroused, pleasured. I was lost, overwhelmed; found, lifted up, exalted. Like a double star once forcibly split, its separate halves wandering and searching for each other through a dark universe, we found each other in brilliant recognition. We came together in flashes of heat and light, we united in a burning, shattering explosion that wed us into one magnificent sun.

The other sun, outside, was dying as I lay in the circle of his arms with the soft, dark, curling hair of his chest beneath my cheek. Slowly I returned to this world. I had always known that Charles would be capable of such passion. What I hadn't known was that I could be so easily ignited and burn with a flame that was equal to his. I stroked the dark line of little hairs down the center of his chest to his navel, and beyond.

He trapped my hand. "That's dangerous territory you're getting into there. It would take very little . . . !"

I moved my head up to his shoulder, where I could see his face. He looked wonderful, he had a transcendent peacefulness I'd never seen in him before. "Please, Charles, kiss me."

He turned on his side and kissed me, long and deep, with the unequalled softness of love so recently shared and fulfilled.

"I've never felt like this before," I said honestly. "You've ruined me for any other man, Charles Charpentier."

"Good. That's exactly as it should be." One eyebrow arched up wickedly. "Will Father Durrell be very disappointed, do you think?"

"I'm sure he will," I said with mock seriousness. I thought for a minute. There was something I was dying to ask. I decided to do it. "Charles, do you really, ah, have sex with Regina?"

He scowled, started to say something sharp, and then thought better of it. He wrapped me more closely in his arms instead. "No. That's something else I have to apologize for. I don't know if I wanted to hurt you, or shock you, or make you jealous or what. I must have been out of my mind. The whole truth is that she'd be willing, she's made that perfectly plain any number of times. I don't deny I've been tempted. She has a way of sensing when I'm particularly, ah, in that kind of need, and sometimes when she'd come to my room on some pretense late at night. . . . But I wouldn't, not with anybody who works in the house. I've never laid a hand on her."

I let out a sigh of relief. "I'm glad. You have no idea what disgusting visions I've had, of you and her, *doing* it!"

"Well, don't have them anymore." He played with my hair, which earlier he'd taken down from its braid. "You have hair to die for, my love. But it's really a mess right now!"

I sat up and hit him with my pillow. I was working up my courage, knowing it was time to leave. I didn't want to go, not back into all the tensions and unknowns that awaited us at Charpentier. The beach cottage was like an enchanted place, our bed a magic circle. I was afraid that once my feet touched the floor I would never know such happiness again.

Charles caught the pillow, wrestled it from me, pulled me down on top of him and kissed me again.

"We have to go," I whispered.

"I know." He looked very serious. "I'll never forget this afternoon, Rosamund. Remember, our love will outlast the storms."

"Our love will outlast the storms." Even as I made the affirmation, tears threatened, as if I knew that something so precious could be fully given and yet soon taken away. I bowed my head and let my hair fall around me so that Charles could no longer see my face.

*   *   *

"You're eating breakfast with me again," I observed. "I'm glad. I've really missed you. You're so unutterably charming in the morning."

Charles came from the sideboard with his orange juice, and paused to kiss my cheek. "I fully intend to have breakfast with you every morning for the rest of my life."

"Be careful! Remember about the ears on the walls." But I was happy. I was glad he'd said it, it was what I wanted too.

He unfolded his newspaper and scowled for a moment, pulling his expressive black eyebrows together. "Yes, I guess I do have to watch myself. As I said yesterday, I've lost my tolerance for this situation. Maybe I should talk to Barkstone. We could push the time ahead, at least by a couple of weeks. I already have a house in mind. It's a rental, and I can see if it's still vacant. But I swear I'd buy one sight unseen just to go ahead with this."

"No, Charles!" My voice was sharp with the alarm I felt. "So much happened while you were away, and is still happening. We're in a kind of continuing crisis situation, and we must let it take its course. Please!"

"So it still matters so much to you."

"Yes, it does." I forced my voice lower. "I still have hopes for that sanatorium. Do you understand?"

"Yes, I understand." He went behind his paper, and I let him be. But only moments later I was aware of his eyes on me, and I turned from gazing out of the box window to see Charles's face transformed. It was a look that was new to his craggy features, a look of love. "I won't complain, Rosamund. I know your tenacious caring is also what makes it possible for you to love a fool like me."

I blushed. He beamed and returned to reading the newspaper. Jenny brought our breakfast, and everything was blessedly back to normal.

But after that nothing was normal again.

I found Ashtoreth strung tight as a wire, the worst I'd ever seen her. I read through the nurse's notes of the previous two days in search of a cause, and found nothing out of the ordinary. I asked her what had happened to upset her, and she replied with, "You know nothing of these things." I was getting tired of that line, and I told her so, to no effect. Still she fluttered and paced and wrung her hands. At midmorning I was sufficiently concerned that I went upstairs for her medication.

"No, I don't want that. It makes me sleep, and I don't want to sleep. My mind, my mind has to work!" She said it with such anguish that my heart went out to her. What torture it must be to feel your own mind barely under your control!

"Believe me, Ashtoreth, as keyed up as you are today, it would take more than one of these capsules to make you sleep. You should know by now that you can trust me. If you take it, I think you'll find that your mind will work better. Right now your mind isn't working very well anyway, is it?"

She didn't reply, but she stopped pacing. I had a part, at least, of her fragmented attention.

Encouraged, I continued. "Right now your thoughts are racing, bouncing around inside your head, aren't they?"

She came several steps closer to me. I sensed curiosity, and suspicion. "How did you know? You can't read minds! Can you?"

I shook my head. "Not the way you mean. But I know some things I don't always tell, just like you. I know, for instance, how minds work. If you take one of these capsules, the only thing that will happen is that your thoughts will stop running like a racehorse. Believe me."

"All right." She held out her hand. I'd won a major victory.

She did calm down, and I tried for nothing more than just to be with her. She read and wrote at her desk, and played with her cards. I tried to read myself, but I couldn't concentrate. She had taken the medication, and a second capsule when the first one wore off. But she was still far from well, and I was worried about her.

Late that night she went out again with Regina. I was writing letters, supposedly, sitting in my little chair with a clipboard on my lap. Mostly I kept falling asleep. I'd opened the window, willing to air-condition the whole outdoors if in return I might hear the sounds of their leaving. The walls inside the house were too thick, but I had hopes that sound might carry on the night air. It did. The opening and closing of the french doors to the patio were clearly audible and brought me immediately out of my drowsing state. I clicked off my lamp and looked out of the window. I didn't see anyone, but I was sure I'd heard those doors. I ran to the gallerylike windows of the hall and impatiently watched the driveway. Still I didn't see them. No shadows where none should have been, no car moving without lights from the garage. Someone must meet them, pick them up down the drive, beyond the oak alley. If I ran after them now I might be in time to see them met. But also they would almost certainly see me. Instead, I decided to continue my search of Arabella/Ashtoreth's room.

Old robe, bare feet, flashlight—I was getting good at this. Check the living room, check the bed, check the curtains. I opened the desk drawer and took out the black book, and thumbed through it with one hand while I held the flashlight in the other. This book's title page had no name, it read, "My Book," and was dated 1984, two years previous. A few moments' scanning revealed a marked deterioration that I hated to see. Her spiky black handwriting had lost much of its character and degenerated into a scrawl. Page after page was no more than senseless, barely legible chaos. But more recent pages were different. By empathy I felt the great effort with which Arabella had begun to teach herself again that which she once knew. Symbols were laboriously copied, probably from her own red book; the strange foreign words were painstakingly printed. There were splendid circular drawings that reminded me of Jung's mandalas. She drew much better than she wrote. She must have concluded the same thing herself, for in recent weeks, perhaps months, she'd abandoned words altogether. She drew animals and strange creatures that might be the demons of her imagination. Suns and moons and stars, ringed planets, heads horned and crowned, pentacles, alchemical symbols I only half recognized. And eyes. Was this the Eye of Horus, or her own eye? I couldn't begin to decipher these drawings, but an art therapist would have had a field day. I put the black book away. It was interesting, but had told me little of help.

I still felt a sense of anticipation, of more to be discovered. I opened the door of the walk-in closet. If I found anything, I would have to be careful. I must not go into a trance or whatever that had been. In the close confines of the closet the flashlight wasn't much help. I turned on the light and closed the closet door behind me. Immediately I had to fight down a sense of claustrophobia. It soon passed. I looked around me in near-disgust. Too much of anything always sickened me, and this woman had far too many clothes. I plowed through them, wasting little time. None of this was what I wanted.

The closet was deeper than I'd realized. I pushed my way through a back rack of evening dresses, the long, fluffy kind nobody wears anymore, and found another door. There was a second closet, a secret closet, hidden behind the first. I opened the door, felt the wall inside for a light switch, which I found and flipped. A shiver went through me. This was it! Here she kept the garb and implements of another life. There were long, flowing robes in red, white, and black, and one astonishingly silver. Here was the black hooded cloak she'd worn in the storm. A shiny cape of midnight blue worked in silver with some of the symbols from her book. On the shelf above was a collection of ceremonial masks that stared at me with empty eyes.

This secret closet was an eerie, uncomfortable place, but I couldn't leave. By the pricking of the back of my neck I knew I was close to a discovery. Against one wall was an old wooden trunk, and on top of it a small chest of finer wood. The small chest was locked, and I remembered the key in the hidden compartment of the desk. It would be worth the effort, and the going back into the dark room, to find out what was important enough to merit its own locked hiding place.

I was disappointed. There was nothing inside the little chest but money. Not even very much money, though there were quite a few silver dollars among the coins. Some currency, nothing larger than a twenty-dollar bill. I was puzzled. Why would Arabella, or Ashtoreth, keep this piddling amount of money locked up as if it were a treasure?

My neck still pricked and urged me on. I put the small chest aside, sat down on the floor and opened the trunk. It was full of occult paraphernalia. On top was the candle I'd given her, burned down to a one-inch stub, also the two books of matches. I removed these, and shuddered as my hand touched a hideous thing that must have been a voodoo doll. A dark gleam in a back corner caught my eyes, and everything else was forgotten.

I touched it. It was round and smooth, cool and shiny, and black as blackest night. *Obsidian*. I heard the now-familiar thrumming in my ears, felt the light-headedness and disorientation, saw my vision blur and waited for it to clear again. These things would pass, I need not be afraid. I touched it again, I took it from the chest and held it, heavy in my hand. A perfect sphere, about four inches in diameter, like a fortune-teller's crystal ball—but this was made of obsidian. I knew it must be rare, unique. But I hated it. I hated it, yet my hands wanted to touch its smooth, round coolness. I wanted to look into its black heart. I put it down on the floor in front of me. I took three deep, calming breaths and counted as I breathed. I looked at my watch. It was 1:35 A.M. I felt the memory coming, and this time I must not get lost in it.

Memory struggled close to the surface, and I did not want it to break through. This was a bad memory. It was why I hated The Obsidian. The black ball was bad, it made my mama cry. Memory seized me, and I became a child again.

All the tall windows were open, and I ran and skipped, playing "In and Out the Windows" all by myself. From the parlor to the verandah, in and out. Mama had said not to bother her, she was busy. I knew what she was doing. I wanted to peek, but I didn't. I was a good little girl, but I did wish Pierre was here. Sometimes Pierre would play with me. There was a breeze today, it blew the long white curtains and sometimes they would get in my face when I went through the windows, like cobwebs. I didn't like that. I stopped running. I wasn't having fun anymore. I heard Mama cry out, a bad, bad sound. I was very frightened. I crept along the verandah to the other parlor, where my mother sat at a table with her back to the windows. Very quietly, because she'd said not to bother her, I went into the room. Mama was bent down over the table, with her head on her arms, and she was sobbing, her shoulders were shaking. Her long black hair covered her face. The obsidian ball was on the table right in front of her. Mama could look in the black ball and see things, but I was never supposed to look into it, and I couldn't play with it either. It was not a toy. I knew what had happened. She would never let me stay in the room with her when she looked into the ball, but I knew. She'd looked in it, and she'd seen something bad, something that made her cry. I crept up to the table and touched the shiny black ball with one finger. I was afraid of it, but it fascinated me, too. I never saw it again, because right after that my mama took me away. And I never saw her again either.

Oh, God! I sat on the closet floor with tears streaming down my face. I cried for little Rosamund who had lost her mother and was too young to understand, and I cried for the big Rosamund who was myself. Why would the memory not let me see my mother's face? I took the obsidian ball in my hand. In her journal Arabella had written, "The Obsidian," she had claimed it for her own. And she had said something about a child going away, that it was not a place for children.

My mother had been able to see things in this ball. If I looked into The Obsidian, what might I see? I didn't dare look into it. It still fascinated me, and still I also feared it.

Piece by piece, as I had tried to understand the woman who was supposed to be my patient, I learned instead about myself. My fascination and fear of the black waters of the Waccamaw had their root in this ball I held in my hand. *This* ball, this Obsidian. Surely there could be no other like it. This was The Obsidian of my deepest and most dread memories. And Arabella/Ashtoreth could be my mother!

My watch told me it was 2:15 and time to go. I put the obsidian ball back in its corner, restored everything as before. I went back to my room and crawled into bed. I lay afraid to move, so sick at heart that I was also sick to my stomach. One thought so filled my mind that I could think of nothing else: I had made love with a man who might be my mother's husband. It was too much to bear.

Chapter 18

FOR REGINA TO BE at my door at seven o'clock in the morning was so unusual, it was a shock.

"Miss Rosamund, I must ask you to come. I cannot awaken Miss Arabella."

I thought crossly, If you didn't keep her out half the night, it would no doubt be easier. But I said, "All right. Just let me get some clothes on."

"Please, I think there is not time." She was as haughty as ever, but her eyes flickered with alarm.

"I'll hurry." I pulled on jeans and a cotton sweater and started to comb my hair.

"Please, Miss Rosamund!" It was the second time she'd said please, she who had never asked my help for anything. I left my hair falling down my back and went with her.

Arabella/Ashtoreth looked shrunken in the great black-pillared bed. Her eyes were closed, her breathing was shallow and her pulse when I found it on her thin wrist was faint, rapid, and thready. Her color was bad. My mind worked rapidly and automatically, sorted through experience and made decisions with an authority I hadn't known I possessed. "You were right, Regina. We haven't got much time. She's going into a coma. Get a small glass of orange juice and put three teaspoons of sugar in it, *fast!*"

"Sugar? But—"

"I know what I'm talking about, just do it!" Regina fled.

"Hold on," I pleaded with the nearly lifeless woman. "Don't leave me, stay with me. Hold on!" I held her wrist and felt her heart struggling faintly, her lifeblood under my fingers. "Stay with me!"

Regina returned. I lifted Arabella in one arm and held the glass to her lips. "You must drink. Your life depends on it. Drink!" I tipped the liquid into her mouth. "Swallow!" Her eyes fluttered. She swallowed. "That's right, that's very good. Again." Little by little I fed her the sugar-laced juice until she had taken it all. Then I put both my arms around her and held her limp, thin body as a mother holds a sick child.

"You'd best call Dr. Barkstone now," I said to Regina. "The danger of coma has passed, but he might want her in a hospital for observation."

"I'll do it," said Charles. I hadn't known that he was in the room.

I could feel life and strength flowing back into the frail body I held in my arms. Just a little life, just a little strength, but she was better. Her breathing deepened and became near-normal. I felt her pulse and found it stronger, but not yet in normal range. Her eyes rolled under closed lids.

I began to function on automatic again. "Open your eyes and look at me." She did. "Can you tell me your name?" This was reality-testing. At the moment the matter of her name had no other significance for me.

Her green eyes were clouded, and flickered like a candle in the wind.

"Tell me your name," I repeated.

"M-my name is, my name is . . . Arabella. Arabella Charpentier."

"That's right. Do you know where we are, Arabella?"

She looked around slowly. "This is my room."

I relaxed a little. She was oriented to person and place. It was a good sign. "Do you know what day this is?"

She made an effort, I could see it in her eyes, but she could not remember. "No, I don't know. I'm too tired now. I want to sleep." The green eyes closed.

"It's Thursday," I said softly. "Go ahead and sleep, you've done very well." I pulled the sheet and summer blanket up to her shoulders. She seemed already asleep. Only then did I realize that she had told me her name was Arabella, not Ashtoreth.

"Barkstone says you probably saved her life," said Charles at dinner. It was the first time I'd left Arabella's rooms all day. I was most inappropriately dressed for the dining room, in the same jeans and sweater. I'd been too tired to change.

"How did you know to do that," he asked, "to give her sugar?"

"I'm not sure. It all happened so fast. When I worked on the geriatric floor in the hospital, we had a diabetic woman and the same thing happened. I guess I just remembered. In the back of my mind I've been afraid this would happen. Arabella hasn't been eating right for a long time now, and her glucose levels have been unstable. When a person doesn't eat and she continues to get even a small amount of insulin, it can be too much. Too much insulin puts a person into shock and then coma—when I gave her the sugar, the insulin had something to work on, and that brought her out of it. Don't worry, Charles. It isn't likely to happen again. Dr. Barkstone sent us a glucometer this afternoon. The instrument gives a much more precise measurement than the dip sticks I've been using. If I weren't so inexperienced, I'd have asked for it before now."

"I wasn't worried. But if you don't eat your dinner, I will worry—about you." His eyes lingered on me with a softness that brought me pain.

I ate mechanically, grateful for the weariness that provided an excuse from conversation.

"I've hired a registered nurse," said Charles. "She'll be here in the morning."

I put down my fork. "I don't want a nurse. Arabella is my responsibility, and I intend to be with her every day until she's on her feet again."

"Don't be stubborn, Rosamund. Barkstone said a week or ten days she'll be recovering from this, what did he call it?"

"Insult to her system."

"Yes. So I got a nurse. I don't want you shut up with Bella for ten days, I want you with me. Tomorrow we'll go to

Charleston to get the new station wagon, and since we'll be there anyway, I want you to meet my mother. We'll have lunch at the club, and—"

I interrupted. "Listen to me, Charles. N.O. No. I made a commitment to do a job, and I must do it my way. Otherwise all the time and energy I've invested already will seem meaningless. I've told you this before, and it hasn't changed. In fact, since she's so sick now, I feel even more strongly."

He clenched his jaw, and his sapphire eyes turned stony. "I need you to drive one of the cars back."

"That's not such a problem. Take Regina—she'll be the one who drives the new car anyway, not me."

"Damn it, I don't want to take Regina, I want to take you! And I want to show you off to my mother!"

I could see in him the boy he'd once been, so proud, so determined to have his own way. A darkly handsome boy with too much hair that tumbled into his eyes. I smiled in spite of myself. "Remember what you said only yesterday about my 'tenacious caring'? You can't expect me to turn Arabella over to a nurse who's a complete stranger, especially not now. There will be time later for you and me, another time for me to meet your mother." I lied, aching as I did so. I didn't believe there would be time later. I knew that I could never stay with a man who had been my mother's husband. *If* she was my mother. And that was the hell of it, that I didn't know, and most likely I could never know.

He yielded reluctantly and said he would take Regina to Charleston. I pleaded my exhaustion, which was real enough, and escaped early to my room. I showered and washed my hair, letting my mind go blank while I scrubbed hard enough to make my skin tingle. It helped. I had my hair half-dry when I realized the little keys were not on the dresser where I always put them when I was in the shower.

My stomach dropped down into the vicinity of my ankles. I hadn't been in my room at all since I'd dressed so hurriedly at seven A.M. Surely I'd taken the keys with me then! Surely I'd automatically stuck them in my pocket before I dashed out to follow Regina! But I *wasn't* sure. I couldn't remember. I searched everywhere, beginning with the pocket of the jeans I'd worn all day, and I didn't find the keys.

Regina must have taken them. Probably she'd had them

for all or most of the day. Soon she would come knocking on my door, she'd stand there with that superior leer on her face, dangling the keys from her hand, and she'd torment me with my carelessness. She'd done it before, now she'd do it again, and I could only wait and feel guilty. I might as well finish drying my hair.

An hour later she still hadn't appeared. My hair was thoroughly dry, and in my robe and gown I wanted nothing so much as to get into bed and read until I fell asleep, but I couldn't. I could confront Regina myself, or I could go to Charles. I went to Charles.

His bedroom door was open, but he was not there. I went on down the hall to his office, and found him deep in a pile of papers at his massive desk. He looked up as if he sensed my presence, smiled, and my heart turned over. Quickly, so that he couldn't misinterpret my reason for being there, I said, "Charles, I have a problem."

His smile didn't fade, but one eyebrow arched. "What, only one? Well, whatever it is, I'm glad it's brought you here. Have I ever told you how much I like the way you look in that pink robe? It's a good color for you, it brings out the red in your hair."

"Thank you." My cheeks flushed, but only slightly. "I feel terrible about this—I've lost the keys to the cabinets in my sitting room. I can't find them anywhere!"

The black brows came together. "That doesn't sound like you, Rosamund. You're too conscientious to lose those keys. Well, never mind. Since Bella's certainly too sick to get out of bed, there's probably no harm done."

"I, uh, I think Regina probably took them, to teach me a lesson about carelessness. But I really don't think I was careless, I think I *must* have had the keys in my pocket all day just like I always do, and that would mean . . ." I let my voice trail off. That would mean that Regina had deliberately come into my room and taken the keys from my dresser while I was in the shower. I let it pass. "Surely you have another set of keys? The important thing right now is to make sure the medication is all there."

"Yes, sure." He took his keys from his pocket, located a small key among the others on the ring, went to a file cabinet and removed a metal lockbox, which he unlocked with the small key. He rummaged around and eventually came up with the three little keys I needed and handed them to me.

"Thanks," I said. "I've meant to ask you for some time, why is it so important to keep these keys with me all the time? No one has ever told me."

"It's a precaution. When the first nurse disappeared, a substantial supply of barbiturates and tranquilizers apparently went with her. Bella was on a lot more medication then. Barkstone gradually worked it down to the one tranquilizer, and from what I understand, you don't even give her that. But before you came, even with the locks on the cabinets medication would disappear. Regina said Bella would get the keys from her aides and throw her own medicine away so she wouldn't have to take it. That's the only reasonable explanation, since the aides would report the missing medication themselves and none of them had a drug problem. Nor, in fact, did the first nurse, or if she did, we didn't know about it."

"I see. Well, Arabella certainly can't have done anything like that today." More and more I was convinced that Regina had my keys. But if not to shame me, which she'd had ample opportunity already to do, then why? "Charles, come back to my rooms with me while I count the medication. I want a witness. And there's still the big question— where are my keys? Perhaps you might question Regina. I hate to confront her myself."

"Of course I'll come with you, but you don't need a witness in my house, my love." He studied me and saw my nervousness. "You sound as if you're afraid of Regina."

"Not afraid. I just don't trust her."

"I thought you were over that!"

"No, I'm not." I said no more as we went through the halls, dim now as night approached outside.

"Show me where you keep the keys," said Charles.

"All right." I led the way through the connecting bath from the sitting room to my bedroom. "I always leave them on top of the dressing table while I'm in the shower—" I stopped short, staring in disbelief. There were the little keys, exactly where they should have been. "I, I don't understand this! I know they weren't here before!"

"Sshh, my love. It's not that important, don't be so upset." Charles came up close behind me and stroked the length of my hair. "You're just overtired, and you made a mistake. If you weren't so tired, you wouldn't have over-reacted."

I turned on him, hands clenched into fists, suddenly angry. "I may be tired, but I didn't make a mistake, and I didn't overreact! Those keys were *not* there before!"

"Oh, Rosamund. Don't be unreasonable. You know there's no other explanation. Regina is with Bella, and she wouldn't leave her tonight any more than you would have left her today. Regina argued just as forcibly against a night nurse as you did against one for the daytime. In fact, I began to think the two of you were in some sort of contest over my so-called wife." He pulled my resisting body into his arms. "Poor darling, you're exhausted. I wish you'd change your mind and let me get a nurse."

"No," I said into Charles's chest. He was right, I was exhausted, and the feel of his hard, strong body worked an instant spell on me. When he kissed me, I had no more will to resist his reasoning.

"Let me take you back to my room," he said softly, his lips against my ear. "We'll lock the door."

"It's . . . too risky." His lips were on my throat.

"Regina won't leave Bella's side until midnight. Let me kiss away this tension here . . . and here . . . and here. . . . I love you, Rosamund. Let me make love to you where you belong, in my bed, that was my father's bed, and my grandfather's—"

His last words, the mention of family, brought me to my senses. I put my palms flat against his chest and gently pushed him away. "I'm too tired, Charles. Not tonight."

It was a poor excuse. I knew it, and he knew it. My heart cried out for him, an anguished sound that I could not allow past my lips. I folded my arms and stared at the floor.

"I don't understand you, Rosamund." Slowly he backed off.

I kept my silence. I bit my lower lip until blood came and I tasted its sickening sweetness on my tongue.

"I'll thank you to toss me my set of those keys," said

Charles from my door, more than a trace of the old bitterness and hardness in his voice.

Arabella opened her still-extraordinary eyes and looked at me. Around the room went the green eyes, then back to me. "You're Rosamund," she said in a flat voice.

"Yes."

"I'm sick."

"Yes, you are, but you'll be better soon. You're already much better than you were yesterday."

"I remember. That doctor said you saved my life."

I smiled at her.

"You should have let me die." The eyes closed.

Those were the only words she said for several days. She ate what was given to her, she used the bathroom when I took her, otherwise she slept, or appeared to sleep. I reported these things to Dr. Barkstone who said, as usual, "Observe."

So I observed, and since observing a sleeping woman was not much of a challenge, my mind was free to trap itself in a million dead-end thoughts. Hour after hour, day after day, I doggedly used logic and reason on a situation that was basically illogical and irrational. It was a frustrating process, often interrupted by onslaughts of emotion from a very simple source: I was in love with Charles, loved him with an intensity I'd previously thought was reserved for the heroines of novels or the soap opera screen. Eventually I harnessed the emotion and reduced it to the one fact: I love Charles. I put that fact in with the others, in a hodgepodge of the irrational and illogical and now the emotional, too.

In the long, quiet days Arabella's rooms became for me a sanctuary, as they had long been for her. Her bedroom, as always, assailed my senses and touched deep, uncomfortable places in me. But in her living room I could think, and laboriously I thought upon my hodgepodge until I forced it into an order I could work with.

First, it was a waste of time and energy to question any further than I already had, what had *really* brought me to Charpentier. I called it coincidence, Lynda called it serendipity, Timothy probably would call it karma. The fact was that I was here, and all the déjà vu had turned into real memories. I had recovered enough of my lost early years to understand why my growing-up mind had protected me from those memories, and Charpentier was the agent of that recovery. I accepted this.

Second, Arabella *could* be my mother. She was the right age, she had come from New Orleans, and she had in her possession the obsidian ball. For my own peace of mind I had to know, and it was this I struggled with longest, because a part of me did not want to know. That part of me argued that where Charles and a private detective had failed, I too must fail and so why try? But my more rational self knew the answer. I had an advantage, I had the grandparents, those heartless people who had not even come to Aunt Henry's funeral. All I had to do was take a picture of Arabella, a younger Arabella, to them and they could say, yes she was their daughter or no, she was not their daughter. They would be bound to recognize their own daughter. I knew where I could find such a picture, in the bottom drawer of her desk. When my time at Charpentier was up, I would take the picture to Vicksburg, and then I would know the truth.

Third, I did love Charles. Given the situation, I found I could be grateful that at least it was impossible for him to be my father. At least I hadn't committed incest. The fact that we had made love did make a difference to me. In a kind of wonder I realized that for me, with Charles, the physical act of love had a meaning far deeper than the words *making love* implied. I felt I had been physically joined to him, forever— as corny as it sounded. Marriage and monogamy suddenly made sense. This was a source of both joy and horror. The horror could only be removed by sure knowledge that Arabella was *not* my mother. After many, many hours of getting lost in a maze of alternating desire and hopelessness, I decided that I must somehow reestablish a physical distance between Charles and me. When Arabella was well enough again and settled somewhere, I would tell him I needed time and space before I could commit myself to him. He didn't have to know that the main thing I would do with the time and space would be the trip to Vicksburg with Arabella's picture. He needed a divorce anyway, with or without me, and divorces take time. What was it I'd said? "If our love lasts that long." Prophetic words!

Finally, dangerous tensions still existed at Charpentier, and they still centered on Regina. I had no facts to go on, only feelings and intuition, and the strange vision about George's disappearance. Whatever she had been doing with Arabella/Ashtoreth, the present illness had interrupted it. I felt Regina's impatience. Sometimes, when she came to take my place at the bedside before dinnertime, she looked at me with such calculated hatred that I wanted to strike her as much as I wanted to run from her. I did neither. I wanted her never to know how much I feared her, not only for myself but also for the woman who might be my mother. And also how little I knew what I could do about it.

So, by day gradually I gained control again over my life. By night it was another story. Dinner with Charles, served now by Phyllis since Regina stayed with Arabella until midnight, assailed and wore down my defenses. It was not easy to put distance between us when he was so determined there would be none. I invented a sense of propriety that I did not feel, and hid behind it with a yearning, aching heart. Charles struggled with my new-found propriety, called it "infernal," and in general fumed like a not-quite-dormant volcano. I would go to bed exhausted. And now into my exhausted sleep every night came the dream with its terrible red and black, the fire on the water. Every night I woke, startled, dripping with the cold sweat of nameless dread. Consequently though I slept, I did not rest well. My eyes, always too big for my face, took on a hollow, haunted look. My vision haunted me.

"Rosamund, what are you doing down here?"

I opened my eyes to the gray light of early morning seeping through the french doors, then to Charles's face bending over me as I lay on the couch in Arabella's living room.

"Regina had to go to Patton," I said. "It was some sort of emergency with a cousin—I thought you knew. I couldn't get a nurse on such short notice, and so I just decided to sleep down here."

It wasn't exactly the truth. I had fallen asleep on the couch and been awakened by my recurring dream in the middle of the night. After that I'd been too frightened to go through the dark halls to my room and so I'd stayed where I was. I sat up now, recognizing the oddness of Charles completely dressed in a suit and tie at this early hour.

"I guess Regina did tell me. I'd forgotten." He ran his hand through his freshly combed hair and messed it up. "I have to go to Charleston. My mother's in the hospital. Apparently she took an overdose of something and then changed her mind long enough to call 911. They don't think she'll make it. I can't imagine my mother committing suicide! I shaved and dressed because she never likes to see me looking sloppy, and then I realized how silly it was to take the time. I wanted you to go with me, but you weren't in your room, and I panicked, went running out the door like a crazy man. Then I saw your car in the garages, and I realized you might be in here with Bella. I'm sorry. The truth is, I'm not thinking very clearly."

I stood up and put my arms around him. "I know it must be a terrible shock, but she's in the right place. Nine times out of ten they can pull somebody through. I can't go with you, though. Did you call Louis?"

"Oh, God, no. A fine brother I am! I'll call him, and then I'd better go. I'll let you know what happens." He kissed my cheek quickly and was gone.

Two hours later Charles called to say that his mother had died without regaining consciousness. By midafternoon he was back at Charpentier, and at my insistence he told his wife the news.

Arabella said, "She never liked me." And she closed her eyes, shutting us out.

Charles looked at her in disgust. To me he said, "I don't know what you expected. It's true, Mother didn't like Bella."

I shot him a warning look. At least she had spoken, for the first time in five days. I touched her hand. "Arabella, open your eyes and look at us. The funeral is in two days. I know you're getting well, and I want you to tell Charles, tell your husband that you will get up, get out of this bed so that in two days you'll be strong enough to go to the funeral with him."

With her emerald eyes Arabella looked at Charles and then at me. "No, I'm too sick to go. You go, Rosamund. If he needs somebody to go with him, you go in my place." Once again she closed her eyes. We left the room.

"I do need you, Rosamund. But I'm surprised that Bella would see that."

"I don't think she did, not in the way you mean. She hasn't been talking, but in a lot of nonverbal ways I can tell she's become dependent on me—too dependent. That's why she said what she did, it's one more thing she can get me to do for her so she doesn't have to do it herself. But still, if you need me, I'm here for you. I'll get a nurse for the next couple of days." Even if Charles didn't need me, a nurse would help to break this unhealthy dependency of Arabella's.

The death of Eleanor Charpentier was taken hard in the house. Phyllis went around on tiptoe. Jenny, who had been very fond of Charles's mother, cried in the kitchen. Regina did not return that night. When the nurse arrived, it was early evening and I'd had my dinner with Arabella. I found Charles in the library, drinking and morose. I said, "Please tell me everything, how she died."

"When she called the emergency number, all she managed to say was 'Help' and her name and address. She never regained consciousness, so she never said anything to anyone. A blood test showed she'd taken an overdose of some kind of tranquilizer—they told me the name of it, but I don't remember. Her doctor was there when I got there. He said he had no idea she was depressed or anxious about anything, and he'd never prescribed a tranquilizer. But he said when people her age decide to commit suicide, it's not unusual for them to go to a different doctor, sometimes more than one, and tell whatever tale they have to tell to get medication. Then they stockpile until they have enough to do the job. What *was* unusual was that she changed her mind and called for help—the doctor said that most elderly people who want to kill themselves are very determined and efficient about it. With the amount of drug she had in her system according to the blood test, it was surprising she'd been able to call."

"Did she leave a note?"

"No. Nothing like that. *Nobody* knew she was that unhappy, nobody!"

I wished he would cry, it would help him to cry. He looked as if he blamed himself. I knew a little of how he must feel. "When your mother, or someone who has been like a mother to you, dies so suddenly like that, you're left with all the things you wanted to say, and all the things you wanted to do, and you know now you can never say or do them. It's hard, I know."

"Exactly." His voice was bitter. He turned the ruby ring around on his finger. I realized that he always wore it when he went to Charleston, and I guessed his mother had given it to him. "I wanted her to meet you. I wanted her to see that I could marry the right kind of wife, a wife she and I both could be proud of. I wanted her to be at our wedding, wanted us to give her grandchildren—!" His voice broke.

Now his pain cut through me, too. I went down on my knees beside him. "That's my fault, Charles. If I'd gone with you that day, the way you wanted me to, at least some of this wouldn't have happened!"

"No, darling, it's not your fault. None of the awful mess I've made of my life is your fault."

"Oh, but it is!" My tears spilled over. "If I'd let you tell her, gone with you to tell her about us, she'd have known there might be grandchildren, it might have given her something to live for!"

Now Charles's tears came, great drops that rolled silently down his face. He pulled me into his lap, and we cried together until we were both wet with our mingled tears.

When the time came, I went to the funeral at Charles's side, I sat with him and Louis and Lynda as part of the family. If I caused a scandal I didn't care, because it was true that Charles needed me. He was paralyzed by his grief. The rector of All Saints' Waccamaw returned a few days early from his sabbatical to officiate for this woman who had been important in his parish. He was assisted by Timothy, solemn and pale. The little church overflowed with people, and I had to admit that the service with all its ritual was comforting.

Afterward I stood with Charles clutching my arm so

tightly it hurt, and watched as the small wooden box that contained his mother's ashes was placed in the ground with the other Charpentiers, under the outstretched wings of the marble angel. I could not help but wonder if my ashes would someday lie there too, along with Charles and Louis and Lynda.

When the burial was over, we all went not to Charpentier but to Leighton. Everyone understood that Arabella Charpentier was too ill to have the party of mourners at the house. And never once, through all of this, did it occur to Charles or to me that his mother might not have taken her own life.

Chapter 19

ARABELLA ROUSED HERSELF AND once on her feet, she acted as if she had never been ill. She wore her glasses again and the colorful caftans.

"Where is Ashtoreth?" I asked.

"I am Ashtoreth, and I am Arabella. You may call me what you like it doesn't matter, we are one."

So, I thought, out of her illness she has achieved a synthesis of her two selves. She had been angry with me for leaving her with the nurse, as I'd expected she would. The anger had propelled her out of bed, but it also made her close to Regina again. You win a few, you lose a few. Regina had come back from Patton the day before the funeral, and in the last few days had been with Arabella every possible minute. However, after I was back on a daily basis, Arabella's anger quickly faded and turned to trust. She still remembered that I'd saved her life. She talked to me more openly than ever, she fairly babbled.

One day I took advantage of this. I asked her something very much on my mind. "Arabella, have you ever had any children? I mean, before you were married to Charles?"

"Children? I don't like children!"

"A lot of people don't like children, but they have them anyway. And then they give them to other people to bring up, maybe to their own mothers and fathers, or to a sister. Did you ever do anything like that?"

292

"I, Ashtoreth? What would Ashtoreth do with a child? What a silly idea!" She disappeared into her closet.

Oh, well, at least I'd tried. She came out of her closet again with something that interested her more than the subject of children. In her arms was a long red gown which I recognized from her secret closet. She held it up to her, then threw it on the bed and went back into her closet.

I got up from the divan where I'd been sitting and perched instead on the foot of her bed. When she came out again, she had a white gown and the midnight blue cloak with its embroidery of silver symbols. "Are you getting ready for something special?" I asked.

"Not really. I'm just going back to work." She threw the gown on the bed and put the cloak around her shoulders. Since she was wearing an orange tunic with a gold sunburst in the center and gold trousers, the addition of the blue-and-silver cloak was blindingly bizarre.

"That's a beautiful cloak. Have you had it long?"

"Yes, it *is* beautiful. Somebody made it for me. I can't remember who, it was a long time ago. These are magical symbols, you know. It's rather grand, but I think I'll wear it tonight. With the white robe. What do you think?'" She held the white robe up so that it covered all her orange and gold.

I told her the truth. "I think you will look spectacular. You should wear those glasses you have on. The mirror lenses compliment the silver embroidery."

"Oh, I don't wear the glasses when I work. Only around the house. Yes, I'll wear these tonight. But there's something else that goes with this, if I can only find it—" She went back into the closet again, after throwing the cloak and gown on the bed.

I pulled the cloak to me and traced my fingers over one of the silver symbols. It really was a beautiful thing. My finger tingled as I touched the silver threads.

Arabella, flushed from her efforts, came out with her arms full of occult junk—voodoo dolls, a crescent moon on a stick like a wand, a clear plastic pyramid—and threw them on the bed, where we were getting quite a pile. She mumbled about not being able to find something and went back into the closet yet again. Next she came out with nothing but the obsidian ball, and threw it on top of the pile.

My heart stopped beating. She had already turned back to the closet, but I stopped her. "Wait! What is this, this black ball?" I picked it up and held it, round and smooth and cool in my hand.

"That? It's called The Obsidian."

"What's it for? What do you do with it?"

Like a child who has lost interest in a plaything until it becomes of interest to someone else, she came now and took it from me. She sat next to me, crushing the blue cloak under her, and held the obsidian ball in her cupped palms. "You look into it. It has magic inside."

"It must be"—my mouth went suddenly dry—"very rare, very unusual. I've never seen anything like it. Crystal balls, yes, but not black like this."

"It is. It's the only one in the whole world, that's why I wanted it so much." Her voice sounded far away, as if she spoke from out of the past. "But it has a black heart. When I look into it, that's all I can see, its black heart."

Her words were enigmatic. I didn't know if she meant that she could see only evil things or that she couldn't see anything in it but its own black glass. She stared into the orb for a long time. My heart hammered. I had to work to produce enough saliva so that I could swallow. At last she turned her head slowly and looked at me.

"You like it, don't you, Rosamund?"

"I suppose, in a strange sort of way, I do. It's . . . fascinating."

"Well, then, I'll give it to you as a present. For saving my life. Here."

"Thank you." I took The Obsidian as she offered it, from the palms of her hands.

That night it was very warm, still in the 80s though the sun was long gone. The humidity was surely in the 80s, too. Arabella had willingly told me, when I'd asked, that she was going out with Regina, that they often went out at night and that was when she did her work. When I asked further, where did they go and what kind of work did she do, all she said was, "Regina helps me. I go with her. I can't work alone." It was nearly midnight now, and I waited with my flashlight, determined to follow them as best I could. I tried to ignore the heavy air that made it hard for me to breathe. There was no moon, and it was very dark.

The light went out in Arabella's living room. I heard the french doors open and then close, but in the sudden void where there had so recently been light I could see nothing. Damn! I thought. I mustn't lose them right at the very outset! They must have eyes like cats to see where they're going in this darkness!

I felt rather than saw them pass me—surely I must be mistaken! Nevertheless I turned and in a moment I could see. Two dark shapes, black-on-black, one of the dark shapes rippled with tiny dots that faintly glowed. That would be Arabella, in her midnight blue cloak. Its silver embroidery seemed to emit a faint light of its own. Of course that was impossible. I found it equally hard to believe that they were headed not for the road but the river.

I followed as closely as I dared. I had worn dark clothes too, my least-faded jeans and a long-sleeved navy sweater that was much too heavy for the warm weather. I had even wrapped my hair in a chocolate brown scarf. Not very attractive, but it achieved the desired effect.

I had to assume that they were going to the dock, because I couldn't leave the shelter of the bushes at the edge of the garden without being seen, nor could I see the dock from the bushes. I strained my ears for the sound of a boat. Soon I heard a slithering, sucking sound, and I remembered. Charles had told me that was the sound of a flat-bottomed boat being poled through the water. I dropped to hands and knees, hampered by the flashlight, and crawled across the open lawn to the edge of the bank. The boat had already left the dock, going upriver. Its unblinking yellow eye mocked that I was too late, I would lose them now. Oh, but I mustn't lose them! I scrambled up and switched on my flashlight. I got my feet in gear. The small circle of light wasn't much help. I had to run or I would lose that leading yellow eye, and I continually overtook my own light-beam.

Too late I realized what I had done, how very foolish I'd been. If I had stopped to think, I would have known that the next plantation upriver from Charpentier was Leighton. Between the two the riverbank receded into a horseshoe shape, and the horseshoe was filled with the overgrown grasses of the old rice fields. I missed my footing and I fell; when I instinctively put out my hands to break the fall, I lost the flashlight. I rolled on the hard bank, unable to stop myself, and then I slipped and slid feetfirst into an evil, sucking softness. The living, murmuring, endlessly moving rice-grass closed over my head.

I couldn't see. I couldn't breathe. I screamed, but not a sound came out of my throat. I fought the sharp-edged grass, my arms and hands flailing in blind panic. The pain of myriad tiny cuts on my hands finally broke through my hysteria. I found I was breathing after all, gulping, sobbing. I calmed myself. I was thigh-deep in muck, but the muck had a bottom. I couldn't see, but I could walk. Maybe I could walk out.

It was like pushing my way through an endless, living curtain of cutting ribbons. The viscous, muddy water slowed my steps, as in a bad dream when we run and run and get nowhere. Yet I kept on. My fear reduced me to a primitive state, and I prayed what must be everyman's primitive prayer, Oh please, please get me out of this and I'll never, ever do anything so foolish again! I thought about poor Alice Leighton in all her petticoats and heavy skirts. No wonder she had drowned! It was hard enough slogging my way through this mess in jeans. Probably she had prayed the same prayer. It hadn't worked very well for her, though. . . .

I saw ahead of me a lambent patch of light. Where did it come from? I moved toward it with my sluggish steps, parting the grasses. I was moving onto higher ground. My head was blessedly above the grass now. The light was brighter too, always ahead of me, swirling within itself. I followed the light, so fascinated that I forgot my fear. The grass was chest-high, and the muck around my legs thinned. I moved faster toward the light. It swirled and became more dense. I stopped and watched, out of danger now. The swirling light became solid from the center outward, co-alescing into a glowing girl with voluminous skirts, a tiny waist, and ringlets in her hair. She hovered in the air, tiny feet peeping from beneath her huge skirts, surrounded by her halo of light. And then she dissolved and was gone.

As she dissolved, I saw a rowboat beneath the place she hovered. "Thank you, Alice!" I said aloud. I reached the boat and rolled myself into it. There were oars, too, but for a while I just lay in the bottom of the boat, shaking and thinking. Fear had been waiting for me in the old rice fields all along. I'd felt it on the night we'd watched for Alice. Saved by Alice Leighton's ghost! Who would believe it?

Lynda would, of course. I sat up and fitted the oars into the oarlocks. I'd practically grown up rowing on the Charles River. Getting back to Charpentier in a rowboat would be a piece of cake! Someday I'd tell Lynda about this, but not tomorrow. For now, how Leighton's rowboat came to be at Charpentier's dock would have to be a mystery.

I gave the rice fields a wide berth, keeping to the blackest black that I knew must be the open river. I rowed strongly, with a surprisingly light heart. I found the dock easily because of the relatively lighter color of its new wood, and tied the boat on the far side, away from the steps. I had lost my flashlight and my sneakers and my scarf, but thanks to tight jeans I hadn't lost my house key—it was still in my pocket. Perhaps the most amazing thing of all was that I let myself in by the West Front door just as the grandfather clock in the hall struck two. I'd been to the jaws of death and back again in just two hours!

"What happened to your hands?"

I'd hoped Charles would be too preoccupied with his newspaper to notice, but no such luck. I had my prevarication ready. "I went for a walk early this morning, and I had a fight with a bush, and the bush won."

Charles took my right hand and examined it carefully. The many scratches were tiny, but they were fiery red. "I'll say it won. You must have been trying to rescue a baby rabbit out of the blackberry bramble."

"Something like that."

"Poor city girl! The rabbits live in there!" He kissed my fingertips and returned my hand to me. The touch of his lips went straight through me, as it always did. I'd been trying again since the funeral to get some distance between us, and again my success was minimal.

Charles went back to his paper, and I went back to my thoughts. After a few minutes, he said "Oh, my God!"

Instantly, he had my attention. "What is it? Something in

the local paper?" Charles read the local paper on weekdays, the *New York Times* on Sundays.

"Yes. I think this is about one of Phyllis's relatives. A twelve-year-old boy was riding a horse along the side of the highway between here and Georgetown. Something spooked the horse, and it threw the boy onto the road. A car hit him and dragged his body before the driver could stop. The child was dead when the ambulance arrived."

"That's horrible!"

"Yes, it is, and if I'm not mistaken that family is among Phyllis's many cousins. Jenny will know. It happened yesterday—I expect Phyllis won't be in today. I'll have to go over there and see what I can do for the family."

I was sorry and said so. But I was preoccupied and distracted by a vivid and disturbing new dream that I'd had during my few hours' sleep. The part of me that was able to see things like Alice Leighton's ghost seemed to be working overtime, and I had to decide whether or not to trust its message, whether or not to tell Charles.

Jenny came in with our breakfast and confirmed that the boy had been a cousin of Phyllis, and she didn't expect Phyllis to be in today. Jenny's earnest face looked drawn this morning, her dark skin dusty-pale. Surely there was no justice when a good woman like Jenny could be so unhappy while the Reginas of this world flourished! Regina alone of all the household had remained unaffected by Mrs. Charpentier's death. Every day Regina looked to me more and more like the cat who'd gotten the cream. I was going to cut off her cream supply if it was the last thing I ever did! I really had had enough of her, all I could stand.

In that moment I decided I could wait no longer. It was more than time to stop Regina. I said, "Charles, I want to talk to you about George."

"Hm?" He folded the paper and put it aside. "All right, I'm listening."

"I think George is dead. I think he was shot with his own rifle, the one you gave him. I don't know where the gun is, or the car, but I know where his body is. It's in one of the creeks in the marshes at Murrell's Inlet."

Charles's expression was wary, guarded. Not the total

disbelief I'd expected. "If you know that much, do you know who shot him?"

"Yes, I think so, but I can't prove it, so I'd rather not say. It could be dangerous for me to tell anyone, even you. In fact, I suppose I shouldn't be telling you this here at the breakfast table, but, well, I get tired of being unable to talk openly with you, and I just don't think I can sit on this all day!"

"It's all right, just keep your voice down. How do you know these things, Rosamund? What's the source of your information?"

I squared my shoulders, ready for rejection, and looked Charles steadily in the eyes. "I saw it in a dream, a particularly vivid dream I had when I was waking up this morning. Actually I had the dream when I was about half-awake, so it was as much a kind of vision as a dream. I've had such things before, Charles, and there has always been truth in them. I know it sounds crazy, that's why I can't tell the police. But *you* could tell them, maybe you could think of a reason for them to look in the creeks." There was more, much more, but if I told him the rest he'd surely think I was crazy and discount everything. There was my vision of Regina driving off in the station wagon with George, his rifle stuck between her seat and the car door. There was the premonition I'd had of death and danger in the creeks when I'd looked out on the marshes of Murrell's Inlet from the restaurant window that night with Timothy.

Charles's face set in the lines of the hard, practical businessman. "A dream isn't sufficient reason to go to the police, though I admit under the circumstances your dream sounds more plausible than you may think. I neglected to tell you that the police found the old Volvo. They called about it the day my mother died, that's why I forgot. The station wagon was abandoned in Garden City."

"That's on the beach between Murrell's Inlet and the ocean?"

"Yes, it is. Which is consistent with your dream. The problem is, the police don't buy the foul play idea. They believe George stole or 'borrowed' the old station wagon—"

"But he had his own truck!"

Charles shook his head. "The truck belongs to me, though I gave it to George to drive. People knew George. If he was going to 'borrow' a vehicle, he'd take the oldest, most beat-up one. When the police went over his cabin, they found a lot of his clothes and his stash of money gone, too. So they concluded that he took off and just abandoned the station wagon when it ran out of gas—the tank was empty. I told them I didn't believe he'd do that. They asked if I suspected foul play. I said maybe, and they asked for a motive. I couldn't think of one. George was mentally retarded, but he was a completely harmless, gentle man. He never got into any trouble, didn't even drink. So, Rosamund, if I go to them they'll ask me again about a motive. Why would anyone want to kill George?"

Dangerous or not, whether he would believe me or not, I had to risk it. I had to tell Charles why George had died. I put my napkin down on the table, pushed back my chair. "I know why. Let's take an after-breakfast walk in the oak alley." No way would I say any more in the house, where I might be overheard.

I made small talk as we walked away from the house. "It's amazing how much cooler it is under the live oaks. Nevertheless, I have to tell you, your summers are terrible!"

Charles grinned down at me. "You'll get used to them. I'll build us a house on the beach. I've wanted to do that for some time anyway."

I returned his smile in spite of the sick feeling I got in my stomach whenever I thought about the future. We reached the pair of trees farthest from the house and I sat down on the grass and leaned against the huge trunk. Charles sat too. The morning sun through the leafy branches of the ancient oaks bathed his craggy features in green-gold light.

"I wasn't ready to tell you any of this, but I feel I owe it to George. He died because he was helping me." I plunged on, not giving Charles time to voice the objections I saw in his eyes. "I asked him to help me keep an eye on Regina, to watch where she went if she went out at night, especially with Arabella. He said he would, and a few days later he was gone. He was afraid of Regina. They're all afraid of her, even Jenny. But he said he'd help me anyway. It was to be our secret; anything he found out for me, I promised I

300

wouldn't say he'd helped. Regina must have seen us together, I don't know. At first I thought she'd just threatened him and scared him off. Now, because of the dream, I think she killed him. But I have no proof. If the police do recover his body, that would be something, a beginning. Charles, I feel responsible for George's death. I'd give anything if I hadn't involved him!"

"What is it you thought Regina was doing? What's so big and so awful that she'd commit murder? Surely you realize you're accusing Regina of murder!"

"I don't know what it is; that's what I've been trying to find out. I only know it involves your wife somehow. Can't you see, Charles, it isn't Arabella who's the evil one? It's Regina!"

"What makes you so sure of this?"

"Intuition. Instinct. I admit I have no proof."

"Rosamund, I'm afraid your intuition is about ninety percent wishful thinking, and the other ten percent paranoia. You and Regina have never gotten along since the day you first set foot in the house. I admit that Regina is so devoted to Bella that she just might kill to protect her. Anything else, I simply cannot believe. Regina is practically besotted with Charpentier and the Charpentiers, she has been ever since my mother rescued her from a difficult situation at Patton. I'm sure she'd never do anything to harm or even to reflect badly on any of us. Whatever you think you have to prove, I advise you to drop it. It's twisting your beautiful mind all out of shape, and I won't have that!"

I felt miserable, and irritated. How could Charles have such an incredible blind spot? "I was afraid you wouldn't believe me," I said. "So you won't tell the police to look for George's body?"

"With only what you've told me to go on, I'm afraid not. Whatever we do, it won't bring George back. It's best to get on with the things we've planned, and forget about all this. We'll move both Regina and Bella out of the house, which is the only way either you or I will have any peace. That reminds me, I've rented a place for them. Why don't you get a nurse in for a couple of days? Since Bella's illness you seem to have given up your regular days off, and what with that and the funeral, you must need a break by now. I'll show you the house, and you can help me with the furniture."

"I suppose I could use some time off," I agreed without enthusiasm. There was no use arguing with him, none at all.

I called the agency and arranged for the nurse for two days. I'd been without a break for a long time, as Charles had said. I'd been so wrapped up in all that concerned Charpentier that even the Fourth of July had come and gone without my notice. Timothy had gone back to Virginia, Lynda had gone on a business trip to someplace that was making money on a house the way she wanted to with Leighton, and here I was coming down to the wire alone. As usual. I wanted the time off, not for the reasons Charles suggested, but so that I could do something to force Regina's hand. I had to be free to move around. Also, I did need information, and I had an idea, a couple of ideas, where I could get it.

At noon I went to the kitchen myself to get the lunch tray, as I'd told Regina I'd do to make up for being late after breakfast. The kitchen was strangely silent, no gospel songs. But Jenny's hands, as usual, were busy. She was chopping celery to go in the tomato aspic that Charles liked and I didn't.

"I miss your music, Jenny. I don't believe I've heard you sing in a long time, and you don't play your radio anymore."

She shook her head, but her hands flew. A food processor had very little advantage over Jenny. "Things is bad, Miss Rosamund. Real bad. A body don't feel like singing."

"I know. Where's Regina?"

"She took that new car and went off someplace. She been goin' off a lot lately, and not to the store, neither."

I eased myself onto the counter-height stool. I felt a bit like a traitor, going behind Charles's back, but I would do what I had to do. "I'm glad she's not here, because I want to talk to you. I talked to Charles earlier this morning, but he doesn't believe me. Regina is not a good person, Jenny. I think you know that."

Jenny's hand stopped in midmotion. She put down the knife and wiped her hands on her apron. Her eyes glinted with a glaze of tears. "The good Lord's name be praised,

302

Miss Rosamund! I never thought as any of the Charpentiers would ever come to see that!"

"I'm not a Charpentier, maybe that's why I can see it."

"No ma'am, maybe you're not rightly a Charpentier, but you're like a member of the family anyways. I seen how you stood by Mr. Charles when his mama died so sudden, and how you looks after Miss Arabella like you really cares for her. That's good enough for me!"

"Thank you." I was glad to see her warm smile again, glad it was for me. "Now, about Regina. I have to show Charles what kind of person she is, I have to have proof. Is there anything you can tell me that will help me?"

Jenny thought. Shadows came and went in her eyes. But she said nothing.

"Jenny, what does she do to you and to other people to make you so afraid of her?"

Jenny twisted her apron in her hands. She decided to talk, and the words came out as if she spat them. "She worse'n a witch. She the one *controls* the witch. And she smart. Uppity, but smart. Everthing she do, she fix it so it look like somebody else done it."

"I know that, I figured some of it out. But how does she do it?"

"She got control over Miss Arabella, and Miss Arabella got the evil eye. Regina say who she put the evil eye on, and Miss Arabella do, and then peoples has troubles. Bad troubles. All them nursing aides before you come, that's what made 'em leave. Regina she gets potions from Miss Arabella, she give the potions to peoples and it make 'em crazy. Sometimes make 'em sleep like the dead. And she got this big black man look like a giant but got a mind like a child, she put a spell on him so he do anything she say, and he do only what she say. He go round with her of a night on her evil bizness."

"Where does she go at night? Does that man take her and Arabella somewhere on a boat?"

"That he do, Miss Rosamund. They has meetin's. I close my eyes and my ears bout them meetin's. I don't know nothing bout them, and I don't want to know. But Phyllis, she know. She young, and curious. Good as gold, but she got enough curiosity to kill a whole bunch of cats!"

I smiled. It was a good description of Phyllis. "Will she be back tomorrow? Or the day after? I want to ask her about the meetings."

Jenny looked troubled. "Well, seein' as how I already told you so much, Miss Rosamund, I'll tell you the truth. But you got to keep it to yourself and let Phyllis tell Mr. Charles in her own time. The truth is, she ain't never coming back, not long as Regina's here. Phyllis be scairt to death right now. She say her cousin dead because Regina got Miss Arabella to put the evil eye on his horse. The boy sneaked into a meetin' and Regina caught him. Phyllis been sneaking in, too, but she ain't been caught, less'n he told on her, and he might of. So now she too scairt to come back."

How very interesting! I couldn't accept the evil-eye-on-the-horse part, but the rest of it made a lot of sense, more than Jenny might realize. "Jenny, you've helped me a lot. I promise you, I'm going to stop Regina somehow. I have to know more about these meetings. Do you think Phyllis would talk to me if I go to her house? I could go tomorrow. A nurse is coming in so that I can have the next two days off."

Jenny nodded. "You just leave it to me, Miss Rosamund. Phyllis would do anything in the world for you, and when I tell her you say you'll stop Regina, she'll talk to you all right! Best you meet her at my house, ain't nobody there in the daytime. Phyllis's place will be busting at the seams with relatives for the funeral. I'll set it up. You come and see me afore breakfast in the morning, and I'll tell you what time and all."

Chapter 20

PHYLLIS WAS INDEED SCARED. She showed a concern for me that was touching, and it took me a while to convince her that I simply would not go away from Charpentier, as she had done and wanted me to do, to protect myself. At last she opened up, and out poured a wealth of information, unedited and uncensored, all preserved by an amazingly retentive mind and an eye for detail.

Phyllis knew that the name Regina meant "queen," and she said Regina acted like a queen whenever Charles wasn't around, bossing everybody, even Arabella. She was even bossier away from Charpentier. She had started the meetings a little over two years ago, and they had been held since the first in the old slave chapel on Freeman's Island. They were supposed to be "secret meetings," but most of the black community knew about them. The whites did not, and only a few white people came. The meetings were held every Wednesday and Friday night, whether or not Arabella was there. But Arabella was the star, the central attraction, because everybody thought she was a witch. The giant black man, whose name was Joe, was Regina's protection because she was none too popular. She never went anywhere at night without him. Some people said he was a zombie, because they'd never heard him talk, but Phyllis knew better. She said he was "nuthin' but a big, dumb black man."

Arabella used another name in the meetings, and many people who came didn't know she was Arabella Charpentier. I asked if she used the name "Ashtoreth," and Phyllis said yes, that was it. Ashtoreth said spells and healed some sicknesses and told fortunes with cards; she asked for payment, but she would take whatever you gave. She could also do something Phyllis termed "call out the animals." Sometimes she would go into a trance and in the trance, she would put the evil eye on anybody Regina told her to. Regina demanded payment for this on her own, a lot of money which was paid to her outside the meetings. Also outside the meetings Regina sold "potions" supposedly made by Ashtoreth. Phyllis said the potions were just some kind of drugs mixed up in fruit juice, and Regina mixed them up herself in her room at Charpentier. Phyllis had found this out by snooping in Regina's room.

In the beginning, anybody could come to the meetings except children. You had to be over sixteen. But for the last year or so, Regina had to approve you. It was more like a club now, a club that in Phyllis's opinion did more bad than good. Now when Ashtoreth called out the animals, which seemed to have no purpose other than as a demonstration of unusual power, one or more would be sacrificed. Not in any ritual, Regina or sometimes Joe just killed them. Now there was more of the evil eye, more asking for harmful spells. Phyllis's fascination was with Arabella's performance as Ashtoreth. To see this, she would sneak in again and again, even though the growing violence of the meetings sickened her. She described for me the place she usually hid. She said she would never go again after what had happened to her cousin, which she was sure had happened because he had been caught.

I praised Phyllis for her good memory and told her I intended to go the next time Arabella would be there. Phyllis promptly said she'd heard Miss Arabella was to be at the meeting tomorrow night, Friday. I thanked her, and assured her I would be careful and use her hiding place if I could.

I drove in to Georgetown with plenty to think about. Regina came across in Phyllis's account as a woman increasingly drunk with her own power. I didn't doubt that Arabella/Ashtoreth was growing more powerful too, or she had been before her illness, and I expected she would soon regain her lost ground. Regina must have gotten the drugs for her potions at least in part by stealing them from Arabella's supply. I faced the chilling possibility that if Regina had killed George, she might have killed others. She might well try to kill me. In fact, if the "evil eye" alone would have done it, no doubt I'd be dead by now.

In Georgetown I bought black denim trousers and a black turtleneck shirt—it was a man's shirt, the only black one I could find, and several sizes too big. I also bought a paisley scarf in dark colors, mostly black. And an expensive 35-mm camera designed to take pictures of sporting events. It was small, had a built-in telephoto lens and automatic everything. There was one more thing I had to do. I drove to Wachesaw Landing to look for Captain John. I had to wait for him to get in from one of his tourist boat trips, but it was worth the wait. He agreed to be my boatman the following night, no questions asked.

I returned to Charpentier with just enough time to take a nap before dinner. I lay down on my bed. Sat up again. I felt as if someone, or something, were in the room with me—an eerie, anxious feeling. My eyes roamed, seeking its source, and came to rest on The Obsidian. It was on my dressing table. Perhaps I should put it in a drawer, or better yet, like Arabella, in a box in the closet. I picked it up.

As soon as the orb of black glass was in my hand, it began to grow warm. It seemed to command, Look at me, look at me! I was afraid to look, and I had to look. I sat down on the little chair and I looked into The Obsidian. Its blackness radiated heat and doom. I knew what that meant, I'd felt it many times now. In fascinated resignation I stared at the tiny red dot which appeared in the center of the black ball, and watched it grow into a leaping, crackling red flame. Fire! The roar and the heat and the smell of fire were all around me. Still I stared. The flames within the black sphere licked its rounded inner surface. Balls of sparks wheeled and fell. Obsidian black turned completely red. The ball was so hot it must surely burn my hand!

The red in the sphere collapsed, fell in upon itself in a small implosion. The Obsidian was black again, and cool again. I took it in my other hand and looked at my palm on which the ball of fire had rested. There was no burn, only the faded marks of myriad tiny scratches.

It is a strange thing to be convinced that someone you know and see every day has killed, and likely will kill again, could even be planning to kill you. For me, it was similar to what I felt in the presence of the ocean—everything else receded, everything else became a shade less important, and individual concerns tended to arrange themselves in a descending hierarchy of importance. Thus, when on Friday I spent a large part of the day in Georgetown with Charles, my focus was already some twelve hours ahead. The small house he had rented for Arabella and which he assumed Regina would share, the discussion of what furnishings could be brought from Charpentier, and the shopping for what had to be bought, all seemed a bit unreal. When I looked at Charles I did not see the strong, beloved face of the man I most likely could never have; I saw instead the iron-willed, stubborn master of Charpentier whom I must convince of Regina's wickedness. I talked of ceilings that seemed too low to accommodate Arabella's pillared bed, but I thought of the pictures I would take at tonight's secret meeting. Pictures that were to be my proof, pictures that would convince Charles first to call in the police, and second that Regina was no suitable companion for his wife. My preoccupation insulated me from the pain I otherwise would have felt as Charles talked happily of the future, a future he confidently asumed we would share. And I assumed we could not.

In the evening I felt a rising, desperate excitement. Within me was a certainty that this night would be significant, decisive. Yet oddly enough, when I'd dressed all in black, wound my hair around my head and covered it with the scarf tied gypsy-style with the ends hanging down in back, and hung the camera around my neck, the excitement left me. From my vantage point outside the house I watched Arabella and Regina leave as they had left before, and I felt as if this were a routine thing, nothing out of the ordinary. And when at last I stood on the dock myself waiting for Captain John, I felt nothing but an icy calm. I did not doubt that he would come, did not doubt that events were unfolding as they should and I would have the capacity to act as I had to act.

Captain John pulled his rowboat up to the dock and I stepped down. There was a half-moon above, and by its light I saw his familiar weathered face and the cap that clung to the side of his head as if it were a natural part of him.

"Thank you for being on time," I said. "I want you to take me to Freeman's Island."

"I figured as much. No other place to go this time of night." He grinned and winked. Trailing one oar, he turned the boat around and headed back upriver.

"You know about the meetings?" I asked.

"Anything happens more'n once on this river, I know about it. You invited"—he looked me over from head to foot—"or are you just gonna crash the party, so to speak?"

"Crash the party, so to speak."

"Taking pictures, are you?"

"Yes, and I hope no one sees me."

He nodded. "Don't you worry none. First sign of trouble, you just get yourself back to this boat and I'll have you off that island faster'n a greased pig can skate!"

"Right," I confirmed, smiling at him. I was glad of his help, and knew I needed it. Though I could row perhaps as well as he, I didn't have his superior knowledge of the river. Besides, it felt good to have an ally.

There were twenty or so boats pulled up on the sloping shore of the island. Though the land was overgrown with trees, I could see the old chapel clearly about a hundred yards away. If not for the boats, I'd have thought it deserted. It looked like an outsize cabin with a squat belfry on top, paintless and gray with age, all the windows boarded over. Not a light showed.

"You remember now, Miss Rosamund, first sign of trouble you come on back. I'll wait right here."

"I will," I said. Still filled with icy calm, I watched my footing carefully but there was no need, the path was worn smooth. I thought as I approached that the hardest part would be getting through the door unseen.

Through the closed door I heard the alien, guttural sounds of Arabella's chanting. Good—attention would be on her. The door had an old-fashioned iron latch. It moved soundlessly. I cracked the door, paused, and slipped in. A second to get my bearings, and then I slid along the back wall to the spot where Phyllis had hidden successfully, an enclosed stair railing in a far back corner. The stairs led to a loft that was no longer safe, so they were never used.

I settled myself on the third step. My height was an advantage. I could sit on the steps and see over the railing without much danger of being seen. There were no pews in this chapel. Men and women, mostly black but a white face here and there, sat on the floor in an irregular circle. A few older people who couldn't manage the floor sat in straight chairs on the circle's periphery. The distinctive odor of kerosene filled the room, from glass-chimneyed kerosene lanterns that were everywhere. There were candles too, in many-branched standing candelabra. The light was golden, quite beautiful. In the center of all this stood Arabella/Ashtoreth in a flowing silver robe, arms upraised, head flung back, silver-streaked hair streaming, pouring from her throat sounds of gnashing ugliness, strident discord. I raised my camera. My work had begun.

Regina stood up now. She looked very tall, resplendent in a long gown fitted closely to her full breasts and then falling straight to the floor in vertical stripes of orange and turquoise. Her head was wrapped in a turban of the same material. She held up her hand. Ashtoreth opened her eyes—even from my distance I could see their astonishing green. I also saw that she swayed a little, unsteady on her feet. Into a heavy silence she barked out a command.

"Gnath!" Or so it sounded.

Ashtoreth was calling out the animals. More guttural commands followed. I don't know what I had expected. Something grander, maybe, awesome and terrible, but not this pathetic parade. A scraggly, half-grown patchwork cat. A largish nondescript bird that fell down from the vicinity of the ceiling as if it had been shot. An old yellow-brown dog that moved slowly and looked either sick or drugged. A pitiful trio, but they did come to her. She seemed unaware, staring over the heads of the people at nothing, until Regina came up behind her, put a hand on her shoulder, and whispered in her ear. I snapped a picture of this whispering. In response to Regina, Ashtoreth bent down and picked up the cat. She held it around the middle, which cats do not like, and it twisted and meowed. Then Ashtoreth brought the cat's face up to hers, she looked it in the eyes and murmured rhythmically to it for what seemed like a long time. Finally the cat went limp in her hands, its legs and head hanging down like so many dirty patchwork rags.

The crowd mumbled and stirred. Some of the faces looked scared. My camera was busy. Regina took the cat from Ashtoreth. Her giant unfolded himself from off the floor and picked up the bird, which looked already dead to me. Jenny and Phyllis had not exaggerated his size. He gave the dog an incongruously gentle nudge with his foot, and it slunk away. Ashtoreth collapsed in a chair that someone had dragged forward for her, apparently exhausted.

Regina, with a gloating smile and malevolence glinting from her tigress eyes, held the limp cat at arm's length and walked slowly with it around the circle. Some people flinched, some turned their heads, and some sat unmoving. Her meaning was clear: What we do to this cat, we can also do to you. She returned to the center of the circle, gathered her strength, and gave the patchwork body a violent wrench. With an audible pop the cat's neck snapped. Regina smiled.

That "pop!" broke through the calmness which had protected me. My stomach turned over, bile rose bitter in my throat. I gagged. But I had the cat's death on film.

An involuntary moan had arisen from the crowd, but Ashtoreth gave no sign of hearing. She sat in her chair near the center of the room, still as a statue. Regina and her henchman placed the bodies of the cat and the bird on a table at the other end of the room. That seemed to signal some sort of break in the meeting. People got up and walked around. I crouched lower behind my railing, only my eyes peeking over. Regina brought Ashtoreth a glass of something to drink and spoke to her in a commanding tone. I heard the words clearly. "You will bring yourself out of your trance now!" So that was it! In order to use whatever powers she had, Arabella/Ashtoreth did a kind of self-hypnosis, and she relied on Regina to help her get back. I knew little about hypnosis, but I did know that if she could hypnotize herself she could also bring herself out of it. Unless, of course, Regina had brainwashed her to believe otherwise. I remembered how anxious she had been to have a candle, "to practice" she'd said, and she hadn't seemed to want Regina to know. Perhaps she had been trying to learn to do this without Regina, without success.

The giant came with a folded card table in one hand and a wooden box in the other. He unfolded the table, put it beside Ashtoreth, and put the box on top. It was the box of money that I'd seen in her closet. Ashtoreth asked for a candle, and one was brought and placed on the table. People came to her one by one, dropped an offering in the box, and then got down on one or both knees and talked to her. I became absorbed in watching this quiet, seemingly harmless activity; now and then I took a picture.

Suddenly, from nowhere, I sensed danger. My fingers pricked, my scalp pricked, icy cold seized me by the nape of the neck. My vision blurred and when it cleared again, I was out on the river. On the obsidian black water. Red flames leapt into the black sky and were reflected in the black mirror of the water below. And there was something else. Through a curtain of flames turned transparent, like rubies, I saw Charpentier as I had seen it for the first time, the great white house rising straight up from the glossy dark water as if it were built upon the river itself. Danger! Fire! called my mind. And the vision vanished. It left behind unspeakable anxiety, a feeling of impending doom.

I blinked. I was not on the river, but still in my hiding place. Ashtoreth still received her petitioners. But there *was* danger, and I knew the danger was at Charpentier. The danger was to Charles, and to the house itself. My frantically searching eyes told me that Regina and her giant helper were no longer in the old chapel. How long they had been gone I'd no idea.

For precious moments I was torn. Here was the woman who might be my mother, with her sick mind and her frail body. She should not be left alone, and Regina had deserted her. At Charpentier Charles was alone, in bed, asleep, unaware, and any moment now Charpentier would go up in flames. I couldn't be in two places at once, I had to choose.

I crept form my hiding place, edged out the door and hit the path running. I had to warn Charles! Captain John saw me coming and had pushed his boat into the water by the time I got there. I splashed in. "We've got to get back to Charpentier, as fast as possible!" I panted. "If we don't, something terrible is going to happen." Please God, I thought, it hasn't happened already!

"I got a outboard motor on this boat, if'n you don't mind the noise."

"Use it! Just get us there as fast as you can!"

In a spray of water, we were off. Over the sound of the motor I yelled, "Did you see Regina and that big man leave the island?"

"Yep. Went thisaway, downriver."

"How long ago?"

"Fifteen, twenty minutes. Not long."

I clutched the sides of the speeding boat, my heart throbbing in my throat. I expected at any moment to see all those identical dreams and visions become reality, to see Charpentier burning upon the river right before my eyes.

Blessedly, it didn't happen. The boat bumped the dock, and I was out before Captain John had it tied. Another boat, flat-bottomed, was also there, as I'd known it would be. I called to Captain John, "Regina and her man are in the house, and they're up to no good. Please follow me in and use the phone in the hall to call the police. And please hurry!"

I heard a "Yes, ma'am," as I clambered up the bank. The camera thumping against my chest as I ran was an irritation, so I tore it off and flung my precious pictures away somewhere in the garden. Running up the steps I tugged my key from the pocket of my jeans, but I didn't need it. They'd left the West Front door open. I dropped the key in the hall, skidded on the oriental runner, and took the steps two at a time, in the dark.

Thank God I was in time! There they were in the South Wing corridor outside Charles's door, the big man on his knees doing something and Regina holding a battery-powered lantern. Clearly, my appearance was a shock to them.

How I hated that woman, how I despised her! I heard myself snarl, a sound I hadn't known I was capable of making. Regina backed a step, never taking her eyes from me, and set the lantern on the floor. I forgot her giant friend. I screamed a battle cry, and my arms and legs took over, letting loose their karate on the real enemy. A running kick to her chest, and she staggered. She hissed and spat and clawed and ripped my shirt. I spun and with my elbow cracked her cheekbone. I jumped away on both feet for distance. I screamed again as I came up with a flying kick to her windpipe, and she went down, hard. She was dazed. I rolled her onto her stomach, pinned her arms behind her back, and sat on her rear end while I took off my scarf and used it to tie her hands. Before I got off her I growled, in a voice that barely sounded like my own, "If you even try to get loose, I'll give you a chop to the back of the neck that just might kill you!"

Then I remembered her big friend, I heard Charles banging on his door, and Captain John came up the stairs. Being a practical man, he turned on lights as he came.

The big guy with the mind of a child was grinning from ear to ear. "You beat her up!" he said.

"Yeah, looks like I did." Suddenly I, too, was grinning from ear to ear. I understood now why he hadn't helped her. "I guess you didn't like her much either."

"She be mean to Joe," he said, swinging his huge head from side to side.

"What the hell's going on out there?" Charles bellowed. There was a crash and a muttered curse as he threw himself against his heavy door. "I can't get the damn door open!"

Captain John shambled up the hall in his rolling gait, as if nothing on land or water could ever perturb him, assessed the situation in a glance, and with a wink in my direction called through the door, "Have you out in a shake of a sheep's tail, Mr. Charles."

Charles's door, which opened out into the hallway had been wedged shut with a triangular block of wood, and as I'd come upon them the big guy, Joe, was completing the job of stuffing rags all around the doorframe. More rags were stuffed in the windowsills and along the baseboards.

"Soaked in paraffin," said Captain John as he removed the rags from around the door. He whacked at the wooden wedge and got it out.

"We was gonna burn the big house down," said Joe.

I wanted to rush to Charles as he came, glowering,

through his door. But I didn't dare move away from Regina. He wore only a pair of short pajama bottoms, and he looked strong and hairy and muscular and angry, and I'd never seen a more gorgeous man in all my life.

"My God!" he said.

"We was gonna burn the big house down," said Joe again.

"That's right," I said, "but it wasn't his idea. It was Regina's. She made him do it."

Charles looked at me, then saw Regina in her splendid orange-and-turquoise gown, face down on the floor at my feet, her hands tied with my scarf. He picked up a rag from the floor, sniffed it, threw it down again.

Joe, pleased with his role as interpreter, beamed and said, "The pretty lady beat up Regina!"

"The pretty lady is apparently stronger than she looks," said Charles. He looked up at the giant. "And who are you?"

"Joe." He beamed again.

I had taken an instant liking to him, probably because he hadn't pulverized me. "He's a big guy on the outside, but inside he's just a little kid, aren't you, Joe?"

He swung his head from side to side, pleased or embarrassed or both. "Yes, ma'am."

"Police is on the way," said Captain John. "You got Miss Rosamund to thank, Mr. Charles. She saved your house, and she might of saved your life, too."

Charles looked confused. He ran his hand through his already disarrayed hair. "I'm sorry, I'm having a little trouble taking it all in. One minute I was asleep, and the next minute I heard this unearthly screaming, and when I finally get the door open, you tell me Regina and, uh, Joe were going to burn my house down. . . ."

"With you in it," I said.

Regina lifted her head off the floor and raised one shoulder. "You, too, Rose-a-mund," she spat. "I thought you were in your room! You deserve to die, both of you, to burn along with the *great* house of Charpentier!"

"Watch your mouth," I told her. There was a wail of sirens coming up the drive.

Finally Charles came to me, put his arms around me.

"Rosamund! I don't know what the hell this is all about, but I'm glad you're safe."

"We'll talk later," I said.

"I might have known you'd say that!" Charles hugged me closer and kissed my forehead.

I wanted to relax in his arms, but I couldn't, not yet. "We have to go back to the island and get Arabella, as soon as the police take Regina away."

"Island? What island? I don't understand any of this," Charles complained.

"I'll go let 'em in," said Captain John, and ambled off.

While he let the police in the East Front door, a black man I'd never seen before came pounding up the stairs. He brought with him the acrid, bitter smell of smoke. He looked at us wildly, recognized Joe, and was obviously shocked to see Regina tied up on the floor. Then his eyes fastened on Charles, even half-naked an authority figure. "Sir, I come to tell Regina, Ashtoreth done set herself and the whole place on fire!"

Fire burned on the water. Great columns of red flame rose high in the black sky and were reflected in the river's black mirror. The fire crackled and roared, it belched balls of sparks that wheeled crazily up and then fell hissing and popping into the water. The heat seared our skin, even from a safe distance. The whole island was burning. With everything so dry from the drought, once the chapel was aflame the trees had gone up like paper. Charles and I and Captain John sat in the captain's rowboat and watched it burn.

It was doom. It was destruction. It was the end for the people who'd been unable to get out. It was the end for Arabella/Ashtoreth Charpentier, who might have been my mother. The reality was a thousand times worse than my vision had ever been. I could not be in two places at once. I had chosen Charles and Charpentier, and now the island was burning.

Tears streamed down my face. "That's what I saw, that night at Leighton with you and Timothy. I saw great columns of flames like this, the red fire on the black water. I saw the island burning." I started to shake uncontrollably, I shook so hard I rocked the boat.

316

Charles wrapped me in his arms. "Captain John," he said, "I think we'd better take her home."

The first thing I saw when I awoke was my clock, which told me it was three P.M. I'd slept an incredible ten hours. Next I saw Phyllis, sitting in my little chair, reading a magazine. I struggled up on my elbows. "Hi," I said, "where'd you come from?"

She bounced up, grinning, eyes sparkling. "Oh lordy, Miss Rosamund! When I heard all about it, I came right here. I said, could I help, and Mr. Charles he told me to sit with you. You done it! Regina be in jail, she won't never get out! That big dumb Joe been telling everybody how you beat up Regina!"

The muscles of my arms and legs reminded me painfully of that, but I couldn't suppress a smile. Physically conquering Regina was one of the more satisfactory things I'd done in my life! I sat up, now recalling other, less pleasant things. "The fire—how many people died? It didn't spread to either side of the river, did it?"

Phyllis shook her head. "No, ma'am. The firemen didn't let it spread. But nobody knows yet who-all died, because people didn't exactly advertise when they was going to them meetings. People what's missin', they might of been burned up but they might be somewheres else, so they just got to wait and see. Miss Arabella, she dead for sure. Them what got out, they say she started the fire by a accident. She gone into some crazy dance, a-whirlin' around, and she knock over a lantern. Whoosh! Caught herself on fire first, then the whole place just gone up!"

I remembered my feeling of doom, of the end. It had been the end of Arabella. Burned to death—what a terrible way to die!

"Mr. Charles been at the police all morning. He say to tell you when you wake up, come see him downstairs."

"Thank you, Phyllis. Perhaps you might tell him for me that I'll be down in a little while. And could you bring me a cup of coffee and a piece of toast?"

"Yes, ma'am, I sure can!"

I showered, took some aspirin for my sore muscles, and had my toast and coffee while I more or less dried my hair. I left it loose on my shoulders both because it was easy and because Charles liked it that way. I dressed in my green slacks and a cream-colored blouse. I found Charles in the library, huddled in the wing chair and brooding. I took the matching chair.

"Phyllis says you've been with the police."

He looked at me, his dark blue eyes almost black, a starless void filled with pain. "Yes. Rosamund, Regina killed my mother. You seemed to know so much, did you know that, too?"

"No! I thought she'd killed George. I knew she had killed animals and done a lot of the things you blamed Arabella for. But your mother! Oh, Charles, I had no idea!"

Charles put his head in his hands and expelled a heavy sigh. "I thought she was loyal, but she hated us." He straightened up and leaned back in his chair, stretching out his long legs. "The police called this morning and said Regina was ready to make a statement, but would only do it if I was present. So I went. She looked at me with such pure hatred—I've never seen anything like it. It was horrible."

. "I know that look." I should know it, she'd looked at me that way many times.

"She had been stealing Bella's drugs for years. She killed that first nurse, strangled her and buried her body in the woods at Patton, sank her car in Winyah Bay. She bragged that she had power over Bella. They had some sort of cult going—I gather you'd figured that out."

"Yes, I did." I made a mental note to look for my camera in the garden. Charles should see those pictures.

"Incredible as it sounds, Regina was convinced that Bella really did have the so-called evil eye, because she could mesmerize animals. Regina thought if Bella would try hard enough, she could kill with her eyes—look at people and animals and stop their hearts. But Bella wouldn't do it, wouldn't try. Regina blames you, says before you came she was making progress but you confused her, got her off the track. So Regina decided she would have to kill them herself, the people she wanted dead. That was her uncle and my mother. She had a way of opening up capsules and taking out the medication, she'd been doing it for a long time. Sometimes she'd put the capsules back together again with

318

crushed aspirin inside so no one would suspect. That's what she did the night your keys were missing, and she took that medication and used it to kill my mother. She didn't go to Patton until after—you remember, she was gone. Both her uncle and my mother, she forced them to take overdoses of tranquilizers dissolved in fruit juice. My mother tried to live, so they knew it was an overdose. Her uncle was old, and they thought he had simply died in his sleep."

"Why? Why did she want to kill them?"

"Crazy revenge, for taking her away from Patton. Regina had an obsession with Phillip Patton that went all the way back to childhood. You see, old man Patton, Phillip's father, did a lot of business in Europe. He married a Swiss woman, and they lived half of every year in Switzerland. Regina's uncle was old man Patton's butler and valet, so he always went with them and since Regina was like his own child, she went along, too. She grew up alongside Phillip, part of the household. She got it into her head that some day Phillip would marry her, and to make a long story short, her uncle and my mother got her out of Patton just in time to prevent a scandal. I always assumed Regina was grateful to them for that, but she wasn't. She hated them for it. She hates me too. She tried to transfer her obsession to me, but as I told you, I wasn't interested. It seems she still had ideas she might make me interested, until you came. You and I ruined her fantasies, Rosamund. She wasn't going to let us live in this house together. She was going to burn it to the ground, with us in it."

"And George? Did she kill him?"

"Yes, she confessed that too. Your dream was right. The police are looking for his body now. But the boy who fell off the horse, Phyllis's cousin, she had nothing to do with that. It was just an accident. Can you imagine, she said she wished she *had* caused that boy's death?"

"Yes, Charles, I don't even have to imagine. I'm sure she's proud of her killings, unrepentant. But I did think she cared about Arabella. Does she realize that Arabella died in the fire?"

"I suppose she does. I don't really know. I was too appalled after listening to her confess to all those murders to even think about the fire." He lapsed into a moody silence.

319

I stared at the decorative brass fan, the summer occupant of the fireplace. Everything in me ached—mind, body, heart, soul. "It's hard to believe Arabella is gone," I said.

"Yes. That fire will be long remembered up and down the Waccamaw. The papers haven't got hold yet of the fact that my wife died in the fire. I haven't begun to think how I'll deal with that."

We sat in silence. I thought that, for me, all was not yet over. Charles would have to deal with the publicity, which was bound to be difficult. I had other things, perhaps more difficult.

Charles got up from his chair. I thought how many times I'd seen him to that, seen his large body unfold with surprising grace. Charles Charpentier was imprinted on my soul forever—the unruly dark hair with its touches of gray, the broad planes of forehead and cheekbones, the strong jaw, the sensual mouth, the expanse of chest, the powerful thighs. The look of him, the feel of him, the smell and taste of him were in my blood. I was shaken by a wave of desire, as if this dark Thor had hurled his thunderbolt and pierced me with it.

"Here," he said, "you need a drink as much as I do, I'm sure."

It was a glass of the sherry I preferred. I took it without a word. I sipped and the amber liquid burned sweetly down my throat.

Charles went suddenly on his knees in front of me. His face was twisted with intensity of feeling, his eyes blazed. "What can I say to you, Rosamund? 'Thank you for saving my life' seems almost trite after all this! You went through hell for me, and I didn't know. When you tried to tell me, I didn't believe you. Forgive me for that! You put yourself in danger, I know that now. Oh, Rosamund . . . !"

With his arms around my legs and his head in my lap, Charles cried. His great shoulders heaved with his sobbing. Dry-eyed, unable to cry, I stroked his hair. I loved him, and I had to leave him, and I might never return. Arabella's death made no difference. I still had to get the picture from the bottom drawer of her desk, still had to take it to my grandparents, because I had to know the truth.

"Hush, Charles," I said softly. "Whatever I did, I did it

for all of us, you, me, and Arabella." I slid from my chair to the floor beside him, into a damp, sweet embrace. We held and comforted each other, rocking back and forth, like unhappy children.

The telephone's ring split our world and interrupted a kiss that had just begun its healing.

"Let it ring," said Charles.

"No," I said, disentangling my arms and legs from his, "I'd better answer it."

"Hello, Rosamund?" The voice was Lynda's, breathless and excited.

"Yes, it's me. Where are you?"

"I'm in Natchez, but I just got back from a side trip to New Orelans. It's so exciting, Rosamund! I've found your mother!"

I was stunned. You can't have, I thought, she died in the fire. Arabella was my mother, I'm almost certain, and if I hadn't left her in the old slave chapel she'd still be alive. "I guess you haven't heard," I said into the telephone. "There was a huge fire here last night on Freeman's Island, and Arabella died in the fire."

"Oh. Your vision, Rosamund. That was it."

"Yes, I'm afraid it was that exactly."

"Louis may have tried to call, but I just got back here. What was she doing on the island?"

"It's a long story, too long to tell over the phone."

"Well, is everyone else all right?"

"Yes, except Regina. She's in jail—another long story. She killed a lot of people, including Charles's and Louis's mother. But it's all over now."

"My Lord!" She paused for a moment, presumably collecting her thoughts. "Listen, I don't mean to sound insensitive, but I'm sure Charles can handle all that. I can't help it, I'm still really high on what I've done the past two days. I was so close to New Orleans anyway, being in Natchez on business, I simply had to try to solve your mystery. I went to the house in the picture, Eauclaire, and I asked around. I have all sorts of contacts when it comes to finding out about old houses. And I found the owners without too much trouble. They gave me the name of this man who rented it from them during the sixties and seventies, Pierre Dorrance.

Would you believe I found him in the telephone book? So I called him and I told him I was trying to help you find your mother, Margaret Collins. He remembered you, Rosamund, as a little girl. And he knew where your mother is. She's in a convent in New Orleans, has been there for years and years, probably ever since she took you to her parents. I called the convent and talked to the Mother Superior. It's a cloistered order, but when I explained everything, how you'd been led to believe for so long that your mother was dead, the Mother Superior said if you will come and let her read your aunt's letter to prove who you are, you can see your mother! You'll come, won't you?"

Now it was my turn to pause and think. At length I said, "Yes, I'll come. As soon as we've had some sort of memorial service for Arabella."

To Charles I said, "I have to go away, very soon. I can't explain now, but I'll tell you everything when I come back."

Chapter 21

MY MOTHER WAS A small woman with a pale, unlined face and eyes the color of mine. Where once she'd had long, abundant dark hair, she now had a white wimple and a black veil. Modern reforms in nuns' dress had not reached behind these walls. Her voice seemed different to me, soft, hesitant, as if she spoke little in normal conversation, which was no doubt true. I remembered her as I'd rememberd the size and shape and feel of the long windows, with a distant thrill of recognition.

The story she told in her soft voice was sad, simple, and in its own way, noble. She'd had a premonition that both she and I would come to harm if we stayed in the house I remembered, so she had taken me to Vicksburg, to her parents, the only place she knew I would be safe and cared for. She had returned the car to her friends at Eauclaire, but she had not stayed. Instead, she had begged a job at this convent. "To atone for my sins," she said. After seven years of working as a servant, during which time she converted and became a Catholic, she had asked and received permission to be a Lay Sister. She still scrubbed the floors and worked in the kitchen, but she joined the professed nuns in the chapel and said the same prayers. She was happy. She believed her sins had been forgiven. After another seven years the Mother Superior had asked if she would like to join the Order. They'd sent her to their novitiate to study and take vows, and then she'd returned to New Orleans, no longer Margaret Collins but now Sister Mary Dolorosa, Mary the Sorrowful, a name she'd chosen herself.

The convent parlor was furnished with gleaming austerity. We sat alone at a bare table on straight chairs in the middle of a sea of polished hardwood floor. The room smelled of floor wax and furniture wax and candle wax. Shafts of sunlight fell from lancet windows, too high and narrow to see out of, and shone upon already-shining wood. My mother was serene with her own inner light.

I reached into the canvas bag I'd carried on the plane and withdrew two objects. I put the first on the table. "Do you recognize this, Mother?"

Twenty-three years of strictest training had had their effect. Her lips quivered only slightly. Her eyelids snapped shut, then opened again. "Where did you get this, my child?" she asked in a whisper.

I placed the second object on the table. "I got it from her. Do you know her?" It was the photograph of Arabella that I had chosen from her desk drawer.

My mother nodded. She kept her hands hidden in her long, wide sleeves. "This is an orb made of obsidian. It is many centuries old. It belongs to a past I have atoned for, and almost forgotten. I will speak of it this once, for your sake, Rosamund, but never again. The purpose of The Obsidian is to see into the future, but it will not show for everyone. The legend is that the orb was made of black glass because it was made for a magician who practiced only black magic. In the days when I wandered up and down the Gulf Coast I met a black magician who possessed The Obsidian, but he could not see into it. I could, though I did not practice black magic, at least not intentionally. He gave it to me. I was just eighteen at the time. He said he had acquired it in Europe, in Budapest, I think. I lived like a gypsy in those days. I was wicked, I did wicked things. You more than anyone must know this is true, since I cannot even tell you with certainty who your father was."

"I believe you were young and confused and perhaps different from other people. But I don't believe you were wicked."

"The Church teaches us that there is no difference between black and white magic. To practice the occult in any form is wicked, and that is what I did. The Obsidian will show only evil and unhappy things, and it shows them in an ambiguous way, so that its messages are hard to understand. But it has a strange attraction, or at least it did for me. Once I possessed it, I found it hard to give up. The woman in the picture is Anabel Johnson. She had come to visit Eauclaire several times and she had linked herself with our group, when I lived there with you. When I left she moved in and took my place. I remember she had the most unusual green eyes, Pierre was fascinated with her. . . ." With a visible effort, Sister Mary Dolorosa fought her memories. She looked at me kindly out of her gray-blue eyes. "When you were three years old, I looked into The Obsidian and saw you drowned in the swamp and myself wandering lost among the cypress trees. That is why I took you to your grandparents, why I gave The Obsidian to Anabel who coveted it. God moves in mysterious ways, my child. I must believe it is God's purpose that has brought you here with these things of the past."

I sighed. I put the black glass ball and the photograph back in my canvas bag. Coincidence, serendipity, karma, God's mysterious ways—by whatever name you wished to call it, I had been set free. "Anabel changed her name to Arabella, and she married Charles Charpentier. I—" I censored rapidly, not wanting to disturb my mother's hard-earned serenity any more than I had already done. "I got to know them, and it was a problem. You see, I never could remember the first three years of my life, but being around Arabella kept jogging my memory. I'd get only bits and pieces, but I knew they were real memories. Arabella is dead now. Before she died I'd come to wonder if she might be my mother. I didn't want her to be, but I had to wonder because of the memories. I'm so glad I found you, that my friend Lynda found you for me. I'm proud to have you for a mother, Sister Mary Dolorosa, and I hope you forgive me for disturbing the peace of your convent."

"Of course." She embraced me. "Before you go, would you like to see our chapel?"

*   *   *

"I don't understand this strange whim of yours. It's much too hot in the middle of July to be out on the river," Charles grumbled.

"You promised to humor me, so humor!" I smiled up at him, blessedly happy. I'd told him everything. Déjà vu, visions, dreams, doubts, hopes, fears, memories, everything. He had listened, scowling, skeptical, and finally simply amazed. Then he had taken me into his arms and into that great bed, the bed that heirs are conceived in, and made love to me. And I, to him. I'd promised to marry him in six months' time.

Now we were on Captain John's boat, which I had rented for just the two of us, for a very special purpose of my own. We slowly skimmed the surface of the dark water. The boat proceeded around the blackened ruins of Freeman's Island, and I said a prayer for Arabella and the others who had died in the fire. I felt the throb of the motor, throbbing in time with the beat of my heart, an affirmation of life in contrast to the reminders of death.

Charles's arm went around me and he held me pressed tightly against his side. "You promise you'll come back to me from Cambridge?" he asked. "You won't get up there and change your mind?"

"I'll come back, and don't *you* change *your* mind about me finishing medical school in Charleston!"

"Barkstone would kill me if I did." He kissed me at the base of my ear.

"No, he wouldn't, because I'd already have done it myself!" We could banter again, it was wonderful.

I turned my attention to what lay ahead. This boat trip was different, because I knew now what was on either side of the river. I recognized the broad grassy banks of Leighton, and the old rice fields which no longer held terror for me. And yet it was the same, the mystery of the black water would always be the same. Charles and I were silent under its spell.

We rounded the horseshoe curve. Charpentier rose before us, straight up from the black water, elegant and shining in the sun. I trembled. I felt the word form in my mind: *Obsidian*.

The boat stopped, idling in the middle of the river as I'd requested of Captain John. I bent down and reached into my leather shoulder bag which sat on the deck. Charles stood back, watching. He did not know what I intended to do.

My hand closed on it, round and smooth and cool. I withdrew the orb and held it in both palms. It shone black, eating the sunlight, black as an evil mirror, black and smooth as the river was black and smooth. It was mine. It said, Look at me, look at me!

I stood at the railing and opened my hands. The ball fell, and left a tingling feel of loss on my empty palms. The water closed over it with scarcely a sound.

"Obsidian to Obsidian," I said.